THE BLOCK ROOM

LLOYD HARVEY

The
Book
Guild

First published in Great Britain in 2025 by
The Book Guild Ltd
Unit E2 Airfield Business Park,
Harrison Road, Market Harborough,
Leicestershire. LE16 7UL
Tel: 0116 2792299
www.bookguild.co.uk
Email: info@bookguild.co.uk
X: @bookguild

The manufacturer's authorised representative in the EU
for product safety is Authorised Rep Compliance Ltd,
71 Lower Baggot Street, Dublin D02 P593 Ireland (www.arccompliance.com)

This work is entirely fictitious and bears no resemblance to any persons living or dead.

Typeset in 11pt Minion Pro

Printed and bound in Great Britain by CMP UK

ISBN 978 1835742 372

British Library Cataloguing in Publication Data.
A catalogue record for this book is available from the British Library.

For Will.

Repetition is useful, but continuous use of mechanical repetition also has harmful effects. It is dangerous because it easily induces habits of sheer mechanised action, blindness, tendencies to perform slavishly instead of thinking, instead of facing a problem freely.

Max Wertheimer

THE WOODCUTTER

1926

Hand steady, he leaned in. The gouge chisel carving u-shaped grooves, his thumb acting as a brake at the end of every pass. Wood flaking up with vitality, sometimes curling like cold butter, a mulch of shavings accumulating around the jig. The woodcutter's back complaining; his hands numb.

He switched to the spitsticker tool – only the finer details now. Each cut testing his patience. To rush, to force, risked losing his efforts to the woodpile. A few scored lines, a few tight corners hollowed out, the slow intense process almost done.

He wiped the block with a flat hand, blowing nibbles of pearwood from the furrows. Then pulling back he admired his work. Another carved vignette complete. One of thirty printing blocks. Each to be assigned its own colour, the wallpaper only complete once all had left their mark.

It was the kind of work the woodcutter relished and

yet for a long time there had been little of it, the visits of Sidney Wallis to the workshop infrequent since 1916. Just once a year with an order for only one set of blocks.

And the woodcutter sensed something different about the post-war designs, as if all that went on back then had somehow infected Sidney's creative mind.

Designs still stunning though, he thought, *beautiful patterns sure to be repeated over and over in many a living room, in many a city.*

After brushing down surfaces and tidying away tools, the woodcutter arranged the blocks side by side and when he leaned back against the bench with a mug of tea, he sensed a cryptic melancholy in the patterns as he tried to take them in all at once. And he wondered then, if after coated with paint and pressed upon paper, their superimposed prints would confess to the world some deep, unspeakable truth.

DEV

1991 – Manchester

I sat in a hospital lobby waiting for a taxi. To my left a pair of sliding doors opened and closed like a hungry mouth. The doors swished open, swished closed, then open again, the corridor space in front of me flushing with a steady flow of people. Two-directional. The young and healthy weaving between sick and old. Currents in a human river that intermingled by the vending machine and further down the corridor in the waiting area.

In came a nurse pushing an empty wheelchair, its grey tyres almost clipping my toes as he coasted by, his light blue scrubs smaller and smaller in the corridor, eventually dissolving into the muddle of hospital traffic. And then my eyes sank aimlessly into the plain magnolia walls, grim details re-emerging as I slipped into the beige; my mind doing its best to scramble away but memories of the desert had already taken hold...

...Dust clinging to everything; rubber buttons, hatch seals, smeared in places by a sweaty hand. The sensation of heat off the lower bulkhead. The man in the hatch next to mine uttering calm and routine words into his helmet. The monologue beside me babbling on: Sunray – this is callsign twelve – message understood – over.

A tap on the shoulder pulling my gaze away from burning oil wells, the helmeted man glanced my way, his paddled hand veering north-east like a weathervane as he relayed the warning, "partisan activity".

It was like he'd thrown a stick for a dog, my binocular vision scampering off over a desert that was vast and empty and indifferent. I searched a gully then swivelled around and scanned the terrain behind, but all I could see was the dust kicked up by our convoy, cut loose and sliding away.

And then of course everything went haywire – our armoured vehicle lurching as callsign fifteen on our left took a direct hit, tracks of another vehicle churning a protective arc also exploding. The sound so loud it affected my vision. My body somehow on sand, the ringing in my ears unwavering as chaos unravelled around me, one of our jets banking and gaining height.

I stayed down, gingerly moving fingers and toes while gazing into the orange glow of a parched winter sky, the routine of army life suddenly rendered insignificant. Everything strangely serene until I felt my body being dragged away, my boots furrowing the sand, my right ear dangling like heavy jewellery. I sat in a makeshift first aid post, streams of blood soaking everything below my ear, the moments before getting thumped glitching on a loop as I looked around for Andy. The view straight ahead hidden behind the face of a medic, his eyes level with mine, his hand shaking my shoulder, his mouth saying my name: Devon... Devon... Devon, but his speech was no more than a silent mime...

Blinking myself into awareness I looked up as the fingers of a delicate hand landed on my shoulder, the receptionist standing beside me, a fatigued smile on her face, her other hand pointing at a taxi that was parked beyond the sliding doors.

Wallpaper Mill

The taxi dropped me on Didsbury High Street, and I walked the rest of the way home. Being out in public something I had struggled with since returning to Manchester unless wearing a hat or donning a hood. Half an ear a small percentage of oneself, but when missing enough to throw self-confidence disproportionately askew. And, of course, before surgery, a lot of unwanted attention came my way. Bemused intrigue mainly, as if I were one of those asymmetrical Picassos that hung on the wall of a gallery. My ear part re-attached, part reconstructed, it had taken three operations to put it right. And now with the dressing off, and the stitches out, my walk through a Manchester suburb on a busy afternoon was like some nervy big reveal.

Textbook had been the initial verdict of the decisions made in the desert that day. But in the moment, stopping for that long had felt reckless, our vehicles basking in low sun, our camouflage glowing gold against carbon skies. Captain Ross's claim that we were safe, as long as "Angel" had eyes on the desert, as if I were his lucky charm.

Angel: a nickname rekindled by my friend Andy when he saw "Dear Angel" on a letter from home. Coined by my mum because I had made a Christmas cake. Conversation over turkey dinner that year a clamour over what part of me came from whom, as if I were layers of a cake, concocted from different recipes. Tight curled hair and the skin of my West Indian mum, the rest of me like my English father.

I continued on below verdant trees that lined the street, the only eyes giving me a second glance belonging to the cat in the hair salon window. Almost disappointed at my unnoticed return to the world of "normal", I cut through an alleyway beside the florists and skipped up the metal steps that led to my flat.

Briefly peering at myself in the bathroom mirror my head looked roughly symmetrical. Right ear slightly lower than the left, a bit chewed but reassuringly earlike.

Fine, so I *looked* normal.

But looks were deceiving and lurking beneath mine there was something not right, something missing that no one else could see.

At the living room window, I scanned the street below. People drinking outside the pub, people in and out of boutique shops, people on the top deck of a bus that trundled past.

Everything busy and vibrant. A lovely sunny Saturday scrolling by. But I could only watch from the sidelines because the world had stopped talking to me. Everything near silent and neutral. I was so annoyed with my ears for not being able to hear. Such a simple everyday thing, but they just couldn't do it. Parts deep inside my right ear – specifically the hair cells in the cochlea – were damaged and deemed unfixable. Only phantom sounds lurked there now. Deep reverberations or mysterious groans as if a glacier crept through its internal channels.

The jury was still out on my left ear. It just lazily snoozed, occasionally waking up to let in sounds before falling back to sleep, test results suggesting its workings were still intact, most likely because they had sheltered from the blast on the leeward side of my head.

So, apparently, the future held promise. The specialist's early prognosis of total deafness now upgraded to unilateral listener.

And as the weeks passed, sounds on my left side did trickle in. To discern a beat or muffled voice, tiny breakthroughs that should have lifted my post-war gloom. But I hardly noticed them because of what loomed ahead. A dread growing inside as the military hearing drew closer. The prospect of an investigation lurking on the horizon, ready to dig up and repeat everything I was desperate to forget.

And then the day arrived, sounds in the courtroom just a series of anchorless rushes and odd clonks. Voices burbling as if my ears were underwater, my ability to hear no better than a fish. I had no idea of what went on until a copy of the transcript came my way. Flicking through to the back I read the summing up.

Act of providence...

Nobody's fault...

Case for the defence built around the Battle of Barnet of 1471.

Friendly fire had – it seemed – repeated through the history books of military conflict. My platoon shot up by our own side forgiven due to the fog of war.

But the "no blame" verdict failed to sooth a trauma that had lurked inside me for weeks: a toxic mix of irrational fears – things in the sky still messing with my head.

I trudged on.

Each week whispering a little louder. New sounds, like gifts my left ear unwrapped and gratefully took in. Music more than a beat now, conversations a broken string of consonants but not the links between them. The acoustic microclimate of home capturing the midrange sounds of taps and kettles and toilets.

My first hearing aid a game changer. The little plastic device reconnecting me to other people. Especially those who turned towards me; my auditory shortfalls compensated by watching expressions and lips.

Three months later, hearing on the left side was back to ninety per cent depending on the conditions. The hearing aid's performance hit and miss outdoors; better inside, if spaces weren't too big or overcrowded. And winning back my hearing, albeit in one ear, tamed my dislike of intrusive sounds. I would just sit and listen and smile – everything bigger, everything richer: taz of a moped, yap of small dogs. Car alarm. The man living in the flat next door strumming a guitar.

And it did feel as if my life had regained a brighter rhythm, some repeated pattern of upbeat normality: I went to a department store every Saturday for coffee and cake before buying homely items for the flat. I started a new job working for a friend of my mum's as an office admin. I embarked on a twelve-week course of therapy: one session every Thursday afternoon in a cramped room, my anxieties crawling out from a foxhole one by one. Guilt, flashbacks, fear of it all happening again. The fear of unexplained delays most of all, my brain convinced that some destructive force would lurch out from above and wreak havoc once more. It was a three-month period in which my trauma untangled so much that by the end of the summer, memories of the incident began fading to lighter shades of beige.

And during the later sessions we focused on good memories and happy times and there were many because my childhood had been a good one, but the memory of my gran's bakery rose above it all. And that got me thinking and the following Saturday when I went to the department store for coffee and cake I came back with a bread-maker.

It was too big for my tiny kitchen; not much worktop left for anything else. But I didn't care. It made lovely noises and lovely smells. The whirring repetition of the paddle, the fist of dough thumping around the tin, the ticking heat and the comforting odours that escaped from the lid.

On weekdays I programmed the cycle to start early, the smells I woke up to setting my mood for the day. On weekends I would try and relax on the sofa with a book, the machine active somewhere beyond the stories I read. The afternoon light changing around me, shadows of my demons alive in the room, the whirring paddle charming them away as if mixing them into the dough.

And then of course, it just felt wrong to eat bread that was full of demons. To be honest the results were a bit grim: texture too dense, the crust limp, shape of the loaves strange and lumpy.

Although at first the waste didn't seem to matter. In my mind the rejected bread that lay warm in the pedal bin was merely a biproduct of a self-invented therapy in which the bread machine somehow sequestered my anxieties and buried them inside tortured-looking loaves.

The pedal bin never went hungry. The bread machine churned. The routine of nine-to-five gobbled up the month – autumn gradually topping and tailing the days. My performance review at the end of October fantastically unremarkable. My manager, Janet, in her lovely way putting a rosy tint on my utter indifference to the world of admin. And then out of the blue she offered me a place on an information technology course, monitor screens on the desks around us leaning in as I pondered what to do.

The following weekend I talked it over with my parents.

IT -- the future, a steady job.

'A no-brainer,' my mum said with the intonation of "you'd be mad to turn it down".

And it was clear that my mum's friend had pulled strings to get me that job, so I just couldn't bring myself to tell her it wasn't for me. The company sold products from an index catalogue. Clothing and homeware shipped in from the Far East, landing on our shores after six weeks at sea. And it bothered me that this was all happening out there in the real world, and I was stuck in an office staring at screens and tapping keyboards. Grumpy and full of unspent energy, I was like some overprotected kid kept inside whilst his mates played down the park. I yearned to be out there, doing something real.

And besides, the office bothered me.

The open-plan space so spectacularly beige my desert phobias felt right at home there; a residue of that fateful day hanging in the harsh fluorescent light. On bad days I caught myself scanning the ceiling grid whilst using the Xerox machine. My state of high alert interrupted by a paper jam, or someone standing a safe distance behind, under pressure to get on, but reluctant to ask if I'd finished. People irritated me, especially those who stood together in groups. Did they not know the risks! The high body count if something went wrong!

And then on better days everything felt innocuous, the office just a busy workplace. My desk on the fringe of a large open-plan area where I skulked with not much to do. The salads I took to work eaten by midmorning I would buy a sandwich from a nearby deli then walk around a cold city park where I sat on a bench eating doorstep slices cut from artisan loaves. Tasty carbs warming my mood, a faint desire to get back on track stirring in my stomach.

And then I stopped using the bread machine and for days it sat out of favour on the worktop. Its job done; that lazy automated method of therapy over. I needed to work harder at getting better.

I walked along my local high street, the bread machine a boulder in my arms; the ladies in the charity shop wide-eyed when I placed it on the counter.

Back at the flat I mixed ingredients in a bowl, working everything into a rough ball with my hands before turning it out on the worktop. And then I worked with the speed and focus of a regular baker. Palm and heel of my hand lightly stretching the dough, all the time aware of the changes, the way the gluten strands in the mixture developed; my fingertips on the lookout for the onset of silkiness. Movements light and firm, never heavy handed. I forgot everything else for ten minutes or so. Fluidity and rhythm taking over.

The rise, the knock back. Everything repeated. The dough transforming as it relaxed into the ingot-shaped tin, heat of the oven doing the rest. The top turning gold as it rose and fissured and doubled in size, the loaf hardly resting before I ran through the knife.

Steam rising from the cut face as butter gilded it yellow. I closed my eyes and took a big bite. The warm bread like a dream in my mouth.

*

Did I forget to mention? I knew much more than the basics because my grandmother, Marion, ran a bakery in Speightstown. Her lime-green shop sandwiched between buildings of old Barbados. It was a town in the north, away from the resorts, a little frayed around the edges but full of Bajan character. I used to work there during summer holidays, and my gran would playfully remind my teenage self that baking was more than just measuring out the ingredients from a recipe book.

'A splash of water if the mix is too dry, a dash of flour if too wet. Hands. Trust your hands, Devon,' she would say rolling her eyes and holding my wrists and turning the palms of my hands skyward. Then she would return to work, smiling on and on despite the daily repetition of what she did. I loved working for my gran. I should have known my heart lay back there in Speightstown.

And with that in mind I took bread to my last therapy session and announced my big idea.

'You actually made this?' beamed my counsellor. 'Best bread I ever tasted,' she said, but her excitement soon shrank. And after talking it through it was agreed that even without the burden of post-traumatic stress, running a bakery would prove to be very tough.

Maybe next year.

The following day I sat on the park bench, pigeons pecking crumbs from a crust I had picked apart. I was so annoyed with myself for allowing my dream to be shot down without a fight. Flinching as pigeons exploded skywards, I got up and left the park and took a taxi to the office. Mayhem of the city too much for my nerves. A bad day unsettling the whole week.

Booking time off I stayed at home, like some lonesome grizzly bear, sleeping and eating and backing away from the telephone whenever it rang. Frankly I was fed up with *just* talking things through.

*

But I had not realised that it was Isla Graham who was leaving the messages. She was an eccentric friend from the past; our families close since we were little. She tried to ring me several times; left messages to say she was there if I needed help. She could sign. That was her job. To be honest I had not got back to her because when we were kids she was overbearing and bossy.

Mum accused me of being rude. 'She's different now. Besides, Roger and Jane would love to see you.'

Isla lived with her parents in a sleepy market town that nestled between moorland slopes. It was a remote place, about an hour north.

'A break from the city is just what you need,' Mum said handing me the address book. I phoned the Grahams' house. And the following weekend I drove north in Mum's car. The journey lasting just over an hour. A period of time in which I remembered playing with Isla as a child. Her wanting to be with the boys a problem because she could not bat or bowl. I winced at memories of her standing behind the cricket stumps pretending to be the umpire. Our all-day park matches descending into massive arguments because we ignored her. The arbitrary decisions she made driven by boredom and not the rules of cricket. She would eventually march off into the outfield, not giving the ball back if it came her way, her rude hand signals from then on, ones you would not find in the umpire's manual.

Thinking back, she had always been good at communicating with her hands. But really, I didn't need to sign. My left ear holding its own as long as the batteries in the hearing aid had plenty of juice in them.

I arrived at their house still not sure that my visit was a good idea. But clearly, I'd got it all wrong. They were lovely to me; treated me like their own. I'd forgotten how like family they were. After dinner Isla and I walked her dogs along a canal that skirted the town. And as we struck out into open moorland, I could see that Mum was right. Isla was not the stroppy little monster I once knew. And, well – I liked her. Funny and bright with occasional outbreaks of endearing sass. And it turned out her year had been torrid too. After living in Manchester for two years she had returned home after an unpleasant split with a cheating boyfriend.

Canal water mirrored the fading sky; a seam of burnt ochre that parted the moor. We turned back. She asked me about the Gulf War. I briefly described what happened. After that we trudged along in thoughtless silence, the light closing in all around us.

Before long we were in town again, Isla pointing out the old canal-side building, a paper mill that was undergoing renovation after decades of neglect; subdivided into spaces for small businesses. Gazing up at the building I felt a tingling sensation in my hands, impulses shivering through me, my grandmother's words repeating through my head: *Hands. Trust your hands, Devon.*

*

Bakery dream rekindled; it glowed inside me for days. Hidden and protected from anything or anyone that might crush it. Lunchbreaks highlight of the day, I walked through city streets towards the deli-bakery, studying the window as I stood in the queue.

Inside: sweet treats at the front. Shelves laddering up the back and side walls, artisan and regular loaves neatly stacked upon them. Multigrain, white, sourdough, rye, focaccia, baguettes. Sticks of grissini like giant pencils in a pot.

It was like I'd stumbled into a bread cave. The smell beyond description – more a good mood that embraced the air.

I soon got to know the owners, Lee and Toby. Although most days they had little time to talk shop with me. Lunchtime their busiest time, but I had so many questions about setting up a bakery. And then one day:

'Come back later, when we're less busy,' muttered Toby, his big curly hair supressed by a hairnet, his hands busy wheeling brown paper bags over the counter to queuing customers.

Later that day they welcomed me into the shop, and I followed them through to the backroom, a windowless kitchen where the tang of fermentation overwhelmed the air. A commercial set-up with enough oomph to supply cafes and restaurants as well as their own doorstep customers. Industrial stand mixers, deck ovens, a whole fleet of wheeled cooling racks parked along the side wall. And being there felt right; excitement tingling through my body, my gran's voice partying in my head.

Initial conversations were awkward and cagey, the owners tight-lipped, until I explained my bakery would pose no threat because it was so far north. And then the floodgates opened. Costs, qualifications, schedules, Toby ran through the lot, and I left with a roughly outlined plan and their words buzzing in my hearing aid: *embrace tiredness, grinding hours, profits to make your accountant weep. Bakery seconds for breakfast, lunch and tea. Make sure you do it!*

The Angel Bakery

'Given it any more thought?' Mum enquired while blitzing the kitchen sink. Not waiting for an answer, she raked draws for cutlery, all the time talking about the IT course, the doors it could open, her words partly lost to the fraught clink of knives and forks.

I served up a roast dinner.

Mum shuffled forward on a chair. 'You need a bigger table – you should have come to ours.'

I usually did, but what I'd learnt over the years was that the best place to make a stand was away from the family home, a place where my childhood conformity still faintly echoed.

'The neighbours have an Apple Macintosh – it's a clever little thing.'

'Mum – it's not me.'

Wine flowed. Dad sat very still. Mum looked messy.

'What are you going to do then?' she snapped. Dad's stillness now skewed towards the television, his eyes squinting at the cricket score.

I left the table, his attention snapping back when I returned with a yellow A4 wallet. 'Actually, I've been giving that some thought,' I said, pulling out photographs of the mill. Explaining its renovation was part of a drive to regenerate the high street, I pointed out the end bay of the building was still vacant, then described my idea of setting up a bakery; mum's silence the reaction I feared; her hanging moment laced with disappoint – my expensive boarding-school education all for nothing. And I knew she would link it with my grandmother, her return to Barbados, her daily toil in a Speightstown bakery. A return to old ways, the old world. To my mother, the island was a place where her ancestors wielded blades at sugar cane and lived in creaking chattel shacks with no running water; these were stories of extreme hardships I had grown up with.

But this was different. My grandmother found joy in what she did. Nothing groundbreaking or technological about that. She had simply discovered what made her feel good and repeated it every day; and, well – she was the most contented person I had ever met.

Mum stared at the photograph of the mill and remained silent as if absorbing the impact of my news, as if shaking off its historical backstep.

'Mum – are you alright?'

'I'm fine.'

'I really want to do this.'

'Is this really – you?' she said looking at me over her glasses.

'Really sure.'

Dad held her hand. 'Can you tell us some more?'

I took a deep breath.

'Well – it's no money tree, but I can make it pay. The area is crying out for a bakery. And at least my army pension will give me something to live off.'

Then I led them through the details of a business plan, costings, forecasts, break-even point on the bank loan. Their look of bemusement switching to one of mild surprise, a glance of unspoken approval passing between them. My dad tentatively offering help. 'I will have to check our finan…'

'We'll help,' Mum interrupted. 'We had money set aside for when you bought your first place.'

She stood and hugged me, her kiss landing silently on my broken ear, her body falling limp as she sat down on the sofa as if months of strain had suddenly deserted her.

'I know it's a messy grind, Mum, but it makes me tick.'

'Okay – I get it – whatever makes you happy. My mother has got such a lot to answer for,' she said, rolling her eyes.

'She has?' I beamed.

We sifted through photographs of the mill, Mum describing the stonework above the entrance doors as quirky.

'The mill's frontage reminds me of the Glasgow School of Art,' she went on to say.

And the mill did have that same infectious aura, some joyous energy that pulsed through its playful facade.

Mum filled our glasses and after toasting the bakery, we drank wine until late and Dad talked of a relative who had worked at another mill, that also made wallpaper.

'Potters were in competition with the Wallis mill. They were only a few miles down the road in Darwen.'

'Didn't even know we had relatives that way.'

'Aunty Minnie died before you were born. Still remember her stories about the Wallis mill though. The owner built a school and housing for his workers, all a great success until the First World War. A lot of Lancashire mills became munitions factories back then…'

Absorbed by the revelations, we sat in silence.

'The mill being requisitioned turned the place upside down. A closed community like that struggled with the influx of outsiders. The goings-on so grim the parish council decided to give the town a new name between the wars – place used to be called Dardale. Anyway, Minnie moved to Blackburn after retiring. Died of emphysema a few years later – bit of a heavy smoker.'

'Bit of a racist…' Mum said, leaning towards me, '… fell out with the family big time.'

'Anyway, this all happened way back. The town's turned a corner since then. Roger and Jane are very happy there. Used to have a reputation but not now. Wish we lived that way ourselves. In fact, your mother and I may follow if you decide to settle.'

My parents stayed over and slumbered in my bed.

I took out my hearing aid and lay on the sofa. My excitement bristling in the silence, leafy shadows cast by streetlights, dancing around the walls as if they were covered with restless patterns.

Could a place really change its name? What on earth could have happened between the wars?

One thought leading to another, haunting memories of the Gulf War came to mind. Then wind whistled down my street, the wall shadows distracting me away from desert carnage. Tree silhouettes swaying, leaves busy, as if scrubbing, as if erasing my war-torn traumas. The wind gusted again, and I closed my eyes and tilted towards sleep, and tried only to think of things to come.

*

November: I waited in the meeting room above the agent's office; big, wild skies above town drawing me to the sash windows. The street outside straight and treelined. Town square at the top end; Wallis Mill at the bottom. Between them a continuous run of two and three-storey buildings. A hotchpotch of civic one-offs that would have looked unruly if not for their shared love of Georgian proportions.

Beyond the roofs lived wilderness. Belts of heather blooming like bruises on a distant ridge, the moor hunched below menacing skies. The town like a ship between green waves. The buildings unkempt and tired and unpicked by time and whipped by the wind.

It was plain to see there was a big push to reverse the

decline. Grand windows overlooking the square now peeking through a lattice of scaffold poles and boards. Clouds of dust and sounds of construction work coming from the open windows across the street.

That energy of renewal not yet echoing through the room in which I sat: the ceiling needed a lick of paint, the coving cracked in places. The wallpaper looked old, maybe a Wallis Mill original. It was grubby around the doorframe and light switch, faded on the walls closer to the window. A pattern of hares printed upon it; some sitting, some on the run. Everything repeated.

Their heads turned back; eyes fearful of whatever they ran from. A chase around the room that drew me in until it all disappeared behind display boards mounted on the wall that marketed the business units; artist's impressions of the internal spaces, red words slashed across the corner of a floorplan that read *Only Two Remaining*.

The stairs creaked. The door opened.

The agent appeared closely followed by the current-day owner of the mill, Rennie Wallis, a silver-haired gent, his tall frame hindered by age; he stuttered into the room wistfully looking about as if stirred by some distant memory. Then his eyes settled on me, and I stood, and we shook hands.

He nodded towards the blurb. 'It was my father, Sidney, who built the mill – have you seen his statue in the square?'

The exchange between us more of a chat than formal meeting; he said his tenure as the lucky heir was drawing to a close as the old money generated by his father's empire had dried up. The Dardale Hall estate where he lived now a burden he was looking to sell.

'But not the mill,' he added, conceding the family's wallpaper business went belly-up soon after his father's death. 'It's been unloved for decades, so finally making something of it is my way of making it up to my father.'

And I'm sure that was true, but it was obvious the venture was not a money spinner; his offer of a cut-price lease too good to be true. Though it came with the condition I used his team of consultants for the fit-out. Which was fine. One of the business units was already home to the architect's practice, so they seemed best placed.

'I should have renovated it years ago.' Most of what he said seemed tinged with regret. 'Just hope I'm still alive to see it all finished.'

Then he explained that in the event of his death a legal company would continue to manage the property on behalf of the beneficiaries in his will, for a fixed term of twenty years. He couldn't guarantee what would happen after that.

His old age a factor I had not considered although a twenty-year lease felt like eternity, so I casually brushed it aside and signed the paperwork and we shook hands.

I slept over at the Grahams' all week and met with the architect every day. A design to suit the budget thrashed out by Friday. The architect prepared drawings and submitted an application to the council.

I went back to Manchester and resumed work at the office. Absent-mindedly cocking things up as I drifted like a zombie back and forth to the Xerox, snatching the telephone from its cradle whenever it rang as if I were an expectant father awaiting news of the birth. And the calls kept coming; estimates from builders, queries from building control, detailed questions about the internal layout of spaces. My baby gestating. Six weeks later the council approved the plans, and we appointed a builder. Within a month work started on converting the end bay of the mill into a bakery and the space above into a two-bed flat. Three months in, the bakery was finished; completion of the flat still some way off.

Refusing to let me travel back and forth to Manchester every day, the Grahams again kindly offered me a bed.

So, I loaded the car with a bag full of clothes and set off, the skies opening somewhere beyond Bolton, lazy sweep of the window-wipers brushing wet weather aside as the road climbed. The journey tortuous; a roadworks diversion that took me over high lanes, the moors shrouded in mist. Then a fleeting glimpse of the town below. The huddle of slate roofs like wet scree that had been washed into the valley, the road angling down, two sharp bends, the town reappearing beyond a third. The canal bridge ahead; pub one side, mill the other.

I parked up, collected the keys from the agent, then opened the bakery door. The shop interior, bare brick walls and oak plank floors, unlived-in coldness hanging in the air, the glass counter at the back like a jewel in the light of a tall industrial window.

I carried on through another door that led to the kitchen. The room silent; sounds dulled by the castle-thick walls. I peeled film from the stainless-steel appliances, read instruction manuals then fired up the deck ovens.

The next day I baked. Pick of the artisan loaves and cakes landing on the Grahams' dining table at the end of each day.

The week before opening I tied up loose ends: snagging lists, inventories, supplier discounts negotiated, recipe cards laminated. As I waited for Isla, I sat next to the ovens and checked costings, then checked them again. Then I left the kitchen and walked through to the shop. Contrast between the two spaces a reflection of where my passions lay. The kitchen full of energy, gleaming stainless steel and buttery smells. The retail space barren like a Soviet-era corner shop that was having a bad day.

Thankfully Isla had offered to help, but she was late – maybe held up by weather that had gone from bad to worse; a series of fronts sweeping in off the Atlantic, the street outside battered by rain.

And then time slackened, and my imagination began to drift; terrible scenarios of what may have happened to Isla plaguing my mind. And then I saw her in the angling rain, walking down from the bus stop. Hands stuffed in pockets, hunched and hooded, her feet stomping over drenched cobbles. She lunged into the shop. Her hood flicked back, her face red-eyed and wretched.

'You're alive.'

'Of course, I'm alive.'

'I mean – are you alright?'

'No. I'm not alright.'

She was late because of an argument with her mother. I took her wet coat and draped it over a stool.

'Want to talk about it?'

'No.'

'Want a hug?'

'Yes.'

Isla was in limbo – like I had been earlier that year.

'I told her I hate Manchester, Dev. I'm not going back there,' she said, chewing a thumb nail.

We unpacked boxes of stock, the swish of wet traffic filtering into the shop; neither of us talking as we loaded up the shelves.

'Why not use your skills locally – start your own business?'

Her face appeared from behind a five-tier shelving rack. 'Has everyone gone mad?'

'What's the matter?'

'Deaf community not big enough.'

'Ah yes – of course.'

She was in the window then, her hands soon busy rearranging the display. 'As I said to my mum – it's probably just your right ear.'

The sass in her voice made me smile as I hung a framed photo of my regiment on the wall by the till. I picked out Andy, a good friend I had lost in the desert. Then I glanced at Isla. Resolved to sulk, staring people into submission as they walked past the shop. Her hands busy wiping builder's dust from the inside surface of the window, a sign that said "The Angel Bakery" above her head, the weather lifting, views of Main Street clearing. In many ways she reminded me of Andy. His no-messing approach. One friend lost; one friend gained.

'Isla.'

She approached the till, grime on her face like she'd been on jungle patrol and forgotten to wash off the camouflage.

'Mm.'

'The whole shop thing leaves me cold.'

'My favourite game as a kid.'

She was at the till then, her eyes all over the keys, and I wondered if her mind had flipped back to selling unicorns to soft toys.

'What I'm trying to say is – I'll need help with it.'

'Is that a job offer?'

'There, if you want it.'

'Cool. Reckon I could do that,' she said without hesitation.

'Well – you've got the job.'

She was so excited. And she was the perfect fit. Trustworthy. Confident with people, could multi-task without losing her cool. And yes, it was partly my way of repaying the Grahams for all they had done for me.

We sat on the floor and ate scones.

'Dev.' She said my name carefully as if it were something delicate.

'Mm.'

'Just one thing – you know this won't be leading to anything romantic.'

I choked on the scone. 'I do love you, Isla – but mixing business with affairs of the heart is a recipe for disaster.'

She smiled, leaned in and kissed me on the cheek. 'Thank you for helping me out.'

'We'll make a good team.'

I wasn't surprised or downhearted by the rejection as our relationship over the years had only ever been platonic.

And, well, in any case – there was someone else. Someone from my past, before the army.

Someone who crashed back into my life, without any forewarning.

Right out of the blue.

DANI

1989 – Moss Side, Manchester

She sat alone in the bar absorbing the sounds that swirled in from the lounge. Heckles, boozy jeers, the blaring television, the clink of glasses, the same noises that had echoed through her childhood. The roughness always rising through the bedroom floor at night. Her young mind tucked up in bed imagining the flat above her father's pub floated above an angry sea, the men drinking below like mad pirates. Ruffians who, over the years, had become as predictable as the tides. Congregating in the lounge on a Saturday afternoon something they always did.

So, nobody noticed her in the corner of the empty tap room, that familiar anxiety hidden in her gut, her hands tightly wrapped around a glass of coke, her feet pushed back against a rucksack, her whole body resisting the urge to flee.

And all the time she stared at the willow tattoos on her forearms, a copy of the pattern that repeated around the walls of her grandmother's hallway. The entwinement of branches and leaves settling her nerves.

She sat and listened and waited, the bar room waiting with her. The row of optics, the pump handles, the pretty woman in a bikini printed on a snack display card smiling into a room that stank of stale beer and cigarettes.

In the other room the television roared. The match kicked off, the jeers got louder, she calmly gathered her things and walked over to the bar, straps of the rucksack looped in one hand as she reached over the bar top and grabbed the wooden bat.

The street outside deserted, the peculiar thin song of an ice-cream van chiming beyond terraced houses. The end house directly before her not lived in since the riots, the windows and doors bricked up. Its frontage blindly facing the head of a no-through road kids used for street games; a goal painted on the wall with white paint.

But the street was empty because the cup final had enticed the kids away.

She had counted on that.

Walking around the corner she stopped by the kerbside, her legs and feet reflected in the polished panels of a car.

A fixed-up Jensen Interceptor SP, that her father loved like family.

And yet her family was broken and in bits.

You cannot fix old family problems, her father's voice grated through her mind as she glared into the car, eyes very wide as if she peered into the chapters of a younger life, traversing the years in a desperate attempt to understand what had gone wrong.

'Damn car,' she whispered.

The tremble in her hand steadying as she gripped the bat tighter, the urge to run in her legs so powerful she wondered if it was due to some hand-me-down gene. Women running away, a pattern that had echoed through the generations of her family. The most recent being her mother, Deepika, who had run from home because her parents' choice of (arranged) husbands did not include Mancunian hardmen. And then of course there was Dani's great-grandmother, Ellen, who had run away from home during the First World War, abandoning her baby before disappearing. And that baby was now Dani's grandmother – a lady called Harriette, a lady with the willow patterns in her hallway.

And there were others, apparently, further back in time, the details of why they ran lost in the fog of history. Which seemed to make Gran Harriette the exception to the tradition of running away. Fabled for being steadfast. Very rarely, if ever, leaving the mill town she was born into.

Dani edged closer to "Jensen". Close enough to feel the warmth from an engine that had raced back from the bookies, close enough to see the finer interior details through the passenger window. The oxblood leather seats triggering memories of when she last saw Harriette, more than ten years before. The memory sticky in her head, because the visit had been so traumatic, the memory always starting with her eight-year-old self, sat inside Jensen, travelling north to Harriette's town. Jensen growling; countryside blurring…

… *'What does SP mean?'*

'Six pack...' Her father snatched at the gearstick uttering something about six carburettors, '...you cannot beat, a muscle car.'

Those trips to her gran's were her favourite days. Sundays normally, sometimes stayovers during school holidays. Although she never enjoyed the journey via the moorland road, desolate greens and browns, stubby old trees like bony goblins hunched away from the wind. And then she would see rooftops in the valley. Nearly there. The shops on Main Street then Gran's lane unkempt and weedy and full of potholes that Jensen didn't like.

The lodges at the top, one her gran's home, the other her workshop, symmetrical either side of gates seized open with rust, a cattle grid between them preventing deer from straying off the Dardale estate.

Dani got out of the car; her feet not touching the ground, she was soon inside the hallway, the willow branches entwining around the walls, her arms soon squeezing Harriette's middle. A kiss always landing on the top of her head.

Then in the kitchen she sat by the window with a glass of lemonade, glancing at the car, searching for the muscles, her father's voice flexing somewhere behind her. And then she felt Harriette's hand stroking her head. A toffee apple and cabbage leaves placed in her hands. Leaving the kitchen, she took the shortest route to the garden through the music room between a piano and cello. Crunching into the toffee apple, she remembered the crackle-

glazed cello was made a long time ago by a man called Goffriller. A man who lived in Venice, a place that had canals instead of roads, his name sticking because it sounded like gorilla (her dad was a gorilla).

At the hutch she lifted the rabbit and carried it to a shady spot on the grass near an open window. The rabbit heavy on her lap, whiskers quivering as it nibbled. Its body flinching as the arguing voices crashed out of the kitchen window.

Dani offered up another leaf and stroked the rabbit's ears.

'That's all folks,' she whispered but the quarrelling went on. Harriette's soft Lancashire tones critical of how her father treated his family, the mistreatment of his wife, his misplaced love for that "Damn car!".

Then something about her brother being dragged into his father's Moss Side ways. Then Dani heard her own name batted back and forth. Harriette's mention of it handled with great care, words either side of it uttered with firmness as if they were protective shields.

'No need to worry about her,' he snarled.

'Hard to believe.'

'I'm sending her away.'

'Where?'

'Away from me and far away from you!'

Her father burst into the garden, pulling her up so roughly she thought her arm might break. Then he saw the rabbit hairs stuck to her fingers.

'If you touch anything you're walking home.'

'But I haven't said goodbye,' she remembered blurting as she got dragged to the car. It was the first time she remembered something snapping inside, that nasty urge to grip Jensen's oxblood insides, twist and pinch them with her sticky little fingers.

But somehow, she managed to stay still for the whole journey, instead imagining Jensen motoring through Venice, water gushing in through door gaps and up through the floor, her metal sibling gradually sinking, gradually drowning. That was the last time she was driven to Harriette's. A year later Dani was sent to boarding school...

Chanting from the pub pulled her attention back to the street. Her grip on the bat tightening, she wheeled it over her head and brought it down onto the bonnet with considerable velocity, the impact sweet like hitting a pillow. Reflections of the sky newly twisted; clouds glitching in and out of the gaping dent.

She waited, her heart pounding; noises in the pub behind her, feverish; football crazy.

After an intake of breath her swings gained rhythm, like an axe felling a forest. Not one panel escaping the bat. Whole sheets of glass torrents of diamonds after one hit. Wing mirrors snapping like brittle limbs, headlights splitting like whacked ice.

She stopped to catch her breath; the car critically wounded; the pub windows singing, "I See the Stretford End Arising". A football song that threatened trouble if you weren't a home supporter. And then the pub erupted – a goal!

Dani let out a defiant roar and again the bat arced through the air, this time landing on the roof like a death blow. Then she edged closer to the car, stooping lower, her head level with a dangling wing mirror.

'You see – I have muscles too.'

Dropping the bat, she backed away, grabbed the rucksack and ran.

*

Through the terraced streets she raced, outwitting the chance of a car chase by improvising a route through narrow ginnels and dead-end streets. Her course set in the general direction of Hulme because Simon lived there. She'd met him a few months before; went back to his council flat after a party, remembered him as kind and considerate. He was at the poly, his flat a scruffy squat. A final-year student, soon to be moving on, his place *going free*, or something like that, she couldn't quite recall. She just hoped he was still there, still living in the Crescents estate.

Dashing over Moss Lane East the straps of the rucksack dug into her shoulders so much, she thought the pub pirates had got her but when she swivelled around nobody was there; the traffic criss-crossing as if cutting her free. And for a while she just looked back from where she had come, through the traffic, the jumbled row of little shops on the far side of the road shuttered and unloved and indifferent. Her breath steadying, she turned and went on her way and walked past St Mary's Church, its thin spire like an upturned spike that left no mark on the passing clouds. The streetscape changing, terraced houses thinning, the strange Crescents estate looming ahead; hundreds of flats locked into low-rise concrete. A two-by-two grid of housing blocks, the crescent shape of each so long she'd seen them from a plane. Four smiles or a puckered frown, depending on the approach to Manchester Airport.

And then she was in the estate, her tiny figure dwarfed as she continued across a sea of scrappy grass. A free-for-all space that flowed unloved between the cliffs of concrete. Graffiti the only feature that marked Simon's block from the rest. She climbed an external staircase to the top deck, his yellow door halfway along. She knocked and then knocked again.

A chain jangled; locks turned. Simon appeared ruffling scruffy hair.

'Hi,' he said with one sleepy eye still scrunched.

He wore only boxer shorts; there was an awkward silence. He screwed both eyes shut and wagged a finger. 'Err...' – finger spooling – 'Er... Dani – right?'

'Right.'

'Everything okay?'

'Fine. Well, actually, I need a place to stay. Just for one night and I was wondering...' She looked over his shoulder into the hallway.

'Right – I see.'

'And I owe you some money. So...'

She held out a ten-pound note. But all he saw was her other hand tucking hair behind an ear, her beauty intensified by the broken nose, the bridge a little flattened. A wild, untamed beauty he'd previously been wary of. And he couldn't remember the money which made the payment seem a bit dodgy.

'Simon?'

'Mm.' He looked up and took the note. 'Sorry – would you like coff…?'

She brushed past him glancing at the rooms either side of the hallway.

He closed the door. 'Come in, come in,' he said pulling on a tee shirt before making shamefaced trips back and forth to the kitchen picking up dirty crockery off the living room floor.

They sat, sipped coffee and chatted, and he calmly listened as stories of her troubled home life tumbled out. When she mentioned the car, he spat out a mouthful of coffee and sprang up and spoke from the kitchen whilst dabbing his shirt. 'I mean – you actually did that?'

'It's bad, I know.'

'Talk about leaving with a bang.'

She nestled into the noisy bean bag. He reappeared from the kitchen. 'Makes my childhood seem idyllic – only real grievance I had was both parents worked long hours.' He raked his hair. 'You've got nowhere to stay?'

'Nowhere.' She shrugged.

'Look – it's fine, you can stay here.'

'Are you sure? It wouldn't be for long.' She offered to share the bills.

'No need. There's no bills. And the place is rent-free courtesy of the architects who designed this dump.'

Her face blanked.

'Wilson and Wormsley – researched them for my sociology degree. Took a lot of shit for this place. Have to say, I feel sorry for them.'

Pulling on jeans and buckling a belt, he talked in a raised voice from the bedroom.

'I mean their intentions were sound. They called the deck access design "streets in the sky" – were meant to liberate folk from the slums.' He reappeared. 'Big shithole in the sky more like and no place for a family as it turned out.'

'Perfect for mine then.'

Sitting on the floor he looked up and smiled sympathetically as he pulled on a pair of grubby trainers. 'It was dangerous for kids. One fell to his death after climbing on the balcony rail.'

Feeling weary she sank deeper into the bean bag and thought of her brother. His body found in a ginnel, his killer still at large.

'Families didn't want to live here after that, so the council shipped them out,' he said from the bathroom, a busy toothbrush garbling his voice. 'Council stopped charging rent. Handed keys to anyone desperate enough to live here. And the best thing – council supplies electricity free of charge…' – he spat – '…compensation for living with rats and cockroaches…' – then he spoke to the mirror – '… hello off-grid anarchy. I mean who'd have thought this shit heap would become an epicentre of counterculture. Place is rife with punks, skinheads, musicians and students.' He walked out of the bathroom apologising for the lack of food in the cupboards. 'I'll nip out and buy some… thing.'

He froze for a second in the living room doorway and then continued on, gently lifting the mug off her lap and placing it on the coffee table. Backtracking to the hallway he grabbed a coat and let himself out and as the door closed, the net curtain above Dani's sleeping body billowed out and then sighed back to the open window.

*

A short while later Simon tiptoed in and quietly placed a saucepan on the hob. Bringing it to the boil he slipped half a packet of pasta shells into the rolling water then checked on Dani.

The Moss Side girl, asleep and purring, her body curled foetal like a cat. Trainers kicked off, her bare feet hanging limp off the edge of his bean bag.

A brave soul, he thought. One who had escaped the grip of a fallen society. He was – at one time – interested in studying her neighbourhood but had been advised not to – by his tutor – because of the dangers. A geeky student like himself investigating "the social causes and consequences of human behaviour" likely to get his fucking head blown off.

The jar of *Dolmio* sauce popped as he twisted the lid.

Dani shifted on the bean bag. 'Is that you?'

'Yes, it's me.' He drained the pasta and covered it in bolognese sauce. 'Hello, sleepy head,' he said, holding out a bowl.

'Thank you.' She took it and ate without pause.

'The flat gets very cold in winter. I'll leave you the bar heater. Don't bother with that thing,' he said, pointing at the portable gas fire. 'Spews out water vapour – makes the walls sweat.'

'You're leaving?' Her words barely made it through the food in her mouth.

'I am.'

'You said you might the last time I was here.'

'Well, looks like you arrived just in time. I'm around for a few days yet. Staying with friends in Altrincham then off on my travels.' He pointed back to the bar heater. 'When it gets cold, just keep it running.'

Her face fell then, her eyes lost in the wallpaper that covered the far wall, the patterns dull and soulless. Not like the graceful willow patterns that lined the walls of her gran's lodge. She had of course considered at length whether to visit her gran but decided not to. Drawing Harriette into the turmoil of Moss Side just seemed so wrong – *Maybe next year.*

'Don't look so worried. It may be a shithole but the anarchy's good-natured here. You'll have friends before you know it.'

He got up, took the bowls and added them to the dirty crockery already in the kitchen. 'I'll wash; you dry?' he said over his shoulder as Dani appeared in the kitchen door.

'Sure.'

Hands busy in the sink he nattered away about finishing his degree and how he planned to study a masters, but only after travelling to Nepal. He was interested in Buddhism.

'It's deeply entwined with salvation, and I like that. You can take my room if you like. I won't be needing it for a while.'

After finishing the dishes, she went to the bedroom and unpacked clothes into the bottom of a wardrobe that had no hanger rail. He lay on the bed and spoke to the ceiling about the virtues of zen living.

Her rucksack near empty and slack-sided she doubled it over and slid it under the bed, the last remaining object inside hard and angled like a broken bone; protection was how she justified carrying a handgun. The media had renamed Manchester "Gunchester" – she lived in the most violent part of the city. Crime her father's religion; his pub like a crooked church; her brother fatally wounded in a shooting.

I've got a gun, big deal.

But it was an item she could not unpack in front of Simon; her world a million miles away from his dreamy idealisms.

He rolled onto his side and caught her eye as she crouched beside the bed.

'Look – why don't you come? I'm interrailing for a few weeks then flying to Delhi. My friend has a houseboat in Kashmir. Free digs. You could join us.'

She half expected to be sleeping rough on her first night on the run. A shop doorway or park bench maybe, so to have a roof over her head, rent free, for the foreseeable future was a minor miracle. In any case, being on the run felt so weak. She wanted to be steadfast, like Harriette. She turned Simon down.

Next morning, they stood outside the flat. Traffic noise from the flyover whispering through the estate. She hugged him. His body a warm oasis amongst the cool concrete.

'See you again then, twelve months maybe.' He stepped back, slung a duffel bag over his shoulder, and set off along the access deck. 'Oh – and give the keys to Bikey if you move on. He's looking after the place while I'm away – he lives in the caravan behind William Kent block,' he said before disappearing down the stairwell.

Closing the door, she turned and hurried through the flat and stood on the balcony and watched him walk across a bare trail that cut diagonally across the grass. He stopped and called up, 'Trust me, you'll have a great time here.' Then he turned and carried on, the space he moved through barren like a clear zone around a prison. He looked back one more time and then disappeared.

Fez

Closing the balcony door, she hid behind curtains, peeked through the gap and monitored the grass below that was split down the middle by a twisting path. But there was no sign of her father or his Moss Side gang. In fact, she saw no sign of life at all, just the opposite housing block. Barren, utilitarian, more like a multistorey car park than a place to live, she thought.

A motion caught her eye. A dog in the play area sniffing puny trees. It zigzagged away, nose scouting the ground. After worrying a bin bag, it circled a washing machine that was dumped beside the opposite housing block. The appliance lying on its side, body deformed, its door like an eye.

Not just children that fall from upper floors, she guessed as a shower of rain stained the concrete walls dark grey.

Her gaze switched between both ends of the path, the spaces there squeezed by the housing blocks as they drew closer together. A place where litter performed manic ariels, a flurry that brought her vigil to an end as the damp concrete walls dissolved into the night.

Then somewhere in the middle-distance rooms appeared. An incomplete matrix of luminous boxes magically floating in darkness. Light filtering through curtains or shining from naked bulbs. And in the very same moment when it seemed the world outside was oblivious to her gaze, she suddenly felt on show, her existence betrayed by the bare bulb that dangled above her head. Switching it off she retreated into the hallway and paced back and forth until the urge to bolt was tamed from her legs.

'You're safe,' she whispered.

No rent... good-natured anarchy... friends before you know it... Simon's words in her head like some Buddhist incantation.

She locked the front door and slid the chain into the keep – it was a waiting game now, just a few days of lying low. Time enough for her trail to go cold, time enough for her father to lick his wounds. Dead son and now a smashed car. Maybe he'd come for her. Maybe he wouldn't.

She didn't know for sure. And that was him. Docile but unpredictable, like a gorilla.

In the kitchen she pulled down the blind and flicked a switch, fluorescent tubes blinking on, overfilling the small room with light that betrayed fluffy dust and greasy walls.

She took stock of food. Enough for a few days she thought, but that didn't include the tatty box of Scott's porridge. On closer inspection she saw that the man in a kilt that appeared on the box had been defaced. Words in a speech bubble that came from his mouth read, *Leave off my stash, wankers!*, the shotput in his hand transformed into a bomb by the addition of a curly fuse.

Pulling out the bag of oats she saw a second cellophane bag in the bottom of the box. It was filled with tablets. Colourful like Love Hearts embossed with various motifs. She spilled them onto the worktop: smiley face, Superman S, the head of Bugs Bunny.

Her college friends took ecstasy at raves. A chemical kick that spurred them on. Back in the day, she never felt the need; dancing into the early hours came easy to her. Born fidgety, she was one of those kids who tormented waiting rooms and shredded the nerves of battle-hardened teachers. A trait her mother moderated by taking her to a boxing club three nights a week.

It was, she remembered, a time when life felt simple, nothing really changing; Mum behind the bar or busy in the flat above the pub. Dani helping her to cook and clean; they were a good team back then. Dani's departure to boarding school spelling an abrupt end to those days. The cracks appearing when she started sixth form. Her brother easing into her father's footsteps, his lack of judgement like an inbred disorder; bruises appearing on her mother's arms. But by then Dani and her mother had grown apart. The bond between them had, over the years, faded away and her mother would not accept any help, would not open up, her state of denial a wall she had built between them. To hit and run had been Dani's desperate attempt to protect her. Give the men in her life something to think about; take the heat off her mother.

Setting aside the bag of pills, she made a bowl of porridge and stood outside on the balcony hungrily eating without pause. Light whiffs of cannabis spicing the air, other smells welling up from the darkness: pungent, earthy, feral decay unlocked by the rain.

Bowl empty, she slipped inside and lay on the bed, the gun beneath her, haunting her mind.

She gave up on sleep at two in the morning and padded through the dark. Threadbare carpet then lino. Her hand brushing a switch, the fluorescent light blinking on. Squinting at the scattering of pills, she picked out Bugs Bunny. Ecstasy guaranteed to make you happy – so her friends claimed. Summers at Harriette's had always made Dani happy. She'd watched cartoons there; loved them so much Harriette bought her a rabbit, and they named it Bugs. She rolled the pill between her fingers and then it was in her mouth, and then in her belly.

'That's all folks,' she said before slumping on the sofa, craving a long run or a session with a punchbag. That usually calmed her demons.

She waited five minutes. Ten, twenty. But there was nothing. All those teenage raves thinking she'd missed out.

She picked another. The letter S set in a diamond. The power of Superman in the palm of her hand; the pill that held most promise. She downed it, paced the rooms then sat again.

This time the sofa a cradle of comfort, the shabby cotton the most luxurious surface her hands had ever known. Warm sensations flushing her arms and legs. The urge to box overwhelming her body, she danced from room to room, furniture and fittings coming under attack, spent toiletry bottles pinging off bathroom shelves.

In the living room she jogged on the spot, arms hanging limp, head rolling from side to side. A break between bouts. The bell; the baying crowd. She fought round after round, fought off demons in every room until her exhausted legs gave in.

Then she lay on the sofa. Her mind calmer, her hands relaxed, her thoughts turning to her gran. How sometimes she would fall asleep holding her hands, the hands of both musician and luthier. Long, slender fingers that not only magicked tunes from instruments but also fixed them. Hands that stroked healing lullabies, hands that could speak, hands that said everything would be okay.

Dani's hands came together, fingers calmly interlacing as something tweaked at the edge of her mind: *Harriette is the mother of my father. How can that possibly be?*

The question of genetic inheritance played on her mind. Were Dani and her father really alike? Over the years people had said that they were.

Fearing there was nothing she could do about herself she turned on her side; the palm of her hand settling on the willow bough patterns that were tattooed on her forearm. And soon enough sleep was her friend. And she was only too glad to let it guide her into the night.

*

She woke suddenly to what sounded like a bang on the door, the hallway as far as she got before vomiting. She slumped to the carpet and lay down, her stomach cramping. *The pills? The porridge?*

More knocking. Three rude thuds that drove terror through her body. Panic surging, she dragged herself across the floor and propped her body against the wall. The letter plate flipped open, the slot an oblong mouth that spoke.

'Si! …Ay, Si! Open the fucking door, will yeh?'

A Scouser?

'I know you're in there – saw yah lights on last night.'

'What do you want?' she said, her voice hoarse, scratchy.

'Fuck me – who's dah?'

Her mind galloped through the logic: *the visitor knew Simon. My dad hates Scousers. If I don't talk to someone, I'll crack.* She slid off the chain, took in a deep breath and opened the door.

A tall punk stood on the walkway, a look of astonishment on his face. White tee shirt, ripped jeans, a black leather jacket embellished with correction fluid. His hair a scarlet sensation amongst the concrete, vertically stiffened with a flat top.

They exchanged glances. Harmless, she thought. Tall and gawky, kind eyes, long neck kinked from bad posture.

'Simon's gone – I'm looking after the place while he's away.'

He straightened, and peered over her shoulder into the hallway. 'He didn't mention anything about you.'

She glared at him, their conversation switching to a staring competition.

'Yeah – well, he didn't mention you either.'

Lowering his gaze, he searched around the concrete deck.

He wanted something. Her Moss Side radar sensed that. But the fist she had instinctively formed behind her back loosened. She liked him. His thoughtful loitering inoffensive, endearing even. So far removed from her smash-and-grab family.

'Names Fez by the way.' He took a step forward and offered his hand. She shook it once then let go, then they stood in silence again.

'You got strong elastic bands if you don't mind me saying.'

'I don't mind.'

'Mm – this is a bit awkward but – Si was going to give me something. He must have forgot.'

'Like I said, he didn't mention you.'

'Yeah – right. Well, did he mention the Scottish bloke – in the kitchen, maybe. Looks after them if you know what I mean.'

She pictured the embellished cereal box, almost smiled and then breathed in deeply.

'You'd better come in.'

'Sound,' he said, recoiling at the smell of vomit in the hall. Three steps further and he recoiled again when he saw the trashed living room: plasterboard dented, cabinet doors ripped off, feathers from cushions lying around like the aftermath of a bird strike.

'You two have a fight or something?'

'No.'

She pulled bags from the cereal box and handed over the pills.

He picked out a yellow smiley face and popped it in his pocket.

'Lucky dip this time.'

He dipped again, his blind hand picking out a purple pill, slot-machine grapes imprinted both sides. 'Nice. A Violet Beauregarde – not a bad pick that, puts juice in your tank. Only payback – outrageous farts.'

She couldn't help but smile then, the dried puke on her lips cracking. 'I had a Superman last night.'

'Superman! Fuck me. Lucky to be alive – what's your name again?'

Her stomach grumbled through the silence. Fez lowered his gaze to her middle.

'Well, whoever – you're a legend. Them Supermans are double strength. Do you mind if I use the lav.'

'Please, go ahead.'

He walked into the bathroom; the door left wide open. She heard everything.

'Gotta be brave to take one on – you pulled through doh, and I like what you and Superman have done with the place.'

He zippered up, flushed the toilet and ambled back, chattering on as if he'd known her for a long time, his monologue switching between how the estate was free from the choking restrictions of a capitalist society to how his mate, Bikey, had the longest clipped toenail he'd ever seen.

'I mean, sick fuckeh. Keeps it in a matchbox and we're talking Cook's here, not Swan Vestas. I told him, get on the blower to Roy Castle.'

She felt sick again, although didn't want him to leave; his company settled her nerves. But she worried about what he thought; the flat looked so lunatic; shadows cast up the wall by a toppled floor lamp straight out of a horror movie.

'So, what brings you to the Crescents?' he asked, eyeing the debris. Then he listened intently to the same stories that she had told Simon. Fez's outrage possessing the warmth of a protective friend, he was quick to reassure her that the Crescents would provide the perfect place to hide.

'Total maze. Might as well be on a different planet, mate. Unless yah dah works at Nasa, he won't find yah. Not even that Indian tracker, the one that chased Butch and Sundance – what's his name?' His eyes searched the floor. 'Lord Baltimore – yeah, not even Balti could find yah here, mate.'

She rushed to the bathroom and spewed.

'You alright in there?'

'I think you'd better go.' Her voice reverberated in the toilet bowl.

'No problem. Sure you're okay?'

The toilet flushed.

'Better already.' She appeared from the bathroom and followed him to the front door.

He tapped his pocket. 'Well, thanks for everything – and if you hear from Si, tell him he's a knob-ed.'

Outside the flat, he lingered for a moment muttering, 'Total legend,' while shaking his head.

'My name's Dani.'

He looked up and smiled. 'Well – you're gonna be alright here, Dani. There's a party on Saturday, why don't you drop in? Top deck – Charles Barry Crescent, just follow the music and you'll find us.'

'Yeah, maybe.'

'I live at one-seven-nine in the same block. Come round for a cuppeh anytime.'

'Maybe see you later then.'

He set off shaking his head and muttering, 'Total legend.' The letter A in a circle on his back shrinking in size as he ambled along the access deck.

'One-seven-nine,' he shouted back before disappearing down a stairwell.

Shutting the door, she went straight through the flat and stood out on the balcony hoping to catch a glimpse of her new friend. But unlike Simon he didn't take the shortcut across the grass. And for a moment she wondered if the punk had been a drug-induced dream. Then she thought of her brother. He was dead. She had not dreamt that.

Her eyes roamed over the featureless walls of the adjacent housing block. Concrete panels, cell-like windows, shoebox balconies. A repeated monotony stark and brutal; residents of the estate left to imagine a better world. But all she could imagine was a massive low-rise filing cabinet. Boxy balconies on a grid, like the drawers in a mortuary wall. Her mother on Valium, father nowhere to be found, she was the one called upon to identify her brother. His body discovered in a ginnel the morning after bonfire night, a bullet through his chest.

She rushed to the bathroom and threw up again, then stayed in bed for the whole afternoon.

Almost-friends

Dani stayed in the flat for three days, pacing the rooms and checking the windows. Her sanity pitched against the views of the estate until the food ran out; her last meal made from stale porridge.

That night she slipped away to a precinct of shops where she bought supplies, then hurried back, her body flinching when she heard a distant gunshot.

The low singularity of it followed by an eery silence, as if for a second the whole world had frozen with shock. But Dani's pace quickened. Fast walk. Jog. Breathless run, her hands fumbling with the keys as she opened the front door.

Slamming it to, she lay in the hallway. The darkness above her pressing down like a heavy weight; the sound of sirens somewhere in the city growing louder and then fading away.

*

Next day she returned to the precinct expecting to see the aftermath of gang violence. But there was no sign of an incident, no blood, no police tape, just a few people wrapped up in coats, their step hurried along by a funnelling wind.

The precinct was, Dani realised, just a route into the estate between the housing blocks where litter played in circles in front of shuttered shops. She looked left then right. The people in coats now just tiny dots disappearing deeper into the huge estate.

Her gaze drew back and wandered across the concourse to a pair of telephone boxes. Red amongst the grey, side by side like old mates, she could almost hear them sharing gossip of who had said what.

'Waiting for a friend?'

The words startled her and she turned quickly, the hot fug of fried food like a wall in the doorway.

'Open early, aren't you?' she snapped.

'Open early – close early. Don't do late nights. Too many muggings,' he said, shovelling chips between compartments of the counter.

'Sounds about right.' She entered the shop and studied the menu board that was mounted high on the back wall.

'Anything you fancy?'

'I'll go a bag of chips.'

'One for the lady,' he said, scooping a portion onto a sheet of paper. 'New here, are you?'

'Just staying for a while.'

He smiled. 'Sounds about right.'

'You been here long?'

'Me? Since the dawn of time,' he said, sprinkling the chips with salt and vinegar. 'Such is the eternal demand for battered cod.'

He handed the warm wrapping over the counter and caught her eye for the first time. 'On the house. Call it a moving-in present.'

'Thanks.'

He looked at the rucksack on her back. 'It's not that bad here. Just watch yourself if you're out late. Best if you're with a friend after dark. Although it seems you're moving on already?'

'Just to the laundrette.'

'Ah, well – you have a good day, then. You know where I am if you fancy some chips and a chat.'

She went to say thank you, but he'd already turned his hand to the business of frying, the sound of crackling fat filling the room as she turned to the door. Her next port of call beyond a few graffitied shutters she entered the laundrette; items of clothing in the rucksack ones she'd grabbed from the laundry basket before running from home.

Emptying them into a washing machine she then sat on a bench and vacantly ate chips. Memories of home life resurfacing as the suds worked away the smell of fags and booze from the load, an aroma that seemed to infect everything in the flat above the pub. Those grim memories persisting until beeps that marked the end of the cycle cut her free from her past.

Gathering the ball of washing into her arms she transferred them to a tumble drier. Her sleeves damp, she rolled them up and studied the leafy tattoos that entwined her arms. Patterns that mimicked the wallpaper in the lodges where her grandmother lived; a pair of quirky buildings that marked the entrance to a country estate.

The drum rotated one way, then the other. The glass window of the drier like a portal that transported her back: the lodges, the entrance gates, the avenue of chestnut trees that lay beyond the cattle grid, the way she would weave between the tree trunks before lying on the grass to gaze up at the jigsaw of greens and blues. Her restlessness briefly calmed before she weaved again, jumping up and grabbing catkins of pale-yellow flowers to take back and show her gran.

Memories of time spent with Harriette kept coming until the clothes stopped turning.

Her recollection of good times receding as the hypnotic effect of the drier fell away.

She opened the machine and packed clothes into her rucksack then swung it over her shoulder. A desire to explore brought on by those better memories, she wandered out of the precinct and followed the vast outer walls of the estate. An orbit that felt never ending until she caught sight of the stairwell that led up to Simon's flat. The route to it over an area of open grass that faced Moss Side.

Her father out there, somewhere, flexing his brawn, her mother blindly defending him, her parents stuck in a blind loop that always came back to the same old story: poor Frank. Driven from his home like that. A terrible event that marred his childhood, something to do with the war, the details never discussed. But it never rang true for Dani because the mill town of his childhood seemed a friendly place. His mother, Harriette, kind and loving.

The stairwell beckoned.

Two hundred yards or so across a muddy path to get there, she guessed. Her journey to the flat nearly complete. The dripping tap, the black mould, the funny smells. She didn't want to go back just yet. So instead, she turned and retraced her steps, the housing blocks grey ogres in the fading light.

Best if you're with a friend after dark.

Of course, over the years she'd had friends. Ones in the playground with whom she'd played football, ones at boarding school that melted away at the end of each term. 'Almost-friends…' her mother had called them. 'One day you will need a close friend,' she used to say.

Streetlights blinked on.

Dani skirted around the estate. Concrete paving, concrete walls, dusk locking everything in like a concrete lid. Graffiti on the walls more prominent in the dimness; foul words big and angry as if written by an unhappy giant.

Why on earth did I come here?

The precinct came into view. The gap between the housing blocks glowing in the streetlight as she wandered through. The chippy, the laundrette, the under croft that provided shelter from the rain. As good as it gets around here, she thought. And in the middle of it all the pair of telephone boxes. Red and steadfast amongst the grey.

The idea of using one to make a call holding fresh appeal.

She imagined dialling numbers, inserting coins, the connection with a person at the other end of the line made without anyone in the world knowing where she was hiding.

*

The following afternoon she returned to the telephones and called her tutor at Loreto College. The reasons she gave for dropping out were, of course, nothing to do with the real situation. At the end of the day, she didn't want the authorities offering her protection. The last thing she needed was the police delving into the reasons why she'd left home.

Back at the flat she moped around thinking of what could have been.

A-level subjects – then geography at university. That was the plan.

But she'd dropped out of boarding school, and now she'd dropped out of Loreto.

So that was it. Education over. Big deal.

All I need is enough to get by. A simple job. Nothing fancy.

Throwing on a coat, she left the flat and walked

briskly to the Northern Quarter, an area on the far side of town known for its sweatshops. But it was clear from the padlocked doors and "To Let" boards that most of the buildings were empty.

Ideas of working in a clothes shop now uppermost in her mind she turned towards the city, her improvised route through the narrow streets soon leading her astray. She stopped and looked back and then looked forward. Then glanced at the pub to her left, the flyer in the window catching her eye: *Bar staff required – apply within.*

A job. In a pub. Are you out of your mind?

The door creaked as she entered, the atmosphere inside different from her father's pub: no television, the lunchtime drinkers older men who quietly played cards.

You need the money. Be nice. Smile.

'Still need staff?' she said, approaching the bar.

The card players momentarily looked up, the landlord's eyes widening as he saw Dani. 'Ever pulled a pint?'

She mentioned places she'd worked at, including her father's pub.

'Great Northern, you say?'

'Stuck it for a year, but I didn't like the people. Landlord's an old-time crook apparently.'

'Heard as much. Well, we're well behaved in here,' he said, scratching his bristled chin. 'Can you work tomorrow? Trial shift – see how it goes?'

'Sounds good. Thank you.'

After leaving the pub she wandered between the buildings until finding Dale Street. Her journey to the shops a cinch from there. A buoyant mood leading her through the Arndale Centre where she wandered for an hour, looking at clothes but not buying a thing. The money in her pocket spent on food she returned to the flat and made pasta sauce, thoughts of her gran stirring as rods of spaghetti relaxed into boiling water.

After eating, she lay on the bed, memories still spooling, one leading to another, her mind exploring the memory of Harriette's workshop as she tipped towards sleep. The cork-faced cramps, the pong of hide glue, the cellos and violins that lay unstrung on the workbench like patients that needed fixing.

The pub proved easy to find the next time round. Her memory of the route jogged by various urban peculiarities. Graffiti mainly and the wholesaler that sold knock-off goods on the corner.

The trial shift going well; her manner bright as she pulled the occasional pint. After last orders, she was offered the job. Four nights a week, cash in hand. The last bus only going so far, she walked the rest of the way alone, through the dark.

The weeks ticked by. Her time on the estate spent locked inside the flat, waiting for something to happen. But after a whole month passing without incident, she concluded that living so close to Moss Side was no less precarious than living in an earthquake zone. The danger always present but mostly dormant. Memories of her geography teacher's theory that Californians were insane for living close to the San Andreas Fault coming to mind.

So, fine. She would live precariously, like a Californian

and wherever possible conduct her life in areas of the city away from Moss Side. Withington mainly where she sat in cafes and watched movies at the cinema and Salford where she joined a leisure centre and signed up for boxercise.

One week no different from the next, her routine repeated unchanged for a month although she couldn't help noticing the changes that occurred around her; the estate stirring into life as the days grew longer.

People appeared. Young people.

Just a few at first, sitting on the grass. Friends meeting up hard to witness from the lonely flat.

Her solitude relieved by working at the pub. Short chats when serving drinks, meagre rations that lifted her spirits. But most of the time she would sit behind the bar, pretending to read a magazine while listening to the old-timers talk amongst themselves: the Tories pledge to save Manchester from decline and England knocked out of the Euros the main topics of debate that night.

She pulled pints of beer, cleared tables, wiped surfaces.

The bell for last orders reminding her of the boxing club. Another round done, she thought, as the men drank up and left the pub.

And soon enough she was back at the flat eating toast and drinking tea. Bath. Then bed. Every night the same thought snuggling in beside her: the wind and rain lashing through the precinct, the sheltering telephone box, her voice entering the receiver, escaping through the wires, to the town up north where her grandmother lived.

Dalek

Wallpaper ripped and peeling off the wall beside the bed… black mould where the ceiling met the wall… marks on the doorframe that recorded the height of long-departed children. These were the things she expected to see when opening her eyes next morning.

But there was something different, something new. The sound of people. Distant, happy, a bit chaotic, it was as if she were lying in the dunes beyond a busy beach. The muffled sounds becoming clear when she opened the balcony door. The grassed area below filled with people as if some great tide had washed them in during the night. The open grass now a sprawling haven of chat and pungent smells. Skinheads, rockers, punks and others of less obvious persuasion; her eyes flitting between them all in search of trouble. But the only sinister thing she could detect was way beyond the crowd, on the far bridge link, slant-sided with a domed top. She inclined her head like a bemused cat.

Is that really a Dalek?

Concrete vibrated in the sunlight. Her vision wavered; her attention drawn back to the crowd as a flash of red hair caught her eye. It was Fez, moving between groups of people, briefly chatting before moving on. Popular. Well known; something she couldn't be. To be well known would be like handing her father a map to her door.

All afternoon sounds of the crowd reached in through the windows and messed with her head. Advance, retreat, advance, retreat, she shuttled to the balcony. Her eyes skipping between the groups of people in search of Fez.

The search frantic because she felt that he was the only person in the world that she knew. Each time the hunt only lasting a few seconds. Marooned in the most remote place and that hair would be a blessed relief for a search and rescue team, she thought.

An hour before work, she closed the balcony door. Space to think opening up as the sounds and smells of the crowd faded away. She ate dinner in peace. Her calmer mind combing through the details of what she'd seen. Or rather had not seen.

Bikey conspicuous by his absence. A big guy with blond hair and beard. A Viking of a man. And yet there had been no sign of him. The introvert. The shy guy. Not surprising he wasn't in the crowd, she thought. On the bus to work she recalled his visit to the flat. He knew nothing of her arrangement with Simon but didn't question Dani's story of why she had the keys.

At work she served drinks wearing an expression of abstraction. Her mind weighing up the risks of having a friend who lived on the estate. But what harm could it do to have a cup of tea with Bikey, the hermit.

The next day she ventured out into the rain and walked through the estate to Bikey's caravan. Covered in moss and overshadowed by William Kent Crescent, from a distance it looked like a piece of sea-smoothed flotsam that had been stranded below a great concrete cliff.

She knocked. Bikey opened the door.

'I was just passing, so thought I'd say hello.'

There was a pause. He stooped and looked into the rain and then back at Dani.

'Simon's friend.'

'Yeah, that's right.'

Another pause. The rain pattered on the hood of her coat.

'Aren't you going to ask me in?'

'Sorry. Yes, of course.'

He invited her in.

'Tea?'

'Please.'

She removed her coat then shuffled along a bench seat that wrapped around a table. An undefined midzone where the smells of fried food and WD40 intermingled. Lounge one side, kitchenette the other, her eye wandering between them until he handed her a mug of tea.

'Cosy,' she said, smiling brightly and shrugging her damp shoulders.

'I'm in the middle of something – do you mind?'

'Carry on.'

He moved into the living area and stooped over a bike frame that was mounted on a stand.

Dani leant forward and watched his hands at work until her role as spectator began to wear thin.

'Is that really a Dalek on level two?'

'Been here since last summer. Lives in Charles Barry Crescent.'

'Keeps itself to itself then?'

He glanced up, disdain on his face as if her remark barely warranted a response. 'Shares a flat with two students.'

Other exchanges followed. Awkward, short, each in

turn shut down by Bikey's reluctance to be drawn into conversation. And then…

'Fez told me about your bikes.'

'Rescued fifteen of them from the canal. Twenty-four off the street.'

He went on to explain that – once fixed – he stored the bicycles in his flat which he chose not to live in because of the bugs and damp smells. The caravan shifted as the wind threw rain at the windows. Dani sipped tea. Bikey tinkered with mechanisms that shifted the chain between cogs.

'What will you do with them all?'

'Take them with me when I move back to Morecombe,' he said, cranking a pedal like he was firing up a vintage car. The spokes disappearing as the back wheel raced round. 'And hire them out to anyone who wants to pedal around the bay.'

Satisfied that he'd opened up, Dani sat back and listened to the details of his plan: the small industrial unit set back from the seafront, the booking system, liability insurance. He would live with his parents until he could afford a place of his own.

Their get-together going from strength to strength, she thought. Sometimes Bikey looked directly at her when talking. On at least three occasions they slipped into a two-way conversation. *A friend. At last, I've made a friend.*

After a further ten minutes of relaxed chat, he mentioned his father.

'A policeman?' she said.

'All his life. We used to live in Manchester when I was

little, but we moved. Dad had some sort of breakdown, so we relocated to the coast. Teenage fights at the local theme park a doddle after the violence of Manchester.'

Dani adopted a more upright position, everything feeling compressed as rain pestered the thin walls.

'Fancy another cuppa?'

'Maybe another time. Need to be on my way.'

Bikey peered out of the window. 'In this?'

She threw on her coat.

'I just love this kind of weather. Don't you?'

Her last words before plunging out of the door and into the heavy rain.

*

Summer came and went, the months made bearable by slivers of friendship: the chip shop owner, the old pub drinkers. When desperate for company she visited the caravan. Her attempts to avoid the open-air gatherings coming to an end as autumnal storms swirled about the housing blocks. The party hardcore shooed off the grass, the estate reverting to an eerie stillness once more.

The longer evenings difficult for her because it grew dark so early and there was too much time to think. Inevitable that with the coming of winter the memory of her brother showed up like unwanted company, interfering and spoiling the seclusion.

And then of course, there was Fez.

He came to her. His visits transactional, like a stray cat lingering until fed. Always three taps on her door; like a code that spelt his name. A cup of tea and a chat before he left with a couple of pills from the porridge box.

And then on November the fifth, he invited her to a social gathering: rockets and sparklers and a few "bevvies" around a bonfire then clubbing in town. 'A fun night out.'

'I can't.'

'Why not?'

'My phobia…'

'Of…?'

'Fireworks.'

She refused to discuss the matter further because fireworks induced memories that were severe and intense.

November continued to unfold like a marathon without a finish line. The occasional fizz or bang plaguing the city as if her route to work meandered through the middle of a fragile ceasefire.

December, like a new start.

The city all decked in lights and tinsel, she sometimes left early for work and wandered through the Arndale Centre, drifting through the shops like a detached stray. The week before Christmas felt barren: Fez back in his hometown of Birkenhead, string lights in the caravan switched off because Bikey had left for Morecombe. Both had offered to take her back to meet their families, but she had politely declined.

Actually, she was looking forward to Christmas alone. A fallow year free from family trauma. Just her and the little tree that glowed on the sideboard. One of many new items she'd bought with money earnt from working extra shifts at the pub.

On Christmas Day she nested on the sofa under a duvet and watched old movies on a new portable television.

On Boxing Day, she ran at dawn wearing new trainers, stopping on the bridge link to catch her breath. No traffic, no people. The city quiet and just so.

Back at the flat she lay on the sofa consuming the pages of a novel she had bought because the word *family* appeared in the title. Reading from cover to cover, her body lay unusually at ease as her mind discovered how *The Swiss Family Robinson* used what they had to make a pleasant life.

She went to the shops the following day and purchased a new saucepan and a new electric fan heater at a discounted price. Two heaters now. One in the living room, one in the bedroom. Last days of the year gripped by savage cold she returned from work and cut across the open grass in her new hat and coat, mud frozen underfoot, roughcast walls of the estate glittering in the moonlight. The heaters always on; bar heater clicking, the fan heater whirring. A drowsy duet that ushered in the new year.

And then Bikey's caravan lights pinged on, and she spotted Fez on the estate. But she avoided the caravan and avoided Fez; her life consumed by routines and new things she was too busy for friends now.

The side-steps, the dodging, it carried on for weeks until, on the way back to the flat she saw Fez at her front door, smoking a cigarette and leaning on the concrete balustrade, lingering patiently. She waited by the stairwell, but it wasn't long before he spotted her and waved.

'Hi,' he said as she approached.

'Hi.'

'Where have you been?'

'To the shops.'

He rolled his eyes. 'We haven't seen you for ages. We thought the Daleks had taken you.'

'They did.'

She opened up.

Fez bounded in.

'Haven't got much time,' she said. 'I'm meeting someone this afternoon.' She wasn't.

'So, who's the lucky man?'

'At three o'clock, in town, it's not a man,' she said, crossing her arms.

'Oh, I see. It's none of my business – fair enough. Got time for a cuppa?'

'Help yourself.'

Fez ambled into the kitchen. 'New kettle. New toaster. New mugs. Splashing the cash, aye, Dani.'

'Yeah. Working every night now.'

'Rescuing the economy single-handed by the look of it.'

'What?'

'You've got all this new stuff. But Dani, what you need is friends.'

'No, I don't.'

'I can introduce you to some mates. Really sound people.'

She insisted that he visited alone.

'You can't carry on like this.'

'Like what?'

A battle of wills ensued, the stalemate ending in a nasty argument. She slammed cupboard doors then threw a mug, which hit the wall beside his head and smashed into pieces.

'Christ, Dani!' he screamed from under sheltering arms, 'I hope that makes you feel better?'

'Not really!' She grabbed another from the cupboard and drew it back ready to throw.

'You should use the old ones,' he said, backing off to the door.

'The new ones are heavier.'

'You're a psycho.'

'Get out!'

'Fine. I'm done with you!'

'You've got the message. At last!' Her final words before he marched out of the flat.

But a week later he was back. Three knocks and the words, 'I come alone' uttered through the letterbox.

She skipped to the door and welcomed him in.

'I'm making some food; would you like to stay?'

'Love to. Smells good.'

While eating they casually chatted about this and that: bugs in the air ducts, a standoff between rival gangs on the access deck of Robert Adam Block. The subject of friendship left untouched, but it was there wedged between them like a third person in the room.

'Look, sorry I lost it,' she said, after swallowing her last mouthful.

'Save it for the judge.'

'I just cooked you a roast dinner so don't sulk.'

Dani made coffee. Fez stood at the balcony window, watching the Dalek as it trundled over the distant bridge link oblivious to the wind-driven rain.

'Built by two engineering students.'

'What?'

'The Dalek – delivers hash cakes to the flats.'

'One way to control earthlings.'

He almost smiled, then took a deep intake of breath. 'You should come to a party – you'd make lots of friends.'

Her face went blank. 'I'm fine.'

'For God's sake, Dani, you smashed up a car. Nobody died. You can't hide forever.'

Memories of her brother squirmed in her gut like a hand pushed into a boxing glove. She carried the drinks into the living room wondering how many years – if ever – it would be before she forgot what had happened.

Fez switched on the television, and they sat on the sofa and watched the local news, a government minister visiting Hulme Crescents the top story.

'Even Michael Heseltine's partying at Charles Barry tonight.'

'I need to get ready for work.' She got up and continued talking from the bedroom as she changed into a pair of jeans.

But there was no response and when she returned it was clear that he'd gone, the television still presenting unsettled weather to the empty room.

Another week went by without knocks on the door. Two weeks. Three weeks. Still no Fez, his absence like an ultimatum. One that she ignored in favour of routines:

pulling pints at the pub, boxercise classes, running the streets.

And then one morning she shrieked when confronted with the Dalek. It was parked right on her doorstep, a scribbled note taped to its toilet plunger zapper:

I am visiting EVERY DAY until you find some friends.
Exterminate fear... not crockery... and get on with your fucking life.
PS... I am NOT a friend.
(Daleks don't count.)

Slamming the door, she stood at the window and twitched the net curtain. The Dalek still blocking the way, feigning malfunction, the note fluttering in the breeze as if pressing the point. She turned away and marched into the kitchen, the act of making coffee executed with extraordinary levels of vigour. What composure she clung to vanishing after taking a mouthful of scalding coffee, her throat burning as she searched the kitchen for something to wield.

Out came the griddle pan.

Two practice swipes and then she was off, striding down the hallway.

She flung open the door.

Momentum doing the rest.

The huge swipe. The war cry. Her angry expression freezing when she saw people, walking past her door, horror struck, recoiling, hurrying away towards the stairwell.

The pan hanging limply at her side, she remained in the doorway. The Dalek in the far distance serenely gliding across the distant bridge link.

Her slow walk back into the living room full of confusion; spiralling paranoia that sucked in the world of machines. Jensen, the Dalek – the gun.

'Get on with your fucking life,' she whispered; her gaze lost in geometric patterns of the living room wallpaper that she disliked so much. Circle in a square, circle in a square, circle in a square.

Dull, severely repetitive, always humming into the room despite her efforts to block them out.

She pulled away and looked down at her forearms. The tattoos free flowing. The pattern a reminder of the lodges and the lady who lived there, her warm embrace, her reassuring words: *don't worry, Dani, it's alright, everything will be alright.*

Fight

Her first party proved to be an edgy affair. On and off she talked to Fez. But most of the time she lost herself to music. The rhythm finding its way into her body, she turned and swayed amongst the heaving crowd and after two hours of dancing she slipped away without goodbyes and ran through the estate, not stopping until reaching the flat. Less than five minutes later she was curled up in bed, counting the beats of her running heart, her mind giddy from glimpsing a new beginning.

Within a month she was a regular at the makeshift club set up in Charles Barry Crescent – two properties knocked into one, walls between the flats smashed through, other partitions stripped of plasterboard leaving the cables and pipes exposed like arteries.

It seemed odd to her that everyone called it The Kitchen. Gloomy and full of ripe smells, the interior was, she thought, more like the innards of a concrete animal, its heart beating Manchester rhythms.

Booze, drugs, euphoria.

People dancing to acid house and psychedelia, an undertaking that connected everyone without the need to talk much. The perfect setting for her shy, fidgety self.

During April, May and June she went back at least once a week. Adapting her routines to fit everything in. She worked at the pub then slept until late morning. On nights off she danced. She ran every day and went to boxercise classes twice a week.

With each passing month she ran further, danced longer and worked additional shifts.

August through to October her regime taking on Olympic intensity. Her body adapting to the additional exertion, she woke before dawn and ran through quiet streets; skipping down stinking stairwells then over the cracked slabs of Dearden Walk, pushing herself hard, as if training for a colossal event.

And then on November the fifth she dropped everything. Pulling a sicky from work she stayed in the flat. Her run next morning long and fast. Her sprint onto the bridge link like crossing a finish line. She pulled up midway to catch her breath, a sense of relief rising because for another year the fireworks that brought her so much pain had fallen quiet.

She breathed in the cold morning air.

City buildings sprawling before her: the distant Loreto tower blocks gathering behind rush-hour traffic like a thuggish crowd, the neighbourhood of Moss Side beyond them.

She read roofs like a map. Her father's pub appearing a little higher, a little bigger, like a knot in the grain of Victorian terraces.

Of course, the sight of home reminded her of him. Her brother. His visitation into her mind so strong it was almost as if he was there on the bridge link, spinning her round and slapping her face. Her shame burning so intensely she sprinted to the flat and hid herself away and tried to forget. But the following week her demons danced at the edges of everything she did until she could take no more. Bursting out of the flat, she paced one way along the access deck and then paced back. The urge to confide in someone almost overwhelming she slammed the front door and strode away into the estate towards Fez's flat, whispering, 'I'm fine' on repeat, to herself along the way.

She knocked and waited.

Fez opened the door with such vigour it made her jump.

'You good?' Not waiting for an answer, he doubled back into the flat.

She could hear gunshots as she walked along the hallway. In the lounge Fez was sat on the sofa.

'You seen *Reservoir Dogs*? This Tarantino guy is genius,' he said to the television.

On screen, a thug in a suit and sunglasses was firing two handguns at the windshield of a police car. Dani raised a hand to her chest. Her heart thudded. Heat prickled beneath the material of her jacket.

'Shit, that's brutal,' he said, sitting back and swigging from a can of lager. 'There's more in the fridge if you fancy one...'

He looked up and then pressed pause on the remote. 'You're upset.'

Dani slumped beside him and picked at a ripped cushion, her urge to confess what had happened to her brother now somewhat diminished.

'I hate myself.'

'Not this again, Dani.' A frozen image remained on the screen. A close-up of the thug, the guns pointing into the room, directly at Fez and Dani. 'Everyone thinks you're a legend. I don't know how to get that through to you.'

'Sorry, just ignore me. This time of year, it just drags me down.'

'Your brother?'

'Yeah.'

Fez pulled her in for a short hug and then he was up and on his way to the kitchen. A few seconds later he was back with a tin of lager.

'Here.'

'Thanks.' Dani swigged from the tin.

'Want to talk about it?'

'Not really. I just want to forget, you know, cut loose.'

They sat and drank lager and stared vacantly at the gun-toting thug that filled the screen.

'Cut loose, you say.'

'Mm.'

'I have an idea.' The guns vanished as Fez pressed a button on the remote control.

'You need a haircut.'

Her face blanked. 'What good will that do?'

'You think you're the only one who wants to break free from their past.' He brushed a hand through his spikey red thatch. 'Why do you think I did this?'

'You have a past?'

'We all have a past. Get a new look. It helps, believe me.'

'That so?'

'I got clippers – a Sinead O'Connor would suit you.'

'Too short.'

Fez ran through the options, her shoulders shrugging like those of a moody kid.

Partial buzz crop, grungy undercut; in the end she settled for Mohawk.

'Your demons won't recognise you,' he said, disappearing into the bedroom. 'Let's do it, before you change your mind.'

She followed him into the bedroom like a skulking teenager. He stood next to a chair, clippers at the ready.

'Skinhead?'

She smiled. 'Fuck off – You sure about this?'

'My mum's a hairdresser.'

She rolled her eyes. He switched on the clippers. 'No peeking.'

A huge bee buzzed the sides of her head, then knitting-needle fingers tugged and weaved top hair from fringe to shoulders.

He finessed a small mirror behind her with salon flamboyance. 'How's that?'

She turned from side to side, the big mirror reflecting an androgynous Mohawk brave. A stranger to herself; a blank canvas on which to paint new pictures. Her fingers brushed the stubble on the sides of her head and studied the plaited top hair that ponytailed down to her shoulder line, her eyes growing brighter.

'I love it,' she whispered. 'Fancy fish and chips?'

'Sound. No salt, lots of vinegar.'

Dani ventured into the estate. Strange to be outside until she remembered that there was nothing between the sides of her skull and the chilly air.

She bought two portions of fish and chips.

'Is that you?' said the man behind the counter.

'Might be.' She smiled.

The people she knew sitting on the bench in the precinct didn't give her a second glance.

Jogging up the steps of the stairwell there was no denying she felt different; a little lighter, a little sleeker.

She entered the flat. The film was back on, and Fez had returned to the sofa. After plating up the food she sat beside him. 'Nobody recognised me.'

'I told you. New you, new start,' he said between chips, his gaze not straying from the screen.

Dani turned her attention to the action. It was clear that something had gone terribly wrong. Two henchmen were holed up in an empty warehouse. One of them had been shot and his shirt was soaked in blood.

'I've got a few things to do before work,' she said, rising to her feet.

'But you've hardly eaten anything.'

'I'm not hungry.'

'You alright?'

'I'm fine. I'll see you Saturday night.'

He saw her to the front door. She said goodbye and set off along the access deck.

'Wait…' said Fez, '…listen.'

She turned and for a moment they just stood, Dani's clothes dancing in a gust of wind.

'What?'

'It's your freedom. Can't you hear it?'

'No. I can't.' She smiled. 'You've been watching too many movies. Thanks for the cut.'

'My pleasure.'

Back at the flat she changed for work and walked to the bus stop, but the bus didn't show so she ran all the way and burst through the door, the card players looking up in surprise, one of them shouting out, 'It's Hiawatha!'

And for a while people did see her in a different way. On the estate she became known as Dawn Squaw, the runaway punk who jogged around the estate. Her fitness levels good, her form relaxed, her route always circular around the perimeter of the estate as if marking a boundary, as if protecting what lay within.

*

Another year passed by. The months following a similar pattern as the year before. Work, parties, boxercise, etc.

With September came rumours that the Crescents had been earmarked for demolition. Sensing the estate was living on borrowed time people began to move out.

October faded away.

*

On November the fifth she hurried home from boxercise, ate a bowl of pasta, showered and got ready. Halfway to the club reminders pounced from the sky, fireworks throwing harsh light. Her shadow squat, like a gorilla.

She ran then, and at the club she squeezed through the hallway continuing deeper until she found the dancing crowd. Popping two pills she swigged them down with a tin of lager, and for a while her mind drifted above the dancefloor. Awareness of her body slowly returning, heavy and tight and out of kilter with the music, time speeding up then slowing down, her vision hazing over than sharpening again. The Stone Roses pelting her ears; memories of her family glitching in; shaky clips of drama behind her clenched eyes: a family fight, her mother slapped. Her mind skipping: a gun, a morgue, a cotton sheet draped over a body.

She focused harder on the music and turned into a dancing machine.

"Pacific State–707" seamlessly merging into the track "PositiveNoise", everyone submitting to its tempo, the room clammy with exertion; clothes clinging to bodies.

"Come Home" – "Kinky Afro" – "Weirdo" – "Fools Gold" – Mancunian tracks one after the other.

As the hours dissolved, her fellow ravers peeled away until she found herself alone on the dancefloor. Fez across the room covering for the DJ, the turntable spinning a track by The La's, a sleepier tune that coaxed Dani to the sidelines. Her journey to the toilet halted when she noticed a flicker of light through a window. Odd because she knew there was only open sward in that direction, her heart racing as she wiped condensation from the glass and saw a car skidding across the mud.

Three lads jumped out and danced in the headlights, two of their voices falling away when her ears latched onto the third. Something cold grabbing at her scalp; her mind now oblivious to the pressure growing in her bladder. It was a voice from the past, whingy, with a hint of Scottish. It was Jimmy – a friend of her brother's; a gobshite that would blab. Time stood still and then slammed into reverse. Her old life surging in as she stared at the abandoned car. And then Jimmy was in the room, behind her, pestering Fez to play livelier tracks. 'Call yourself a DJ?' he said, grabbing records from the pile.

Fez plucked them back. A shoving match ensued. 'That's not your stuff.'

Dani resumed her journey to the toilet, her face hidden behind a raised hand, but she couldn't ignore the escalation; the needle zipping across vinyl; Fez reeling from a punch.

Turning into a monster of knowhow she calmly changed direction towards them and gripped Jimmy's neck, her knee jerking into his groin sending him to the floor. Her rage not seeing he was done she delivered a kick to his ribs before dragging him outside. His whimpering body pushed against the balcony rail, his eyes glaring down at the slabs three storeys below.

'If you tell my dad…' she screamed.

He craned his head to one side. '…Dani?'

She shoved him a little further; his feet barely touching the concrete deck, his weight gradually tipping towards the three-storey drop.

Then arms wrapped around her middle as Fez pulled her back. She released Jimmy, and he ran along the access deck, turning at the stairwell. 'Fucking psycho – you nearly killed me!' he shouted.

She struggled in Fez's arms, but her exhausted body was unable to wriggle free.

'Utter one word to my dad… and… I'll fucking KILL YOU!' she screamed as she squirmed in Fez's grip.

Silence followed – as if the whole world held its breath. Then…

'Didn't you know he's been nicked?' Jimmy shouted as he edged closer to the stairwell. 'He's in the slammer – and your mum's left the pub – vanished.'

Then Jimmy was gone, his words left hanging in the cool twilight air.

Fez released her and she backed away from the whispering crowd. The gap between her and the group ever widening as if a river flowed there, swelling and rough and alive with shame. She turned and ran along the access deck. Her bladder screaming as she sped across the bridge link. And at the flat she rushed to the bathroom, yanked down her pants, her backside finding the toilet just in time, the feelings of both disgrace and relief triggering a memory in which she was seven and playing in the grounds of the Dardale estate…

… her brother teasing her for not wanting to go for a pee behind a fallen oak and after a fight she ran back, over the cattle grid and through her grandmother's garden where her need for the toilet was charmed away by the sound of a cello; the same note repeatedly plucked followed by rolling scales; intrigue reeling Dani into the hallway where she stood quietly, peering through the door gap, catching glimpses of a man at the piano and her grandmother's arms set and ready around the cello.

Then the thrusting bow made her flinch – the sound too much; heavy and deep, peaking and rolling, rushing through the gap like a storm. Her grandmother whipping it up like an enchantress, one hand firmly bowing, fingers of the other pinching and sliding.

The cello alive; demons banished from its hollows; spirits freed from its taut strings. Dani stood wide-eyed, engulfed by tragedy, melancholy and joy.

And then a flurry of plucks.

And then silence.

Tip of the bow resting on the floor, a few strands torn and hanging. Hairs on Dani's arms standing on end as if statically charged by the performance. Her eyes scrunching shut and body tensing with shame because she'd not made it to the toilet.

And then – out of the silence came her grandmother's embracing arms, her kisses peppering down. And Dani remembered looking around at the willow boughs printed on the walls, and remembered feeling the secure entwinement, and remembered thinking that all the walls back home were ever so bare…

…the memory fading away she opened her eyes and pulled up her sleeves. The willow boughs tattooed around her forearms a reminder of that moment: the piss, the snot, the tears. And yet, just like the cello, Harriette had embraced her, banished her demons and raised her spirits, her words still fresh in Dani's mind: *it's alright, Dani, everything will be alright.*

And Dani still felt indebted, because what she had received that day was much more than compassion; it was an encapsulated memory of it. A short while after, Dani had figured out the name of the composer (Elgar) and she bought the cassette recording of the concerto. And whenever she felt the need for an embrace, she would listen to it, and a warm feeling inside and that golden memory of her grandmother would always flow. She sighed. *Why didn't I bring it with me?* The cassette was in her bedroom above the pub.

Drifting into deep thought she ran a bath and lowered herself in, excitement flushing through her body as the news of her father's detention rang through her head. Not wanting to drag Harriette into Moss Side woes had been her reason for not visiting. But Jimmy's revelation had unlocked that door; she just couldn't wait to see Harriette again. Dani's only loving relative; the one-time professional musician turned luthier. And she had so many questions: What went on during the war? Why did this mysterious scandal wreck the family?

Knowing would help, she thought. *To understand would help me cut loose.*

But as the bathwater cooled, her excitement sobered and Jimmy's other departing words echoed through her mind: *your mum's left the pub – vanished.*

Her glee drained away with the bathwater, as she knew that before going anywhere, she needed to find her mum.

The Great Northern Inn

The following night she stood on the bridge link, the distant lights of Moss Side quaking beyond the Loreto tower blocks as Jimmy's voice echoed through her head.

But it didn't make sense. Why would her mum leave Moss Side now, now that she was free of her father?

Setting off through the dark she skipped down steps, ran through the precinct, then along Clopton Walk and out of the estate. Rolls Crescent, a line she'd not crossed for eighteen months soon well behind her.

Then she was over Moss Lane East and running past the piercing spire of St Mary's Church, and then on, through the terraced streets and ginnels, her feet steadily pacing over the same cracks in the paving slabs that were there when she was a child. Then suddenly The Great Northern Inn was before her on the corner of two streets. And through the windows she could see a different face behind the bar serving customers she did not know.

The landlord's name above the door not her father's, she carried on past the windows and after taking a few calming breaths, she backtracked and walked in, conversations carrying on as she weaved between tables, the landlord behind the bar, bald-headed, stocky build, a fixed smile revealing gaps between his teeth. 'Be with you in a minute, love.'

'Been a while since I drank in here,' she said, lifting herself onto a stool.

The landlord served another customer. Hands exchanged money then he whipped the till shut.

'You've probably noticed some changes then. What can I get you, love?'

'Coke, please.' She looked around. A few tables repositioned, otherwise everything the same, the ghost of her mother busy behind the bar.

'I'm just caretaker landlord. Brewery has been pretty straight with me. They plan to shut it down. Selling it on to a developer. Too much history, if you know what I mean. Landlord ended up in Strangeways, you know.'

'Yeah – I know.'

'Knew him, did you?'

'My mum was close to his wife.'

'Oh, aye. Met her briefly, bit short on chat, mind.

Although, to be fair, she wasn't in good health… name's Dee, isn't it?'

'Deepika – Is she still around?'

'Left a while back.'

'Know where to?'

'Not exactly. Other side of town; moved in with family apparently. Flat was emptied by a clearance company. Brewery padlocked the place after the police finished picking it over.'

Her heart sank. She'd left stuff behind, including the cassette of Elgar's cello concerto. There was no way she'd get any of that back now.

'Terrible business…' a flurry of pub chatter drowned his words, then, '…slapped her about, you know.'

'Pardon?'

'Frank – the landlord. Right piece of work.' He shook his head with mock sorrow. 'Fancy one more?'

'No thanks.'

The landlord served another customer.

She finished the coke then left and lingered outside on the corner. Christmas lights flashing in windows along the street smudged by a freezing fog, surface of the road shiny like liquorice.

Dani looked up at the blank windows of the flat above the pub and remembered the occasion when she stood between her abusive brother and her mum, the three-way struggle that followed, how her brother backed off when her well-delivered punch made him think again. What a fool she had been for believing she'd fixed her family for good; everyone playing happy families for a week or two. A ceasefire that ended when she watched her brother place a handgun between them while they sat on his bed. A present from their father; an antique firearm from the First World War. She would never forget the shock when he aimed it at her and threatened to shoot her if ever she laid a finger on him again. It looked rusty and old and defunct, but she never forgot which drawer he pulled it from. One up from the bottom.

Fog thickened. Christmas lights in various windows flashing in unison for a few beats as if through the murk the street had unlocked a secret. Dani turned and walked away and then ran, occasionally looking behind, the pub soon taken by fog. Her face wet. A mat of dew forming on her front. Her pace steadying as her mind ran through the losses. *No father. No mother. No close friend. No confidant.*

DEV

…Two Weeks Later

I had new kit.

A double-size proofing cabinet where I could store resting dough. An Artofex mixer capable of working two whole sacks of flour. Both previously owned by a bakery that had ceased trading, but it was in good condition, a game changer. A gentle, slow mixer that replicated the kneading power of twenty hands. Its unique mixing patterns working irregular-sized bubbles into my artisan bread.

But of course, it wasn't just about the kit. I spent a lot of time forging links with good suppliers. Flour from a miller in Stockport. Dried fruit and spices from an importer in Manchester. I visited each one and checked every label to make sure the produce had been ethically sourced.

To sit in an office and buy blindly was to compromise. And that was not how I wanted to run things. I wanted my business to be simple and honest, and I relished the prospect of listening to my customers. The shop a part of the neighbourhood; the neighbourhood part of the shop. An old-fashioned bakery where the bread was made every day, the life span of the product just that – a day. And then everything started again from scratch, which in reality meant long hours – seven days a week.

And I hadn't stopped for breath on the day before opening.

My mind and body whirling with the creation of my first offering, of all things it was an unusual sound that broke my concentration. Still sensitive to those incoming noises that I couldn't label, I suppose. I looked up and sure enough seconds later through the small side window I saw a livestock trailer rattle past, its idling engine vibrating through the old oak floor as if it had stopped outside the front door.

Walking through to the shop I watched it pull away, reducing in size as it disappeared into town.

And then I saw her, clear as day.

Punk hair dyed, shaved on the sides. Long and plaited on top like an Indian squaw; her changed look pushing me away from any chance of instant recognition. One of those déjà vu moments when you know someone but can't place them – a spirit from the past or previous life.

I traced her ghost for a week. Her name eluding the tip of my tongue, I worried the thump in the desert had affected my head. And then busy with work, it came from nowhere and I realised memories had been blurred not only by the change in her appearance but the surreal circumstances in which we had been pitched together, when we played the parts in a school production of *South*

Pacific – her character name, Liat. Her real name, Dani.

I remembered her not because she was my first love or even a steady friend, but because we were both unwittingly plunged into an awkward spot, like puppets on a stage, everyone around us trying to pull the strings. We were the frontline of desires pent up from years of segregation in single-sex schools.

It was a tradition cooked up by the headteachers. As if bringing the boarding schools together for a few weeks at the end of the year would magically resolve any hang-ups we had regarding the opposite sex.

That year however, the co-ed experiment careered off the rails, because on the first day of rehearsals, the girl who played Bloody Mary proclaimed Lieutenant Cable (me) kissed Liat, in the movie.

Our director, Miss Gimmet, insisted that a kiss wouldn't feature. She even banned the word from stage as if its utterance may corrupt young lips. And although she'd briefly stifled the matter it refused to go away, her evasive approach only allowing the load of expectation to grow. July turned oppressive. Hormones stirred. Pressure built.

Absurd how one small kiss could throw the whole production off course like that. But it did and with only one week to go before the first performance it was clear we weren't ready.

Every day we fumbled through. Miss Gimmet visibly bracing, in advance of the scene when I held Dani. And when the cast demanded, you know what, a strange calmness came over her and she just closed her eyes, and for a second, we all imagined victory. But then she winced and with arms rigid by her side she did this funny little thing with her hands. And then she roared, like an animal.

'No kissing! We *shall not* stray!'

And that was that – the *South Pacific* volcano blew. A riot of vested sailors and grass-skirted dames surrounding the director, all insisting on the kiss; threats hurled like hot chunks of lava.

To be honest, nobody had asked if either Dani or I were comfortable with performing a kiss. I should have just kissed her because that moment of dissent had provided the perfect distraction. But I took no part in the rebellion, stayed on the sidelines, followed teacher's orders and throughout the commotion we just stared at each other's lips.

It was awkward. Girls were an enigma; I had no idea of what she was thinking so I just closed my eyes. And then – well – she bloody kissed me, our lips together for just one second, a big smile on her face beaming away as Gimmet swiftly came between us.

The show ran for three nights. We all rose to it and apart from the odd forgotten line and a few ad-libbed moments we got through. After the final night performance there was a huge sense of relief. No party. Term ended and we all went home.

But Dani's kiss looped through my mind all summer and I couldn't wait to get back to school. Final year students were allowed off the grounds and I imagined various scenarios in which we met in the local town during lunchtime or after school. But during the first term I saw her only once, on the sports field playing hockey.

And then for weeks no sign of her, October bringing news that she had dropped out of school. And with the pressure of impending A levels, the heady memory of the girl who defiantly kissed me faded by Christmas. Exams were sat then I spent the last dreamy summer of my youth with my gran in tropical Speightstown.

I didn't join the forces straight after school but was sponsored through university on an army bursary. A couple of years later I went to an alumni reunion (Dani didn't go). I learnt from friends that after dropping out she'd returned home, worked in her father's Moss Side pub, enrolling at a local college to study an art foundation course. A lot of rumours circulated about her family; *her brother shot by his own Moss Side gang; Dani kicked out of her own home.*

I watched her walk up Main Street and disappear into the square.

Was it really Dani?

The girl who played Liat. I didn't see her again for weeks, but I couldn't stop thinking about that unfinished kiss.

*

My move to the moorland town came by chance. Some months later I learnt that Dani returned because of a family tie. The fact was we hardly knew each other although the thwarted kiss remained a connection we could not ignore. So, our lives gradually entwined and believe me, in the spirit of controlling my own fate, I took the initiative, made the first move and suggested we met up.

But the memory of Gimmet's snub seemed to moderate the excitement of my voyage into self-charted waters. I suppose as time passes people's voices fade. But of all the ones I would never forget, Captain Ross, Andy, my grandmother, it was Miss Gimmet's that came to me whenever I met up with Dani. I don't know why; it was just there prompting my limited intuition. And after what had happened in the desert, I was of course a disbeliever when it came to superstition. But, like I had been Captain Ross's protecting omen, it was as if Gimmet's voice was my guardian angel. Her two words repeating over and over in the back of my head.

'No kissing.'

DANI

Eviction

'Concerto?'

'Yes, Elgar's Cello Concerto – I can't find it.'

Dani's fingers flicked through the vinyl racked below C to F in a shop called King Bee Records.

'Classical concerto?'

'Yes.'

'Well, you won't find it here.' Fez coughed and spluttered. 'Look – we got the Chrissy presents – why can't we go home?'

'We will, soon.'

'But this is the third record shop we've been to.'

'One more – Market Street.'

He rolled his eyes and walked behind her mumbling that he didn't want to go into a shop opened by Mr Bean. But before long they were sifting through the HMV megastore.

'I've found it,' she said with gleeful eyes.

In the queue she held the cassette box in both hands

and read the blurb. It was a better recording than the other one, the cello played by Jacqueline du Pre.

'Jeckel and who…' Fez doubled up in a coughing fit, but he pulled away when she rubbed his back, the tone of his poorly voice like that of a hormonal teenager.

'Wha? I'm fine.'

'You look like an addict.'

He stared at her face for a long second. 'Thanks – I feel much better now.' He coughed and sneezed simultaneously. 'I could murder a bifter – see you outside.'

Through the window she watched him slouch on a bench and scowl at a busker and after a long wait in the queue she came out and they went to a cafe. She ordered drinks at the counter and then they sat next to a steamed-up window framed by a string of multicoloured lights. "Mull of Kintyre" playing on a radio; Paul McCartney's voice lost to chatter that filled the room. She sipped a hot chocolate whilst rereading the blurb on the back of the cassette box.

'Didn't know you were into classical.' His words spluttered out.

'Heard my gran play this once.'

'She played the cello?'

'Used to play in the Halle Orchestra.'

'You were close, weren't you?'

'Mm.' She looked up. 'Haven't seen her in years though.'

A waitress placed hot drinks on the table. They both thanked her.

'Still thinking of going to see her?' His words set off another coughing fit. 'Crescents has given me the plague.' Fez's face contorted.

She leant back as his sneeze built then ebbed away. Twice. Then 'Ahhh-chooo!'

'Maybe next year – Fez – you need to see a doctor about that.'

'Mum's already booked me in. Look, come back to Birkenhead. I hate the thought of you being on your own. Be good for you to get away for a few days. My folks are fine with you staying over.'

'Thank you – but I'll be okay.'

Fez sat back, his face perplexed. 'You're a right billy no-mates, do you know that?'

'They want me to work at the pub over Christmas. And the gym has asked me to lead some boxercise sessions. Instructor's off ill.'

'Join the club.'

'And I have this.' She waggled the cassette box in front of his face.

He rolled his eyes. Bagpipes of Kintyre blared from the radio.

Tipping back, she drank the sludge from the bottom of her mug, then after planting a chocolatey kiss on Fez's forehead, she went to the counter and paid the bill.

*

After Fez left for Liverpool, Dani worked in the pub every day of the week, festive tunes on the jukebox repeating on a loop.

Her Christmas day simple and monkish: no festive television, no decorations. She woke early and read, *A*

Farewell to Arms. A romance set in Italy, a book she'd bought in a charity shop because she'd seen it before at Harriette's. The chapters interspersed with visits to the kitchen where she warmed tea in a saucepan. Chai style: cinnamon stick, crushed cardamom, cloves and brown sugar just like her mum had taught her. And in the afternoon, she made a lasagne as the cello concerto played through the headphones of her Walkman. She ate a humble portion and placed the rest in the fridge. And then she sat in bed for the rest of the evening, finishing the book while nibbling at segments of a chocolate orange.

Christmas fell away. The rest of December dragged its heels. January and February two little months crushed by well-trodden routines. The year so far, a reprint of the last one; going through the motions automatic and stale.

Work at the pub resumed. Her morning run, religiously performed through chasms of cold that lingered between the housing blocks. The leisure centre full of New Year's resolutions; Dani's boxercise class fully booked; the room so full every punch felt like a near miss.

And at night, when the heaters were too weak to stop ice fronds forming on the window, she stayed in bed, her ears warmed by headphones, the sounds of a cello transporting her back to Harriette's hallway, the willow patterns vivid in her mind as she drifted off.

Revisiting the Great Northern, she sometimes lingered on the street, watching the windows. Occasionally she sat inside with a glass of coke. But there was never any sign of her mother.

No sign of Fez either and she had no way of contacting

him. Then, on the first of March, she woke to the letterbox snapping shut.

'That you, Fez?' she shouted, flinging off the duvet. She opened the front door, but there was no one there, just a postcard by her feet which she took back to bed. On the front the word KATHMANDU appeared below a pagoda-ed building. Flipping over she saw Simon's name below a paragraph of text, his departure from the Crescents so long ago that she could hardly remember his face.

Hi Dani, hope this gets to you.

As you've probably gathered, I'm in Kathmandu. Amazing but had shits all week.

Hey guess what! I've met a girl called Danniela!

Have decided to put education on hold indefinitely.

As now learning about this thing called love.

We're heading to Mongolia and then down to Aus.

So, I officially hand over the deeds to you. (Oh, there aren't any ha-ha!)

Congratulations, you're officially a homeowner!

Have a good life.

Tell Fez to fuck off!

Si.

Would if I could, she thought then scoffed at her "homeowner" status. A burst of harsh laughter spilling out as she slipped under the duvet and gazed up at the rash of black mould and peeling wallpaper.

The postcard dropped to the floor as she clambered out of bed. Wrapping herself in the duvet she padded into the kitchen and gazed out of her window. Nobody outside, not even the Dalek. It was as if all life had been absorbed into concrete along with the rain. Everything clammy as if she were camping in a loveless concrete tent.

God, I hate this place.

*

The following night she worked at the pub. The old drinkers sat at wobbly tables and played dominos and cards. As usual, a man named Percy sat at the bar twitching a newspaper, occasionally announcing random headlines to no one in particular. He swivelled on the stool. 'It's a goner!'

The card players ignored him. Lights of a fruit machine blinked for attention. Dani mopped the floor behind the bar. Percy read on.

'They're actually going to knock it down,' he muttered between sips of his pint.

A flat voice rose from the card game. 'Who's knocking what down, Perse?'

'The Crescents. Council's starting demolition next year.' Swivelling around he faced into the room. 'Finally, they're actually cleaning up that mess.'

One of the players threw down his cards. 'Whatcha say, Perse?'

'John Major. Giving us £30 million to demo the Crescents. Regeneration on the way...' – he took another sip of beer – '...well, that'll be the end of Tarzan then.'

'Who?'

'Michael Heseltine, that's who. Been in and out of Hulme for weeks, hanging around like he's looking for Jane.'

'Has nobody told him she's been with a cheetah?'

Laughter died down. And as they swapped stories, she realised they had all grown up in the back-to-back houses that had preceded the Crescents estate.

'Outside toilet, no bath. But I have good memories.'

'They called it slum clearance, but they weren't slums. Them streets were our playground.'

'Aye, the Crescents – now that is a slum and good riddance to it.'

None of them knew where Dani lived and now, she didn't want to tell them. In any case, the newspaper article came as no surprise; rumours about demolition had circulated for weeks and the music scene had already dried up. Bailiffs were filling toilets with concrete and most of the fair-minded anarchists had moved on.

Her feet aching from the long shift, she took a taxi back to the flat and slept solidly. But she woke at six in the morning. She didn't immediately understand what she heard, though she thought she did.

There. Again, the unmistakable sound of a scurrying creature.

Rat!

She jumped out of bed and burst through the balcony door, icy coldness striking up from the concrete, the adjacent housing block basking in the dawn sun like a gigantic cold-blooded monster. Taking a deep breath, she shouted Fez's name – very loudly. The echo of her voice fading. The faint sound of wheels bumping rhythmically over joints of the flyover the only comeback. She crouched down out of the cold breeze and thought how the word "balcony" sounded so exotically Mediterranean, so Romeo and Juliet. But hers was just an icy ledge that even rats rejected. She slipped back in, made instant coffee, pulled on thick socks then ventured back out. And as she wondered how to get rid of the rat, she noticed a figure in the distance, moving between the travellers' buses parked on the grass. A man with a walking stick, lumbering around, peeking into the vehicles. It was the limp that gave him away. An old-school gangster who had turned his back on crime and started the boxing club. It was the man who had taught her eight-year-old self to fight.

It was Erol.

She whistled using her fingers then called his name. Looking up he squinted into the morning sun. 'Dani… that you?'

Curtains in a bus window twitched.

'Who wants to know?' she shouted down.

'It's about – your mum.'

She could sense burden in his voice. The wipe of a brow with the sleeve of his coat laced with relief. Then he steadied his stance, more of his weight taken by a walking stick as if bracing himself for the delivery of bad news.

Clambering down the stairwell she ran out into the open space, the heavyweight figure of Erol waiting for her like a broken giant, his big shoes planted amongst the litter.

She stood before him catching her breath.

'What is it?'

Head bowed; his eyes avoiding hers.

'Erol?' she pleaded.

His scarred face became restless as if chewing on words he couldn't express. He swallowed then looked up.

'I'm sorry, Dani. It's your mum – she passed away.' He looked down again and bothered rubbish with the end of his stick.

Her chin quivered. 'When?' She placed a hand over her mouth, her eyes filling with tears.

'We've been trying to find you, Dani. Jimmy told us you were here, but this place…' He waved the end of his stick at the concrete, as if casting a vengeful spell.

'Erol?' Mascara streaked her face.

'Three days ago – funeral's in two weeks. Look, come back to mine. Don't worry, it's safe.'

Erol's long arms and walking stick parted like a saint, his gaping trench coat consuming her. Wind picking up; litter drifting away. He hugged her trembling figure, and they swayed gently from side to side.

Funeral

The hearse crawled along Barlow Moor Road. Dani sat in the car behind gazing through the rear window at the motorcade. Turning into the crematorium they drove through neatly tended gardens. The car park busy but the bays either side of a prison van remained empty. Suits and dresses flapped in the wind as her mother's coffin was carried away.

Dani walked into the chapel; everyone followed. She assumed most were regulars at the pub who didn't realise she was the girl who helped herself to packets of crisps from behind the bar.

Alone on the front pew, she glanced behind and searched for Harriette, but the only person she recognised was her father who sat motionless between prison officers. Older and knackered looking, like prison had aged him.

She turned to the front. Somebody read a poem about the sea.

The vicar asked everyone to stand for a hymn; organ music filled the chapel. Dani focused on a round window; a stained-glass full stop set high in the back wall of the chapel. And it struck her then that her mother was gone, and she would never see her again. Her eyes made another sweep of the chapel, but she only saw mouths singing without conviction. A confused anger growing in her chest, she wanted to scream out that her mother loved Thin Lizzy, Terry's Chocolate Oranges and sang "Band of Gold" when plaiting her daughter's hair.

"Band of Gold" she thought – it was so her mum. Upbeat tune – sad story, a fitting eulogy if ever there was one. Dani closed her eyes and saw herself dancing with her mum, the feeble hymn giving way to the pop song in her head, her hand tapping her hip, her mouth shaping the words, the lyrics streaming through her mind until she heard a loud cough.

Opening her eyes to the sight of everyone seated, she

dumped herself down on the pew and stared at the floor. The final words of committal were uttered. Organ music played softly, the coffin disappearing through a curtain. Then nothing, just the fading organ and her thudding heart. A long silence finally broken by the vicar's voice, his calm words an automated murmur that gave way to dull pre-recorded music.

As mourners filed out, she caught glimpses of her father, his gruff charisma defused by a grey uniform. He seemed benign, like a Silverback dulled by captivity and for a mad moment she pitied him. Then she felt the weight of his cold eyes and any hope that he might have changed instantly vanished. His handcuffed fists clenched, the band of gold on his finger an insult to the memory of her mother. His gaze loaded with blame, it was as if he knew she'd smashed Jensen, as if he knew what had happened to her brother. Staring him down she clenched her teeth; it took all her strength not to throw herself at his throat.

Last to leave the church, his shoulders hunched as guards bundled him into the van; doors clanged shut, then the van barrelled through the gardens, pigeons on the road flapping up at the very last second.

Dani stood with Erol and a few others beside the chapel. While they discussed details of the *serene* service she shivered and snatched quick glances of people who gathered in groups on the lawn, specifically the tall lady moving between them chatting, shaking hands, her headscarf ballooning in the wind.

The graceful step, the stylish attire, her soft voice playing hide and seek with the blustery weather. It had been years, but Dani knew it was Harriette and despite the biting chill she felt very warm, and wings fluttered in her chest, and she floated away above the chatter, the deep timbre of Erol's voice pulling her back down. 'You alright, love?'

She opened her eyes and offered a thin smile. 'I'm okay, thanks.'

And then she was there, beside her; the floral greys and blacks of her dress misbehaving in the breeze, silver strands of hair teased from the headscarf fluttering across her elfish face, a little more lined than Dani remembered, although her bright eyes still smiled with vim. As a raised hand tucked away wisps of hair, the tall lady introduced herself as "Dani's grandmother" then looked to Dani for confirmation. Their eyes searching one another, catching up with the physical changes that had occurred over the course of a decade. Dani much taller, her eyes now level with Harriette's, they smiled at one another. Everybody shook Harriette's hand, and they all bemoaned the terrible weather.

Erol offered Harriette a lift to the wake.

'Are you sure? That's very kind.'

Dani and Harriette walked arm in arm to the car park. Erol opened the back door of his old Jag like a chauffeur. Before getting in, Dani turned to Harriette, placed her arms around her and they hugged. Harriette looked up at Dani's severe hairstyle. 'My... haven't you grown.'

Dani reigned in glee and beamed. An impish smile broke across Harriette's face. They climbed into the car and Erol closed the door.

*

The mood inside the Great Northern Inn was solemn. Everyone gathered in the bar and ate cold finger food. Dani and Harriette stayed close together and picked at the crisps. They chatted with Erol, Dani mostly quiet, gazing at the greasy marks on her paper plate; being back at the pub like being in a vault of bad memories: *How can this place have so much power over me?*

Harriette turned to one side. 'My taxi's due soon. Can I take you home?'

Dani looked up. 'Could do with a lift into town.'

'Sure. I'm staying in Manchester tonight – Can I buy you dinner?'

Dani smiled. 'I'd like that.'

After thanking Erol for arranging the wake, they left the pub and climbed into a black cab, conversation flowing freely as the taxi inched through city traffic; the journey done in what felt like minutes.

'I'm starving.'

'Me too, Gran.'

'Shall we eat early?'

The taxi pulled up in front of the Midland Hotel. Harriette paid the driver, and they climbed out. And for a while Dani stood motionless looking up at the stone arches and the flags and the tapestry of windows above them.

'Shall we?'

Harriette led the way and they set off up the steps and then walked through the lobby and into the restaurant where they sat amongst the columns of a grand room, the space brightly lit by a huge lantern rooflight. A waiter floated between tables taking orders. Happy sounds of cutlery and crockery escaping into the dining room whenever he set the kitchen doors a-swinging.

Dani searched for roach droppings, but the marble floor gleamed. An ornamental tree grew vigorously towards the rooflight glow. She tipped her head back, closed her eyes, breathed in her grandmother's perfume and half expected a minor miracle to unfold at any moment.

'Are you alright?' Harriette placed her hands on the table. Dani's eyes blinked open, everything soft focus, her grandmother's smiling eyes a little like those of an older Grace Kelly.

'Yes. I think. Just a bit tired.'

Harriette nodded. 'Me too. Sure you're okay?'

'Mm… just got this weird lingering guilt. Wanted to cry earlier but there was nothing – think I've turned into a cold-hearted bitch.'

Harriette sat back. 'Grief is the bitch, dear. Pops up whenever it pleases – and you weren't alone with the guilt.'

Dani searched her gran's face. 'You feel guilty?'

There was no reply; Harriette's eyes lost for a few seconds, before finding Dani's face.

'Well, your father made her so unhappy.'

'Unhappy? He beat her up, Gran.'

Harriette shifted and looked up to the ceiling. 'Oh God.'

'You're not blaming yourself for that?'

Harriette bit her lip, then rolled her eyes. 'He is my son.'

Dani placed her palms over Harriette's hands. 'He's not a little boy. Anyway, Mum kept it from most people, denied it was happening. Got worse when I was at boarding school. Apparently, she covered the bruises on her face with make-up.'

Harriette shook her head. 'I'm really sorry.'

'I don't hold you responsible or anything weird like that, Gran.'

Harriette's eyes filled. She looked away from the table, shielded her brow with a raised hand.

'Christ, Gran… think we need a drink. Fancy a glass of wine?' Spotting the waiter Dani waved him over.

Harriette wiped her eyes. 'Not a bad idea.'

'I really appreciate you coming, I really do.'

'Didn't think I was going to make it. Train was delayed because of debris on the line.'

The waiter handed them padded menus. They ordered a bottle of wine. Dani asked for carbonara. Harriette pondered. Her Gran Harriette – the orphan.

Dani's father had always made a big deal about that when she was growing up. The name Ellen would be uttered, Great-grandmother Ellen, the reckless one who had abandoned his mother, had, apparently, ran off with a man. But there was never any detail, no back story, it was just this bad thing that shamed the family, disadvantaged him in some way, led him into a life of crime.

Harriette picked something off the menu, then chatted to the waiter about his home city of Rome, said she was there in forty-eight then spoke some Italian. He laughed a little then replied in his native tongue. Dani listened to them chatter, bemused. How could such a class act have mothered such a rogue? Then she wondered if her father had ever been a good boy, then wondered if Harriette had been a terrible mother.

The waiter left.

'What was that all about?'

'Asked for a pepper mill.' She nudged the little glass shaker on the table. 'Never been a fan of white pepper – it's like eating dust.'

The waiter delivered a bottle of wine and filled their glasses, then he left and weaved back towards the kitchen. After taking a big glug Dani confessed to smashing up her father's car and running away. Harriette showed no sign of being shocked, just patiently listened then confirmed that she hated the car too. 'Well done, dear.'

And then they reminisced about bygone summers when Dani and her brother stayed at the lodges. The exchange of anecdotes cut short when the returning waiter placed bowls of food and a large pepper mill on the table. '*Buon appetite*,' his parting words.

Dani readied her cutlery. 'Dad refused to bring us over in the end. Should have made my own way. I knew you weren't a good traveller.'

'A pathetic weakness I'm afraid. I still drive the Mini on the estate sometimes, but it stays in the garage mainly. Better for everyone that way.' She took a sip of wine. 'And it's not because he didn't want to, he wasn't allowed to. Court order prevented him from coming anywhere near my town.'

'He used to deny that.'

Harriette twisted the pepper mill with vigour. 'Oh, it's true for sure. Made a terrible nuisance of himself. Had such a chip on his shoulder about the town. Harassed my closest neighbour – got caught up with the law.'

Dani twisted spaghetti onto her fork. She wanted to ask about the past, about what happened to Harriette's mother, Ellen, but instead she held off and scoffed tangles of eggy pasta. And for a while Harriette spoke about her town and how it had started to recover from the recession.

'Look… the past, it's not important. We can start afresh.' Harriette finished her wine, then gestured the empty glass at Dani's bowl. 'As good as mine?'

'Not quite. It's good though.'

They continued eating without conversation until Harriette placed her spoon and fork beside her bowl. 'I just wanted to say… I'm here for you.'

Dani focused on her gran's face while chewing.

'I don't mean in place of your mother or anything like that. What I'm trying to say is I don't want you to feel like you're having to cope on your own… so please, if there's anything you need…'

Still chewing Dani held up both hands and fixed her gran's eye as she swallowed. 'Is there a bath in your room?'

'Well – yes.'

'Please can I use it?'

*

Harriette swiped the card and opened the door. The suite generous; three tall windows sided by silk curtains. Dani sat on the ottoman at the foot of the bed. Boots off, her toes pressed into deep-pile carpet kneading like cat paws, her walk to the window like crossing a bridge of clouds. She looked down at the bustling street and then wheeled back and explored the bathroom.

'It's a lovely room.'

'Well, enjoy. I'll leave you to it if that's alright. Need to go over to Forsyth's for bow hair. Haven't been in the shop for years.'

'It's fine, take your time,' Dani called out, turning on the bath taps.

Harriette rummaged through a bag and pulled out a purse. 'Won't be long,' she called back and then the door clunked shut.

Dani scattered salts into the water from a chrome jar then eased her body into the bath, everything twinkling in bright spotlights.

She dozed off, then woke, then set about untangling her hair, washing it through with hotel shampoo that smelt of peaches. Pulling the plug, she stood and looked at herself in a full-length mirror, malnourished, ribs pronounced, runner's legs, face gaunt, sides of her head stubbly, long, wet hair on top slicked back to the middle of her back.

Look at you, Dani Hey.

The door buzzed open.

Wrapping a towel around her body she ventured out and stood by the bed, dabbing her hair. 'That was quick.'

Harriette glanced at the willow bough tattoos that entwined her granddaughter's arms. 'I recognise the pattern.'

Dani rotated her arm back and forth.

Harriette sat in an armchair and slipped off her shoes. 'As if printed by Wallis and Hilton themselves.'

'Stayed with me since the day I heard you play; it's literally become a part of me. Always wondered if the wallpaper was made at the Wallis mill.'

'You've got it spot on.'

Dani slipped behind the ensuite door and pulled on her clothes then reappeared with her head lost in a busy towel. 'How did you get on?'

'Got what I needed. They usually post me stuff, so it was nice to pop in and chat. Put faces to people I normally speak to on the phone – would you like me to re-plait your hair?'

Dani's head appeared from the towel. 'Please.'

They sat on an ottoman and Harriette's hands began to weave with steady rhythm. 'Hulme Crescents sounds like a tough place – do you feel safe there?'

Dani mentioned the newspaper article about its impending demolition and how living there during winter was awful. A bus rumbled outside. The gap between curtains suddenly dark; a motorbike revved, then screamed away as if in a race.

'Can't tell you how much I've enjoyed seeing you. I really am sorry about your mum.'

'Gran?'

'Yes, dear.'

'What happened to your mum?'

The plaiting stopped. Dani turned. Harriette looked a little thrown.

Dani faced forward again. 'She – she was called Ellen, wasn't she?'

'Yes – she was…' – plaiting resumed – '…but it's a long story. Can I tell you another time? I'm pretty exhausted.'

'Yes, of course, me too. That's fine.' *Where's your patience? Can't believe you asked that – give her a fucking break!* 'I really need to be heading back, Gran.'

'It wasn't a hint. Stay as long as you like.'

'No, really. I've got work tomorrow; need to get some washing done.'

'Oh – okay.'

They hugged. Dani pulled her coat off a chair.

'Sure you're going to be alright?'

'I'll be fine, Gran.'

Harriette scribbled on a scrap of paper. 'Here's my number. Call me any time.'

'Thanks.'

'Will you come and see me?'

'I'd love to.'

'You're welcome to stay for as long as you like.' Harriette became flustered as she walked Dani to the door. 'The place is undergoing a revamp. I guess it's not as exciting as the city. Haven't got a Hacienda or anything like that, but the high street's coming back to life; we've got a Pizza Express now, you know – even the Wallis mill is being renovated.'

'Gran – you don't have to sell it to me. I really would love to come and see you.'

Harriette opened the door and watched her granddaughter shrink in the corridor.

'Your number. I forgot to ask you for your number.'

Dani turned before disappearing through doors. 'I don't have one. I use a phone box. Don't worry, I'll call you. I love you, Gran.'

Dani drifted through town then caught a double-decker back to Hulme, her feelings curdling with every lurch of the bus, the odd assortment of hats and coats that sat before her all moving in unison. Watching the bustling streets she thought of her mum, tried to picture a happy version of her face but couldn't. She thumped her thigh with a fist, her hidden face screwed up, her coat sleeve roughly wiping away tears that spotted her skirt.

*

Two weeks passed; still no sign of Fez.

She went to his flat and tapped on the door, once, twice. The door drifting open after a firmly delivered third knock.

'Fez. It's me, Dani. You in there?'

An uneasy stillness greeting her as she edged along the corridor. Her visit cut short once it was clear to her that the appliances had been looted and the furniture had been trashed.

Next morning, she visited Bikey and they sat at a fold-away table in his cramped caravan, rain drumming on a plastic rooflight above them.

'I'm thinking of leaving.'

'Same here. Never thought I'd say it – but I've had enough.'

'Had one of these yet?' Dani placed an eviction notice on the melamine surface.

'No, but I've had one of these.' Bikey slid a business card onto the table.

'Anthony Gibbons? Who's this?'

'Fez. He called by when you were at the funeral. He's got a job in Salford; moved into a yuppy flat with a girl called Julie. He's left us for another woman, Dani.'

'Thought he was ill.'

'He was. Pneumonia apparently. His mum kept him home till he got better; made him apply for a job and, well, the jammy toerag got it.'

'Anthony? Surveyor? Oh my god.'

'Yep, Antonio. He's going places, that lad. Didn't recognise him in the baggy suit. Shaved all his hair off.'

He slid the card towards her hand. 'Look him up anytime, he said.'

She flipped it over, shook her head. 'Anthony?' Disbelief colouring her voice.

'Actually, I'm leaving next week – Brother's offered to tow the van up to his site in Morecombe; going to work there as a maintenance man.'

'But – your bicycles?'

Bikey looked up at the rooflight and sighed. 'Stolen.'

'All of them?'

'Yep.'

'Oh, Bikey – I'm so sorry.'

'Well, what do you do? At least they can't nick the skills that fixed them. What you got planned?'

'Not decided yet. Need to bail out, that's for sure.'

'Well, be careful, mate, the drugs have got harder in this place. If you ever need to get away, come up to the site.'

'Yeah, maybe – thanks for the offer.'

Dani said goodbye then ran through the puddled estate, momentarily sheltering under the flyover. And when the rain eased off, she carried on to a cafe that nestled under one of the railway arches on Whitworth Street West.

After ordering food she clamped on her headphones and sat at a table, conversations in the room and traffic swishing the wet road outside all overpowered by the sounds of a busy cello. And before long she was savouring a fried egg sandwich, her bites desperate and messy, egg yolk dripping onto a plate that lay next to an unravelled note. The paper torn and creased, the edges tatty, but the numbers written upon it remained neat and bold and unmistakable.

The Road North

She approached the precinct with a sense of unease. Chip shop boarded up, laundrette vandalised, the phone boxes like sentries that had grown weary of guarding their patch. One smashed, its frame askew; the other concealing a potent funk like that of a public urinal.

Crunching over broken glass she held her breath, heaved open a door, and dialled the number.

Harriette answered and they both spoke at once – then not at all.

'I'm so glad you're coming…'

Dani gagged.

Harriette rambled on about a church fundraiser, her words sometimes lost to a booth that whined in the wind.

'…I mentioned you did aerobics classes – what do you think?'

Boxercise – I do Boxercise.

'Yes, I can help. I've only got one coin. May get cut off soon.'

'I'll make up a bedroom above the workshop. Oh, and there's a job going at the pub. I'll let them know you're a dab hand – is that alright?'

'Sounds great. Listen, the pips have gone – I'm out of coins – should be with you by teatime tomorrow.'

'What's that, dear?'

'Tomorrow, I'm coming tomorrow.'

The line went dead.

Dropping the handset, she fought her way out and paced up and down, catching her breath as the stinking phone box closed to like a giant clam. Back at the flat she packed as much as she could fit into the rucksack then climbed into bed and built a picture of the route she would take to her gran's. The square, the alley, the lane. And then she visualised the lodges. One Harriette's home, the other the old gamekeeper's lodge that had been converted into her workshop. Sometimes she would let Dani and her brother sleep in the bedrooms above it and when they came down in pyjamas, she would be working at the bench. And Dani remembered the pong of hide glue and the tools with wooden handles and the cork-faced cramps all arranged in size order on the wall. She would never forget how Harriette carried that little cello she called a viola and the way she gently placed it on the baize-covered worktop. And she remembered sensing that her care for it was motherly as if the viola were delicate and alive, like a baby.

*

Next morning, Dani stood outside on the balcony and held the urn at arm's length. Gently tipping it over the balustrade, a veil of cinders gracefully coiled away, swirling and hanging between the housing blocks as if her mother's spirit clung onto life before realising she was free.

Love you, Mum.

Pulling on the rucksack, Dani left the estate and walked under the flyover, and got into a taxi that was parked beside the railway arches. She had just enough money to get out of the city.

In Clifton she stood in a lay-by and thumbed passing traffic. A lorry pulled over, a whiff of animals spilling from the open slots of the trailer.

She opened the cab door. 'I can take you most of the way,' said the driver.

Clear of the suburbs they rattled through Bolton. Then beyond leafy Egerton, houses gave way to countryside. It was the same route she'd travelled as a child. The truck lumbered up hillsides. The landscape passed slowly. High in the cab, she saw previously unseen vistas; reservoirs, dry stone walls, farmhouses stranded below bare moorland hillocks. Driving through a managed area of spruce, branches bowed in the wake of the truck, the landscape suddenly opening again, the neat edge of forest getting smaller in the juddering wing mirrors until the treeline stretched from road to the barren flanks of Anglezarke Moor.

'You're not one of them vegans, are you? There's nowt in back – already dropped them at market.'

She stared at him. 'No, mate.'

'You've not said much, that's all.'

The truck heaved for breath as the driver shifted gear.

'It's fine, it doesn't bother me.'

As they approached a fork in the road the driver looked at his watch then scratched his chin. 'I've got time for a detour. I'll drop you in town. It's been a while since I've driven through.'

They continued in silence, wheels jolting over potholes, overhanging branches snagging the trailer.

'What brings you to this neck of the woods then?'

'It's where my gran lives.'

'Oh aye. It's where my sister-in-law comes from – her mum still lives here.'

'Small world.'

'Place used to be called Dardale.'

'Yes, I knew that.'

And then the memories came at her like punches; her gran's town all over the news. 1982 or was it 1983 when the man from the planning department was found dead in the canal? Her father suspected but released uncharged; nobody convicted, the death unexplained.

'Mill was a big employer back in the day. Went bust in the 1930s, mind. Our Jen's mum said the Wallises were Luddites. You know – hated machinery.'

'Oh, right.'

'Made wallpaper the old way with printing blocks carved all fancy like. Very labour intensive – top-end stuff. It's the big boys who survived, of course. Potters are still banging out mass-produced stuff.'

She looked at him blankly.

'Potters in Darwen? Owned by Crown? You know, the paint people.'

She sensed the driver looking her up and down, his eyes lingering on her chest.

'Town's been on the ropes for a long time. Pretty place, mind – on the up apparently.'

Pulling her sleeves down she pushed a foot under the rucksack and felt the straight edge of metal inside.

'Sister-in-law wants to move back and look after her mum. She's getting on a bit.'

Trees thinned and the road cut into the side of the valley like a contour line. There was a fleeting glimpse of roofs gathered below then the road turned and began to fall. The town reappearing as they rounded another bend. They crossed over a canal bridge and passed between a pub and the mill.

'Just here will be fine.' She thanked the driver and got out. The truck disappeared into town. It was a bright day. Windows of the mill towered above her, each a tapestry of old glass that shimmered in the sunlight. She turned into town. The grandeur of Main Street like the wardrobe of an old dame, the glamorous clothes of her youth a little moth-eaten and crumbling at the seams. But Dani could sense the vibrancy of a past era. Like her gran, the place had class; boutique shops, people sitting outside an attractive cafe, flowers in upper-floor window boxes. She walked below the mature trees that lined the street and then paused in the square and studied the brass statue of Sidney Wallis, his figure sitting upright, his eyes glaring back through town, an epitaph etched on the plinth below his feet.

May Humanity be Rediscovered in all we Create.
Sidney Wallis
1864–1944

Continuing through the square she cut through the cobbled alley, followed the lane. The crumbling wall on one side marking the estate boundary; middle of the track and verges either side covered with weeds and wildflowers. Then ahead, the white lodges, symmetrical either side of open gates, big roofs sweeping down over windows like heavy brows. Opening the front door, she called out then entered. The hallway smaller than her child's eye memory of it; willow branches on the walls a little faded.

Slipping off the rucksack she placed it under the coat hooks then ventured further in. The kitchen different, extended out to a new wall of oak posts and glass, views of the estate beyond dotted with solitary oaks and elms standing majestically in the heathland.

But it was the two panels of wood hanging on the

wall that caught Dani's eye. Each two-foot square, their surface carved with intricate patterns all grey and fissured like driftwood. Her fingers lightly traced the stems and petals... *carved all fancy like. Very labour intensive.*

Sun spilled through windows; leaf shadows shivered on walls. She heard the front door open.

'Hellooo...'

'I'm in here.'

Harriette breezed in, her tall figure lost in a navy smock that was marked with spots of dried varnish. They hugged. 'Hello, you.'

Dani smiled. 'Here at last.'

'Cuppa?'

'Mm, please.'

Harriette went to the sink and filled the kettle. Dani went back to studying the panels.

'Been waiting long?'

'Just arrived. Have you been in the workshop?'

'No, no. I've been helping Rennie pack.'

Harriette rinsed the teapot then pointed its spout at the carvings. 'Beautiful, aren't they?'

'They look very old.'

'Older than me – so pretty ancient.'

'Well, I think they've aged very well.'

Harriette laughed. 'You can come again.'

'How is Rennie?'

The boiling kettle prevented Harriette from hearing the question. She gathered cups and a milk jug and filled the teapot. 'Wallis and Hilton printing blocks. I rescued them from the skip actually. Stored in the stables for decades. That particular print didn't sell well but I just love the carvings.'

'Is he going on a holiday?'

'Sorry, dear?'

'You were helping Rennie pack?'

She smiled at the confusion. 'No, no, he's downsizing. Struggling with the upkeep of the hall, so – finally moving on.'

Harriette placed tea on the table and they sat by the windows.

'He's sold it to an American company. They're converting it into a spa hotel. Conferences, weddings, Michelin chef.'

Dani searched Harriette's face.

'Don't worry, he's not selling the lodges; he wouldn't throw me out onto the street.'

'Is he moving away?'

'No, no. He's converted the stable block. Never was good on a horse.' She smiled as if for a moment imagining him on a horse. 'They've done a good job – all very modern.'

'He was good on the piano. Do you still play together?'

'Most Fridays.'

Harriette picked up the teapot and filled the cups.

'He's not been right for a while though. Sees letting go of the hall like some final betrayal.'

'Betrayal?'

'Mad, I know. Still feels guilt about the demise of the wallpaper company, but it was his father who wouldn't modernise. Rennie was just left holding a sick baby.'

'I saw people in the mill – has that been converted too?'

'Mm – divided up into business units. An architect's office and bakery so far. Letting out the other spaces when he finds the right tenant. He's very particular about his tenants. It's been empty for over thirty years, spent a small fortune maintaining it. Just glad he's finally clawing something back.'

'Every cloud has a silver lining.'

Harriette smiled. 'Supper?'

She warmed through a bolognese sauce and boiled a pan of spaghetti. They ate by the window, views across the estate glowing in the late evening light.

Harriette explained that she would be at the hall helping Rennie for at least a couple of weeks.

'Sorry I won't be here for you.'

'I'll be fine. Can I help?'

'No, no, wouldn't dream of it. You spend some time settling in. A removal company is packing up most of the rooms. And to be honest Rennie is not much fun to be around. Clearing his father's study is dredging up a lot of troubled memories. He won't let anyone in there apart from me.'

Dani cleared the table and began washing up.

'He's probably just tired, I expect.'

Harriette joined her at the sink.

'Moving a hundred years of family life does feel like moving a mountain. I did mean it when I said you could stay for as long as you like. You should register at the doctor's – use the lodges as your home address. They know you're coming; I mentioned you to the doctor. Please, leave the rest. You look tired. Why don't you turn in?'

'Wouldn't dream of it.'

They finished the dishes together.

'Love you, Gran.'

'Goodnight, Dani.'

Walking to the other lodge she stopped midway and watched the windows of Harriette's lodge blink on and off, ground floor, then first floor, the bedroom the last to flicker out.

An owl. A breeze. Canopies of ancient trees coming to life; clouds above riding east.

Mirrored forms of the lodges either side of the cattle grid, pure dark of the estate beyond. A stately old world, one of quiet order and balance. She sensed life in the hedgerow, deer nibbling the heath, bats on the fly. Compared to the concrete Crescents the landscape around her seemed soft and cushioned and permeable like a big, forgiving sponge.

*

The lodges were in a peaceful place. Sandwiched between grounds of the estate and farmers' fields. Days quiet. Nights pitch-black. Dani could go for hours without seeing another soul.

She went into town most days and walked along Main Street. Everything slower, friendlier, no screeching of trains that weaved into Manchester Piccadilly, no drone of traffic on the flyover. The sound of a gun sometimes echoing through town, cracks of shot in the fields. But there were no police sirens; nobody even blinked.

The following week she helped out at a public event; throughout the day leading a number of sponsored keep-fit sessions; nearly a thousand pounds raised for repairs to the church. The job interview at the Navigation pub lasted ten minutes. After questions about previous experience the landlord offered her the job.

Everything seemed to be going well. And then she opened a bank account. The assistant manager looking at her oddly after her surname appeared on the paperwork.

After that, little doubts began to tug at her shoulder.

And she felt alone because her grandmother the luthier, the one-time professional musician, the only relative she thought she could rely on, remained aloof, whispering in and out of the lodge, her drill-cloth overalls covered in vintage dust. And Dani had made no headway whatsoever in understanding the truth about the scandal that was supposed to have dragged her father down. It was probably bullshit; it usually was with him.

That evening she ran on a track that forked away from the estate and rose up onto open moorland. Stopping to watch the sun slowly sink behind a heathered hillside she then ran back to the lodge in the dusk light. After showering she ate supper in Harriette's lodge then fell asleep in the living room and woke hours later sprawled on the sofa, the plate still on her lap.

She walked to the kitchen; hands on the wall clock at half eleven. Harriette's coat already hanging on a peg, her shoes on the hallway stand, the upper floor of the lodge quiet and sleeping.

In the dim cabinet light, Dani noticed a cardboard box on the worktop, its lid splayed open, novels stacked around a roll of wallpaper that rose up like a periscope. Wrapped around it was an old magazine, the front page entitled *The Fuse*. Carefully freeing it from the elastic band she placed the curled pages on the table. A floral pattern on the front. Inside the cover a black and white photograph of a lady from the past who stood in front of the Wallis mill wearing boots and a boiler suit. Her posture relaxed and self-confident. Her happy eyes and easy smile suggesting close rapport with the photographer.

Chilled – in control – If only I were like that.

Then she noticed a scribbled word under the photo. Dani held it closer, squinted through dimness and after deciphering the handwriting she looked up and whispered.

'Ellen.'

DARDALE

1915

I

Heath Bumble Bee – *Bombus jonellus*

Study for Wallis and Hilton Wallpapers. Plate No. 101 – Bee Lines [see sketch on next page]

Facts: Social insects living in colonies of up to 200 workers. Each queen lays about a dozen eggs that hatch into workers (sterile females).

Quaint beliefs: If a bumblebee buzzes at your window, it signifies that a visitor is on the way. If a red-tailed bumblebee, a man will come.

Ellen waited under the grocer's awning, rain scuttling across canvas like the feet of scurrying mice. Distant moorland disappeared behind cloud, the sky low and blank as if wallpapered flat grey. Watching sheets of drizzle sweep through town she convinced herself war would soon be over and everything would return to normal, and for a moment she dreamt of returning to Manchester.

She plunged into the rain, hurried past shops and turned into Albert Street. Her birthplace. A terrace of houses built by Sidney Wallis for his mill workers, each graced with a small garden, a two-storey bay window and a fanlight over the front door etched with the letters W. H.

Smaller details: perforations in airbricks like honeycombs, lintels carved with the stylised motifs like those printed in the mill. Door knockers cast in the shape of creatures: bees, ladybirds, damselflies.

On her front door an owl.

An owl that her mother used say came to life at night and swooped by the windows to check that all the children were tucked up in bed.

Of course, the magic had worn thin, for years her mind occupied with thoughts of leaving. And then it happened. Women at university rare as hens' teeth, she'd been lucky enough to win a scholarship to study at Owen's. But three months in, a combination of the war and her father had stopped it. Some women at the college volunteered as nurses. Her father insisted she return to Dardale, work at the mill and look after the home, which since losing her mother was a role she had assumed by default, a role that hung over her like a cloud.

Stopping at her house she opened the squeaky gate and walked up the path, the owl always astonished to see her back, the hand of gravity closing the gate behind her.

Maybe her father would announce the war was over, and that she was free to catch the next train out. Everyone said the fight would be done by Christmas. She entered the house, the smell of tobacco greeting her in. Placing eggs in the larder, she heard the strumming of a washboard and her auntie's voice rumbling above it, her tone combatant, dismissive. Then her father's voice in the living room, grumpy and full of pipe smoke.

The strumming stopped. Ellen froze, drips forming a moat around her shoes. And then her aunt's voice. 'Nobody's broken the law.'

Strumming resumed. Her father's reply competing with the vigorous rhythms.

'Not yet – but that Miss Banks is a militant type. Women should be pressing for vote, but loitering outside church, giving out pamphlets, it just gets everyone's gander up.'

The washboard fell silent. 'Told you before, Tom, our Ellen needs outlet. They're spreading word, not throwing themselves under King's horse. Quite frankly, you should be proud of her.'

THRUM, THRUM, THRUM…

'Tha knows everything is different now, Lil. War is a matter of national importance that needs addressing first.'

The washboard missed a beat. '…By men!'

Tom rolled his eyes. 'Saints preserve us. As suffragettes won't be fighting with us, then yes, for now, by men.'

The strumming stopped dead.

Ellen peeked through the door gap and saw her aunt standing in the scullery doorway, soap suds dripping from raw fingers.

'What do you mean – with us?'

'Made my decision. I'm joining up with the lads on Saturday.'

Ellen stopped breathing. The damp coat suddenly heavy around her shoulders.

'For goodness' sake, Tom, you're thirty-seven. What about Ellen? What about mill?'

'Tha means filling factory twenty-four.'

'They'll still need good people like tha self to manage it.'

Lily returned to the tub, Tom's words shadowing her into the kitchen.

'The Ingrams' lad changed my mind. Sixteen, and they let him join just like that.'

'You did your bit in Africa.'

'Exactly. These boys need old sweats like me. It's not been an easy decision, and, well, Mr Wallis…' Tom cleared his throat, '…Mr Wallis respects my decision and will be making up shortfall in the rent an' all. Said there's a job for me when I get back. You can't ask for any more.'

Ellen closed the larder with enough force to fake her arrival home, then she swept into the living room, moved a chair in front of the range and draped her coat over the back of it.

'Hallways are where we hang coats.' Tom pressed tobacco into his pipe.

'Coats don't dry in hallways.'

Lily appeared in the doorway again, wiping her arms with a towel.

'Hello, flower, bet tha could do with a bath. Get them clothes off and I'll put them in the wash.'

Tom struck a match. 'I hear print room's almost cleared.' He sucked the flame into his pipe.

'It is, and we've moved blocks to one end of the block room, so workers have a place to change.'

'Well, hope you've stacked 'em right.' Tom wedged the pipe into the corner of his mouth.

'Yes, Dad. So both sides breathe – so they won't bow – I wish you wouldn't talk to me like that.'

Tom threw the smoking match like a dart, and it found the centre of the coal bucket. Both women glared at him.

'What? Blocks are as good as firewood if they won't register on paper. That's all.'

Ellen shared a quick look with her aunt then said breezily, 'Have you heard the news?'

'What's that, dear?'

'Mr Wallis had a baby boy, there's talk of a street party.'

Tom raised an eyebrow. 'I don't think it's Frau's son everyone's talking about.'

'Come off it, Dad, you don't believe the gossip.'

Lily marched into the scullery, tipped a bucket of suds into the sink, her voice fighting with the gurgling drain. 'I don't remember accusations of treachery when his dealings with Germany kept you in job – and so what if his wife's German, she's hardly about to overthrow country.'

'Well, sorry for casting aspersions but doesn't seem right time to be throwing street parties. Lads will be gone before bunting's up.'

Lily reappeared, hands on hips.

'Mr Wallis had faith in you as mill manager, Tom Parry. He deserves loyalty in return. Bread eaten soon forgotten, that's all I can say.'

Tom removed the pipe from his mouth and aimed the mouthpiece towards his sister.

'Authorities won't let Mr Wallis anywhere near the mill. So, what does that tell tha? Just look at Royal Navy. Dismissed Sea Lord Battenburg only last October. Same principles apply if tha ask me. When at war, tha must see everything with fresh pair of eyes.'

Lily laughed mockingly then returned to the sink. 'Nobody is asking tha. Anyway, can't be standing around like cheeses at fourpence talking colonels and sea lords. Bunting or no bunting, this washing won't get done on its own.'

The strumming resumed.

Ellen placed nuggets of coal onto the dying fire.

Tom turned to the window and stared at his clothes twitching on a rope line.

'About your meeting with this… NSS, well, I've given it some thought.'

'NUWSS.'

'Whatever. Tha needs to stay home and help our Lil. I'm joining up and leaving with the lads next week. I'll be back before tha knows.'

Ellen poked fading embers then stood and brushed herself down.

'But we're moderate. We don't protest like the WSPU…'

'Munitions work begins next week and that can't be counted on if promoting other causes.'

'What if you don't come back?'

A breeze picked up. Embers glowed. Clothes on the rope line inflated like body parts.

'I'll be back.'

'How can you know that?'

'I do not know that. I will do my best to come back.'

'Would you be going if Mother were still here?'

Tom fixed his daughter's eye. 'Quiet now, Ellen.'

Then he dragged his gaze up to the ceiling mumbling unintelligibly as if complaining to somebody above about his daughter. Then he levelled his gaze and shifted the pipe to the other side of his mouth.

'Mr Wallis would like to see tha. Got a special job for tha.'

'Oh. And what job is that?'

His eyes switched between his daughter and sister. 'Well, he didn't tell me – did he?'

'Maybe he doesn't trust tha – with such matters of importance,' said Lily.

'When does he want to see me?'

'When things have settled at the mill. Cedric will know when. Go to the lodges and gamekeeper will take tha down to the hall. All settled then.' Tom kissed Ellen's head then checked his pocket watch.

'Our Lil. Belly thinks me throat's bin cut – what's for supper?'

'Brawn and potato, maybe carrots and beans if tha lucky.'

In the hallway he pulled on a coat. 'I'll be back five thirty.' He complained about the wind before closing the door, his voice fading away as he called out to a neighbour.

Lily stroked Ellen's arm.

'He'll come round. He's got lots on his mind, that's all.'

'Pamphlets say we're suspending the campaign, but he doesn't give me a chance.'

'I know, pet – he's got worse since tha mother passed. Tell him later when he's calmed down. Anyway, you'll soon be busy with changes at mill. Lots of new faces arriving in town.'

Ellen stood, but her voice wobbled. 'What if he doesn't come back?'

Lily pulled her in for a hug.

'Don't worry, petal. He's fought with Manchesters before. Africa no less. Lions, mosquitos, native tribes – survived them all. Now get them mucky things off and run tha self a bath.'

Ellen headed to the bathroom, her aunt's voice chasing her up the stairs.

'And don't be soaking too long – taters need peeling.'

*

A month later Ellen stood in the grand reception of Dardale Hall, harking back to the mill workers' Christmas dinner. The annual gesture never sat well with her father. *Remember your place* he would tell her. *Eating from the same table doesn't change a thing. We are the servants – they the masters* and then he would remind her not to stare at the portraits as if doing so might fill her with dangerous ambitions.

But now her eyes explored the portraits that cluttered walls, and the portraits glowered back at her. Lowering her sights, she focused on the portrait of a young woman that hung above the bottom step of the grand staircase. Flawless beauty: auburn curls set around a porcelain face. She radiated status and yet her expression seemed meek and sad. *Should I envy or pity her?*

'Stunning, isn't she?'

Ellen flinched, looked up. 'Is it your wife?' The words bolted from her mouth.

Sidney laughed graciously as he swept down the staircase.

'No, no, but Elizabeth is related. It's in the eyes, don't you think?'

They shook hands, then Sidney turned to the portrait.

'Louise Mecklenburg Strelitz. Wife to a former King of Germany. Don't ask me on what count my wife is related. Simply put, Elizabeth is a Strelitz, and most definitely not a Mecklenburg. Lines of descendancy very complicated.' He waved away the confusion. 'It's good to see you. I appreciate you coming.'

'I was just thinking back to the last time I was here.'

'Ah, the Christmas dinner. Elizabeth's idea.'

They climbed the staircase then continued along an impressive corridor.

'Any news of your father?'

'I received a letter. He's already looking forward to leave. Shouldn't be long, I expect.'

Opening a pair of double doors, Sidney vanished into darkness, seconds later magically reappearing as he flung open tall drapes.

'Come in, come in.' He hovered around a desk and tidied scattered paper.

Entering the study was like seeing pages of an enchanted book all at once: walls covered with butterflies, pearlescent beetles and hairy moths all mounted in box frames and arranged according to species. Botanical sketches between them. Watercolours of plants, both whole and in cross-section, the anatomy of flowers and seeds laid bare as if sliced through by a surgeon's knife. Her eyes skurried around the room. Rolls of wallpaper, brass telescopes, barometers, a stuffed polecat, her gaze finally resting on the twee details of a wall clock.

'You like my Black Forest oddity.' The captain's chair creaked as he leant back.

'It's – different.'

He laughed. 'Random, I know, but I like it. A gift from a Bavarian client – please, be seated.'

Performing a half orbit around a freestanding globe, she perched on the edge of a chaise longue and stared at a painting of a huge beetle. Its armour coal black, thorny limbed, a hellish war beast that could have climbed out of the fireplace before settling above the mantelpiece.

'About the size of your thumb in real life.'

'Oh – that's a relief.'

'Stag beetles have been around for 300 million years, although I've never seen one. Southerners apparently, New Forest is a good place to spot them.'

Whirring chimes drew Ellen's eye to the wall clock, her interest then switching to a sketch pad that lay open on a bureau below it, the pages filled with a honeycomb pattern. A grid of bees in every other cell. Fleetingly a line of them appearing more obvious. Horizontal, vertical, sometimes diagonal and then just a grid again. The captain's chair creaked.

'I was so relieved when I heard you were staying on at the mill. Although I gather we now call it factory twenty-four.'

'Will you be overseeing munitions work?'

'I thought your father might have told you.'

Looking away from the geometric swarm, for a moment she struggled to find Sidney within the busy room: his figure behind the desk partially eclipsed by earth, the axis of it tilting to one side, the land mass of Russia curving both towards and away from her.

'He just said you wanted to see me.'

'Ah. Well, the authorities have decreed I stay put, a prisoner in my own home so to speak.'

'I'm sorry... I don't understand.'

'My connections with Germany have suddenly become very unfashionable.'

Her heart thumped; her wrists pulsed. Disquiet regularly held back bound itself to words before she yanked them up and shoved them out.

'Having a German wife doesn't make you a criminal and... besides, it is your mill!'

Sidney straightened as if Ellen's defence had sharpened his pride, but then he relaxed again into the chair. 'A mill repurposed as a munitions factory. I appreciate the sentiment but unfortunately, I'm considered a considerable risk.'

'But they can't just take your freedom like that.'

'I'm a rabbit in a snare according to my legal man. The more I struggle, the tighter it gets. His advice: sit tight – hope the war's a short one. Government has powerful wartime jurisdiction I'm afraid.'

Interlacing fingers around his middle, Sidney leant back. The silence interrupted by a miniature wooden bird lunging out of the clock and cuckooing three times. A door snapped shut, mechanisms sighed.

'At least the man in charge has allowed me one concession.'

'Man in charge?'

'Military man. A colonel no less. I may appoint someone who reports back to me, so I retain some kind of connection with my mill. I was hoping you would be my eyes and ears.'

'Of course.'

He slapped the table softly. 'Good then. Come for dinner once a week. Fill me in on all that's happening.'

She looked up at the empty eye sockets of the stag skull mounted on the wall above him, its antlers stabbing into the room.

'In return, I'll equal whatever the ministry is paying you. I've asked Cedric to sort it out. He said you'd be up for it.'

'Thank you, Mr Wallis. I haven't seen Cedric for a while.'

Cedric: her best friend since childhood. Son of the vicar. University graduate. He'd briefly worked in the city, but a year before the outbreak of war he got homesick so returned to Dardale.

'Probably because he's been buried alive under ministry paperwork, so much so he can't commit to the launch of this new publication.'

'Yes – he mentioned that. A works magazine?'

'Ministry of munitions wants factories to publish them monthly. Help bridge the gap between management and the female workforce. As Cedric's hands are full, I wondered if you would take it on.'

'I'd love to.'

'Good. I'll get Cedric to run it by the colonel. A chap called Joe Stander is due to arrive next week. Journalist from the *Leeds Times*. Ministry has employed him as our editor – and dare say censor. Young Australian fellow. Cedric's already met him. Very handsome apparently.'

'I've never met an Australian.'

'It's a case of you liaising between him and the workers. Put forward anything the women wish to include. Cedric will give you the full brief.'

'Looking forward to it.'

It was only after Ellen walked through the grounds and reached the lodges that she realised she'd forgotten to ask after Mr Wallis's baby. Her mind swimming with so many other thoughts: Sidney's house arrest, Dardale and the surrounding villages bereft of men, women arriving on trains to make munitions, the absence of her father. The arrival of a man. A handsome man from Australia.

DARDALE

1915

//

Common Green Bottle Fly – *Lucilia sericata*

Study for Wallis and Hilton Wallpapers. Plate No. 102 – Green Bugs and Blooms [see sketch on next page]

Facts: Common in temperate and tropical regions, including Europe, Africa and Australia. Female lays eggs in carrion of all kinds. Favours domestic sheep in particular, and sometimes lays eggs in the wet wool of living sheep. [German Entomologist Johann Wilhelm Meigen found that fly larvae debrided the wounds of humans.]

Symbology: Ancient lore depicts the fly as a symbol of impurity and a temptation to diverge from the path of righteousness.

Joe sat quietly on a wooden chest. His fellow traveller, a brakeman who wittered on as he hogged the little slot windows that gave glimpses up and down the line: worked the trains all his life but this route had frayed his nerves, his sleep ruined by the prospect of explosive disasters. And then for a while just the sounds of silvery rails and creak of the brake van; at times easy to believe that they had uncoupled and blindly coasted through the countryside.

The brakeman fidgeted about the wagon checking the tail lamp, gazing out of the rear door, switching between the duckets, one side then the other. The ritual repeated a second time, a third, as if those little glimpses of the outside world stopped his fears from racing away.

He rambled on; this leg of the journey not so bad, mostly a climb, couplings taut, the wagons full of empty shells. Not until the return journey would he have to prevent the load from ganging up on the locomotive.

The train ground to a halt at a signal and again, when they helped the fireman chase sheep off the line. And then as wheels and track settled into a monotonous chatter the railwayman spoke of the requisition. The mill well away from big cities. Tools of hand printing easily removed. A bridge connecting its upper floor to the station platform. 'Ticks all of the ministry's boxes.'

It was the most beautiful building he'd ever seen; more glass than stone – wallpapers once made there, high art. Shame to see it dragged into the war like that. But then again, the country was gripped by a shell crisis.

A viaduct, a tunnel, a steep-sided cutting. And then a slow snaking screech through a series of points. They lurched to a stop. Wagon doors drawing open, the voices outside confirming their arrival.

Dardale. End of the line. The brakeman already off and checking couplings.

Joe paused on the rear veranda, sensations of movement draining from his body. To the east, roofs clustered either side of a long, sloping street. Next to the platform, filling factory twenty-four. And behind the train to the north where the track curved away, heathered moorland, the summer skies above him, big and hot, just like the skies at home.

He walked along the platform and approached a soldier, artillery shells gathered behind him in an orderly line.

Joe shouted above the hissing steam. 'I'm to report to a Colonel Bacon?'

The soldier checked his papers then handed them back.

'They're expecting you, sir. There's no access over the link, you'll have to use the main door. Take steps down onto Main Street, can't miss the entrance from there.'

After a three-minute walk, Joe presented his documents to another guard, then entered the building and climbed the lobby stairs. Two doors on the landing; a line of gold lettering across one of them: *Lt Colonel C Bacon. RA – Director of Works.*

He knocked and entered. At the back of the room stood a thin old man, stripey shirt, annoyed, or was it just his face? and beside him another man. Much younger: bow tie above a belly, buttons of his waistcoat under pressure, hairline crack through one lens of his glasses.

Neither – thought Joe – would last an hour at the front.

The colonel stood on the far side of the room, looking out of a window, his uniformed figure very still, not a wisp of smoke from the pipe in his hand. Joe closed the door and walked to the middle of the room. 'Joe Stander, sir.'

The only reply, a distant steam whistle, then just the sound of a fly skittering up the glass above the colonel's head.

'A little late… aren't we?'

'Sorry, sir. The train…'

'Anzac – I gather?' The officer looked into the room, his gaze vague and unfocused.

'Yes, that's right.'

'Mm.' The colonel eyed Joe's feet. 'Your boys are in Gallipoli.'

'Yes, sir.'

'Well, you should count your blessings.'

Joe counted dead flies on the windowsill. One still alive. Its wings fizzing, its body spinning.

'Sir?'

The colonel turned away and talked to the window. 'Had the honour of serving under General Hamilton myself. Man can muster any troop of foot draggers into a big fight… let's hope you don't let him down.'

'You can count on us, sir.'

'We can?'

The other men gazed at the floor as the colonel talked at length about the virtue of punctuality. The lecture unnecessarily militaristic, as if Joe's late arrival had somehow jeopardised the lives of others. The colonel leant his backside against a desk, closed his eyes and shook his head.

'Nobody is counting on you – Stander.'

'Sir?'

'It's the politicians who need your bookkeeping. I don't believe our boys at the sharp end are counting on your nicely balanced ledger.'

The colonel's eyes remained shut, his head thrust forward as if inviting a response.

'But, sir, I'm a journalist and...'

'So that... the situation is crystal clear between us, Stander' – the colonel's eyes opened and blinked upwards – 'can I ask? Do you think our PBI is bothered about... how much this bullet... or that shell costs?' The colonel's gaze slowly fell from the ceiling until level with Joe's eyes.

'No, sir.'

'Right answer. We seem to be getting somewhere.'

The fly's death rattle boring into Joe's head, the portrait of Kitchener on the wall triggering memories, the ghost of his father snarling Kitchener's name and spitting in the dust. It was all so clear in his head as if the events of thirteen years ago happened the day before. That dreadful moment crawling back under his skin – flies swarming around their feet and over the maggoty carcass of a springbok shot by the British – views of their scorched farmhouse from the highveld – the taste of smouldering cattle hides in their mouths – their commando disbanded and on the run like animals before a wildfire – Joe was fifteen, a bandolier slung across his chest, a Mauser rifle in his hands.

The colonel tapped the bowl of the empty pipe into the palm of his hand. 'We military men always stick together, Stander. No accounting for that code of honour. Can you show me a civil servant who can quantify honour?'

Joe was no Australian. He was an Afrikaner, his soul marbled with veins of bitterness.

'No, *sir*.'

Overcome by the warmth of the room Joe drifted again and saw himself in the Kalahari sheltering in the shade of an acacia, its flat canopy hovering above the shimmer.

Heat stroke, peeling skin, close to death he continued west – always west.

'Keep this in mind and I believe there won't be any confusion between us.'

'Thank you. I will, sir.'

His mother dying in a British concentration camp; his loyalties imprisoned with the ringleaders of the failed Boer rebellion. No country, no family, his allegiance reassigned. The Germans saved his life, and it was they who had sent him.

'Let me introduce you to the team. Cedric Hodges, principal clerk. Harold Yates – foreman and factory manager.'

The colonel leant over the desk, his weight propped on straight arms. The neatly pressed cloth of his uniform hanging, cracks on leather strap across his chest opening up.

'That will be all. Hodges will show you around.' The colonel replaced the pipe in his mouth and walked to the window. 'Yates, stay behind.'

Joe and Cedric left the office.

'What was that all about?'

'Military code for things are done my way.'

'And what's a PBI when it's at home, cobber?'

Joe's accent near perfect, picked up from Aussie uitlanders employed on his father's farm. They'd been bullied off the Witwatersrand gold fields by big mining corporations and needed a wage to get by. Joe spent so much time with them that people said he spoke more Aussie than Boer.

'Poor Bloody Infantry. The colonel loves his abbreviations.'

'Glad he loves something.'

'And Anzac? …Cobber?'

Joe laughed.

'Australian and New Zealand Army Corps. Although I'm not in the army, and I'm no bloody Kiwi either. And cobber? Cobber means – good friend.'

'Cedric Hodges.' He held out his hand. Joe reciprocated and they shook.

'Look, there's been a mix-up. I'm a reporter, a journalist.'

'We know. Your role was explained but as you probably gather, the colonel doesn't listen… which is why it's chaos in here.'

Cedric opened a door, and they walked through a large office.

'He doesn't like the idea of the *Fuse* magazine; in his eyes that makes you a bit of a floater. So, I guess you've got the job. It's fine, I can show you the ropes. It's just counting the casings in – shells out, like a simple stocktake. I do all the wages and the costings.'

Doors of opportunity already opening Joe couldn't believe his luck.

'But what about the magazine?'

'Oh, you've got that job too.' Cedric grinned. 'Bit of advice – just to keep your head down, don't question the colonel's decisions and oh, don't mention Sidney Wallis, colonel hates him.'

'Sidney who?'

'Owner of the building.'

'Ah, gotcha.'

'Colonel's made the boardroom HQ. Even replaced Sidney's portrait with one of his beloved Lord Kitchener. Mr Wallis *is* married to a German, but openly accusing him of being a spy is sheer paranoia – barred him from coming anywhere near the place.' Cedric leaned in. 'If any of the guards sees Sidney, apparently the colonel has ordered them to shoot on sight.'

Pulling back, he spoke openly again.

'You'll be sharing this office with Mr Yates. But before you make yourself at home.'

Cedric made his way to the back of the room and opened a door, and they walked into a very small lobby, a second door appearing almost immediately ahead, to the left and right very long, narrow spaces.

'This is the block room. They may look like corridors, but both are dead ends. It's where our printing blocks are stored.'

'Blocks?'

'Hundreds of them. Used for printing wallpaper.'

Peering into the dimly lit room Joe could make out the blocks at one end neatly stacked on shelves like picture books in a giant's library.

'Only part of the mill that Sidney still controls. A concession by the ministry. Mothballed until the end of the war.' Cedric edged past Joe. 'Now for the best bit.'

Pushing open the second door he turned back to Joe and whispered with glee, 'Behold the colonel's army.'

Ahead of them in the middle of a large industrial

space a group of women gathered around a man wearing a white lab coat.

'See the tall lady at the back. If you need to know anything about this place, ask her. She's the mill manager's daughter.'

Cedric whispered Ellen's name loudly. She turned and walked towards them. Her features caught in a glow that spilled down from a long strip of rooflights.

Up since five that morning, Joe's journey had been like a slog across the bushveld. But now his feet ached a little less, and his heart pumped honest blood. And for a moment he was back home on the great escarpment, the Berg wind clearing a bitter fog from the landscape of his thoughts. Beauty emerging before him. Imperishable. Luminous.

'Sorry to tear you away.'

'No problem, Ced – he's just about finished. Heard it three times already.'

'Joe, this is Ellen. Ellen – Joe.'

'Nice to meet you at last.' She offered her hand.

'Likewise.' He shook it.

Cedric waved at the women. Nobody waved back.

'Leave you to it then; must get on.' They watched Cedric disappear into the block room and by then a number of women in the group had turned to eye Joe.

'Sorry for all the attention. Young men are a rare breed these days.' She smiled at the floor.

'Wouldn't be here myself if it weren't for these.' He lifted spectacles off his nose, lenses plain glass, no magnification. He could shoot a running hare at five hundred yards without them.

'Army didn't want me shooting our own blokes.' He shrugged.

'You're a long way from home. Why here?'

'I'm a journalist. Reporting on what the blokes are going through seemed the next best thing.'

'Who do you write for?'

'*Melbourne Truth* back home. Here I've been writing articles about wounded lads recovering at Allerton for the *Leeds Times*. My face didn't fit, mind. Editor wasn't keen on Aussie straight talk.'

Joe surveyed the room, noted the lack of guards and location of the exits.

'Hoping for a posting at the front, but army isn't allowing press at the moment.'

'Well, if you're looking for action you won't find it here. There's just Cedric and a few old codgers and the Lancashire rain.'

'And a hundred women.'

She wiped her nose boyishly with a sleeve. 'Sixty-six. And they don't need distracting from their work.'

'I think it's Cedric you need to worry about.'

Her eyes fixed him. 'It's alright, we trust Cedric. I've pencilled a meeting in your dairy for Monday to discuss what to put in the first edition.'

'Didn't know I had a diary.'

'It's on your desk. Just you, me and Cedric unless he's busy.'

'Actually – I'm very fond of the Lancashire rain.'

She smiled. 'I'd better get back,' then turned and rejoined the group.

Joe walked back to the office, pausing in the narrow block room, his fingers trekking over a printing block, patterns in the room bristling with life. Leaves, stems and flowers propelling him back to what he thought were his last moments, his wrecked body staggering through the Kalahari sands, life evaporating from him, words of the Boer oath croaking from his parched mouth.

And then droplets from the night sky. A cruel mirage, he thought, until the rain thickened and peppered his cracked face. So heavy, he drank from the air and sandy rivulets. Waking in a sluit, he sat up, thought he'd died, the dune veld all around him blooming into a miraculous carpet of colour.

He staggered on. One last day sheltering under a tree, one last sunset, one last star-filled trudge through the cool semi-desert, his body found next day by settlers who worked on a remote farm in Namaland, German south-west Africa.

DEV

Gymkhana

Isla drove the bakery van as if we'd stolen it, my guts shifting with the rise and fall of the lane. On the way back from the hotel, we'd argued. Isla said I was working too hard.

'Don't come crying to me when you burn out.'

Like an idiot I played everything down, claimed I didn't need help.

Our meeting went well; we'd agreed on a contract to supply the hotel restaurant. A moment to celebrate, but Isla just ignored me.

A heavy shower passed, skies brightened, she snatched sunglasses from the dashboard. I squirmed as the van lurched through another bend. We crested a hill and as the moorland road straightened, I secretly gazed at lumbering columns of grey that dragged cloudbursts across distant peaks. The road dipped and vistas vanished behind tufted hillocks and once past High Tor, the moor fell away and at the foot of the valley the church spire and wet roofs of town came into view.

The turn off was marked by an ancient oak post that rose up from the bracken. The horizontal finger of wood that once displayed a placename detached and missing. The road streamed with run-off; sun broke through cloud. Shimmering tarmac twisting down the heath like a silver adder. I looked at Isla hoping she would say something, but she remained aloof.

She was a good friend; twenty-five, an eccentric with orange hair. School years a nightmare because of dyslexia, her young life a traumatic drama until she met a deaf girl who went to the same dance class. And it so happened that Isla loved learning snippets of sign from her new friend; disadvantaged when it came to the written word, the ballet of arms and hands came naturally. So, she went to night classes, became fluent, her interpretative skills called upon by the police, NHS and a television company. Mostly her happy hands attended court hearings and bereavements, but the relaying of grinding truths got to her, and she disliked Manchester and had boyfriend problems – hence her move back home.

She was doing a good job of running the bakery shop. I guessed she was happy doing it, although long term I knew it wasn't enough for her. She'd tried and failed to teach me sign language. I was a hopeless student; my hands too busy working dough had no time to learn another language. Lately I think everything about me annoyed her. The silence continued; her driving did the talking.

We raced through the dripping shade of a tree tunnel; dappled sunspots strobing the windscreen. And then we hit the fringes of town. A metal-clad industrial unit, a petrol station then roads of terraced houses leading to Main Street.

Passing the mill, I looked up at my apartment above the bakery and saw the bloom of builders' dust on windows. Work delayed for one reason and another, but at last they were finishing off and I was due to move in the following week. In the meantime, I stayed with Isla's family, and we were heading back to their home of steel and glass that sat in an acre of woodland. It was designed by Lassiter's; the architects who were overseeing redevelopment of the mill.

A mile out of town we pulled onto the driveway. I followed Isla to the front door.

'Sorry we're late.'

The smell of a Sunday roast greeted us in. Isla's mum – Janet – handed us both a glass of wine.

'Well – how'd it go?'

'Fine, they liked us,' Isla said flatly, then fussed the border terriers who trembled at the window. 'Have you seen a squirrel, Sadie? Where's the squirrel?'

The ground floor was big and fluid, a long wall of sliding glass running across the back. Kitchen, dining, living room one space, all looking out onto a grassy glade edged by thick woodland.

'Muntjac.'

'What's that?' asked Isla.

Her grandmother struggled out of an armchair. 'Muntjac deer – every day.' Shuffling down the hallway she disappeared into the toilet.

Isla opened the sliding doors. The dogs sprinted across

the grass barking at the trees. She squeezed a small purple ball. It squeaked. The dogs wheeled around and scampered back.

Isla's mum gave me a thumbs-up. 'Glad they liked you.'

Re-emerging from the toilet the grandmother yelled up the stairwell.

'Dinner!'

Seconds later, feet of young children thudded downstairs and ran into the garden. A commotion ensued. Uncle Les, Isla, her siblings and the squeaky ball all enticing the dogs out of the woods and into the house. Huge sliding doors closed; everyone sat down.

Conversation flowed. Voices merged. My left ear turned to the table, head inching forward as if tugged by threads of chat. I soon lost the gist; stories floating away like balloons cut loose. Starved of speech, my tongue turned to food. Soon I was full, a bit tipsy.

Pudding was served. I wondered if my batteries were fading and then, as if the hearing aid were especially attuned to detecting her name, I heard it – very clearly.

'Devon knows the Hey girl,' Isla proclaimed.

'Oh, she was a sweet girl... what was her first name again?' Janet said, distributing the wine.

'Gymkhana,' Grandmother blurted.

Conversation fell silent as we studied one another's bemusement, the grandmother repeating the word with a hint of irritation. Then Janet became animated, as though she were on a quiz show.

'Yes! Yes, the gymkhana – on the Dardale estate. The Hey girl was a good rider... we poor parents looked on with hearts in mouths – you were all very young.' She swigged a mouthful of wine.

'Mum – they were Shetland ponies.'

Everyone laughed. Janet, unamused, shovelled more pudding into bowls. 'I remember talking to her gran, Harriette – she was a lovely lady. She hoped her family would move up here, think they lived in Moss Side at the time. Dani was her name, wasn't it?'

Les shifted in his seat. 'Thank God they didn't. Frank Hey, remember him, always in and out of prison?' He turned to Isla's dad. 'Didn't he get accused of shooting the chap pulled from the canal?'

The dogs were at the window again, their noses leaving a tidemark on the glass.

Les chuckled. 'Eighty-two. Will never forget – same year they raised the *Mary Rose*.'

'Poor chap. Planner at the council, wasn't he?' Janet chipped in.

I sat back and took in the revelations. Some words lost but I got the gist; it was all new to me.

'Conservation officer. Was in the reeds for days. Could smell him from the pub terrace apparently – body all bloated up.'

'Not at the table, Les. Please,' Janet protested.

Isla's dad placed a tray of mugs on the table, filled a cafetiere with hot water. 'Police couldn't make it stick. Mishandling of forensic evidence – still ended up in Strangeways, mind.'

'For another murder?' said Isla's wide-eyed little brother.

Les slouched back from the table massaging his

belly. 'Our dad reckoned Frank harassed Rennie Wallis something rotten, chased him through the maze at Dardale Hall, beat him up. Poor bloke had a breakdown. There was a restraining order or something after that. Stopped Frank from coming anywhere near town.'

Isla's dad nodded. 'Sounds about right. Anyway, he's in for life for multiple offences. His wife went to the police and spilt the beans. Dropped him right in it apparently.'

Les burped under his hand. 'Sad, isn't it – family, turning on itself like that?'

One of the terriers jumped up onto Isla's lap. Holding it away from the table, she stroked back ears, which made the dog look extremely cheerful. 'Anyway, she's back in town, working in the Nav. She's so pretty.'

Janet poured coffee. 'Ah, there you go – happy ending. Very talented rider. Won that gymkhana hands down. I remember Harriette being so proud. Probably needed some joy in her life, had a bit of a rough ride herself. Didn't her mum disappear or something?'

'Ellen,' Grandmother muttered as she gazed at the trees.

'That's right, didn't she run a…?'

'Fucking traitor.'

Stunned silence. The table a forum of raised eyebrows.

'Mum! What's got into you…? I think it's probably time for a lie down.' Janet ushered the grandmother away. Lots of eye-rolling whilst everyone helped clear away. Isla slid open the doors, her brother gleefully mimicking his grandmother's words before chasing after the dogs who were already at the trees.

I went to the kitchen area with Les and Isla, and we did the dishes.

'I really didn't know her that well.'

'You fancied her though; I remember you telling me.' Isla smirked.

Les laughed. 'Can't get away with much here. You knew her?'

'Same school. And I did, well, all the lads did. Bit shocked by those stories though, seemed a nice lass at school. Anyway, what was that all about?'

'Bad blood from way back – Don't ask; long story.'

Isla's mum came over and took the tea towel from my hand.

'You look tired, pet.'

'It's been a long week.'

'Why don't you have a nap?'

I thanked her for dinner then excused myself, Isla's dad calling after me as I headed towards the stairs. 'I'm leaving for Manchester early doors, if you want a lift into town.'

'That would be good – thank you.'

In the bedroom, I closed the curtains, lay on the bed, my mind buzzing with stories of Dani and her family. Lifting an arch file off the bedside table I opened it, slid wads of my paperwork over the rings, mainly records of site and council meetings. At the bottom, historical stuff about the canal, railway and mill I'd previously ignored; talk over dinner now sparking my interest. I scanned the articles but there was no mention of Ellen the traitor, Frank the murderer or riders at gymkhanas. Digging deeper, I read text below photographs of po-faced mill workers: Wallis and Hilton switched to paper production after the 1860 cotton famine. In 1902, the partnership split; Ernest Hilton emigrating to Canada to develop a patent for mechanised production. Sidney Wallis stayed and continued to make wallpaper the old way until the national shell scandal of 1915 when the mill along with others were requisitioned by the War Office. I flicked further back to an article about the canal. Building it across the moors costly; its bankruptcy sealed by a railway that arrived twenty years later. The waterway redundant for over two hundred years it was now overgrown and polluted although there was talk of restoration.

After looking at heyday pictures of horses on towpaths I closed my eyes, imagined lying on a barge, a clopping stride towing me along.

*

The alarm went off, the file still open beside me – so tired, my evening nap had merged into a good night's sleep. Isla's dad was already up. I put new batteries in my hearing aid. We drank coffee whilst he shuffled papers into a briefcase. Then we left and drove at a stately pace through the morning mist.

'Business, okay?'

'Yeah – had a good month.'

'Glad it's paying off – couldn't have timed it better. Place has been a basket case for years. Council washed their hands of it after the death of their chap.'

We slowed at a junction, then smoothly pulled onto the B road.

'Nearly moved away actually, but Jan's mum was a tie. Not complaining mind, land for the house was cheap. And, well, this place – the moors, the town. Gets under your skin. Hate being away from it.'

'It's a great house… and the town is buzzing.'

'Mm – becoming popular again. Good luck to you. I think you're sitting on a little gold mine.'

We travelled between misty fields, and after crossing the canal, he dropped me off in front of the mill, the car's rear fog light soon fading beyond the canal bridge. Then for a while I watched the deserted town and wondered what ghosts might be hiding in its streets. Had its troubles really been that bad? The murk lifted; details of the street becoming clearer. It was just a Lancashire town – not the Wild West. Unlocking the bakery door I began shouldering a delivery of flour sacks into the back room.

I got through the week.

*

The following Sunday I moved into the apartment and at first, I was hardly there, just a few hours' sleep on an inflatable mattress every night; each day starting with strong coffee. My kitchen clutter free: only the essentials unpacked; most of the boxes still sealed up and stacked in the hallway.

The bakery directly below the apartment, my journey to work was also zen, a one-minute commute, down a grand staircase, out of the main entrance, thirty or so steps beside railings before entering the shop. The rhythm of the bakery beating ever faster, I normally spent the whole of Sunday recovering in bed.

Although this Sunday I was meeting up with Isla at the Nav. I woke late morning, drank coffee, emptied a whole week's post from my mailbox and worked my way through it before leaving. Within minutes I was sitting with Isla on an outdoor terrace that overlooked the canal and countryside beyond. A group of friends she'd known since school at the same table. They seemed pleasant enough, but the wind repeatedly ushered their voices away and I soon lost focus, my gaze drifting through the open back doors of the pub.

It was busy: drinkers at the bar, others eating at tables, men playing darts. Then in the thick of it I spotted Dani. My pulse quickening as I watched her take orders from a large group; chatty and bright as she did so. She shared a joke with customers as she cleared their table and then disappeared deeper into the pub carrying a stack of plates.

Was it really Dani? Daughter of a criminal? To be honest I couldn't believe it. Boarding pupil. Quiet at school. And here in the pub she had been so courteous even though she was grafting.

Then from nowhere she appeared beside me. Punk hair grown out, swept back, shoulder length, so close I could see individual strands playing with the breeze.

Her stance straightened when she clocked me, her gaze retreating to the pad, thought flooding her face. She worked around the table, her eyes checking mine between scribbles. I watched her lips repeat everyone's order then she glanced at me again.

'It is you, isn't it?' she said looking at the scarred side of my head; I rubbed my tatty ear. I could feel my face getting warm. Words deserted me.

'Devon – right?'

'Hi, Dani.'

We talked about school but not the kiss. She asked me why I was in town.

'No way? My gran loves you.'

We shared a joke; it was shallow and frail. The coincidence of everything throwing us off course, we nearly forgot why we were there. The table silent, everyone our audience; we were on stage again, but we'd forgotten our lines. Awkward. I caught myself biting my lip; she rubbed hers with the back of a hand. She turned away and breezily asked if anyone wanted another drink. Nobody did.

'Good to see you.'

'Yeah, you too. See you around.'

She left the table and disappeared into the pub. Other staff delivered food and cleared away. I made my excuses and said goodbye to Isla's friends. Walking out I caught Dani's eye. She waved; I waved back. I didn't see her again for a while. Work pinned me down like that.

The council began repaving Main Street; parts of it newly pedestrianised. A Café Rouge opened at the top end of town. Saturday market traded in the square for the first time in twenty years. The place pulsed with renewed energy. We gained an ever wider following, a foodie review describing us as the best artisan bakery in Lancashire. Apparently, we were in line for an industry award. Workload increased. I floundered. No wonder my dreams were full of panic. The one I slept through the night before the most unnerving of them all: paddling an inflatable boat through reeds I searched for a body. And then out of the blue shots were fired; bullets strafing the water all around me. Paddling hard I somehow managed to escape uninjured but then the wind picked up and I drifted across open water and into the eye of an incredible storm.

Canal

Isla cornered me. 'You need help.'

'You make it sound like I'm an addict.'

'You know what I mean. A helping hand – like an assistant.'

'It's fine.'

'Devon – it's not fine. I found you asleep on bags of flour. Thought I'd lost you – almost called the police.'

'You're overreacting – I'm coping. We're going to win an award.'

'You have such a bloody ego. I've got customers waiting. Go home. Brush your teeth. Your breath smells.'

'Sorry for the false alarm.'

It wasn't the only one.

The fire alarm triggered at least twice a day. Nobody knew why. A fault with the smoke sensors maybe. I just reset the system and ploughed on. Early starts no longer enough, I burnt through the hours and pulled all-nighters. I just needed to get to the end of the week. Sunday a sleepy atoll where I fumbled around like a dazed castaway. And I was nearly there; home and dry. Friday night through to Saturday morning the last big push to satisfy weekend demand.

Before the shift, I sat on the stone edge of the canal and leant against a mooring bollard sturdy enough to take the lines of a sea-going ship. Too tired to eat chips, my eye was drawn to poplar trees on the opposite bank, leaves in the warm breeze like a wall of butterflies.

Below my feet a forgotten backwater hidden away from busy Main Street. The low point of town. A sump where history fermented.

Sheltered on both sides, sounds bounced off the water and walls of the mill – the brassy call of waterfowl an unadulterated symphony my hearing aid rarely enjoyed. And the seclusion of it normally steadied me. But not today. Because those historical articles were haunting me; the canal builders going bankrupt nagging at the back of my mind. They tried so hard to pull it off: canal widths narrowed, locks shortened, the underside of bridges and tunnels lowered. It limped on. But when the money dried up construction stopped a few hundred yards from where I sat.

A monumental effort that ended in failure.

Ripples of self-doubt washed over me as sultry breezes stroked the surface of the canal. Deep down I knew I couldn't carry on like this; a once easy-going subordinate now fully fledged control freak who couldn't let go. Had I taken control of my destiny or had it taken control of me. Maybe I did need help, but I was just too tired to come up with a plan. To be honest, the thought of handing anything to others plain terrified me.

I looked towards the railway bridge. Another relic; the line not in service since the sixties. A barge, a hundred yards beyond its arches, moored to the opposite bank. It was back. Which was odd, as pleasure boats rarely passed through the cramped tunnel that lay a few miles out of town. And yet it had appeared on and off all summer. Its hull and upper flanks undercoat grey, no name on the bow; rope fenders and an odd tilt its only distinguishing features.

I shared my dinner with a frenzy of ducks, the narrowboat in the distance lifeless, seemingly crewless.

Chips all eaten, the ducks lost interest and swam away. Waterborne lullabies soothed my worries: water ruffled by a breeze, a dragonfly droning, a slew of bubbles, sunshine dancing through the water persuading my tired eyes to draw time on the fusty redundancy of it all – and then a falling dream.

A plunge no more than five feet that ended wet, freezing, the murky surface of the canal smacking me like a wall. I was underwater for just a heartbeat then thrashing, gasping panic. The stone quay looming over me; soft silt sucking at my feet. Knees tucked up, arms frantically sculling, steps or ladders nowhere to be seen. The opposite bank a mass of thorny branches that snagged litter. Hull of the barge a long way off I flipped onto my back, arms and legs trouncing like an overwound bath toy. Would I get there? No chance.

'HELP!'

Cars passed over the bridge, a single contrail streaked the sky, an audience of drakes and mallards preened themselves on the quay.

'HELP!'

Nothing.

Was this it? The end? I shouted louder. I thrashed harder. My efforts rewarded as I pulled alongside a return in the quay, the rusty side of a ladder coming into view.

Clinging on I caught my breath then climbed out spewing water and mashed potato. Something wrong. No sound. No hearing aid.

Glancing at the barge, I saw movement. A silent silhouette.

Someone onboard!

I marched to the boat and stopped. Net curtains fluttering out of portholes like a patronising dismissal as I spat like a spud gun.

I shouted angry words.

My voice a blunt noise muffling through my chest and head. Nobody appeared. Maybe there was a reply, but I couldn't hear it. I shouted louder.

'Why didn't you help me!'

Nobody appeared. Nothing… then more nothing… then a bit more.

'Fuck you then!'

Stomping away, my trainers sucked and gurgled with every step. At the flat I showered off bugs and duck weed.

I felt like a complete idiot.
I felt wide awake.

*

I worked through the night, the kitchen my little safe haven. *Why didn't the person on the barge help? What kind of a place was this?* Once I had my new hearing aid, I was going back there to confront them!

I went to bed at two in the morning and then woke at seven to the smell of sodden clothes in the shower tray; I shoved them in a plastic bag and dumped them in the bin.

Isla was busy serving customers when I explained how I lost my earpiece. Her reaction one of mocking laughter and annoyance. In the face of zero sympathy I sulked, worked through Saturday morning harder than ever, Isla's irate hand signs the only connection I had with the outside world.

We locked up. Her shoulders softened and her hands did the talking again, both flat, one facing her tummy, the other sinking behind it. 'You could have drowned,' she mouthed.

I drew circles around my heart with a fist – Sorry.

We went back to the flat, Isla cooked me a meal then we watched *Silence of the Lambs*, with subtitles.

*

The following Monday, after the morning bake, I drove to the audiologist to collect a new hearing aid. Road noise crashing in on the way home, like crazy musicians rehearsed inside the van. And by the end of the journey, I felt terribly weary: my head achy, my stomach unsettled. But it was a busy day, and stocks were low, a second bake a sound commercial decision. I set the ovens to preheat and removed dough from the fridge. And then Isla's head appeared through the doorway.

'I thought I told you to go home and call the doctor. That canal is full of crap – you've probably picked up a bug.'

'I'm fine.' I carried on.

She telephoned the surgery and booked an appointment and when I protested, she replied with angry hands then stomped away into the shop. Sign for "Grow up", I guessed.

Next morning, I worked the early shift. My appointment not until eleven but when Isla came in to open the shop, she rounded me up and chased me out of the door. I went back to the flat, showered and then decided to call in on *HMS Selfish Bastard*.

But there was no sign of it.

I followed the towpath right out of town, Dardale meadow appearing beyond a slow bend in the canal. I stopped at an old wooden footbridge beyond which the canal ran unwaveringly straight through wayward moor, the bridge beside me half rotten and mossy; some planks missing. A real shame as the field beyond looked so attractive. Nonetheless the view of it was enough to provide a fresh perspective; space opening in my head as I watched the uncropped meadow acknowledge the moorland breeze. The shifting interlude enough for me to finally accept that I couldn't continue without a change; the boat I'd set off in now too big to sail by myself.

The choice? Recruit or fail.

I needed someone with a good attitude who could learn from me. I had to get used to the idea of trusting others – bastard on the barge need not apply. I couldn't imagine turning my back on someone like that. Where was the compassion? Morals?

Then again, like me, they could have been deaf – I let it go.

It was a lovely day. I was alive. I turned back towards town.

The doctor's surgery was at the top end of Main Street, a big Georgian house that backed onto a pay and display car park. It still felt homelike. The old living room a waiting area, consultations conducted in the bedrooms, anaglypta wallpaper, creaky floorboards, the definition of radiators lost to decades of redecoration.

I sat in the living room, the atmosphere strange; people silently waiting like a family that had fallen out. Sitting on uncomfortable plastic, we flicked glossy pages, stared blankly at restful pictures on the wall – the receptionist called me through.

Doctor Penson was in his forties, thinning red hair, shirt sleeves rolled up, his manner cheerful and efficient. We talked about my PTSD and how I was coping without the medication, a serotonin booster I'd taken on and off since leaving the army.

'I feel good.'

He took my blood pressure.

'General health?'

'A little fatigued. Well, tired most of the time.'

I described the mishap; he asked if I'd swallowed water.

'Yes.'

'Any chills, diarrhoea, rashes?'

'No.'

'If those symptoms show, come back and see me. Unlikely you have contracted Weils, but we'll keep an eye on you. Any other concerns?'

'Not really.'

'Working hard?'

'Yes – I've just started a business.'

'I know – my wife loves your bread. And – our daughter is good friends with Isla.'

I slipped on my jacket. 'I'm getting used to the idea that everyone knows everyone else's business here.'

He smiled. 'It's not Manchester, that's for sure. Can't get away with much here. Word soon gets around.'

The body, in the canal – somebody got away with that.

'I don't make a habit of discussing my patients, but Isla was at ours last weekend. Devon – she's worried about you; thinks you're overdoing it.'

'She's probably right.'

'It's not a crime to get help, you know. Unfortunately, I can't prescribe anything for that. Your business – your call.'

'You're both right. It's time I did. Can you prescribe anything for a stubborn nature?'

The doctor smiled.

'Yes, she's called Isla.'

*

I sat outside a cafe at one of the tables that spilled into the square, drank coffee and wrote a job advert on a postcard. Workers erected scaffold over the stone facade of the bank opposite. I paid for the coffee then went to the post office and pinned the card to the noticeboard.

Angel Bakery in need of baker's assistant.
Full training given. No experience needed.
Good hourly rate.
Call Devon on: **** ******

Already feeling lighter, I breezed back and walked into the shop. Isla glared at me.

'What are you doing here?'

I told her about the advert. She gave me a big hug then shooed me out and offered to lock up. I went back into town, bought some fresh ingredients, cooked myself dinner then slept heavily.

*

Within a week I'd employed a local lad called Jack. Nineteen, rugby player, wide shoulders, keen and a quick learner it wasn't long before he moved seamlessly from one task to another without asking too many questions.

Should have done it months ago.

Then I employed another. A friend of Jack's called Blake. He was at a catering college and needed money to run a car. He worked the morning shift then studied during the day.

So, I had my own mini platoon and I looked after them as if they were my own. I insisted they wore ear defenders when the mixers were running and we all worked in silence, moving around like a well-drilled team. On Friday evening before the night shift, I treated them to fish and chips which we ate sitting on the quay. Jack flung a chip into the canal. Then a question.

'Boss?'

'Yes.'

'How are the swimming lessons?'

'Funny.'

Much hilarity: my mishap, apparently on everyone's tongues in the Navigation Inn.

But not the chapter about the barge. I'd made no mention of the barge – to anyone. I don't know why. It made me feel stupid I suppose, like I had been regarded as not worth saving. Besides, there had been no further sign of it and I wondered if it had sunk or was just a figment of my imagination. A grey ghost. My memory tugging it away to some far-off graveyard in the depths of my mind.

On Saturday morning I slept in, started the day at a leisurely pace. A proper breakfast, a skim through the newspaper, all very civilised. I arrived at the shop and helped Isla by manning the till, ten minutes passing before the fire alarm decided to let rip. Everyone's reaction cavalier – here we go again.

Then I saw the smoke through the kitchen door porthole.

Fire extinguisher in hand I rushed back, but soon realised the smoke was in fact a cloud of flour dust, the ghostly figure of Jack lost in the middle of it, his arms swiping at the swirling miasma. The sixteen-kilo sack of flour he was carrying ripped open and hanging limp over his shoulder.

I reset the system. Another day began. Wheels of the bakery steadily churning – mixing, proving, baking, cooling; principles a thousand years had not changed. And yet mounted on the ceiling directly above the mixers a marvel of hi-tech detection ready to disrupt the cycle for no good reason. Its pesky red light blinking unfailingly every thirty seconds, a round plastic Peter that cried wolf.

And the wolf we now knew was a fine cloud of flour dust that drifted up whenever a sack of flour flumped into the mixer. The smoke detector had in fact been doing its job all along, but like me, it was just a little lacking when it came to intuition. I arranged a meeting with the architect. Easy enough. His office was in the same building, his front door across the landing from my apartment.

Glass Meeting Room

Through the glass door I could see two men standing in reception, one in police uniform, the other in a suit. The door buzzed open, the secretary looked up. 'Take a seat – be with you in a minute.'

The suited man pushed a business card across the reception desk. 'Could you give this to Mr Lassiter?' The other glanced my way – a stop and search conducted with the eye. I stared back, wondered if his nose was as faulty as the smoke detector. They made for the door, their aftershave overpowering and cheap.

The receptionist lifted a telephone. 'Mr Enoch is waiting. Yes, they've just left.'

She performed a quick smile. 'Won't be a minute.' Her eyes returned to the computer screen. The keyboard rattled.

I studied a print displayed on the wall. To have wallpaper framed a bit odd, but apparently it was rare. A hundred-year-old swatch printed in the Wallis mill, a stylised pattern of tulip heads.

Karl swept in, his tailored figure slight, his face boyish. He'd grown a beard, his hair flicked to one side like the singer Tony Hadley from Spandau Ballet.

'Devon. Good to see you. Come through.'

The receptionist looked up. 'Inspector Craven left this for you.'

'Thanks.' Karl tucked the card into his pocket. I followed him into the offices, the space impressive, the walls bare brick. My apartment just a modest slice through the building; the architect's office over half of the cake. A long volume not dissimilar to a church. Trusses and rafters high above. Tall industrial windows to the side. I followed Karl down the central aisle. On the left, a row of people sitting along the window wall, eyes glued to computer screens, hands sweeping and clicking. On the right, easy chairs and a coffee table encircled by a freestanding library of journals and white cardboard models. Ahead our destination. A glass-sided meeting room, its polished surfaces glinting like a museum display case, the table thin and techy, chairs like white leaves carried by a colony of legs.

We entered, office noise melting away, the sound of Karl's voice crystal clear.

'Please, take a seat. Isla mentioned your mishap with the canal. Glad to see you in one piece.'

'Seems to be talk of the town.'

'Oh to be famous.'

He rubbed his chin and smiled. I wondered if he'd grown the beard to look older. It didn't suit him. He rolled his eyes.

'Just had a visit from the police.'

'I saw them in reception – everything okay?'

'They're reopening an old case. Happened over ten years ago. Victim was a conservation officer apparently, worked for the local council. They've come by new evidence – wouldn't tell me much more than that. Asked if I'd seen anything suspicious by the canal.'

The barge? Was it suspicious? A boat, on a canal – not really.

Karl reached for a stack of folded drawings. 'I told them, just ducks and swans. Made it clear I'd only been here a couple of years. Still questioned the life out of me – just being thorough, I guess.'

The receptionist walked down the aisle carrying a tray of hot drinks. I got up, tended the door, a wafer plate of glass, opening and closing it almost a mime.

She swept in and out. We thanked her. Karl poured coffee. 'The electrician tested the system, but he couldn't find any faults.'

He pulled a drawing from the stack and unfolded it on the table. But it was a drawing of my apartment and not the bakery. Bedroom, bathroom and mezzanine landing.

He's picked the wrong one.

'I talked through the problem with the building control officer. He suggested replacing the smoke detector with a heat detector. It shouldn't mistake flour dust for smoke.'

'Sounds simple enough. Isn't that a plan of my bedroom?'

'Yes. There's something else. He was a bit surprised when I mentioned you were hard of hearing. For some reason it hasn't come up before.'

'Sorry, I don't follow.'

'The building control officer – he suggested we fit a VAD in your bedroom and lower floor of your flat.'

'VAD?'

Karl smoothed paper creases with the palm of his hand.

'Visual alarm device – safety net for those with impaired hearing. Flashing light conveys the warning.' His hand pulsed like a jellyfish. 'He's not insisting on it, but as you live alone, he's made it a recommendation. I admit, it's something I missed at the design stage.'

'What if I'm asleep?'

'High intensity strobe, designed to wake you, needs installing above the bed and a vibration pad under your pillow. Again, a recommendation. We're talking a few hundred pounds. I'll ask the electrician for a quote, if you want to go ahead.'

'Sure, sounds sensible.'

'Believe me, if there's a fire anywhere in the mill, you'll know about it.'

Shelly appeared in the aisle again, thumb and little finger splayed against her head like a telephone. She mouthed, 'Line one.'

'Sorry, have to take this – shouldn't be long.'

Then it was just me and my thoughts in the glass room. Sounds dampened, views crystal clear in all directions. I was in plain sight of the whole office, like an actor in the spotlights. My mind wandering back to the school stage. Dani standing next to me. The memory so vivid I could feel the sensation of her breath on the side of my neck. And then I recalled the pub terrace and the implausible serendipity. Unfinished business of the kiss an elephant stampeding around us. Dani taking our orders, everybody waiting for me to decide, words on the menu swimming in my vision. The kiss, all I could think of.

Then I caught a reflection of myself in the glass. Pulse racing, an urge inside wanting to make good the regret. I was the product of public schooling, an institution that supposedly produced tough, self-reliant men: colonels, judges, prime ministers.

So why didn't I kiss her; why had I not talked to her about the way I felt.

And then I saw the glass room in a different light. Not so much the flashy stroke of an architect's hand, more his halfway house that lay somewhere between the ethereal and the real. A crystalline nursery where inklings could blossom into ideas.

I had my own. And the flash of inspiration glowed warm

in my chest. I knew where to find her, and I imagined going there. But the glow soon faded: maybe burble of the pub would drown my hearing aid, the disjointed conversation, the awkwardness. I sank into the chair, bone heavy, slow and tired, logistics of reality chipping away my confidence.

I needed a plan.

I drank more coffee and watched the office: Karl on the telephone gazing out over the town, a group of four gathered around a big screen pointing at computer-generated drawings, three people in the library area, sat at a coffee table talking over a pure white model. One of many that littered the office. The biggest and most impressive of all on the end of the table at which I sat. The Wallis mill, glowing in the beams of halogen spotlights.

Impossible not to get drawn in by the magic of it. Details inside and out painstakingly replicated. A labour of love so faithful to the real it was as if a wizard's wand had shrunk the building and frosted it white.

Karl swept in. 'Sorry about that. Ah, the model. You like our self-portrait?'

He lifted off the roof, the inside volume diced by an array of walls. The most prominent of the rooms a straight, narrow space that ran through the middle stretching from one end to the other. A doorless corridor. A blank slot. I ran a fingertip along the parallel walls. 'This part not finished?'

'Used to be called the block room according to Rennie. An old storage space that runs behind the back wall of our office. Sealed up for eighty years apparently.'

'Never knew it existed.'

'Seems no one did. We wanted to open it up – reestablish a link between front and back of the building. But our hands are tied, can't touch the walls until they've been investigated.'

'By the police?'

'No, no. Historical boffins from the V&A when they get round to it. In the meantime, the planners have protected the walls with a temporary preservation notice.'

More technical jargon. I felt myself drifting. I focused on the modelled version of my bakery, the small windows of the backroom set into the gable, a castle-thick wall that kept temperatures steady. The deck ovens like hot caves, I could almost smell the earthy tang of leavened dough, the overtones of a warm crust, the golden aromas attracting customers like bees to nectar. I was itching to get back.

'…and it's not just parts of the mill they're protecting. The speed of the turnaround has caught everyone out. Over half the shops were boarded a few years back, now businesses are clamouring for a foothold. It's led to the council tightening their grip. After years of indifference, they want to list most of the buildings on Main Street.'

Karl stirred a pen inside one of the bigger rooms. 'It's this wall here, facing into the old print room, they're interested in. It was used as a full-size mock-up for the wallpapers, back in the day. Clients stayed at Dardale Hall, then came here to preview the goods before placing orders. European royalty, no less…'

Karl in full flow, I studied the internal spaces of the model. The sealed space, I noticed, also ran behind my apartment.

'…so, this layering of hand-crafted wallpaper tells

a story. Gems of the Arts and Crafts Movement. It's not only increased the significance of the building, but also the town. A heritage asset of national importance, so the boffins claim.'

He removed another level leaving the lowest floor exposed. 'Did I mention we have a new neighbour?'

'You did – months ago. Another business?'

'Car upholstery – repairs and refits. One-man band called Steven Ruskin moving in next month.'

His pen danced in the model again. The partly subterranean space at the end of his pen below ground on the town side, opening out at the back where floor levels matched those of towpath and canal; ground levels around the mill sloping down from front to back.

'Timed that well, should be in before the opening ceremony. Is that still going ahead?'

'I'll say. Ribbon cutting. Speech. Champagne. The whole shebang. Rennie's even booked a string quartet. Then down the Nav for beers. It's turned into a double celebration. Mill's rebirth and the town's change in fortune. Councillor Webster's idea.'

'Looking forward to it.'

'Should be a good knees-up.' Karl reassembled the model. 'Anyway, glad you came in. Would have liked a natter but I've got a meeting. Sorry to rush off.'

We gathered our things, and as we walked through the office, I glanced back at the meeting room. The long white table stretched out like a body, the model of the Wallis mill at one end like a head, everything entombed in glass, glowing in the spotlights like an apparition.

We shook hands in reception.

'Contractor said he'll be in next week to do the detectors. I'll let you know which day as soon as I can.'

*

The shop was quiet. Isla was behind the counter reading a magazine. I mentioned the detectors and then told her about the visual alarm device.

She looked up. 'You're not stone deaf. Surely you can hear that bloody thing even without a hearing aid.'

She was right. It was very loud. A screamer.

'Suppose they don't want to take any chances. With my track record wouldn't mind a little extra backup, to be honest.'

We chatted for a while. Last-minute customers came and went. We closed for the day. I tidied the shop whilst Isla cleaned the glass counter.

'Saw your waitress friend today.'

'Oh right.'

'Jogging through town.'

Isla made a cup of tea. We ate a couple of unsold muffins.

'Well?'

'Mm.'

'Come on. We all saw the chemistry between you in the Nav. I want to know all about her.'

I told her about *South Pacific*, the kiss, the riot.

'A love story.'

'I don't think so.'

'Love spurned. Of course it is. I think you should ask her out for a meal or something. What are the chances of you both being here? A sleepy market town in the middle of nowhere. It's fate. Good fate and it's on your side. She's lovely.'

'Well – maybe.'

Out of my league? Chasing rainbows? I could feel my face flushing. Isla playfully slapped the side of my head. 'You're overthinking things.'

Isla Graham: I loved her, like an older sister. Reliable. Annoyingly supportive. She mind-read my desires, then dragged them out kicking and screaming.

'I'll think abou…'

Isla's sharply raised hand stopped my flow, her eyes shut, she didn't speak. Then she was at the sign language again, like doing so was the best way to get through to me. I think she signed "Just do it".

We hugged then went our separate ways.

DARDALE

1915

III

Honeysuckle – *Lonicera periclymenum*

Study for Wallis and Hilton Wallpapers. Plate No. 103 – Honeysuckle Fantasy [see sketch on next page]

Facts: Honeysuckle is prized by bumblebees. Honeysuckle's scent is strongest at night. Its berries are poisonous, but the leaves, flowers and seeds have been used for medicinal purposes for a variety of conditions.

Symbology and quaint beliefs: Long considered a symbol of fidelity in Victorian times young girls were banned from bringing honeysuckle into the house because it was believed the strong smell would give them suggestive dreams.

The yard behind Hetty's tearoom was small. A few square yards of flagstone and gravel. Metal chairs set around five tables. Joe sat and waited in a shady corner.

Ellen had suggested meeting there because it was a sunny day and the food was good, and yet she was late, and doubts had begun to churn in the pit of his stomach.

They know?

Tremors of suspicion begged him to leave. But gripping the chair seat, he tilted back and tracked martins that swooped across a patch of sky hemmed in by brick walls and guttering. Not good that the only exit was through the tearoom. He took slow, steadying breaths of the pristine air. Trumpet petals of honeysuckle flowed over a sun-drenched wall, the smell of cakes and warm scones rolling up from the kitchen. He closed his eyes and for a moment he owed nothing to anyone, and the war seemed a long way off and although he felt very alone, he at least felt himself.

'Joe.'

His eyes snapped open. Ellen stood beside him. Her feminine lines hidden in a drill cloth boiler suit; her hair big, wavy, alive. He righted the chair and stood. 'Everything alright?'

'Problems with production. Sorry I'm late.'

They sat and studied a menu.

It was meeting number three. One magazine already published. More a limp pamphlet: a welcome from the colonel followed by an exhaustive list of rules.

Their meetings were held during breaks and sometimes after work. It was the only way to commit the time needed to produce something worthwhile for the women, a publication that might bind their souls and offer a little joy. And it was joy – Joe realised – that they needed most because their work was dangerous, their hours brutal, the chemicals harsh. And he felt sympathy for them as their precarious existence was not unlike his. One careless move could spell the end.

A waitress came to the table and made tight scribbles on a pad, now and then giving Joe a look. Maybe she suspected him or maybe she just didn't like that he was there whilst other men were away fighting. Or both. He had no way of knowing.

Without uttering a word, she disappeared into the tearoom.

Ellen leant forward and placed items on the table. 'We've got some drawings and poems by the ladies. Photographs of loved ones from the front line.'

'Looks good.'

'We need more though.'

They sat in silence. A baby cried somewhere inside.

'We could include an article about the building's former life. Maybe a wallpaper pattern on the cover of each issue, so the spirit of the place isn't lost.'

She smiled and thought of her father. 'I love that.'

'Whoever carves those blocks has a rare gift.'

'Woodcutter makes them off site. For a long time, nobody knew where they came from.'

'Ooh, mysterious.'

She laughed. 'Yes – I suppose there was a sense of magic when a new set of blocks arrived. Some of the details only a hair's width, it seemed impossible they were made by mere mortals.'

'Conjured by wizards and elves. You've sold me the magic.'

'They come from Bowland. My father took me there once. A workshop on the edge of a forest. Walls inside carved with flowery details, like the place was hollowed out of a huge tree. It was a magical place. But with age you appreciate the magic is in the hands of the carver and designer, and you realise you have to search inside for your own magic.'

'And the magic inside you?'

She smiled. 'Left it in Manchester. So, heading back there to resume my studies when the war is over.'

'And then?'

And then she opened up. People did that with him. Kind face, easy-going charm, easy to trust.

'Become a teacher, like my mother. And then travel. Teach in countries far away.'

'Like your mother?'

'She didn't travel. She died eight years ago.'

They watched a nervous bird take a crumb from the flagstones and then flutter up and settle on a gutter.

'Sorry to hear.'

'My father is lost without her. He struggles with the unfamiliar. His magic lies in printing the same patterns over and over.'

'Did you do any printing?'

'No, no, don't have the patience. Repetitive stuff leaves me cold. Librarian of the blocks was my job before the war.'

'Well, I hope your father remains safe whilst in France.'

'How did you know he's there?'

'Cedric told me.'

The waitress delivered a pot of tea and food. A sandwich for Ellen, cake for Joe.

'How about a flower print on the front cover?' asked Joe.

'Sure. I can get one. There's a book of swatches in the block room.'

He sipped tea and squinted into the sun. 'Sure you'll find it? It's so dingy in there. And yet the blocks are works of art. Seems odd to hide them away like that.'

Ellen smiled at the straight talk. 'Swings in temperature can warp the blocks. So – the deepest, darkest room in the building is the best place for them.'

'Ah – I see.' Joe jotted a few words then removed his spectacles and forked cake into his mouth. And while they ate, birds darted in and out of a mud nest that clung to the wall above them. Ellen sat back and wiped her lips with a paper serviette. 'And your magic?'

He looked directly at her. 'Raise some livestock. Lead a simple life. Write a novel.'

'Do you miss home?'

He crossed one leg over the other.

'Yes, I miss home.'

The waitress approached, cleared the table and then left.

Joe leant back and lit a cigarette. Ellen topped up the teapot with hot water.

'The block room is a good place to be on a hot day. Nice and cool. I could show you around after lunch. Explain how it all works.'

'I'd like that.'

The waitress reappeared, wiped down tables and watered an old chimney pot repurposed as a planter. Ellen struck up conversation with her. Small talk. Her words straight up and innocent, the antithesis – Joe thought – of his own guarded existence. He tipped back and blew cigarette smoke vertically. Skies so blue. Clouds extinct. Leaning back further, he put all of his weight on the back legs of the chair. A balancing act teetering on the brink. Just like his daily act of weighing deception and sincerity. Too much of either, enough to undo his charade and bring the world crashing down upon him.

He closed his eyes and listened to Ellen's beautiful voice. In his mind everything clear cut. In his heart, loyalties floundered in a storm-battered boat, his appetite for revenge washed overboard.

The waitress left. He tipped forward and stubbed out the woodbine.

Ellen finished her tea. 'I need to buy pegs next door. Meet you out front?'

'Sure.'

She disappeared from the yard. Joe tilted back and for a while watched the martins as they swooped into the nest, every time a chorus of chicks greeting the parent into the mud bowl.

He paid the bill. Ellen waited outside. They walked through pools of shade cast by trees on Main Street. Ellen's hands engaged with the management of hair. Removing pins, placing them between lips, her eye fixed on Joe as she regathered and looped her hair into a loose bun. In the lobby of the mill, she placed the hairpins in a box labelled: *REMEMBER! Metal makes sparks*. Factory rules: no hairpins, no jewellery, no intimacy between workers.

They slipped deeper into the building until alone in the block room. The air inside cool and serene. The faint light from Edison bulbs just enough to see shelves that laddered up either side. But in front and behind, the slender space had now faded to darkness and for a moment Joe imagined the corridor infinitely stretching beyond the mill, like a secret tunnel that looped the earth, a secret tunnel that would lead back to Africa.

Ellen led the way; Joe followed. Carved blocks filing past, they walked between pairs of slender columns that all the shelves ran behind, arching metalwork above, ornate stems branching off, a glass petal lampshade at the end of each.

She drew his attention to the letters and numbers stamped into the edge of each block. A system that organised them into families. Each family joint author of a wallpaper design. The more complex the print, the larger the family.

'Mix up the blocks or lose a family member and the system unravels,' she said.

Joe so close behind he sensed the aromas of summer still clinging to her and he breathed them in deeply; her scent inside him, conjuring magic, confusing his mind.

Who is the enemy now?

He exhaled. Ellen turned. Her elfin face square to his, peering through wild strands of auburn hair that seemed to blend into the carvings either side of her head, the space like a womb from where she was born. 'Such a big sigh,' she said.

He couldn't help but smile at her. 'Smells good in here. Earthy but sweet.'

'That will be the pearwood.'

She explained it was dense, but not brittle, an even hardness across annular rings that tempted the woodcutter's tools into leaving the finest traces of detail. The blocks built up in layers. Two of redwood topped by an inch of pearwood. The grain of each glued perpendicular to the one before.

'Prevents warping. Promotes stability.' Ellen led him further in. Deep shadows lunging around every time they passed between a pair of lamps, his instincts telling him to turn back. But he blindly followed, blocks filing by, carved lines swirling at the corners of his vision. They reached the last pair of Edison lights. Joe saw a trapdoor in the floor ahead.

Not a dead end after all.

'What's that for?'

'Waste chute for old paint and flock. Better to discard it well away from the print room. There's another at the other end.'

Joe swivelled around – the other end nowhere to be seen. Wrought-iron posts and high organic metalwork a forested tunnel. He sensed her close behind, her fingers tenderly interlacing his. She placed his hand onto the surface of a block and together their fingertips traced the carved lines.

'Close your eyes. Tell me what you feel,' she said.

Joe took a deep breath. *Weak? Spellbound?* His fear falling away, his arms relaxed, his hands under her control.

'Freedom?'

He opened his eyes and slowly turned. She removed

his glasses, her fingers exploring his hair, her eyes scanning his face. Their lips closer, one inch apart, the ether between them electrically charged. And then faint voices filtered into the adjacent print room. Their heads froze, and they hoped. But the voices became louder, more numerous, the next shift gathering pace. She pulled back and looked about his face.

'I know somewhere else.'

DARDALE

1915

IV

Melancholy Thistle – *Cirsium heterophyllum*

*Study for Wallis and Hilton Wallpapers. Plate No. 104 – Mauve Meadow
[see sketch on next page]*

*Facts: Has a distinctive, usually solitary purple-red thistle-like flower that
initially droops. The name of the flower derives from its historical use as
a potion to prevent "melancholia".*

*Symbology and quaint beliefs: Throughout Celtic regions thistles represent
bravery and devotion. However, the Victorian language of flowers
identifies it as the flower of intrusion – a warning against unwanted
meddling.*

They left the building separately and met on the towpath
under the railway bridge, then walked alongside
the canal and when the town was out of sight, Ellen
looped her slender arm through Joe's.

'Meadow's not far.'

After half a mile they left the towpath and walked
across a wooden footbridge that spanned the canal. They
stopped midspan and leant over the handrail and for a

while watched insects row their bodies over flat water.

'Wasn't difficult to get away. Reckon Harold was asleep when I left.'

'What were the ministry thinking when they employed him? He couldn't organise a flock of sheep.'

'He's just an old pit pony, you give him such a hard time.'

He glanced up but Ellen was no longer by his side, and she called back from the far end of the bridge.

'Harold Yates is a lazy old nag.' She laughed. 'Are you coming?'

He followed and they waded through the long grass. Ellen, thirty yards ahead, turned and circled and then disappeared, the furrow of her wake leading him to where she lay, her body a diameter line across a flattened patch of meadow.

At first, they lay on their sides sharing stories, their hands picking over trampled flowers, both feeling the joy of being away from the filling factory. Now and then glancing at one another as if curious to learn if what had happened in the block room might develop now that they were alone. They rolled onto their backs and gazed up at a blue circle of sky set within a circle of wildflowers.

'He's alright, I get along with Harold. He actually winces when you bang on the office door.'

'He says I should knock, so – I knock.'

'Thor's knock.'

'Stop defending him, Joe. He's supposed to be overseeing production. I'm just keeping him on his toes. Truth be told, we could all get on without him.'

'And that's what I like about you.'

She rolled onto her side. 'And what's that exactly?'

'You're an upstart.' He gripped her waist, kneaded her hips. She let out a scream.

'Shh!'

He knelt and searched the landscape, the whole meadow shifting in the breeze.

'Coast clear?'

'Not a soul.'

She pulled him down.

'We're fine. Nobody ever comes here; the canal's been redundant for decades.'

Plucking grass from his hair she then lay on her back. Raising hands skyward she surveyed her ragged fingernails. Saxifrage and mallow swayed in the breeze. A plump insect foraged among the strands of a thistle flower.

'My fingers are as buttery as the stripes on that bee. Handling the chemicals is slowly turning us yellow.'

'Still no gloves?'

'Nope. I've requested them a hundred times and smocks and bonnets but it's like Harold's deaf to it.'

She rolled onto her stomach, their bodies at right angles, her face hovering above his. The sky wrapping around her errant curls like a blue halo, insects and birds criss-crossing at various altitudes above her.

'The chemicals have turned Laura's hair yellow. What would you think if my hair turned yellow?'

'I can't believe that's happening. It's terrible.'

'Can you talk to Harold? He listens to you.'

'Is that why you've brought me here?'

'Hush now, please.' She silenced his lips with a finger

and left it there as if holding a partly tied knot. Then slowly lowering her head, she replaced it with a kiss. And then they kissed for a long time.

'That's why I brought you here.'

He smiled. 'I had my suspicions. And yes, I'll talk to Harold.' Then the smile fell from his face. 'Shh. Was that a voice?'

She knelt. Looked around the meadow. 'Sidney comes here sometimes to sketch the flowers but he's housebound. There's no one. Must be the meadow talking.'

'Are those stories about him meeting the Kaiser true?'

She laughed. 'Utter rubbish.'

He pulled her back down.

'Did you know there are no guards on duty at the mill? The colonel has reassigned them to the entrance gates of Dardale Hall to check everything that goes in and out.'

She kissed him again then pulled back.

'The colonel's wasting his time. Sidney wouldn't hurt a fly.'

'The colonel has a cold heart. Not sure he cares either way. You do know if we get caught together, we're for it?'

'Bit nervy, aren't we? My mother used to say it's the suspicious ones that have something to hide.'

Then Joe held a finger to her lips. Then he craned his head up and they kissed again.

*

When Joe returned to the office, he found Harold asleep in the easy chair, a newspaper on his lap, his head jutting from a collarless shirt like that of a tortoise.

Joe gathered papers in readiness for the next consignment and as he closed the filing cabinet Harold jerked awake.

'Thought that'd gone back to Aus.'

'Wouldn't dream of it. You'd miss me too much.' Joe nodded at the newspaper. 'Anything juicy?'

'Usual claptrap and a spy story.' Harold reached for his empty pipe and shoved it into his mouth.

Joe looked down from the big window and checked the street. Quiet. Dardale a soft touch compared to Leeds, a place of near misses and lucky escapes. It was a relief to be away from the city. The newspaper he had reported for regularly whipped up fantastic stories of enemy infiltration. Of course, Joe knew the reality was more prosaic. German espionage a frayed strand of dilettantes rather than a network of insidious spies.

And Joe knew that half the agents were already captured. One a former acquaintance. Carl Lody, tried for treason, executed by firing squad at the Tower of London. Joe had once worked with him on the Hamburg-Amerika line, a shipping company German intelligence often recruited from. Sharing a cabin between Oslo and Hamburg they'd become friends. Lody charismatic, a likeable person of many pleasing ways, very popular with the ladies. A good spy that got careless. An uncoded message he'd sent picked up by British counter-espionage. Joe often wondered if his lapse had been due to romantic involvement. *Maybe it was love that had killed him.*

Harold's eyes closed again, pipe in his mouth drooping.

Sounds of a train whispering through the open window, the commotion of steam steadily rushing towards them.

'How's the new puffer, mate?'

'What's that?' Harold muttered as his eyes blinked open.

'How's the new pipe?'

'Empty... So where have you been then?'

'Oh, waiting on the platform. Train delay – points jammed near Blackburn.'

'Dare say tha copped it from Parry girl, an' all.'

'Pardon?'

'Lass was here this morning, banging on bloody door again.'

Joe continued to eye the street. 'She's got the bit between her teeth, that one.'

Train in the station hissing like a pantomime audience, Harold shifted in the chair.

'Every morning. Bang, bang, bang on bloody door. Gives me bloody heart attack. Chemicals gone to her head, I tell tha. Lost her chump her has.' Harold removed the smokeless pipe from his mouth. 'She's only threatened to strike. Never heard such twod. Strike, a tell tha – over some bloody hats and gloves.'

Continuing his vigil, Joe watched a figure loitering by the trees, a wretch in uniform, pack on back, rifle over shoulder. 'They've got a point. Have you seen their hands?'

Harold sat upright, like a king presiding over a trial, his hands cupping the armrests.

'But hazards come with territory. And therein lies the difference. Blokes just get on with it. You don't hear them…' Harold's face contorted as if in terrible pain, '…moaning this and… and moaning that…'

Harold wittered on. Joe studied the uniformed wretch: everything about him plaintive, eyes glazed over, entranced by the birds darting between trees as if the spectacle of living things moving freely without threat of death overwhelmed him. The birds flew skywards. The soldier trudged on. Puttees wrapped around his shins slouching above muddy boots, his steps slow, almost a shuffle. Joe could only guess what horrors those tired feet had wandered amongst.

'…women don't know how to endure – cheek of it is they're demanding same pay as men. But they can't turn out a piece of work on same level – no – they stay at home for trivial reasons. A day's washin' may be very serious thing for a woman but it isn't for bloody employer.' Harold's restless backside buffed the chair. 'I keep telling the lass. I put in requisition weeks ago, it's out of my hands now. I don't know where her bloody hats and gloves have got to.'

'Sounds settled then, cobber.'

'Not according to her it's not. Said she's coming back every day until matter's resolved.'

Joe gestured towards the doors that led to the workshop. 'You'd better lock up the block room doors then.'

As soon as the remark left Joe's smiling lips it crystalised into an idea. His task of souring industrial relations made much easier if the physical link between workshop and office were severed. And at last, something solid to report back to his ambitious quartermaster. Joe's meddling like a currency. Each tangible act one more instalment towards his ticket back home. And for a moment he saw himself there, on the porch, the sunset gilding the drift as the sound of cicadas lured him towards sleep.

'Tha may joke, but I've already decided appropriate steps need to be taken,' said Harold.

'She just wants what's best for the women.'

'Maybe so, but this time she's gone beyond her station. I'll be suggesting to Colonel that the doors be locked permanently, and all further communications be made in writing. End of. It's reached the point where a line must be drawn. Offices for men. Workshop for lasses.'

Replacing the pipe in his mouth, Harold spread the newspaper on the table. Ironing it flat with his hand, his eyes scanning the lines of a story that lay inside the front page. 'About this factory explosion near Leeds?'

'What about it?'

'Caused by a cigarette, so the rumours say. But truth is coming out now.'

'Usually does.'

Harold swivelled the paper, so the article faced Joe.

'Sabotage all along, see for yourself.'

Joe remained at the window, his throat parched, a bead of sweat trickling down his back. He watched the soldier stroll down the street. 'I'll take your word for it.'

'Belgian refugees working at the plant. German sympathisers. All there in black and white,' said Harold, nodding at the paper.

'Just as well we've been issued with that poster, then.' Joe gestured towards his desk.

The poster so large, it almost covered the desktop. The word *Sabotage* printed across the middle. The letter S much larger than others, winding up one side like a snake, the top of it crowned with a spiked German helmet. Other words warning the public to be watchful for unusual behaviour, to be on guard for spies.

Joe's eyes remained on the street. 'Colonel has got two more, he's asked me to think of places to hang them.'

Harold joined Joe at the window. 'One in the workshop wouldn't go amiss. Looks like you've seen a ghost.'

Joe nodded at the wretch that was now peering through a window of the Navigation Inn. The rifle slung over his shoulder a Lee Enfield short magazine, standard issue. Joe's Mauser better; higher velocity rounds, more accurate over longer distances.

'Bloody hell. It's the Corbett boy. Didn't recognise him. They said he was due back on leave. Well, he won't find anyone in there. Not open until seven these days.'

The train whistle blew three times.

'I'd better go.' Joe grabbed the clipboard off his desk and paperwork and a pencil and then froze and stared at the office chair that was pushed away from his desk. His mind descending into a nightmare in which he was strapped to the chair, blindfolded, the firing squad only fifteen yards away, their breaths the last ones he would hear before dying.

He left the office, paused between the doors of the block room, carved blocks shelved either side, his fingers reaching out, the memory of Ellen's guiding hand bewitching him.

Close your eyes. Tell me what you feel.

His thoughts switching to the soldiers of a firing squad, unsettled by the prospect of cold blood. Eight clammy fingers wrapped around eight steely triggers.

He knew the stakes were high. And yes, he'd probably get caught. And yes, he'd probably get shot. But he was less afraid now.

Because oddly, in a place where he'd planned to sow revenge, he'd found someone. Held her, kissed her, even one breath of her more powerful than a world's worth of hate. And he had only known her for a single beat of time and yet the love was fast growing; hard hitting; whatever had triggered seemed irreversible. It was inside him, glowing in his chest, something that could never be taken away, even if strapped into that firing squad chair. In the end everyone died. But his death would be swift. A clean death. Because if it came to it, those eight sorry eyes peering down their cold steel barrels would never be able to miss a heart that had grown as big and warm as his.

DANI

Orphans

Nearly a month had passed since Dani started working at the pub, but she still felt uneasy being so close to where the man had been found.

From behind the bar, she scrutinised every wink and elbow, every word to one side, every glance. And yet after a month of serving drinks, there had been no comeback whatsoever. In any case, how would they know she was the daughter of the accused? It happened more than a decade ago. Water under the bridge.

Her shift ended. She walked along Main Street, lights of the town fading as she left the square. Surfaces of the lane silvered by the moon. Faint gold glimmers in Harriette's lodge filtering out from the deeper spaces. The sound of bowed strings unwinding from open windows.

Dani stopped, looked up and breathed in the starry night. Parched leaves flirting with a warm breeze; July ambling back after a day on the moor, sun-kissed and loaded with the scent of heather. The rest of her way to bed fret free, the onset of sleep was swift.

The following morning, she ran through town, past the mill, along the towpath then across the farmers' fields. Ground beside the hedgerow uneven, her feet lightly skipping over furrows of baked mud, they followed a track that looped back to the lodges.

She showered, changed then walked over to her gran's. The Mini parked on the drive, coat on hook, shoes on the rack, keys in the bowl, too. All in their place simultaneously, for the first time in weeks. Only the day before, Harriette had said Rennie's move to the stables was nearly complete. Must be some truth in that, she thought.

She wandered through rooms. Kitchen, study, lounge; all lived in and cosy with hints of chaos. The music room different: tidy, self-possessed, its uncluttered nature reflected in the glossy sheen of the cello. One chair, one stool, one music stand, one large picture on the wall, a knee-high sideboard, photographs of family and friends upon it, arranged in neat rows like an audience.

Sitting on the floor she stretched her legs. Faces in photographs sharing her line of sight. Harriette's husband, Reginald Hey, front row. Killed in the Second World War, shot down over Salerno. A story told to Dani with more affection than sadness, Harriette dwelling on their shared love of opera and Italian food. Reginald looked handsome in RAF uniform, his kind eyes and smile not like her father's at all. Dani felt diffident and out of place then, a messy blemish in such a calm place.

Harriette stirred in the room above; bed springs crumpling then her feet padded floorboards. Dani withdrew to the living room and turned on the old television, singed dust spicing the air as its innards warmed up. Images appeared. A diver leaping, his arching back and splayed arms momentarily hanging above the Sagrada Familia.

There were footsteps on the landing and then Harriette called out as she came down the staircase, 'Has it started?'

'Just a recap.'

'Coffee?'

'Yes, please.'

Harriette pottered in the kitchen then joined Dani on the sofa.

'Our first proper morning together,' Harriette said.

'You okay with the Olympics? We can walk if you prefer.'

'Quite happy on the sofa. I've been looking forward to this. Any horse jumping?'

'Later on.'

They watched judo for a while, in silence.

'Nav seems friendly.'

Harriette's eyes remained on the screen. 'Popular again since changing hands – bet they're glad of your help.'

Silence again. Competitors on the mat fought for a hold.

'Me staying still okay with you, Gran?'

Harriette glanced to one side. 'Of course – for as long as you like. Sorry, dear – I'm still half asleep.' She smiled then sipped coffee; fighters stood and reset.

'I appreciate it. Felt lost after losing Mum. Made me realise what you must have gone through – you know – when you lost yours.'

Judo fighters crashed to the floor. Dani placed her mug on the coffee table. 'Gran?'

'Mm.'

'Hope it's okay, me bringing that up.'

A big struggle on the mat; one of the Olympians yielded.

'No, dear. It's just – there's not much to tell. I was a baby so wasn't really aware of what was going on.' Harriette smiled then took Dani's hand. 'Honestly, there's not much to it. Sidney took me in; loved me like his own. One happy family. That's about it.'

'Must have been difficult for you, though.'

'Stiff upper lip, dear. That's, I'm afraid, what our generation do.'

The bouts continued; scores levelled.

'I feel bad for asking but I feel a bit in the dark about the family's past. Nobody really talked about it much at home.'

'You shouldn't feel bad about it.'

'With all that went on I can't believe you turned out so normal, Gran.'

Harriette's accent thickened. 'Just a rumour, lass.'

They both laughed a little. Harriette's gaze returned to the screen.

'Gran?'

'Mm.'

'What did happen to your – you know...'

'My parents? Oh, it's all a bit melodramatic. The stories are half fiction, I'm sure.'

'I'd love to hear.'

There was another big struggle. The referee awarded a Koka. The crowd cheered.

'Well, you see…' Harriette's eyes wandered the room as if answers lay somewhere amongst patterns on the wall, '…my father, Joe, wasn't a local man. Australian apparently. During the summer of 1915 my mother fell for him. They were close – but it didn't last.' Harriette placed her mug down. 'Then things get a bit patchy. And of course, the chaos of the Great War blurred everything. There were different stories – not sure which is true.' She relaxed into the cushions. 'My mother stayed for a while after I was born. But him leaving proved too much. She followed her heart and ran after him. Always hoped she would return some day. Sentimental, I suppose. Well, all in the past now. Nobody knew where they went, some say Ireland.'

Judo competitors stood either side of the referee waiting for the result.

'I'm sorry, Gran.'

'Oh, you've had it much worse than me. I can't really complain. In many ways I've been fortunate.'

'I wouldn't have left, if you were my baby.'

Harriette smiled, her hands caressing the sides of Dani's head, her thumbs gently sweeping her cheeks. 'Heart on sleeve, just like your mum. It's life, dear. Sometimes you can't control where it takes you.' Harriette stood. 'Come with me.'

Dani followed her into the music room.

'Take a seat. I'd like you to meet my surrogate parents.'

The cello was presented to Dani, the body of it

soon between her knees. Harriette positioning her granddaughter's fingers on the neck and her other hand on the bow.

'Movement from the elbow, soft wrist and fingers.'

The cello burped. Dani shrieked, 'Foghorn!'

They stopped laughing, Dani's fingers stroking the shoulder of the instrument.

'How long have you had it?'

'Eleventh birthday present from Sidney. It was actually a gift from one of his clients in Munich. He very generously passed it on to me.'

'It's such a beautiful thing.'

'And I played it quite well. He saw potential, arranged my lessons, came to my performances. He was good like that, you know, looked out for me, made sure I played to my strengths. I loved Sidney but it was the cello I bonded with. Playing it every day was how I coped with being an orphan; saw the cello as my mother and the bow my father. Sounds a bit crazy, no?'

'I don't think so.' Dani lightly patted the cello's shoulder. 'Not many people can say they've played with both great-grandparents.'

Harriette looked down and smiled at the floor. 'Dare say not.'

'The piece you and Rennie played that day – you know, when I was younger.'

'Elgar's Cello Concerto? We played it a lot. His part quite dull, a simple muse, but he never refused. It helped me through, you see, meant I could have good times with my imaginary parents.'

'I have the tape. Listening to it helped me through bad times.'

Harriette looked a little emotional then. 'Oh, I see.'

'The thought of you playing comforted me. I used to think Rennie was my grandad.'

Harriette laughed then picked up a photograph from the sideboard, the one of her stood with Sidney and Rennie by the entrance to a maze. Dani placed the cello on the stand and then stood beside her grandmother.

'I was upset when I discovered he wasn't my brother. He's a good man, too nice really; doesn't have his father's hard nose for business.'

'Gran. The man in the next photo – is he a relative? I don't recognise him.'

'No, dear. That's Sir John Barbirolli. Never met a man like him. Women didn't play in the Hallé before he became principal. Opened the door for us, actually.'

'You played in that orchestra, didn't you?'

'For sure, two hundred and fifty-eight concerts in 1945.'

'Two hundred and fifty-eight! You played in them all?'

'Most of them. Thinking back, some of those were in 1944, performed in front of troops stationed in Holland and Belgium. It was madness really. Those places had only just been liberated. We were whisked away after one performance – they hid us in open trucks under blankets, it was that close to the front line. Eindhoven, I think.'

'Bloody hell, Gran.'

'Well, being away from home, it helped me move on from losing Reg. We lived on Albion Street back then.

Frank, I mean your dad, stayed at the hall when I was on tour. Sidney looked after him.'

'Must have been a very exciting time.'

'Exciting for sure – but hiding under that blanket I felt stupid, it all seemed a bit reckless, I could have been shot or blown up, I just wanted to get home, look after your father. World had enough orphans to contend with.'

'So, you stopped playing?'

'Still played in Manchester for a while, just didn't go on tour – I...'

Harriette went to take a sip but realising all the coffee had gone she swirled the mug and stared into the emptiness.

'...I finally left the orchestra because of something else.'

She looked up, steadying herself with a deep breath.

'It was when I was away in Holland that Rennie saw my mother. She'd come back, apparently.'

'What, Ellen? Here, in town?'

'He caught a glimpse of her on Main Street, reckoned it was definitely her.'

'What happened?'

'Disappeared again. I'd just returned when Rennie told me. The orchestra toured again; I stayed here. Didn't want to risk missing her a second time.' Harriette walked to the French doors and gazed into the untidy garden; leaves inside out from night-time gales. 'Waiting for her, staying here, turned into a bit of an obsession, an indefinite tie.'

'And what about my dad? He must have still been a boy.'

'He was, and it wasn't easy for him either. I mean, he was safe up at the hall but when I was away, our house on Albion Street got vandalised.'

'Why, Gran?'

'Oh, the wars. Difficult times, anger and resentment swirling about the place like a storm. Sidney's wife was German, you see, from Prussian nobility. Wallis and Hilton exported most of what they produced to Germany. As you can imagine, after the outbreak of war, all that soured and unfortunately so did Sidney's standing.'

'Sounds a bit harsh.'

'Many of the local lads didn't return from the fighting which as you can imagine stirred up bad feelings. Frank spending time at the hall didn't go down well either; all caught up with us in the end.'

'Is that why he left?'

'Stuck it out at first. Difficult to believe, I know, but back then he was a good boy. Studious. He had a place at grammar school – and people seemed to have put the first war behind them – then Hitler came along. Bad feelings resurfaced. By then he'd had enough – he left town soon after VE day.'

'Oh, I see.'

Cheering from the television drew them back to the living room; coverage had switched to boxing. They sat and watched in silence for a while.

'You boxed, didn't you?'

'Mum used to take me – think she hoped it would tire me out, but I reckon it just – kind of weaponised me.'

Harriette laughed. 'You were a feisty child; she

probably thought it would keep you out of trouble.'

'Suppose so. Haven't boxed for years, although I did a boxercise class when I lived in Hulme.'

'Boxercise?'

'Keep fit. Like aerobics but based on boxing moves.'

'Isn't that what you did at the fundraiser?'

'Yes.'

'I heard people loved it. I could see you doing something like that.'

'Oh, it was just a one-off.'

'But you enjoyed it.'

'Well… yes.'

'And I heard they were turning people away.'

'Because the church hall was so small.'

'Sounds like there's a demand for it. Could be a nice little sideline for you. I'm sure there's bigger spaces in town.' Harriette disappeared and rummaged through drawers in the utility room. 'I'm calling Rennie later; I'll ask if he knows of anywhere.'

'Oh, okay – Do I have a say in this?'

'Play to your strengths, dear – what do you say to that?'

Dani thought for a while. 'Have you always been this persistent?'

'Always.'

Harriette appeared from the utility room holding secateurs then wandered down the garden towards the cane wigwams.

Dani changed clothes then left for work. It was the liveliest night of the week. Cars full of boys; fathers dropping off daughters. The pub terrace crowded with sixth-formers who studied at the local school.

Last orders. Another shift done. Stepping onto the street she turned to the canal and walked onto the bridge where she inhaled the smells that came from the bakery. Windows of the mill dark apart from a small one set deep in the gable wall. She watched until catching a glimpse of Dev then she remembered him sitting on the pub terrace. Damaged ear. Scar in his hairline. That haunted look. Something had happened to him. She sensed a kindred spirit, sensed they were both here to seek shelter.

She took another deep breath, the bakery smells lifting her beyond description – more like a good mood that embraced the air, embraced her senses, kissed her soul. Walking back between the old buildings and trees, she smiled at drunken laughter that came from a back street. With town soon behind her, she looked ahead at the lane, memories of her past waning, her future faint, flickering but alight. Then she drew level with Harriette's lodge. The lights were on so she decided to drop in and say goodnight.

'I've spoken to Rennie, by the way,' said Harriette.

'Oh, how's he doing?'

'Settling in – He's invited us for tea tomorrow. You're not working, are you?'

'No, it's my night off.'

'Good. By the way, he knows of a place that would be perfect for keep-fit classes. A nice big space. It's the top room at the back of the mill. He said it used to be called the print room.'

Stable

Turning off the lane, tyres thrummed the cattle grid, the car picking up speed as they passed through a colonnade of trees. Windows open, hair disturbed, Harriette spoke above the wind rush. 'Just to warn you, he's a bit out of sorts.'

'What do you mean?'

'All this change – it's unsettled him.'

They bobbed in unison as the road rolled about. Landscape of the estate a refined version of the surrounding countryside. Old trees loners in the heathland, drifts of silver birch in dips and hollows flickering in the breeze. The landscape graceful, everything a little more composed than Mother Nature had intended. Everything blurred past. Harriette not paying much attention to the way ahead, her eyes often elsewhere, lingering on streams and clearings as if looking out for old friends.

'You drive fast.'

'Only road I've ever driven on over the years. Do it with my eyes closed.'

There was an unsteady silence.

'Can you drive?'

'Yes.'

'I'll put you on the insurance.'

Harriette explained the laws of her road. The places where deer tended to cross, treacherous bends that iced over in winter. She stopped twice to point out nests of woodpeckers and owls, and again by a huge elm that had fallen in the storm of 1987.

'Sometimes I wonder why I tax and insure. It's a private road. Nobody ever uses it.'

And like she'd tempted fate the front of a removal truck filled the road ahead, its cab rocking from side to side as it shook out an emergency stop. Harriette manoeuvred the car onto the grass. The truck pulled level.

'Nearly done, Mrs H – Mr Wallis wants us to bring the portrait up to the lodge if that's alright.'

'Yes – Thank you.'

'Tell us where, and Jimmy will hang it for you.'

'End wall of my workshop – already showed him. Thanks again.' Her reply a little short she wound up the window before fumes from the truck swamped the car.

They sat in silence. Harriette's face still turned away, taking in the heathland and deer that grazed in the shade of a distant tree.

'End of an era?'

She turned back and smiled. 'Probably the most that's happened here for half a century.'

They set off, weaving between rhododendrons and monkey puzzle trees. And then the road straightened and swept down to manicured lawns. Tarmac surface changing to gravel; the car slowing, tyres crunching the driveway. The stately frontage of Dardale Hall inching by; stonework edges worn by time, paintwork peeling. Then the car accelerated as gravel reverted to single-track tarmac, the stables ahead backed by forest. They passed through a brick archway, the enclosed courtyard not as Dani remembered. The paddock now a walled garden: a lawn, a neat border, rosemary bushes in Greek urns. The building also recomposed: stable doors removed; arches infilled with modern glazing. The car came to a standstill.

Rennie appeared from a glass door, his tall figure frail, slow-moving, his clothes loose, like he wore hand-me-downs from a former robust self. Dani met him halfway along a garden path. Harriette lagged behind.

'It's been a long time,' said Rennie.

'Nice to be back.' She shook his outstretched hand. It was warm, grip feather-light, his demeanour restless.

'Ponies have gone – sorry about that.'

'I was sorry to hear you were moving out of the hall.'

Conversation stalled. Rennie's presence beside her faint, like he might flail away if a breath of wind blew through the garden. They both turned and watched Harriette who was standing by the car pruning dead flower heads with pinching fingers. 'I saw a van outside the hall, you were supposed to be out midday,' she said as her hands worked through the flowers.

'Stay of execution. Americans gave me till the end of the day.'

Rennie turned to Dani and rolled his eyes. 'It's just a big old draughty house. To be honest I should have moved years ago.'

Harriette caught them up, then Rennie turned and led them up the garden path.

'Come in, come in, welcome to my new home.' He opened a door, and they entered a lofty space. Kitchen, living room, library all playing nicely together in one long, open room, smells of fresh plaster and old oak vying for attention.

'Well, what do you think? Architect's done a wonderful job, such a talent. All the mod cons – underfloor heating.' He tapped the floor with his foot. Dani looked up at the roof timbers, all split and peppered with pin holes; stout rafters above massive oak trusses, just like an old wooden ship had capsized above them. 'It's beautiful,' Dani said her eyes still up in the timbers.

'Please, make yourself at home, dear, we'll put some tea on,' said Rennie.

The old couple drifted into the kitchen area, engrossed with talk of ailments and doctors' test results. Dani moved towards a corner sofa that angled around a cast-iron stove. The living room chic: wiry sculpture displayed on blocky side units, modern art on the walls. The position of everything carefully considered as if arranged by a gallery curator. She wandered to the far end of the space where a huge picture frame leant against a wall. Cocking her head to one side she could see it was a portrait of Rennie's father, Sidney Wallis. The canvas damaged; something pasted over it. A poster – incomplete – most of it ripped away. The bottom third still stuck on, a big sentence like a headline printed across it.

Realising the chatter had stopped she looked up. Harriette rummaged inside the fridge; Rennie stood holding a teapot as if he'd been given something to do. 'It's my father. Found him whilst clearing the study. Badly damaged as you can see, but Harriette won't let me throw him out.'

'No – I won't. You just can't treat family like that. The removal men are hanging the portrait in my workshop tomorrow.'

Harriette loaded the trolley and then Rennie set off. Pushing an odd assortment of crockery, a round fruit cake and a teapot covered by a duck-shaped tea cosy.

'Smells good.'

'Made by one of my tenants in the mill. The Angel Bakery.'

Harriette poured the tea.

Rennie dithered over the trolley. 'This black cake is my favourite. He's created quite a following already.'

'I run past most mornings; always seems busy.'

'Ah – Harriette mentioned you were a runner – used to do a bit myself.'

Harriette glanced Dani's way and rolled her eyes. 'Rennie dear, please sit down – you're supposed to be taking it easy.'

The room fell quiet as they drank tea and savoured cake. Rennie took another bite, his mouth chewing, his thoughts running away, memories strobing as he leant back in the armchair: the terraced houses on Albion Street, the tearing sound of a woman's high scream, the scream of a bystander, the scream of a witness…

…and then he remembered running full tilt after Frank, a fifteen-year-old boy with a knife in his hand and blood splattered on his clothes, male wrath gathering in the street behind. They both ran onto Main Street. Frank much quicker, already twenty yards ahead, disappearing down steps. On catching up he found Frank pacing the quayside, choking with panic, the knife thrown into the canal.

Rennie remembered digging in his pocket for the key. He always carried the key.

'Into the mill, quick, back door.'

They moved deep into the building, and he opened a trapdoor above them. A hatch normally invisible within the coffered ceiling. A hatch with a history, a hatch through which dregs of paint were lowered and disposed of in the canal. A practice stopped after fish were found floating in the water. Those who knew of the hatch and dead fish never returned from the Great War and anyone else who remembered the block room thought it had been sealed up for many years. It was the perfect hiding place. Clear as day he could remember his next words to Frank.

'Don't touch a thing. Stay until nightfall, slide the catch back and the hatch will drop. Follow the towpath to the tunnel. Legger McGinty's boat is there, under a tarp. Turn right at the Junction – canal will take you all the way to Manchester.'

Then Frank's legs disappeared into the hatch above, and Rennie remembered closing the trapdoor; the black opening turning into a coffered ceiling again. Then he saw himself running out of the mill and onto the quayside, the mob already on the bridge. And he waved them on towards the head of the canal and he heard himself shouting, 'Just seen the back of him, he's beyond the bridge… beyond the bridge!' and they waved back before running away in pursuit of Frank's ghost…

…and then the flicker of another wave: Harriette trying to catch his attention. 'The architect – I said, what did the architect come back with?' Harriette's eyes rolling again, irritation colouring her tone. 'Karl – the architect? You said – you spoke to him,' she said, stretching her words out as if speaking to a child.

'So sorry…' He brushed crumbs off his lap. '…may have to make an application to the council. He didn't think it would be a problem – just a bit of red tape. Apparently one of the councillors said a keep-fit club is just what the town needs.'

'What do you think?' Harriette turned to Dani.

She froze. Her mind wrestling with the reality of it; the awkward pause unsettling the room. Rennie leant forward. 'You can use it for free as far as I'm concerned. See how you get on. Nothing ventured and all that.'

Harriette smiled quizzically. 'Any thoughts?'

Dani's mind a battlefield of thoughts. Word would get around she was Frank's daughter. A member of the Hey family back in town. Maybe she could change her name. Maybe it would be an amazing success. And then out of nowhere for the first time in weeks she remembered the gun, still in the rucksack, hidden under the bed, which would be the first place police would look – *idiot.* Teeth grinding, she glared at her plate. *I need to get rid of it.*

'Dani? Are you alright, dear?'

But where? She placed the plate on the coffee table. 'I don't want to sound ungrateful – it's just a lot to take in. A big step.'

Harriette and Rennie sat forward.

'Of course, dear.'

'Take your time – just come back to me whenever. There's no hurry,' added Rennie.

'I really do appreciate your offer.'

'No problem.' He downed a last mouthful of tea. 'Well, I think it's about time I gave you the grand tour.' Rennie levered himself out of the chair and showed them all the rooms, then proudly showed off the walled vegetable garden, and new greenhouses. And then another round of tea and cake and talk of old times, the horses, Dani learning to ride, the gymkhana.

They said goodbye, climbed into the Mini and set off.

'Sorry about Rennie. Not quite himself.'

'It's fine. It's so kind of him to offer me that room.'

'He likes you.'

'He does?'

'I can tell.'

Harriette changed gear as the road shimmied around a huge Lebanon cedar.

'Doesn't trust anyone with that room. Says he can't let it out, but actually he doesn't want to.'

'But he's had viewings.'

'He's had one.' She smiled Dani's way then looked back at the road. 'We're not forcing you. We just thought it was – well – very you.'

'I'd just like to sleep on it, if that's okay.'

The cattle grid thrummed; they pulled onto the driveway.

'That's absolutely fine. Maybe we could chat about it again at the opening ceremony. Rennie and the architect will be there if you wanted to ask any questions.'

'Forgot about that. Next Sunday, isn't it?'

'Mm – should be fun. About time this place patted itself on the back.'

Harriette shifted and grabbed as she got out of the car. 'These opportunities rarely come along; my advice – grab them before they pass you by, dear.'

*

It was Sunday evening. The pub quiet; people away on holiday. Just a few chatting regulars in the bar. She overheard certain words. Something about a white tent.

Another word: investigation.

At first, she couldn't stop her thoughts from racing away. But then she calmed down and tried distracting herself with jobs behind the bar. After all, they were just random words plucked from the air, she thought. Their conversation could have been one about a camping holiday. The investigation of a blocked drain, maybe?

After the shift ended, she walked to the bridge, her eyes adjusting to the darkness. And as she watched spits of rain draw circles on the canal other details emerged from the night. The edge of the quay, stone steps running up the back wall of the mill. The door at the top that gave access to the print room. She imagined people coming and going, imagined herself conducting fitness classes, aerobics, boxercise. Then distant skies flickered. Flashes of far-off lightning. Rolling thunder fading to the west where the canal disappeared into the darkness. Rain thickened as she jogged up Main Street, heavier rain catching her up in the square. The statue of Sidney Wallis gleaming with run-off. She thought of his portrait, and where it hung in the workshop, over a patchy bit of wall left damaged when the lodge was converted into a workshop. The plaster pockmarked, and a brick displaced when gun cabinets were prised away, so Harriette had told her.

She ran up the lane, ducking through the weather into Hunter's Lodge and then she was in the workshop. Sidney on the end wall peering through the gloom. Standing next to the canvas her fingers traced the torn edge of the poster that was still part attached, her eyes staring at the words printed upon it:

AT ONCE!!!

ISSUED BY LONDON EMERGENCY COMMITTEE, AND PRINTED AT FOULTENEY PRESS MIDDX 1915.

She looked up, her head so close now a series of brushstrokes was all she could see. Her gaze slowly lowering until falling upon the only thing in focus – the smaller words printed close to the poster's bottom edge. The date. 1915. The country at war. The words commanding. A call to arms? And then something clicked.

Bounding upstairs, she slid the rucksack from under the bed and pulled out the revolver. Within seconds she was back in the workshop, carefully angling the portrait away from the wall, her fingers slipping behind it, feeling for the brick-sized hole.

Tent

She'd avoided the canal all week because of the gossip.

Tip-off... new evidence... oh, David's poor wife and daughter... maybe another body has been discovered... maybe that's why the police tent has appeared...

Collective wisdom settled on the most plausible explanation. A deranged serial killer had struck again. But Dani knew it was about the man who had died a decade before. A well-respected local; author of a book about the town's history or something like that. Difficult to tell from behind the bar. Multiple conversations garbled like a radio constantly retuned. But one thing was clear. The ghost of unexplained death had planted the seeds of morose conjecture in everyone's minds.

And after a fretful night Dani lay in bed thinking of the canal. For a while she watched the sun and cloud tussle behind the curtains. Then turning over, she checked the clock. Awake since three her worries had disintegrated the hours – *I should go there and see for myself.* Facts were better. Her gran taught her that; life more connected to logic since living at the lodges. And then she was up and dressed and jogging down the lane, hopping over potholes filled by night-time rain.

She made no eye contact with the volunteers who were setting up the square: brooms sweeping cobbles, bunting going up, half a dozen staging blocks being shunted into place beside the statue of Sidney Wallis. And then she was on Main Street. Shops, trees and cars all ignored by her straight-ahead gaze. Slowing to a walk she approached the mill, her eyes closing as she wandered out onto the bridge, the cold metal siderail guiding her along.

At first, she could not look. Her other senses taking in the scene. A small aeroplane droning above, birds landing on water. Nothing unusual.

And then the flapping.

Peeking to one side the first thing she saw was the tent. Its ripstop fabric pitched on the far bank shivering then snapping flat.

Tinges of vertigo. The canal below her feet an oceanic abyss.

Backing off she turned and ran. Her movement laboured, town never ending, the lane full of water traps. Plunging through it all she barged into Hunter's Lodge, clambered upstairs and buried herself under the duvet, her hands gripping the sheets; that fierce urge to run soon surging through her again. But also a mulish desire to stay; two armies of will battling it out under the covers.

Her heartbeat levelling, she focused on the glowing curtains that angled into the room. A summer breeze purling through an open window. She could sense the garden brimming with life; beehives stirring, raspberries fruiting, French beans coiling up, lively chat coming from the other lodge. She rolled out of bed, her mood lifting as she tidied the room, flurries of laughter now spilling from the other lodge; the joy of Harriette's musician friends a gust of brightness that blew straight through her.

She put a brush through her hair, pulled on clean joggers then walked to the other lodge pausing in the hallway for a moment, listening to the chatter that bubbled in the kitchen. Old age the topic of conversation. How its onset hindered them: stiff hands, finger control, difficulty with vibrato.

Dani took a deep breath then entered the room. 'Good morning. How did the rehearsal go?' she said.

All four ladies, grey-haired and full of smiles, looked up. 'Good morning… very well, thank you, dear… we're due at the square any minute for a final run-through.'

She sat at the table, a mug of coffee placed before her, the musicians radiating warmth, all sounding off at once: doting words, fussy noises, compliments about her looks insatiable.

Too much. And then the questions: How long was she in town? Could she show them boxercise moves – did she have a boyfriend?

Shaking her head she yawned, 'No, I don't have a boyfriend.'

They all leant back. 'Look at the time. We should clear away.' None of them moved from the table. Their chatter turning to matters of performance. Acoustics of the square, how to keep music from blowing away. Harriette rummaged in the utility room for pegs. Dani sipped coffee. 'I'll clear away if you want to head off.'

They moved untidily, via the sink, the toilet, one up in the bedroom retrieving a scarf. The quartet reforming by the front door, slipping on footwear and outer layers. Harriette rubbed shoulders with Dani at the sink, the hallway nattering behind them. 'Sorry, dear – we don't get out much. Are you alright?'

'Yes, fine. Didn't sleep well, that's all.'

Placing a hand on Dani's arm Harriette smiled. 'See you in the square?'

And Dani sensed then that she knew about the tent. Hand on arm, reassuring smile – all code for carry on, stiff upper lip, *everything will be fine.*

'I just need to shower. Won't be long.'

Harriette rubbed Dani's arm then joined the others, their happy voices fading, silence in the kitchen doubling in volume. After clearing away, Dani returned to Hunter's Lodge and showered before changing. A new look: summer dress, flat sandals, long-sleeved cardigan. And yet the same person in the mirror. Chip off the old block, daughter of the accused. She pinned up her hair, applied make-up, her eyes screened off by sunglasses as she left the lodge.

*

Dani helped Harriette position chairs and music stands in a corner of the square then carried instrument cases into the church and after wishing the musicians luck she disappeared into a small marquee, where champagne was served from a trestle table. Downing a glass, she took a second and repositioning herself in the shadow of a tree she watched people arrive; sounds of the quartet gently unfolding, stately but not pompous. The "music of friends" so Harriette had described it. Chamber music the accord of four instruments, one introducing a melody, the others replying. Conversation and laughter coalescing in the square Dani had no idea who was who. The day before, she'd overheard Rennie explain to Harriette that her audience would consist of mainly outside interests. House builders, estate agents, the new owners of Dardale Hall; a celebration, but also an event to showcase the town.

So lost in the music Dani didn't realise that an old man stood beside her.

A row of medals on his chest, a young girl tucked in beside him.

They had come not so much for the opening ceremony but for the music. The man knew of Harriette. The girl's big eyes looked up. 'I play the violin,' she said quietly.

'Grade four with distinction,' he added, the medals on his chest pushed out a little further. The conversation developed, questions about the town filling Dani's head. But before she had chance to ask them, the music stopped, and the musicians took a bow. And then a man walked across the stage and adjusted the mic stand. Dani knew it was the architect. Sometimes on Friday afternoons he would be in the Nav buying drinks for his staff. He tapped a champagne flute next to the mic, the audience's attention turning to the stage as glassy clinks bombarded the square.

After thanking everyone for coming along, he then talked of the town's origins. When did it all start?

'A settlement of weavers that crafted checked cloth and calicoes for hundreds of years, their yeoman cottages huddled either side of the old Roman road. The next big change not until the Industrial Revolution, the whole world on the precipice of change. A chapter of the town's history covered by our next speaker. I hand you over to Councillor Mike Webster.'

The councillor moved forward, medium height, thickset, head shaven. A thug if Dani had not known otherwise. He paid tribute to Sidney Wallis; rattled off biographical trivia: a follower of the Arts and Crafts, not an advocate of mechanisation, he predicted the problems of mass-production, depletion of resources, damage to the environment et cetera, et cetera.

Bunting flickered above the silence as Mike looked down at a cue card.

'He drew inspiration from the countryside, incorporated his sketches into wallpaper designs. His business a success, but also one based on a mission to keep us connected to the natural world. His designs destined for our homes a daily reminder of its beauty and fragility.'

A nearby tree seemingly in agreement as its branches violently twitched, two pigeons exploding out, flying up and then swooping down behind the roofs of Main Street. Mike flipped another card.

'Sidney loved William Blake. References to the satanic mills in his poem "Jerusalem", sickened him. He wanted a better deal for his workers. The mill they worked in was, I believe, his attempt to create his very own Jerusalem. A place where people would be valued – *may humanity be rediscovered in all we create* – those were Sidney's words and I believe he tried to live by them.'

He briefly glanced at Rennie who sat stage left.

'Today we are lucky to have with us the living custodian of the Wallis mill – Sidney's son – Mr Rennie Wallis. It is down to him that we can celebrate the rebirth of such a splendid building because despite being empty for decades, he has carefully maintained it. Bringing it back to use only possible because of his good stewardship. I'm sure you will want to join me in thanking him for that.'

Rennie stood. Applause died away, everyone expecting him to speak. But he just stared into the distance. His frail figure eclipsed by the statue of his father. Sidney's brassy features glowing in the sun, lines of pigeon mess streaking the furrows of his forehead. An awkward pause. The councillor turned and spoke to Rennie, the microphone broadcasting his concern. Rennie nodded then sat down.

'Well, once again, thank you all for coming. And if you would like to make your way to the mill, Mr Wallis will be cutting the ribbon. Thank you.'

More applause. Then Dani followed the crowd. Everyone gathering in front of the mill and focusing on the ribbon strung across open entrance doors. A sense of dread trickling through her bones because the forensics tent could be seen from where they all stood. Its white roof peeking above the road bridge.

She looked away and searched for Harriette in the crowd, but the only familiar face she saw was the man who looked like her brother. Smile, swagger, hair colour, all so familiar it was like a sick joke. The distance between herself and Moss Side suddenly eroding, like her past had sold up and moved to her gran's town.

The lookalike's name was Steven Ruskin, a regular at the pub. He re-upholstered car seats and had recently moved his business into the Wallis mill. She knew of this because he spent most evenings telling everyone in the bar that he fixed up classic cars for the great and famous. To

Dani's relief he was much taller than her brother Matt. A difference that erased her anxiety.

The councillor, the architect and Rennie stood on the entrance steps, everyone clapping as a theatrical pair of scissors cut through the ribbon. Dani closed her eyes and everything seemed to fall away. No tent, no family lookalikes, just the sun on her shoulders reaching deep into her bones.

'Dani, isn't it?'

She turned quickly. A bald man beside her. Puckered scar across his chin, ears roughed up. Rugby player? Boxer?

'Councillor Webster.' They shook hands. 'Pleased to meet you at last.'

'Likewise – that was a good speech you did.'

'Oh, I fumbled through. Forgive me for getting straight to the point but Rennie has told me about your idea. And, well, Karl and I had a chat to the planners, and they seem very positive.'

Skies blue and billowing white. A colossal edge brightening as it inched across the sun, the town plunging into shade, the white tent at the fringes of her vision dimmed away.

'Dani?'

'Sorry – I mean yes, thank you – it's very good of you to help me.'

'No problem. A project like this needs somebody energetic like you. Rennie said the room needs a good clear out. Council's health and leisure manager is on our side. She'd definitely support an application for a change of use, they're always keen to improve wellbeing of the community.'

'Change of use?'

'Business to leisure. Look, don't worry. Rennie's already instructed Karl to proceed.' He smiled. 'People are rooting for you.'

A voice from the crowd called Mike's name. He inched away. 'Maybe catch you in the pub later.'

'Yeah, okay – thanks again.' It's like an arranged marriage, she thought – *and the whole town's in on it.* She moved through the crowd towards Harriette and Rennie.

'You played lovely, Gran.'

'Thank you, dear. You've met Mike then.'

'Yes, I have, and he mentioned something about an application.' She turned to Rennie. 'I don't know what to say. I'm very grateful for your help.'

Everyone acting in her best interest. Everything handed to her on a plate – impossible to say no. But the guilt that trundled up from her gut marred everything – *if only they knew.* She saw blood then, creep through the fibres of her brother's shirt. She only meant to warn him off. Make him back down.

Harriette hugged her. 'You'll be amazing.'

They chatted for a while. Harriette seemed happy as if the performance had satisfied her deeply. Rennie over-exuberant as if dread had fallen away now that the proceedings were done. Dani kissed him on the cheek. He smiled. 'Coming to the Nav?'

'Maybe in a bit. Need a moment to myself.'

'Of course, join us later.' They crossed the road and disappeared into the pub. She set off in the opposite direction, her route hugging the mill. A sloping side road, then another corner, the mill towering above her, the rear wall a poor side of scruffy brickwork.

Reaching the canal, she stood on the quay and looked back at steps that ran up the gable wall to a door she knew led to the print room.

Play to your strengths, dear – what do you say to that… You'll be amazing.

She climbed the steps and tried the door, but the door was locked.

The stone landing she stood on, raised like a lectern, framed by a waist-high wall. She surveyed the view. Ducks and swans and fish and the countryside beyond. Jovial noises drifting down from the pub drawing her attention that way. The tent beyond the road bridge lurking above the reeds. Snapping her gaze away, her eyes ran in the opposite direction along the dead-straight canal. And through the tall arches of the railway bridge, she fixed her eye on a boat. A narrow boat painted dark grey that leant into the bankside bushes. So reticent, so indistinct. Like a shadow – she almost missed it.

DANI/DEV

Frogmen

Dani opened her eyes. Her first thoughts of the day tainted by the sound of gunshot. Three weeks had passed since the opening ceremony, a period of time in which she'd not seen her brother's lookalike, but now this. Slaughter on the estate; another shot whispering through the countryside. A sound that led her directly to the memory of her brother.

Diving under the duvet she tried to focus on her memory of the deer stalker instead. Wax jacket, smell of damp dog, too jolly by far; Harriette hated him. Employed by the new owners he'd asked them to avoid the estate until after nine. It was yet another event that seemed to taunt September.

She thought back to the opening ceremony, how the town had seemed in denial ever since, the days sequentially stranger as everyone ignored the circus on the far side of the canal. The tent replaced by a Portakabin. The search area extended. A grid of spoil heaps appearing as if a labour of moles was colonising the canal bank.

And then frogmen joined the show. An audience of kids sometimes watching from the towpath. Slimy oddment after slimy oddment raised from the bottom and laid out like inanimate casualties pulled from a shipwreck.

Her grandmother disappeared into the garden a lot. As much at sea as the rest of the town, although hers a solo voyage, absorbed in projects that drifted nowhere. She spent the last week of September quietly raking the first fall of leaves; her efforts undone by gales. Then the weather calmed, and one big smouldering heap emerged, the sweet fug of autumn enveloping the lodges for days.

And as if – along with the leaves – Harriette had swept away the bother, October came with good news. The application successful. Paperwork rubber-stamped. Permission granted. A wave of happiness travelling through her grandmother when Dani announced she would give the exercise classes a go.

Reaching out Dani took the key from the bedside table, big, heavy, its brass tulip head flipping over and over as she rolled its shank between her fingers. The builders had cleared away their mess the week before, but the print room needed a deep clean. Which was fine; she had been looking forward to it. Glad she could do something in return for Rennie's help.

She got out of bed, stood by the window, autumn more beautiful than any she could ever remember. The estate running on and on, acre after acre, grass, bracken, damp ribbons of air hugging the shins of distant woods. Grazing deer trotting on, spooked by another shot. The new silence broken by the slamming and fastening of her neighbour's window as though a whirlwind of anguish had sucked it shut.

Dani rolled out of bed, a cat lick in the bathroom, old jeans and a frayed sweatshirt hastily pulled on. Key and money shoved into a pocket she walked over to the other lodge. She knew Harriette would be quiet, her anxiety braced behind that stiff upper lip.

And there she was, her legs wedged under the kitchen table, the end of a pencil between her lips, a column of handwriting on the pad before her.

'It's his last visit,' Dani said. 'Not back for a couple of seasons, apparently.'

'Mm. So he reckons,' Harriette replied then changed the subject. A few words about jobs in the garden before returning to her list, the pencil lead chit-chatting across paper while Dani made a cafetiere of coffee.

At the table they sat in silence for a while. The garden diary filling with tormented scribbles, *Falstaff last seen on the 14th* scrawled down one side of the page.

Dani looked through windows, the garden fence just a couple of horizontal iron rods; otherwise nothing to suggest what was heath and what was garden.

Then she realised the chit-chatting had stopped, Harriette sitting back sipping coffee, sharing the same view.

'Need to go, Gran – busy day.'

'Fine – see you later.'

Dani kissed her grandmother's forehead, said she loved her. 'I'm sorry about the deer.'

Harriette smiled. 'Thank you for the coffee.'

Dani left the lodge and was soon crossing the square thinking of ways to cheer her gran.

The view of Main Street different now the trees were shedding leaves. More of the mill and the Angel Bakery filtering through. Divine aromas escaping into the street. A jingling bell on the bakery door stirring memories. A school bell, a curtain call, the summer production. The dress rehearsal. The gentleness in his face, his good behaviour worth a thousand kisses. And yes, since serving Devon at the pub, of course she'd thought about him. But she wasn't thinking now. She was just feeling. That same rare delight galloping through her chest. And she remembered reading his heart, remembered feeling it thump through his body and clang against hers as they gazed at one another.

Maybe just a quick hello, a brief chat with an author of better memories. For old times' sake. That wouldn't do any harm, would it?

The bell jingled above her head. In the shop, she joined the queue and watched a young lady with orange hair work the counter.

'Morning. What can I get you?'

'Breakfast bagel, bottle of water – oh, and this.' She placed a packet of biscuits on the counter.

'Biscotti – I'm addicted to them.'

'Present for my gran – she loves anything Italian.'

'You work in the Nav – Dev's friend, right?' Tongs fished inside the glass counter.

'Just briefly – way back.'

'Setting up in the room behind us, right? Welcome to the family. My name's Isla.'

'Thanks. Cleaning it out today, actually.'

'I'll definitely come along to your classes – loved your aerobathon.' She handed Dani a paper bag. 'I'd pre-order lunch if I were you, means you won't have to queue.'

Isla served other customers. Dani studied the blackboard menu.

*

On seeing her through the porthole of the kitchen door, I hurried through to the shop.

'Hi, good to see you again.'

She turned, looked a little startled. 'Oh – hi. Good to see you, too.'

'How do you two know each other then?' Isla called over whilst serving a customer. I knew what she was up to, knew where she was headed.

'We were at school together,' Dani answered.

It was like watching a slow-motion car crash.

'Oh, so you're Dani. I've heard all about the kiss.'

Customers exchanged glances, eyebrows were raised, my face flushed. Isla smiled. I could have killed her. She sidled up and placed her arm around my waist. 'This one's forgotten how to. Nearest he comes to lips these days is reading them.'

'Oh.'

'He's a bit deaf, especially when I'm talking.'

I placed a hand over my ear. 'Which is most of the

time. My hearing aid doesn't pick up everything.'

Isla squeezed my waist. 'You two should meet up some time.'

'Yes, we should do,' Dani replied still gazing at my ear, lost in thought. A short silence.

'Maybe sometime next week?' I suggested.

'Okay, I'd like that.' She turned to Isla. 'Pastrami sandwich on white, please.'

Isla scribbled. 'Got it... And make sure you hold him to that. He needs tearing away from this place.'

There was no reply from Dani at first; her face turned to the photograph of my platoon, her big eyes piecing things together. Then she turned to me and smiled.

'See you soon.'

'Yes, sure.'

She left the shop. Isla served the other customers. The moment slipping away, the loose arrangement like sand escaping between my fingers.

*

Dani stood on the quay for a while, spits of rain forming rings on water, the Portakabin beside the canal, the embankment around it cordoned off. More and more equipment arriving on site every week – strimmers, spotlights, generators, a metal detector, little flag markers pushed into the ground; an overnight security man guarding it all.

The canal bubbled and wetsuits bobbed up under the bridge. The shoulders of two divers higher than the others.

The word POLICE on their backs appearing above the waterline.

She stumbled up the steps and entered the mill, waiting behind the closed door for a moment, details in the cramped lobby exposed by a bare bulb; thoughts of monstrous crimes seeping in. And for sure, her father was likely to have killed the council man, but the investigation was unsettling her, as if its searching fingers roamed through her stomach, raking guilt previously lost to denial and time. Climbing a narrow staircase to a top lobby, she walked into the print room. A lofty space topped by iron trusses. Dim skies above the rooflights subduing patterns that covered the back wall. A lattice of daisies, thistles and honeysuckle. All wilted and past their best and loaded with meaning. And when she spread her arms across the wall, she felt part of the sombre story, but also oddly safe as if her leafy tattoos merging with wall patterns might hide her from all the forensic examination.

Breaking off she edged away until her back was against the opposite wall. Patterns that appeared random close-up now slowly forming coherent imagery: the subtle outline of five deer skulls emerging side by side along the wall.

And then the rain came down harder and skies darkened further; antlers and eye sockets fading away.

Switching on the lights she sat on a stepladder and ate breakfast. Factory lamps highlighting the muck: dustsheet in a deranged heap, old newspaper, offcuts of wood, empty pop cans. At first, she cleaned using a dustpan and brush, tipping the rubbish into a yellow chute that dropped to a skip below. Firing up the industrial vacuum, she swept the head of it through the room; footprints in the sawdust cleansed away, oak boards revealed. She dragged step ladders between the metal cone lights that dangled from flexes, each covered in a film of dirt. She cleaned them all. And high on the ladders she could see down through the only window, down to the quay, down to the canal. The water rasped by windy rain, neoprene heads bobbing like seals in a rough sea. And then she saw Devon in a raincoat on the quayside talking to the divers. Her ladder descent almost a fall, she went to the window and watched him turn towards the back of the mill, towards the steps.

The divers disappeared; the canal bubbled. Dani retreated to the ladder her chest throbbing with panic, her mind full of thoughts she couldn't clear: the night sky full of colour, her brother's shocked eyes, his gasping mouth.

Rain pummelled the rooflights; watery shadows ran down walls. The steps creaked; a figure appeared.

*

She stood next to a pair of ladders frantically wiping her face.

'You okay?'

'Fine… dust in my eyes… from cleaning the lamps.'

'Your lunch – We thought you'd forgotten it. Was taking the diver's order for tomorrow so thought I'd drop it by.'

Letting go of the ladder she took the paper bag.

'Thank you… What's the time? In my own little world up here.'

'Three o'clock. You've been busy.' I walked deeper into the room. 'Love this space.'

'Been here before?'

She slid out the sandwich from the paper bag, halfway, so her dirty hands didn't touch the bread.

'Nearly had it for my apartment; went for the space above the bakery in the end.'

'Oh, I see.'

'Anyway, I'll leave you to your lunch.'

'Stay if you want – a bit too quiet up here, to be honest.' She sat back on the stepladder and nibbled the sandwich. 'Lovely, isn't it?' she nodded at the back wall.

'Demonic is the word I had in mind, gets me every time though.'

I sat cross-legged on the floor a few feet from the ladder. Rain drummed on the rooflights above us.

She took a bigger bite and chewed for a long time. Our first time alone, no lines to say, no audience, our eyes locked and sharing the simple pause.

'Tasty,' she said from the corner of her mouth. 'Isla seems nice.'

'She's lovely… I'm sorry about all that, you know, the *South Pacific* thing. I don't go around telling everyone about the kiss – well – I mean, half a kiss.'

She smiled; my heart rate quickened.

'Seems a long time ago – It's something I've regretted ever since.'

'Me too. I was such a goody two-shoes back then.'

She focused on the floor and looked a little embarrassed.

'I meant – I regret leaving school.'

Idiot.

'Sorry – yes, of course, must have been a tough decision. What happened?'

She stopped chewing, her face deep in thought.

'Bit of a long story.'

She took a big bite. Enough to prevent conversation. We looked around the room whilst she chewed. She swallowed.

'You joined the army then?'

'Mm. I did.'

She tilted her head and looked at the scarred side of my head. 'Did you get that in a fight?'

Rain came down harder. I felt hot. A bit flaky.

'Bit of a long story.'

She ironed the paper bag on her thigh and neatly folded it over.

'Is that what you would call a ceasefire?'

'Yes, well, more of a blockade actually.'

A happy stalemate: we both smiled. She stood and I watched as she swept her hair into a band.

'You and Isla just friends then?'

'Since we were kids. She's running the shop for me. Only until she's worked out her life.'

'Oh, okay.' She nodded. 'I'm lucky the owner is letting me use this space. Must be pretty amazing living here.'

'Yeah, my apartment is amazing.' Waves of weather washed over the rooflights; rainwater trickled through drainpipes. 'You should come round, see it for yourself.'

She gave me a serious look, like she was about to say no.

'I'd like that.'

'Sundays are my free day.'

'I work Sundays.'

'Ah.'

'Got the twenty-third off, though.'

'Twenty-third it is then?'

'Okay.'

We paused for breath. Smiling, nodding, looking around the room.

'Do you like Caribbean food?'

'Never tried it.'

'I'll make you some.'

She smiled. 'You like feeding people, don't you?'

I got up, my knees cracked. 'Get it from my gran. It's a Barbados thing.'

At the door I glanced back. 'Twenty-third then.'

'Twenty-third.' She was beaming. My heart singing.

Nodding once I turned and skipped down the steps.

DEV

The Kiss

Everything was set. Dinner simmering; the flat tidy. I went out to get some air. The bridge had been closed off all week; blue and white plastic tape stretched across either end. From behind the cordon, I watched the Portakabin being craned onto a truck. Searching the bridge had, it seemed, been the old bill's forensic finale.

The pub's extractor belched smoke; last week's oil still in the fat frier by the stink of it. The bridge really wasn't the best place for fresh air. To be honest, I'd come to see if the police were still fishing for clues, and it was a relief that they weren't. Rumours had floated around all week about them pulling out. Apparently, they'd only found odd items of interest in the canal. Junk from the fifties and sixties, a few old mill tools from the last century. But that was it, no solid evidence – nothing juicy.

The truck drove away. A pong wafted up from the canal and a coot called from under the bridge as if celebrating the return of its territory. Ambling back, I thought about what Isla had said about the old bill's belated grope for facts; a door-to-door plea for anyone who witnessed suspicious behaviour twelve years before. They'd set up a phone line – information treated confidentially, et cetera, et cetera. It seemed a bit desperate to be fair. Too little too late and it was clear everyone resented it especially as the police bungled the original investigation all those years ago. And then Isla mentioned how awkward it must be for Dani and her grandmother.

To be honest, that hadn't even occurred to me. Not wanting the investigation to colour my view of Dani, I suppose, subconsciously I'd separated her from it. I decided not to make any mention of the police when she came over and was glad the windows of my apartment looked over town and not the search area by the canal.

Back at the flat I switched off big lights and turned on floor lamps; the wine-red corner sofa glowing in the middle of the room like a big heart. My place looked cosy. Isla had unpacked the remaining boxes, arranged cushions and throws, hung the two Rothko prints side by side on the back wall. For the first time it felt lived in.

Dani was late.

I paced around the sofa, Isla's last words repeating in my head – *relax, be yourself, don't go on about work.*

I checked the curry then went to the window. Sunday on Main Street filtering through the trees. People dawdling through town, a couple pausing at the estate agent's window, a man folding a buggy as his family entered Café Rouge. Dusk settled early. Streetlamps flickered awake. Ribbons of cobbled paving damp and shiny like the skin of a reptile. A blackbird swooped between trees; its outburst fractious. I checked the time.

She was forty-three minutes late.

Unexplained delays like this always took me to a dark place, a place where my perspective slipped, a place where I always feared the worst. But please not there, not now. Heart racing, mouth parched, without rhyme or reason my head flipped back:

> *Dust clings to everything, rubber buttons, hatch seals. Smeared in places by a sweaty hand. The man in the hatch next to mine utters calm and routine words into the microphone of his helmet. Within minutes he will be dead. I can sense heat off the lower bulkhead, feel the throbbing tone of diesel engines. Then everything goes haywire and I'm reeling from a blow that has slammed me onto sand and then I'm checking myself, checking to see that my legs are still attached...*

The blackbird flashed between trees, its livid chorus snapping me back.

I should look for her.

But as I reached for my jacket, the intercom buzzer stabbed the air – reflexively, I snatched at the handset.

'Hello!'

'It's Dani.' Her voice was thin and faint and trampled by hissing traffic.

'I'm on the first floor.'

I buzzed the lobby entrance, her steps echoed in the

stairwell, her ascent quick and feline. Not enough time to rein in my wobble. My palms wet. Breathing wrong. *Calm yourself. Inhale, exhale; inhale again.*

'Hi,' she said, smiling, her hair tucked behind one ear.

'Come in.'

'Sorry I'm early.'

'Early?'

'We said four, didn't we?' She grinned at me. 'Clocks have gone back – Did you forget?'

'Yes, I did.'

Handing me a bottle of wine she removed her jacket and hung it on a peg, the hallway capturing her scent, its feminine quality sculpting the air: outside freshness mixed with musky perfume. She moved below the under croft, the sheen of her hair captured by spotlights, the space transformed into a catwalk. I followed her out into the triple height living area.

'Shall I take off my shoes?'

'No, it's fine.'

She took them off looking up at the metal roof trusses. 'Same as the print room.' She glanced back.

'Yeah.'

Then she was at the windows, her face tilted up like an excited child; eyes smiling.

'There's so much sky.'

'Pretty cool, isn't it?' I raised the bottle. 'Thanks for this.'

'Actually, it's from my gran, I don't know much about wine. Chianti's her favourite.'

'Tell her thanks from me. Like some?'

'Mm – yes, please.'

She sat on a bar stool, one leg crossed over the other. It was surreal. The girl from *South Pacific* sitting in my kitchen. That was six years ago, and yet I felt like a teenager again. Tense and confused. 'How's it going?'

She watched me clumsily twist the bottle opener into the cork.

'I've been on a coaching course; keep-fit instruction, personal training.'

'Bet you can't wait to get started.'

'Started classes a couple of weeks ago, actually.'

'Oh. Right.' The cork squeaked out.

Fiddling with my dud ear was one of those involuntary tics I did when nervous. The scarred nobbles on its top edge grotesque, like a rocky edge. Jerking my hand down I dropped the corkscrew in the drawer and whipped it shut, utensils inside violently shifting which made her jump a little.

'Thought you may have heard us; we're next-door neighbours, aren't we?'

I poured wine.

'Not strictly. There's a room between us.'

'Didn't know that.'

'It's a narrow space that runs behind my apartment. Sealed up… during the war or something.'

Sipping wine, we both eyed the back wall, her foot performing little rhythmical bounces. Then her beautiful eyes went big. 'Sealed off, you say?'

'Yeah. Well, so the architect reckons.'

'Just as well. I mean, we play the music pretty loud. Steven has already complained about us.'

'Isn't he below you?'

Glass to mouth, she gave a little nod. 'Mm.'

'Seems like a nice guy.'

She delayed answering, her foot switching from little kicks to little circles.

'He gives me the creeps; reminds me of my brother.'

'Ah, right. You didn't get on then.'

'With my brother? No. No, we didn't get on.'

'Right.' I knocked back wine. Conversation dried up, our eyes drawn to the big industrial windows, tree branches brittle in the street light as if the slightest breath of wind would snap them off.

Ear fondling, corkscrew fumbling, one hour behind everyone else. I'd blown it big time.

She nodded at the pot. 'Smells amazing.'

Little wisps of steam eked out.

'Bajan curry and homemade naan bread.'

'Bajan?'

'Exotic term for anything that comes from Barbados.'

'Like your gran.'

'Yeah – she's definitely exotic.'

She smiled and nodded.

I lifted the lid and stirred. 'Isla said you're staying with your gran?'

'For a while. I was desperate to get out of Manchester. She kindly offered me a bed.'

'She sounds nice.'

'She's lovely.'

'I lived in Manchester for a while after the army; Didsbury?'

'The posh bit.' She smiled again. 'I was roughing it in Hulme.'

The wine was loosening us up. 'How long were you in Hulme?'

Her eyes fixed on mine. 'Long enough.' She took a slow sip.

'Hungry?'

'Yes – very. Thought you'd never ask.'

She carried the bottle to the table and refilled the glasses. I served up. Our forks soon busy shifting food around plates, sounds of my own eating ridiculously loud in the hearing aid.

She asked me about work. I explained we were flat out. I kept it brief. But the questioning continued: keeping accounts, national insurance contributions, advertising. She leant on the table, her chin propped by a hand. 'You're not daunted by it, then?'

'Mm?'

'I mean financially.'

'A bit, at first. Having multiple streams of income helps – makes your business robust.'

This was something I'd picked up at a seminar although it was clear that she'd worked that one out for herself. As well as aerobics she was holding boxercise and tae-bo classes and had just finished a course in women's self-defence. Apparently, there was a demand for that. Questions kept coming and I found myself in full flow and whilst picking at food we traded quick glances.

'Sorry for all the questions.'

'It's fine.'

'One more?'

'Go on.'

'Does it make you happy?'

She addressed the question to the side of my head, to my scarred ear, then she sat back. My audience of one. Her foot brushed mine, a kiss of the ankles. I twitched but her foot remained there, very still, no tics. My mind scampered around for an answer.

Happiness: glimmers came and went like it had a will of its own. I loved the bakery, but it was all-consuming, an unhealthy obsession. Isla regularly reminded me so. And I knew there was something missing, a gap that I tried to fill with the wrong ingredient. I needed other elements in my life. I needed balance. I needed... a way to express all this without sounding desperate. I looked up from the table to see that her expression was a little jaded, a line of puffiness below her eyes. Who knows what sights they'd seen. She smiled often enough but her lashes rarely blinked. And I sensed turmoil behind her cool composure. I guessed we must be in a similar place. Bouncing back after tough times.

'Yes, it makes me happy.'

We sat in silence whilst her boyish jaw worked a last mouthful.

'That was lovely. Thanks.'

'My pleasure.'

Knocking back wine, she then stood and made quick work of clearing the table.

'You've done that before.'

She smiled. 'Between you and me, I'm handing in

my notice. Keep-fit classes and working at the Nav is becoming too much.'

'Fair enough; something has to give.'

From the sink she walked to side units that hugged the back wall and looked at framed photographs. I joined her.

'They look happy.'

'My parents. Mum's from Barbados, Dad's from Manchester; they live in Didsbury.'

She switched her focus to other things on the shelves, fingers speedily flicking through CDs, cassettes, books. She didn't dwell; it was like a detective searching for clues. Picking up a chess piece she weighed it. 'Do you play?'

'A little.'

We moved the game to the coffee table. Sitting on the sofa she tucked up her legs. I sat on the rug. She frowned continually whilst playing opening moves. I made early errors. After taking a third of my pieces she relaxed, sat back, her eyes looking up for the first time.

My moves took forever. She maintained the upper hand.

'Who taught you to play? Kasparov?'

She laughed. 'Girl in my dorm was chair of the school chess club.'

'Oh… right.' I dragged it out.

I could tell she drew pleasure from that, like a cat toying with a mouse that wouldn't play dead. And focusing on the game seemed to release us from inhibition. She sat on the rug beside me. We forgot ourselves, took breaks, drank more wine, talked about the game, how the twists and turns of it were a bit like life. She spoke of her friends that lived in the Crescents and how its demolition had rendered them homeless. I spoke about friends in the army. We switched to talk of school, the songs in *South Pacific*, Miss Gimmet. The kiss.

Executing my demise, she smiled at the inevitability of the closing moves. I laughed at my strategic ineptitude. We both sensed what was coming.

Sharing a side view of the board we sat closer. Her perfume stronger, I studied the downy hairs on the nape of her neck while she gave a short analysis of my downfall.

Too many "country" moves early on, stronger pieces frustrated by pawns, other pieces left undefended, my spite check driven by ego.

'You should have castled earlier.'

She turned away from the board and looked me in the eye. The last time our heads were this close we were on a stage.

'I think I get it… Anything else?'

Her face so close I could feel her breath intermingle with mine. Realising we'd past the point of no return, the last few inches of the long and overdue journey were unrushed and tranquil.

The sides of our noses gently docked, and our lips came together.

DARDALE

1915

V

Damselfly – *Odonata (Suborder Zygoptera)*

Study for Wallis and Hilton Wallpapers. Plate No. 105 – Damsels and Dragons [see sketch on next page]

Facts: The damselfly has been on earth for over 300 million years. Their six legs cannot walk; instead, they use them to catch prey and perch when resting. Females go underwater to lay eggs on plant stems.

Symbology and quaint beliefs: Folklore of many western cultures holds that Odonata are a snake's companion and Satan sent them into the world to cause mischief.

Rates of production increased. The length of trains grew ever longer. The factory at full tilt in the sultry heat of late July. Thousands of four-and-a-half-inch shells clanked through the workshop. Each carefully passed around like an unwanted baby. Each fed a block of explosive, a cordite igniter, a bursting charge, a fuse. The women's bustle carving swirls in a fumy haze that angled in from the rooflights. The finished deadly product wheeled away in cart wagons, across the bridge link and onto the platform. A place from where Ellen would watch the loaded trains heave out of the station, until the brake van disappeared beyond the bend in the track. And when the sound of wagons faded, and moorland surrendered to silence, the whole of Ellen's body itched as she imagined the German equivalent careering towards the front, their cannons shooting, their shells exploding, hot fragments tearing into the battlefields, an anxious knot tightening in the pit of her stomach as she wondered how on God's earth her father would survive the coming together of it all.

Another shift done, she went home and bathed, scrubbing arms and legs until they prickled and when the redness faded, she surveyed her skin obsessively. And then dressing in a long-sleeved blouse and long skirt she left the house and walked along the street following a route that steadily lifted her above the town, a route that led her to Joe.

Passing by the lodges and turning away from the estate she walked onto moorland, the track a narrow channel through broom. The spring of peaty ground warmed by the sun soothing her feet, the scent of wild heather cleansing her airwaves, the sight of open fells taming the beat of her industrial day.

She continued on, land falling away, hem of her skirt playing with cloudberry and bracken until heath ended and the trail sided a sloping field of crops. On joining the towpath, she saw Joe waving from the canal bridge. She waved back and broke into a run.

And then together they set off towards the estate and scrambled through a break in a dry stone wall. Passing through the dappled light of a wood they soon reached a pond and sat thoughtfully on its grassy bank, their bare feet disturbing calm water, the sparkling wavelets drawing her eye to low branches and languid insects that seemed to hover above aquatic iridescence. Summer haze trembled.

Glancing to one side she watched Joe, his gaze lost to watery rhythms as his hand absent-mindedly picked at the grass. She reached out and placed a hand on his. The picking stopped and after a brief delay his face turned and beamed. She smiled back.

'You were miles away.'

'Water's so clear.'

'A spring comes up by the rocks on the far bank.'

Nobody said anything for a while. Ellen's eyes returned to the pond.

'Muriel went home sick last week.'

'Mm – She alright?'

'Not sure – complained of stomach pains, couldn't eat a thing at break. And Beth refused to leave home yesterday because of the yellow marks on her face.'

He lay on his side, head propped by a forearm, tension in his body dispersing into the grass. 'Reckon you lot are just guinea pigs for the ministry.'

Ellen sighed. 'I keep telling Harold it's the chemical dust. It's got worse over summer; the girls are breathing it in…'

Swirling a hand over grass Joe watched a swan etch crystal lines on the pond.

'…he won't let us sweep with damp wood shavings – *too much moisture's not good for explosives* – it's just like he's talking about his tomatoes.'

He laughed at her impersonation, then saw the grave look on her face and her upset eyes. He stopped grinning. She held out her stained wrists as if presenting them for shackling.

'Meanwhile, half of us turn yellow.'

Joe slowly unbuttoned her cuffs, his eyes fixed on hers as he rolled up the sleeves of her blouse. They both studied her stained forearms, then he kissed them.

'Does it go any further?'

She said nothing. An intense silence ensued, then she watched him remove his own shirt, her eyes travelling across his broad shoulders before falling upon the scar that ran up his side.

'It's my little beauty spot.'

Head to one side she studied his damaged torso. 'How did you get that?'

'Werner.'

'Oh. What's Werner?'

'My friend Werner Wid. He shot me,' he said matter-of-factly with a shrug.

'Shot you!'

He lifted an arm and gazed dumbly at his flank. She couldn't help but smile at the shooter's name; supressing an urge to laugh she wrestled with the excitement buzzing in her chest.

'In what world do friends shoot each other, exactly?'

He looked up and smiled. 'In the bush.'

Feeling hot and heady she pushed words through tight laughter.

'So, your friend – Werner Wid – shot you, in a bush.'

Eyes beaming up she laughed freely then, which made him laugh too, the muscles in his skinny middle contracting then relaxing.

'Not in "*a*" bush. In "*the*" bush. You know, the land. What you pommes call the countryside.' Lowering his arm Joe placed his palm on the grass. 'Our countryside is hot, endlessly massive and full of hares. We were hunting and, well – I got in the way. We were just young blokes mucking about – Werner's eyesight's no better than mine. It was – an unfortunate accident.'

He gazed back at the water and took a deep breath.

It had taken a huge effort to reveal all of this – because it actually happened. It was like he'd heaved open a heavy door behind which lay the real Joe Stander. The slither of openness so fine he could sense the sweet air of truth seeping in. At the time they feared he might die but somehow, he recovered; nobody wanted to hunt with Werner after that. Joe smiled, then ushered his old friend back in, and then, once again he closed the door.

'You're lucky to be alive; it's such a big scar.'

'Wound got infected but eventually healed. The scar had a growth spurt when I did.'

Ellen reached out, her fingertips gently tracing his ruined skin.

He went to kiss her, but she recoiled and with heart beating harder she unbuttoned her blouse and peeled away the fabric, her bare shoulders rounded as if shivering in an icy wind, her gaze fixed awkwardly on the grass.

Sensing him slowly lean in, she closed her eyes. His warm mouth poised on the nape of her neck, lightly brushing over the shoulder strap of her camisole, his lips continuing with deliberate firmness tracing slowly down the discoloured arm she'd been so ashamed of revealing.

Her tension softened. He looked up. 'Do you ever feel sick?'

Removing his thumb from her wrist there was no pale imprint in the yellow. And then he felt huge pangs of frustration because he didn't know how to fix her.

'No, I'm fine.'

'Is it all over?'

'Body and arms.'

Joe kissed her forehead then stood, and she watched his scarred middle wade into the pond. 'Coming in?'

She followed. And they undressed their submerged bodies until naked. Items of clothing joyously lobbed as bundled projectiles, the drag of air opening them up mid-flight, spray from cartwheeling body parts strafing water before making landfall with sodden slaps.

Her body lightened by buoyancy she wrapped her legs around his waist and placed forearms on his shoulders, her head raised high above his; she had lost all inhibition. His hands flattened on the sinews of her back, his mouth exploring her front, she relaxed around him. His kisses ever higher as her body gradually lowered. She sensed his firmness as if her soft contours moved against the tectonic edge of a continent. He kissed her neck then lips, their immersed bodies convergent and concealed from a cruel world.

The natural world continuing on around them.

A carp surfacing, a swift hunting. A damselfly hovering

by them before heading to a white blouse draped over the grassy shore. Attracted to the movement of a soaked hemline it darted back and forth until the easy rhythm of incoming waves ceased to flow.

And then their bodies were still and as one, the sides of their faces pressed together as they watched glowing insects dance close to water in the low shafts of sunlight.

They swam for a while, their happy voices echoing about the close air of the glade. And after hanging clothes on branches, they lay and looked up and watched the oak trees redden ever deeper in the setting sun.

And when darkness finally fell, the silhouettes of overhanging leaves and branches transformed into a pitch-black coastline of headlands and coves and their innocent eyes drifted, together, across a quivering ocean of stars.

*

They bathed at the pond most evenings, the heatwave breaking late August. And as summer receded, the Lancashire autumn and a great buffeting wind invaded the town. More women got sick, and the number of shells made at the factory fell short of production targets. In the colonel's office, Ellen stated the problems over and again: chronic fatigue, long hours, exposure to chemicals, no factory canteen. These, she argued, were the reasons for shortfalls.

After exactly one day she was summoned back to the office. Harold in the corner, toxic happiness smeared across his face. The colonel behind a desk, rattling off emphatic decisions like bullets from a machine-gun: all leave withdrawn doors of the block room to be locked, the workers' magazine shelved. From a large cupboard he produced a stack of work smocks and handed them over.

'To be worn over skirts... women barred from wearing trousers.' His eyes lifeless. 'That is all.'

She left with the smocks. The block room doors were locked. Meetings to discuss the magazine erased from the diary. Ellen's other meetings with Joe non-existent. Then September marched into October, reports of "a brilliant, allied victory" in a French city called Loos inspiring a brief upswing in production. Then the bombshell hit.

After being off work for a week, Muriel died. Requests for compassionate leave ignored, everyone worked through their grief, the misery only compounded when a self-righteous medical officer visited the factory. Examining Ellen and all the other ladies he then, in a mocking tone – as if obvious all along – proclaimed they should all drink milk; a cure for the yellowness, so it was claimed. So, the women drank milk and for most it relieved symptoms. But not Ellen's. She continued to vomit and yet her health remained as good as ever. And it came to everyone's attention that her symptoms appeared to be unique: a newfound abhorrence of certain smells and certain foods, her period overdue.

She arrived at the factory ready for another shift and whilst at her bench she watched Cedric meander through the workshop like a lost soul, swiping through papers attached to a clipboard. Eventually he pulled up next to her.

She glanced his way. 'Lost something?'

He stood motionless.

'Cedric?'

Head scratching. 'Figures don't add up – I'm missing two shells.'

'Two? But we've filled thousands. Maybe the ladies have stowed them in Harold's saddlebag…'

'No joke, Ellen. It's explosives gone missing, not rolls of wallpaper. I've told the colonel, but he's not interested in little anomalies.'

'He is a little anomaly.'

Cedric rolled his eyes. 'Can you walk back with me after work?'

'Yes, I'll walk with you.'

They met on the entrance steps and then set off, Cedric dropping into the post office to deliver a bundle of letters along the way. Ellen waited outside and watched women spill from the factory, their chatter criss-crossing with the next shift before disappearing into town. And then just two children playing chase under trees that shivered in a cold breeze, leaves ragged and yellow and whispering to a rat-grey sky.

Cedric emerged and they continued along Main Street.

'You look troubled.'

'Keep feeling something's wrong – getting myself worked up for nothing, I suppose.'

'Very dramatic – been reading *Father Brown* stories again?'

He laughed at that and at the corner of Ellen's street, they stopped and continued chatting. Cedric in full flow, rambling on about a new munitions factory that was located further north, by the coast, purpose built, huge.

It began to rain.

Cedric squinted up. 'Look, come back for a cuppa. I've got cake that needs eating up.'

'I will, thank you.'

They crossed Main Street and entered the square.

'I know why the Davidsons weren't at church on Sunday.'

'The Davidsons who live in the hamlet?'

'They got the dreaded telegram. Charles died instantly. Loyal North Lancashires took heavy losses apparently.'

Ellen clenched her eyes and thought of her father. 'Oh God, I feel sick.'

Realising she'd stopped, Cedric looked back. Ellen motionless, the disbelief on her face oblivious to the strengthening rain.

'You alright?'

'He was my age. I can't believe he's gone...' Her eyes found Cedric, '...but the papers say we surprised the Germans – took prisoners.'

'This is what I mean. The real story. It's held from us, censored. That's what Joe tells me, anyway.'

Her mind wheeled about; her gaze fixed on the surface of a puddle twitching in the rain. She thought of the pond, her skin against Joe's.

Cedric squinted upwards again, his eyes blinking into the rain. 'Ellen – we're getting soaked.'

She hopped over the puddle and ran towards him. 'I haven't seen Joe lately. Is he alright?'

'He's in Leeds, attending a press bureau conference. Staying with his "journo" friends. Back next week, so he reckons.'

They hurried into a narrow passage. A cut-through between buildings that lined the square, on the far side a cobbled path, the wisteria-clad vicarage and a mews of cottages. Unlocking a front door, he ushered Ellen into his home then shut out the lashing rain.

He handed over a towel which she used to dry her hair; her voice engulfed by the rubbing. 'What is happening then?'

'According to Joe the autumn offensive was a complete botch. Battle of Loos a bloodbath. Courtesy of Field Marshal French's incompetence.'

Her face reappeared, hair big and wild. 'Meanwhile, everyone takes it out on the Wallises.'

'Town has it in for them, for sure.'

'How does Joe know these things?'

'Hack grapevine. If the truth leaves a bad taste in the mouth, they're not allowed to print it. Doesn't stop the whispers, though. Light the fire, would you, while I rustle up some tea?'

Ellen arranged kindling and scrunched newspaper in the hearth. Reaching for the matches she admired the twisted wreaths of straw and dried flowers on the mantleshelf.

'I like the display.'

'Present from my dad – decorations from the harvest festival service. I've got pumpkin pie if you want some.' His voice mingled with sounds of clinking china.

'Prefer cake if there's enough.'

After all these years Cedric was still a loyal friend. A friend who wouldn't judge her for being so close to the Wallises. Son of the vicar, weedy as a child, a misfit who spent most of his time alone. She still remembered the day he came back with a maths degree. He wasn't the butt of jokes after Sidney employed him to keep books and manage the payroll.

He entered the room carrying a tray, a bigger man under the low beams of his own living room. Striking a match, she lit the mound of paper and wood.

'Ooh. Carrot cake.'

'Last of my mother's sugar went into that.'

He placed the tray down and they sat and talked about the food shortages, the likelihood of rationing and the lady on Gladstone Street who was caught hoarding flour in her bath and how it had gone bad and clumpy and no use to anyone.

'The cake's so good. Say thank you to your mum.'

'I will.'

Conversation turned to Muriel's death and as Cedric refilled the teapot Ellen sat on the edge of her seat, her hand busy scratching her scalp.

'Her family told me she died of toxic jaundice; said she'd suffered from a bad liver since childhood. Conveniently the cause of death made only reference to that. No mention of the amatol that's attacking our health and turning us yellow. Feels like a bloody cover-up to me.'

Cedric swilled the teapot in circles.

'I hear the medical officer made recommendations. At least something good has come of it.'

'Huh – you mean the old goat who stayed in town for an hour, stating the bloody obvious. After sending Laura and Polly home he instructed us to wipe benches with damp cloths and sweep the floor with wet sawdust. I've suggested this for weeks. And of course, that nitwit Harold's agreeing to it now that a *man* has stuck his oar in.'

'Any news on the leather gloves?' He poured the tea.

'None. Harold's decided to hide behind a locked door and tell us nothing.'

'So I heard. He kept complaining about your "intrusions" to the colonel – not sure you're going to win that battle, Ellen.'

'Someone has to stand up for the workers. Any more cake going?'

He cut another slice. 'Look, it's not what you're saying… it's how you're saying it. You'll be seen as a troublemaker if you carry on like this.'

'I don't give a fig if I've dented the precious ego of Harold Yates. Anyway, whose side are you on exactly?'

She swallowed a last mouthful of cake.

'Made short work of that.'

'Talked to Joe recently?' she said with sledgehammer nonchalance.

'Briefly. Wasn't his normal self. Cut up by news of Gallipoli. One of his family is in the thick of it.' He placed his cup and saucer on the tray. 'I get the feeling you were quite close.'

She ignored the comment.

'Gallipoli?'

'Peninsula jutting into the Aegean. We're fighting the

Turks there, but it is not going well. Thousands of Aussies killed.'

A relative? In the thick of it? But whenever she asked about family Joe clammed up. She felt sick, the sweetness of the cake upping her heart rate. Cedric stoked the fire; flames licking at the newly added log. He looked up from the hearth.

'It's alright, I wouldn't tell a soul. Factory rules and all that.'

'Sorry?'

'You and Joe.'

'Yes – close. Well, we were. I mean, things have cooled.'

'Thought you'd give the other ladies a chance?'

She laughed but without enthusiasm. 'Feeling left out, are we?'

'Sort of – you lot only seem to have eyes for Joe the Adonis.' There was a loud crack from the fire, sparks disappearing up the flue. 'Don't you think, well – he's a bit too good to be true?'

'What do you mean by that?'

'It's just, I have an aunty who lives in Frankston. She and my mother send telegrams all the time.'

Ellen felt her patience shorten. 'Sorry. I don't follow.'

'I was talking to Joe about Manchester Piccadilly, said it probably wasn't a patch on Flinders Street. He didn't seem to have a clue what I was talking about. Which was odd because my aunt said anyone from Melbourne would know Flinders Street Station. There's a grand ballroom there.'

'It's probably a misunderstanding. Lost in translation maybe. These Aussies speak a different language half the time.'

'Well, that's the other thing.'

'Oh, saints preserve us, Ced. What other thing?'

'His accent. It's probably nothing but the tobacconist fought in the Boer War, reckons he can hear traces of Afrikaans in Joe's voice.'

'Yes, Cedric. It's probably nothing. Like your missing shell is probably nothing. Look, I'd better get to the grocers before they close. Otherwise, I'll have *nothing* for dinner.'

'Stay for supper if you like.'

'Thank you, but I'd better get back – housework to do and all that.'

Cedric followed her to the door and held the handle but delayed turning it. She pulled on her coat.

'Ellen. Look, I'm going away for a while. In the meantime, this Joe fella seems like a nice chap, but... just don't rush into anything.'

'Anywhere nice?'

His grip on the handle tightened. 'Er – White Lund, near Lancaster. Munitions committee have asked me to visit the new projectiles factory, help set up the accounts.'

'Ooh, nice, you'll have to pop along to Morecombe. It's a lovely walk along the seafront.'

'Ellen, all I'm saying is – just be careful. We don't really know him from Adam.'

Ellen slowly removed his hand from the handle then opened the door and walked away from the cottage.

'Ellen...'

'Thank you for the tea and cake.'

She turned and waved then disappeared into the alley.

DANI

Demons

The evening with Dev had given her a boost. The memory of the kiss outshining her well-worn worries and fears. And no way was she bothered about winter. Not this year. This year would be different. And yet as October took a bow, she prayed for biblical rain, a damp-squib, a fallow year, sparklers waved half-heartedly below dripping umbrellas. That would be good.

And it did rain for three days but then skies cleared. First night of the month crisp, creeping needles of frost unpicking her innocence. Ghosts seeping in – memories exploding out.

*

She spent the first evening of November with Harriette and Rennie and before dinner they agreed to play Elgar's Cello Concerto. They all sat in the music room, Dani on a chair wedged next to the sideboard, her eyes closed and waiting with blind anticipation, gentle noises of preparation tickling the air: the soft clonk of the cello against something hard, rosin cake applied to the strands of the bow, Rennie fussing over the height of the piano stool. Dani's mouth dry, the first blows of music only seconds away, the demons in her mind painting terrible images: judge's gavel about to fall, queen's neck below a raised axe, stag in the crosshairs of a rifle sight.

Then the big sounds came. Ubiquitous, devastating. Assaulting her ears, her body absorbing vibrations, the demons kicked out of her head and mauled around the walls of the room. The music shaking her soul to the core, dismantling her, reassembling, rearranging, reforming. Hairs on the back of her neck and arms standing on end. Her backside rooted to the chair, everything else aerobically violent.

Then those plucks at the end beyond which she felt modified but not entirely sure how. Her demons subdued and scattered; a while yet before they could regroup and clamber back in.

'Joining us for something to eat?' said Harriette as the musicians creakily stood and moved to the kitchen without flamboyance.

'Be with you in a minute.'

Dani lingered on the chair but was unable to find words adequate enough to describe what the elderly duet had given her. Peace? Freedom from strife? Something like that.

She joined them at the table and while eating dinner they discussed the concerto, its abruptness, the mix of anguish and hope, how the music ached. The musicians talked on. The piece composed in the first spring after the Great War; Elgar's elegy for the millions who had died. They apologised for their performance, something about ragged strings and the piano slightly out of tune. Ignoring Dani's claims that it was perfect, they pitched into the technicalities. The nine-eight-time signature – Wagner's *Ride of the Valkeries*? Dukas's *The Sorcerer's Apprentice*? all composed in nine-eight.

Dani was lost, so Harriette put it to her in relatable terms.

Running.

Whilst jogging, count each step – one, two, three, four then repeat. Steady, simple, like music composed in four-four-time, like the opening movements of Vivaldi's *Winter*. Nine-eight just a more complicated way of breaking down the rhythm. Of course, they loved that she showed interest. It sparked them up, took years off their age. Like excited children with burning secrets, they played a recording of another piece – Vaughan Williams' *The Lark Ascending*.

Dani closed her eyes and soared. Her demons now tiny and far below, like scurrying ants.

*

After that night Dani counted a four-beat rhythm whenever she ran. The method lifting her to a higher place, her mind opening up like the carved flowers that hung on her grandmother's wall.

She vowed to run twice a day until December. Fields

too muddy, she weaved through the streets on the north side of town. A sprawl of Victorian terraces that once housed families who worked in a cotton mill that was no longer there; burnt down in the seventies – an insurance job according to Harriette.

One, two, three, four.

Later that day, she'd be in the Nav working until late. So, it didn't matter that it was November the fifth; the fireworks, the sparklers, those damn bonfires.

Just focus on the running, focus on the counting.

The terraced streets so long and straight she could have been back in Moss Side. Front doors opening onto paving, the slabs below her padding feet scrolling past like a film reel of the past.

Step on a crack and the bear will jump on your back.

Her brother was the bear that made her laugh on the way back from school. She was young and thought he would never change.

One, two, three, four.

His final moments crushing those distant recollections, the sickening images coming with ease: his body pulling back with shock, like he'd run into an invisible tree, his eyes staring up, mouth gaping like a fish out of water sucking in the bangs and the phosphorous pops; colours blushing across his face.

She sprinted.

Parked cars careening past. Her breathing all wrong, her breakfast welling up.

Slowing to a walk she stopped and retreated into a gap between the terraces, her shoulders rising and falling. Both her hands flat on a brick gable, feet wide apart, as if ready to be frisked as if under arrest. Head hung low she spewed and for a gut-wrenching moment her head blanked. And when her breathing normalised, she walked back onto the street. The sky Martian clear, the quiet street in solemn shade. She looked ahead to the three-storey villas which ran across the end of the road, brick frontages topped by slated roofs glowing gold in winter sun, thawing frost dripping from dormers like jewelled fringes.

Heading back, she ran fast and loose and soon she was back at the lodges. Harriette's kitchen a sanctuary of calm. Relaxed and tidy, the Aga radiating a steady warmth, views of the misty heath beyond the big back windows. Breathing it all in, Dani's shoulders softened. Being there, being with her gran like a therapy.

A cello was on the table, on a blanket, as if struck down by illness. A peg loosened, one string removed and draped over a dining chair. Her gran stooped over the instrument, berating herself for not replacing strings earlier.

'Sorry, dear, but do you mind if I carry on with the re-string?'

'No, fine, can't stay for long – got a few jobs to do before my class.'

'Bit busy myself. Good to see you, though.'

Dani reached for the kettle, Harriette's voice following her to the sink as she filled it with water. 'Everything alright? You seem a little restless.'

How does she know there's something amiss – she's not even looked up from the cello!

'Just got back from a run. I'm fine. I'll make a cuppa. How often do you change them?'

'Depends,' Harriette replied while seating the end of a new string into what she called the fine tuner. 'Did you have a nice evening at Devs?'

'Mm – did a lot of catching up. He said thank you for the wine by the way.'

As she made tea Dani remembered that the evening with Dev had been a little awkward. Of course, the kiss, being equal to a thousand words, had settled them both. It had been very pleasant, felt right. But on reflection it seemed unfair for her to draw him in like that and now she felt like a fraud, like an imposter.

She heard the faint melody of her grandmother's voice, then a silence, a hanging cadence, like Dani had missed her cue; she'd been distracted like that for days, her head lost in chasms of torment.

Harriette looked up from the cello and smiled. 'Are you sure everything's alright?'

'Yes, fine. It's the fireworks, they put me on edge – sorry, what did you say?'

'One string at a time, dear. I mean, you can't rush these things.' She unwound a peg and the tension of another string loosened off. 'He's a nice fella.'

'We're just friends.'

Dani placed mugs of tea on the table.

'Pass me the pencil, would you?'

'Sure.'

Harriette rubbed graphite into a groove before seating the new string and as they drank tea, she methodically replaced all the other strings and listened to Dani talk about Dev and how they had met at school.

'I'd better make tracks, Gran.'

Harriette walked Dani to the door.

'If it makes you feel any better, I hate them too.'

'Sorry?'

'Fireworks. They spook the deer and me, to be honest.'

They hugged. Dani thought: *I don't want to go.* 'See you tomorrow then' – a kiss on the cheek – they both had jobs to be getting on with. Dani walked across to the other lodge; burning leaves peppering the air, orange skies marbled with grey, the estate blurred by a thickening mist.

After cleaning Hunter's Lodge, Dani lay on the bed thinking of the future, weighing up the possibilities. She'd made a good start; already three classes a week and there was demand for more. Dozing off, phantom explosions brought her round. She sat up, her shoulders and neck tensing, mist at the window so thick she could hardly see the other lodge. Blurred light from Harriette's kitchen illuminating piles of leaves hunkered outside the back doors as if drawn by her worldly gravity.

Dani showered and changed into gym clothes. First a boxercise class then a shift at the Nav. *Keep occupied, keep your mind distracted, it will all be over by midnight.*

*

The class was good. A real buzz in the room. She'd pushed them hard, hit them with Manchester music: *Happy Mondays, The Charlatans, Stone Roses, New Order.* Then the warm down. Stretches to slow music, then everyone lay on the floor very still. She counted twenty-seven bodies. And for a terrifying moment her exhausted mind turned apocalyptic. *I've overdone it – I've killed them.*

Then out of the stillness came vital signs. Breathing, fidgeting limbs, twitching fingers. And beyond the bodies, the back wall. Its wallpapered surface almost alive, branches and leaves and the animals amongst them multilayered, like a hologram. Its beauty on a level with Monet's *Lilies* or Van Gough's *Wheatfields*, she thought.

Music stopped and the bodies awoke but the group didn't linger. Most were headed for the firework display and soon Dani was alone, hoovering fluff and restacking mats. The wallpaper on the back wall glowing in the fading light. More mural than repeated pattern, she thought. The only obvious recurrence a horizontal line of stag skulls subtly formed by entwinements of flora, everything dark and full of demons. Foreboding, like a warning that said stay away.

She took one last glance, then flipped the light switch and left the building.

Exhumed

Locking the back door, she descended steps that led onto the quay. Pausing for a moment beside the canal, she watched cars on the road bridge and remembered passing over it as a child, and how its hollow thrum triggered excitement because it meant they were nearly at Harriette's. She'd not paid much attention to the canal back then, its slice through town so underplayed. But now it intrigued her. Whether her father was guilty of murder or not had been, it seemed, assigned to the uncertain realms of decomposition. The strip of water a master of concealment, dissolving the layers of time into a sludge not even the police could unpick.

Her mind turned to the gun she'd so hastily stowed behind the portrait. The place so obvious, so discoverable. The murky water just beyond her feet a much better place, she thought.

A firework screeched into the air. Pulling on headphones her immediate response. She pressed play and soon enough classical music shielded her ears. Streetlights on the bridge flickering on as she climbed steps up to the road, rotten odours of the canal falling away, last moments of daylight clinging to the horizon.

Town too quiet. The calm before the storm. No teenagers larking outside the chippy. The abandoned hatchback the only car parked in the pay and display. Last-minute customers in the ironmongers queuing between push fit plumbing and pungent pet treats, clutching boxes of low explosives.

She cut diagonally across the town square flinching halfway as if dodging a bullet. A screech from nowhere creeping into the headphones. Cursing, she ramped up the volume, the remaining journey passing through a tunnel of orchestral music that led her back to Harriette's lodge. And beyond the front door, a calm smell of baking greeted her in and said welcome, take off your coat, *everything will be fine.*

The kitchen a scene of serenity: Florentine biscuits on a

wire rack, Harriette asleep in an easy chair by the window.

She stirred to the sounds of Dani making a pot of tea; tired from raking leaves, Harriette had fallen asleep whilst reading a novel. They chatted as Harriette transferred biscuits to a plate.

Dani knew why she'd made them. Florentines were her brother's favourite.

'I make them every year,' Harriette said in a shaky voice as she held out the plate. One side coated in wavy chocolate; the other side bejewelled with glace cherries.

Dani couldn't face them, but how could she refuse?

She swilled one down with a mug of tea. Their subsequent conversation meek and hesitant. The subject of her brother's death like an iced lake over which neither wanted to venture too far. Another biscuit, another mug of tea and then chat settled on the future: Christmas together, the spring, the summer. Oh, next year, what a year it was going to be.

Dani noticed the time. 'Got to go, Gran. Shift starts soon.'

They hugged, Harriette's hands performing a little squeeze. From the door Dani briefly checked the scene, her grandmother sat in the easy chair, book in hand, commemorative ritual complete, respects to her grandson dutifully paid.

*

Dani changed her clothes then set off for work, volume of the Walkman on its highest setting, sounds of Vivaldi's

Winter pulsing through the headphones. Everything fine along the lane until the batteries in the music player began to fade. The headphones falling silent as she drew level with the statue of Sidney Wallis.

Noises seeped in. The music giving way to the sounds of people passing her by. The town's excitement undercut by warlike booms. The fronds of sky glitter drifting over Main Street like a phoney sunrise. Distant lights of the Navigation Inn mere stains in a man-made fog. She walked faster, tacking through people, her nerves flinching at the flares and flashes and the thin speaker announcements that wafted down from the rugby club. Memories spooling as paving slabs passed below her feet. She lunged into the pub and crossed the lounge area and sat on a stool behind the bar.

Every year… it gets worse… calm down… count to four.

She made herself take a few minutes before doing anything else. She sat on a stool by the till and breathed deeply until feeling more capable of work; not long before the three men in the tap room would need a refill by the look of their empty glasses.

The lounge devoid of people. Just the speakers piping music into the room and millworkers in old photographs behind the pool table glowering over the baize like a disapproving audience.

The pub quiet; just what she'd hoped for.

'Hello, love…'

She flinched and turned to see her boss, Geoff, appear from behind the cellar door.

'…thanks for coming in.'

'No problem. Where's Kathy?'

'Took the twins to the rugby club.'

She forced a smile.

'Bet they're excited?'

'That's putting it mildly. Can you hold the fort? Need to clean out a few more lines.'

'No problem – doubt I'll get overrun tonight. Surprised you've opened.'

'Kathy thought that, but we have to keep the diehards happy,' he said, nodding towards the group of men before disappearing behind the cellar door.

Time dragged.

Alexander O'Neal played through the speakers.

Dani thumbed a magazine; her reading of an article on Princess Diana interrupted by a coldly conveyed order. 'Two pints and a whisky; when you're ready, love,' one of the men called out from the bar area.

She poured the drinks and delivered them to the table, clinking away empties without eye contact. Her cast-iron indifference wiped away as she turned back to the bar, the sight of a man waiting on the lounge side of the servery stopping her dead.

His jawline, his jacket, his short-brimmed bucket hat.

My... brother?

The framed mill workers glowered across the room. A faint screech somewhere outside tore through the sky.

Every part of her body flushed with blood, the tray in her hands slowly tipping. A glass tumbling to the carpet sparking laughter from behind. 'Can't get the staff these days.'

Her skin prickled with irritation, but all she could do

was stand and stare at her brother's ghost, his eyes peering from under the brim as his head tilted up. The confusion resolving as his ghost rose from the barstool. Too tall. *Not my brother.* She grappled for a name...

Car... upholstery...

Her powers of recall hindered by the rude chorus that came from behind.

'I hear you're leaving us'; 'Not good enough for you, are we not?'; 'These beers taste like piss water'.

The name Steven Ruskin coming to her as his voice boomed across the pub, 'Shut it, Declan, before I come over and break your weird face.'

Within seconds Steven was through the lobby, standing over the other men, his figure posturing for a fight, her mind flashing back to home life above the pub.

But there seemed no escape as she veered away towards the bar, her steps freezing again as she caught sight of Geoff near the back entrance, his finger levelled in her direction, the man beside him dressed in police uniform; her evening spiralling into an ever-darker chasm.

The gun. *They know.*

She wheeled round, the room tilting, the others already gone, her chest thudding, her hand gripping the bar rail. *Run!*

But the policeman was already there beside her, the cold, smoky street radiating from his uniform, a look of worry all over Geoff's face.

'This is Dani.'

'I'm glad we've found you, Miss Hey.'

Heart pounding, she glared at them both.

'I'm afraid your gran has had some bad news. We didn't want to leave her alone. Mr Wallis said you were the closest relative.'

His voice nonsensical, just a stream of foggy words, she glared at Geoff.

'Yes, yes, go, that's fine. I can cover. Kathy will be back soon.'

She grabbed her coat and followed the officer out of the pub. *He's out of shape - I could outrun him.*

'It is open.'

She stood beside the car staring at the inactive strip lights fixed to the roof. *It's the most low-key arrest in history.*

'Miss Hey?'

'Mm?'

'I said it's open – we'd better get to your gran's – are you okay?'

'Yes, of course – sorry, I'm fine.'

The car interior smelt like a Happy Meal. They pulled away, trees of Main Street filing past. Then a voice on the radio reported an incident: Minor collision. M65. HGV off the carriageway.

'Going to have to drop and run, love. Need to take a look at that.'

The officer talked back to the radio. Main Street blurred by. Trails of silent rockets rose to the west, frittering up as if traced by the sweep of a starved ballpoint pen. And then out of nowhere super nova explosions expanded over the Dardale estate.

'Don't look so worried, your gran's safe.'

'What's happened?'

'It's to do with the remains.'

'What remains?' Her head ached.

'The remains we found in the canal – your gran's not mentioned that?'

'Mentioned what? Look, just tell me what's going on!'

He gave Dani a quick glance then looked back at the road.

'Alright, love, no problem, thought you might know. You are Dani Hey, aren't you?'

Lights on the dashboard swam in her vision, a rush of guilt strangling her airways. She took a deep breath.

'Yes, I'm – sorry, bad night at work.'

'Tell me about it.' He glanced at her again as they pulled into the lane. 'Just trying to do what's best for your gran.'

'Yes, of course, I'm sorry.'

The officer's eyes returned to the challenges of the lane, his hands tussling with the snatchy wheel, the car lurching and pitching.

'Look, I shouldn't be the one filling you in.'

'I'd appreciate it if you did. It's just – my gran – she's a bit old school. You know, stiff upper lip.'

Glancing at the rear-view mirror his face softened. 'The forensic boffins, they've been trying to identify the person found in the canal. Your gran gave a DNA sample. Well, it seems the remains are that of your gran's mother, Ellen Parry.'

'My… great-gran.'

'Appears so.'

The car pulled up beside the lodges, grassy details in headlights vanishing as the engine died. Their short walk to the door, illuminated by a concluding volley of fireworks exploding nearby, the night sky above them filling with brilliant plumes of colourful light.

*

Harriette came to the door and thanked the policeman. He smiled then left, their faces glowing red in tail lights that rolled about the lane until the squad car disappeared.

In the hallway Dani hugged Harriette tightly.

'Why didn't you tell me?'

'I didn't want to bother you; didn't think for one minute it would come to this.'

'Oh, Gran.'

'Seemed like a wild goose chase at the time. They asked me a lot of daft questions I didn't really have answers to.'

'How sure are they?'

'Ninety-five per cent.'

She saw the stress in Harriette's face.

'Have you eaten?'

'Not a jot.'

'Let me make you some pasta. Glass of wine?'

Harriette nodded. 'Yes, please – there's a bottle already open.'

Dani gathered ingredients then began to cook. Her gran sat on a barstool beside the worktop, gazing into a glass of wine. The hob came to life: pancetta spitting in a pan, pasta rolling in hot water, parmesan grated, eggs beaten, tension in Dani's shoulders loosening as she swigged back a second glass of wine. Bringing everything together she sensed a quizzical look.

Dani froze. 'I've missed something?'

'Looks good to me.' Harriette sipped wine then placed the glass down, all the time her eyes fixed on her granddaughter. 'Thought it was me who was supposed to be in shock. Looks like you've seen a ghost.'

They sat at the table and Dani tonged spaghetti into bowls.

'Difficult night at the pub.'

'Oh, love – sorry about all this. I asked the police not to bother you – told them I was fine. It really isn't a big deal.'

'It's fine, Gran – To be honest, I'm glad to be back early.'

Harriette praised the carbonara then spoke of the big storm that was due at the weekend. Her chatter then pitching into trivial matters she looked a little shocked when Dani interrupted.

'I'm sorry for being so direct, but what's happening is a big deal… as in, I think you're putting a brave face on it. You know, doing your stiff upper lip thing.'

Harriette simultaneously puckered her mouth and twizzled a finger inside her right ear. Dani sighed.

'Can we talk – about your mum?'

Silence.

'Gran?'

Harriette looked up; her brow furrowed. 'If we must.'

'We must.'

She took a deep breath and sat back. 'There's no criminal case to pursue; not that I was expecting one.'

Dani got up, fetched the bottle from the worktop and topped up Harriette's glass.

'Thank you, dear. Rennie refuses to pay extra for the Chianti Riserva, but it's so much better.'

'You're straying again.'

'Sorry.'

Another sip. A sigh. 'The forensic pathologist – lovely man – said the silt had preserved my mother's skeleton.'

'Did they say anything about how she got there?'

'Not really. He said the skull was damaged, but no real chance of identifying cause of death. Forensics degrade as the years go by, apparently.'

They wound spaghetti around forks.

'The other man, the inspector, now he was a grim chap. Bit insensitive – suppose that line of work sends you that way.'

They ate through a brief silence.

'Apparently, they triangulate the evidence. My DNA, carbon dating. Quite clever, really. The inspector suggested my mother accidentally fell in and drowned; said they pull bodies from canals in Manchester all the time. Mostly misadventure after alcohol – Cheers.' She slugged back a mouthful of wine.

'You said triangulate.'

'Parish records. The only missing person registered in 1916 was a Mrs E. Parry. Ironic really, probably hundreds of local men missing at the time.'

Dani poured the last drops of wine into her glass. 'Actually, I did see a ghost tonight.'

'Really – well, this place is full of them.'

'That Steven Ruskin, there's something about him, reminds me of dad… and, well, he looks exactly like…'

299

– the single syllable lodged in her throat like a stone – '…
Matt.'

Harriette surveyed Dani for a moment, then looked
away.

'Oh, that rat, he's Sheila's son. Surely, you've heard that
rumour by now.'

'You know him?'

'Your father owned a couple of houses on Dean Street
– leased them out.'

'Didn't know that.'

'Well, let's just say, when rent wasn't forthcoming,
he used to take alternative methods of payment – that's
the rumour, anyway. Who knows, it could have been the
milkman. She was a bit of a slapper.'

'Gran! Oh my god, Gran – So, you're saying – he's my
relative?'

'I wouldn't worry. They do say we're all more closely
related to one another than we think.'

Then Harriette's face turned glum and explained that
according to the laws of exhumation her mother would
have to be reburied within a couple of days. Opening
another bottle, they drank more wine.

The alcohol loosening Harriette up, her painful
memories disentombed like the bones of her mother.
Stories about the town and Dani's father flowing. Then…

'I'm so proud of you for getting out of Moss Side and
making your own future.'

'I love you so much, Gran.'

They hugged clumsily, Harriette finally agreeing that it
was time to go to bed. 'Goodnight, dear.'

Dani walked between the lodges, and for a moment she lingered in the workshop and stared at the portrait of Sidney Wallis, berating herself for not finding a better place to hide the gun. Pulling the gilt frame away from the wall her fingers searched for cold metal.

Still there.

Then stepping back, she focused on the paper strip pasted over the bottom of the portrait and read out the words printed just below its torn edge.

'Report suspicious things and persons. At once.'

She cursed, rolled her eyes, and then turned and made for the stairs vowing that she would throw the gun in the canal as soon as an opportunity arose. *Let the redundant canal work its magic.*

Funeral #2

Dani paced about the music room wracking her brain for consoling words then dismissing everything as incongruous. *My gran's burying her estranged mother. It's bizarre. What am I supposed to say?*

At the French doors her eye followed footprints across the frosted lawn until they disappeared into the fog. Then there was movement: colours of an Etro headscarf filtering through bare branches. Then Harriette appeared from behind the hedgerow, walking the path that ran beside the crumbling wall, her mac flared at the waist, swaying above the stride of dark tights and patent leather loafers, her gloved hand caressing frosted fennel heads.

She sat on the wooden bench, her figure dwarfed by big winter oaks that reached through the fog and over the wall. It was the first time that morning she'd seen Harriette settle. Dani followed her gran's footprints to the bench. They sat in silence, Harriette seemingly entranced by the winter decay.

Dani looked back at the lodge, its lichen-covered chimneys closed in by the fog. Leafless strands of creeper forked over its walls like arteries. The exposed render a little crazed, woodwork around windows fissured. And Dani felt uncomfortable then: her youth conspicuous amongst the patina of time, new blood from the iffy side of the family, flaky and insubstantial.

Then she worried if the ongoing silence was Harriette's way of saying that she wished to be left alone.

And where was Rennie? Surely, he should be the one consoling Harriette.

A single leaf lazily flickered to the ground.

'Oak is the last to fall, you know.'

Dani shuffled closer and placed an arm around Harriette's shoulders.

'You okay, Gran?'

Harriette rubbed Dani's hand. 'Bit confused, that's all... suppose it's all sinking in.' Clouds of vapour followed her words into the chilled air. She turned, her eyes searching Dani's face.

'I used to go to church on Sundays – prayed my mother would come back. Stopped going after my fiftieth... assumed she'd passed away by then... Had this stupid fantasy that maybe one of her offspring might travel back and visit me. Feel a bit foolish now.' Her gaze returned to the garden.

'The vicar has written a short eulogy. His father knew Ellen. Shame nobody else will be at the church to hear it.'

'Isn't Rennie walking to the church with us?'

Harriette ignored the question, her leather gloves brushing her lap, her lips puckering.

'I've had a good life here – will be forever indebted to the Wallises for taking me in.'

She turned to Dani.

'I can't trust him now, though.'

'Trust who, Gran?'

Harriette's eyes tracked a slow circle around Dani's face.

'Can I tell you about it after the service? Rennie will be there… please don't say anything.'

'For sure.' Dani nodded. 'Why don't we go in and get warm? I'll make you a cup of tea. We're not due at the church for another hour.'

Harriette stayed motionless, her face blank.

'Or I can just wait inside – if you prefer.'

Harriette's face softened then, to a gentle smile. 'Thank you, dear, but I think it's time I came in from the cold.'

*

They sat in the kitchen sipping steaming mugs of tea. The room cold and still, even the radio that normally jabbered in the background had nothing to say. Sounds of winter outside muffled by the fog. Harriette gazed through the window, her eyes lost in the murk. 'Your father never told me about Matt's death.'

Dani's shoulders tensed; she'd managed to keep him out of her head all morning. 'I didn't know that.'

'Your mum wrote to me a month later. That's why I didn't come to your brother's funeral. Always felt bad about that.'

Dani surveyed her grandmother's forlorn face.

'Believe me, it wasn't a good day. I mean, I know it's not meant to be a happy occasion, but it was so… dominated by Father.'

'Why doesn't that surprise me?'

'Anyway, he wasn't the same boy you knew – just went the same way as Dad.'

'Feared as much. I feel partly responsible, I was so absent. Wish I could have seen more of you; maybe I could have prevented it.'

Dani broke eye contact, her gaze loitering in fog beyond the windows.

'Police reckoned it was a rival gang, a revenge killing. They didn't catch them.'

Liar – you don't deserve her.

Harriette shook her head as if in pain. 'Oh God. Must have been difficult growing up in your father's shadow. Your brother was such a lovely easy-going boy.'

Dani pictured him months before his death, all pumped up and full of shit, remembered how easily she could dominate him in a fight, *he was so useless in a scrap.*

'I was afraid you would go the same way, but you didn't.'

'To be honest, Gran, I've not been a saint myself.'

Harriette took Dani's hands and pushed up the sleeves of her jumper.

'Sweetheart, this is the pattern you chose.' She weighed Dani's forearms. 'Never really been one for tattoos, but I like yours.'

'The pattern stayed with me. I had no problem describing it to the tattoo artist.'

'I'm so proud of you for getting yourself out of there, you know, running away. I think it was a very brave thing to do.'

Dani pushed her sleeves down and kissed Harriette on the forehead.

'I reckon it's time to go, Gran.'

As they reached the bottom of the lane the fog thinned, and the church came into view. Dani took her grandmother's hand and they walked into the square side by side.

*

Harriette's arm looped through Dani's and pulled it tight as they entered the church. Incense hung in the stony air; the aisles lit by candles. Rennie sat on the front pew facing forward. The vicar waited at the end of the nave; a small wooden casket made of old printing blocks behind him. They levelled with Rennie and sat. The vicar acknowledged the exceptional circumstances of Ellen's discovery.

'Today we shall commit her body to its resting place and pray that she may now rest undisturbed.'

A simple service unfolded in which the vicar delivered

a eulogy describing Ellen's role in the mill during the war years. Then soothing classical music played as the casket was lifted and carried away by two undertakers. Everyone followed. Emerging from the church, they walked single file between the headstones of a graveyard surrounded by arthritic trees, a low blotch of hazy sun glowing through the branches. Ahead, an opening in the ground between two raised tombs, blocks of stone shrouded by branches of a yew tree. They stood beside gaping turf, cut ends of roots within the dark earth. The wooden box lowered; rites conveyed. The vicar's steady tone seamlessly moved into prayer. Then for a while just crows spoiling the silence as the group doubled back through the graveyard.

They talked briefly in the square by the church porch, Rennie adding very little, his countenance reduced to that of a child. And after a round of shaking hands and expressions of gratitude, he followed the vicar into the church.

Dani wiped her eyes and nose with a sleeve.

Harriette hugged her tightly. 'I know, it's sad...' then pulled back and smiled, '...we seem to have run out of mothers.'

'I wish I'd come here sooner. You know, to be with you.'

'Well, thankfully, dear, it's not my funeral – we've got plenty of time. Let's go home.'

*

They entered the lodge and pulled off coats and shoes. 'Is Rennie not joining us?' said Dani.

Harriette walked away, her voice disappearing into the kitchen. 'I'll put the heating on.'

They made tea, cut slices of cake and carried everything into the living room, Harriette soon kneeling beside the fireplace, setting light to a mound of paper and kindling. Dani sat knees to chest in an armchair and gazed at her grandmother's hands as they charmed away wisps of smoke. The fire began to draw, bricks around the fireplace glimmering in the dimness. Crackles. Pops. A shoal of sparks swam up the flue.

'Have you fallen out or something?'

Harriette looked up, her face timid, glowing in the flames. Stiffly rising she brushed off her skirt. 'We're not talking.'

'Mind me asking why? It's just – something's been bothering me.'

Harriette slumped into the other armchair, her crossed arms defending the silence.

Dani picked up the teapot, swilled it in small circles as she made her way to the bay window, views of the hedgerow on the lane just a black band below amber skies. Then a voice from behind.

'No. I don't mind.' Harriette was up again placing a log on the fire.

'The family story about your mum running away?'

'Oh, that.'

Dani continued swilling the pot. 'She was found here, in town, so it can't be true. And earlier in the garden, you said you couldn't trust Rennie. You were going to tell me about it.'

'We had words – last week.'

Harriette fell quiet again. Dani placed the pot on a side table then perched on an armrest. 'Gran. Will you please tell me what's going on?'

Harriette hugged a cushion. 'We've had an almighty fall out.'

'Sorry to hear that. I'm sure it will all blow over.'

'I'm not so sure.'

'That bad?'

'It got nasty, horrible things said. Good friends all these years, but now it seems – he's not been straight with me.'

'Oh, really. How?'

Harriette blew on her tea, looked at her granddaughter, her will slowly ebbing away. She placed the cup down. 'The forensics chap…' – leaning back she gazed into the fire – '…said my mother died somewhere between 1915 and 1920. So, turns out Rennie's story about seeing her in 1945 was a lie.'

'But surely, he wouldn't make that up?'

'He's admitted he did – bloody liar.'

'Why?'

'Didn't want to be left on his own. I get it. He had to take all the flack after the war. The Wallises were resented by pretty much everyone when the company collapsed. But he didn't have to do that. He didn't have to lie to me.'

'Dad used to talk about the Wallises like they were traitors.'

Harriette rolled her eyes. 'Oh, he's going back to the First World War. Sidney did most of his business in Germany, had aristocratic connections, members of Prussian royalty, and of course a German wife. A teutophile, by all accounts.'

'And then the war started?'

'Mm. History really wasn't on their side. Press stirred up anti-German sentiment. All claptrap, of course, but it made the authorities paranoid. Sidney Wallis suspected of this, that and the other. Very odd times – even the King of England changed his German name to Windsor.'

Harriette plumped a cushion, then settled back with the cup of tea, glancing at her granddaughter between sips, gauging whether she'd done enough.

'There's more, isn't there?'

Harriette stopped mid-sip then placed the cup down. 'You don't give up, do you?'

'I'm my grandmother's granddaughter – you used to tell me not to bottle things up.'

A wry smile. Then Harriette cleared her throat, 'My father…' then rolled her eyes, '…he was the final nail in the Wallises' coffin.'

'The Australian?' Dani sat perched on the edge of an armchair.

'Joe Stander. Never met him, of course; apparently not many people did. He was an outsider. My mother fell for him. I was conceived. He was accused of being some sort of infiltrator, you know, gathering intelligence for the other side?'

'A spy? Dad never said anything about that – he was always light on the details, mind.'

'As were the powers to be at the time. Rennie said

my father had nothing to do with the Wallises, but the authorities couldn't resist putting two and two together. Virtually destroyed what was left of their reputation. And I was left an orphan, daughter of a spy, nobody wanting to touch me with a barge pole. That's when the Wallises took me in and sheltered me from it all. Which was fine. But then Sidney died. And of course, Rennie inherited the estate, the failing business and all the backlash that went with it. He just couldn't cope.'

'Makes me feel sorry for him.'

'Well, don't.'

Dani got up, went to the bay window, views of the lane lost to darkness, Harriette reflected in the glass that faceted around her.

'He clung to me; was terrified I would leave him. So, when I came off tour, he told me he'd seen Ellen, in the hope that I would stay here and wait for her to return… and I did.'

'Christ, Gran, that was so bloody weak of him.'

'I was so mad – oh God, I really didn't hold back, I gave him both barrels.'

'Not what you need on the day of your mother's funeral. Are you alright, Gran?' Dani leaned in and held her.

'Think so, dear. It's just – staying in town all this time I've now got this awful claustrophobia, got this overwhelming urge to get away, for a while, anyway.'

'And you should. Thought my life was dramatic.'

'Well, drama does seem to run in the family.'

'Which leads me on to Dad. I suppose he got caught up in all of this.'

'You're right, he did, but I'll have to tell you that story

another time, after a stiff drink maybe.'

'Of course – it's been a long day.'

Harriette jabbed the fire with a poker, whiffs of peppery smoke seasoning the room. Dani felt hot and lightheaded. 'I need cake.'

'Me too.'

The fire took hold; bigger logs burning steadily.

'Getting away for a while will do you good, Gran; I can keep an eye on things here.'

'Well, actually, I have been planning a trip over new year. Just me and an old friend from the Hallé. We've booked flights to Venice, arrive New Year's Eve.'

'Ooh, running away to Venice. Very romantic.'

Harriette laughed. 'Nothing like that... more revisiting my ancestral home.'

Dani chewed cake, for a moment her face blank. 'Yes, of course. Your cello was made there, by... gorilla?'

'Goffriller...' Harriette laughed. 'Matteo Goffriller.'

'Yes, yes, of course.' They both laughed.

Then Harriette explained that his workshop had been in the Cannaregio district of the city. She'd always wanted to visit; saw it as a pilgrimage to the birthplace of her surrogate parents.

'Time for a negroni, I think?' Harriette's tone upbeat as she left the room.

'Sorry?'

'It's an Italian cocktail,' she called back from the kitchen.

Sounds drifted through the hallway: cabinet doors clapping shut, the clink of glasses.

The fire glowed.

*

Dani woke the next morning with an aching head and dry mouth. Rolling over she buried herself in the duvet, wind whipping the lodge, overhanging branches scratching the rooftiles.

She'd lost count after the second "nightcap", the rest of the evening a bit of a blur. Harriette so excited about the new rail link to Manchester Airport, the new terminal, the bigger choice of destinations soon to be on offer. Dani had sensed a certain deep-seated regret in her grandmother, some pressing need to go on tour again. And they talked at length about taking weekend trips together, planning adventures well into the early hours: Vienna in spring, Helsinki in summer. Rome in the autumn; a visit to *Antico Caffè della Pace* imperative! They served the best negronis ever. *'Fancy another?'*

Dani dragged herself out of bed, threw on some layers and peered between the curtains. Conditions not too blowy; still no sign of the big storm due to hit that afternoon. Better to go sooner rather than later. Hangover aside, she had jobs to do, errands to run, writing off the day not an option. First the electrical shop. The music player she used for classes only working if a hairgrip held in the play button.

Downstairs she pulled on a coat and a big woolly hat. And within minutes she was on Main Street standing before the shop window, the JVC model she'd previously eyed no longer on display. She went in and asked if they had any more at the reduced price.

'Sold out – sorry, last one went yesterday.'

She lingered in the shop looking at the other players. And then the televisions caught her eye. All tuned to the same channel. Multiple mug shots of her father, a whole wall of his cold eyes glaring into the shop. She retched a dry heave as the televisions simultaneously switched back to the newsreader – moving lips; no sound – a ribbon of words spooling across the screens.

...Hey's appeal case... police found guilty of gross misconduct... falsified evidence unearthed by defendant's legal team.

She ran for the door and threw up in the gutter, the grey sky boiling overhead. Then she hurried back to the lodges, rain slicing down like ice-cold daggers.

DARDALE

1915

VI

Canary – *Serinus canaria domestica*

Study for Wallis and Hilton Wallpapers. Plate No. 106 – Caged Canaries [see sketch on next page]

Facts: Each breath of a canary can take in double that of a human. Hence, their use in coal mines to warn of poisonous gas.

Quaint belief: The Greek and Roman societies believed that the canary was able to see ghosts and spirits of ancestors and people who were too preoccupied in the materialistic world could not hear the song of this bird.

llen wished she'd stayed at Cedric's when she saw people queuing outside the grocers. Dorothy Holt at the front, wife of the postmaster, knew everyone's business before they knew it themselves. Joining the line, Ellen glanced at the rabbits in the window, skinny fur dangling over five eggs and a box of tea leaves, Mrs Holt blethering on to Mrs Martlow, all puffed up and full of her own importance. 'Vicar needs new cleaner,' said Martlow as she sat on a tea chest rubbing an unshod foot. 'Don't look at me – feet think tha's marched to Wigan and back.'

'Bad knees.'

'What tha say?'

'Fossdyke's knees couldn't tek it. Twenty-three years she washed them floors.'

'Clean tha Lord's house and that's what tha gets.' Martlow shook her head spiritedly.

'Very sad what happened to her Freddie – died instantly they say.'

The awning billowed up, its trim shimmying. The wind's muscle having no effect on rabbits in the window or the fly that danced between their glassy eyes.

'Did tha know Frau Wallis's brothers were fighting with Germans?'

Holt shook her head with surety. 'Probably shot Freddie at Marne.'

Ellen couldn't hold back any longer. 'Ypres, actually.'

They glanced down the queue, their faces stunned. 'Beggin' your pardon.' Martlow reshoed and got to her feet.

'Always a good idea to check your facts. Freddie died in Ypres not Marne.'

Ellen nodded at the inverted rabbits, their stubby front legs reaching down as if straining to grasp the last jar of honey.

'They look all sad strung up in there, Mrs Holt. Maybe you should try one in a stew, although you're not too short on rabbit it seems.'

With lips pursed and long blinks, Martlow and Holt disappeared into the shop, the queue behind Ellen talking in hushed voices, the lady next to her glaring at a shopping list. Not the first time townsfolk acted strangely in her presence.

Because she visited the Wallises?

That was Cedric's view on the matter. He reckoned guards at the estate were now there to protect them rather than prevent their escape. Ellen hated how town had rounded on Sidney. It stank. Her aunty had got that right: *Bread eaten soon forgotten, that's all I can say.*

Martlow emerged from the shop, synthetic flowers in her hat bending in the wind. Holt came out and shot Ellen a sly smile then disappeared into town.

In the shop Ellen bought onions, potatoes and duck eggs. Halfpennies and farthings changing hands, conversation at the counter sparse. Her way home a gauntlet of turned heads and averted eyes, a stare from the telegram boy the only shared glance.

Opening the gate, she sauntered up the path.

'And what are *you* looking at?' she muttered at the owl as she unlocked the door. And then after hanging her coat, she noticed an envelope against the skirting board, mauled by the door swing, its crumpled edge torn.

At the bureau she sliced a blade through the top of it and pulled out a telegram, the words seeming to move on the page. Eyes screwed shut, she placed a steadying hand on the bureau. Heart galloping over timorous breaths, she counted twenty tocks of the mantel clock before her eyes revisited the piece of paper and read the words below her father's regiment.

Missing believed injured.

The falling telegram reeled in her wake as she hurried

to the closet and vomited in the toilet. Staying down on the floor, her mind scrambled for memories of her father, his routines around the house, around town, at work. Always where you'd expect him to be. His habits repetitive like patterns on wallpaper.

Hearing voices in the street she hauled herself up and climbed the stairs and from a front window she saw a man in uniform standing at the door of the opposite house. Rifle slung over a shoulder. Khaki caked in mud. Then the Baggaleys embraced him, and she realised it was their Albert. Neighbours emerged: Mr Horton calling from a sash window, one of the Gumley sisters from a doorstep. Albert raised a tired arm and waved back to them.

Ellen edged away from the bay window and looked about the tidy room, everything in its place, nothing missing. Opening the wardrobe, she ran fingers over his shirts and jacket. The smells definite and of her father: shaving soap, tobacco, mothballs. Her daddy's cap hanging inside the door, his pipes on the dresser. His things patiently waiting; how could he not come back?

Lions, mosquitos, native tribes – survived them all. He'll be fine, you'll see.

She returned to the bay window, but the street was now deserted, October chills making inroads on three sides of her trembling body.

Downstairs she lugged coal from the cellar, cleaned the grate, lit the fire and after supper she placed cushions on the floor and lay upon them with blankets, losing herself in orange caves of the fire, ghosts of her family moving about the room. And placing a hand on her belly she searched for what might be forming inside. But there was no bump as yet, and no internal murmurs – just a curious sensation that she was not alone.

*

Waking early Ellen went to the toilet but there was no sign of her period. Other women at the factory had also missed theirs, but not three in a row. And she still felt grim, her breasts sore, her head gripped by the mother of all headaches.

Working it off she threw herself into chores. The act of scrubbing and polishing exorcising bottled-up irritations: *Father didn't have to join up – so why did he? ...I expect rain is spoiling Cedric's seaside jolly... Why had Joe left for Leeds without mentioning any word of i?. Why can't I hold on to the men in my life?*

Coal dust banished from every surface, clothes washed, floors scrubbed. Enough for one day. She collapsed on the settee. Smell of Sunlight Soap on her front. The cast-iron range clicking as it cooled, the Gumleys next door muffling through the wall.

The ambience of her body different, like it wasn't hers. She sat very still, hand on her belly, the unthinkable creeping in. Panic scrambling through her chest. How long could she keep it a secret? Would she know what to do?

The house offering no clues, the sense of isolation overwhelming but who else could she turn to. Her aunty was so besieged by two young children and baby of her own.

She gazed at the patterns on the opposite wall, a haunting chiaroscuro of dark teal and jasmine. A gift courtesy of the Wallis and Hilton company. End of a run or an imperfect second, one or the other, she couldn't remember. Her focus lost in the flowery print, she began to envy the Wallises' incarceration. A blissful lockdown isolated from judgements, isolated from the war. And she imagined what it must be like living there with all those spare bedrooms that looked out on the splendorous estate. Her mind then full of dreamy ideas she washed and changed into best clothes and polished her shoes. Pulling on her coat she left the house, her route cutting straight through town, her gleaming shoes avoiding mud on the lane and deer droppings on the estate road. And before long she sat in the grand dining room of Dardale Hall, discussing this and that but mainly the welfare of workers, the thorny subject of war avoided.

But then Sidney asked after her father and Ellen couldn't hold back the tears.

'Missing?'

'I received a telegram yesterday.'

Sidney sprang up and stood by a tall window, his blushing face turned towards the gardens. Rubbing the back of his neck he spoke to the glass. 'Is there anything we can do?'

Searching for an answer she looked about the room but could only think of Sidney's own twisted predicament: the mill prised away from him only to be used for the manufacture of shells destined to be fired at his wife's fellow countrymen. Swallowing hard she wiped away tears and composed herself.

'I don't blame Mrs Wallis for what's happening.'

He slowly turned. 'I get the feeling most people do.'

'I'm beginning to realise most people aren't driven by what matters.'

A tiny smile liberated his face from strain.

'You remind me of your mother when you say such things.'

Sidney often spoke kindly of her mother: good teacher, principled woman, sorely missed. Ellen felt proud then and her awkwardness faded away.

'May I ask how your wife is, Mr Wallis?'

Sidney turned to the window, his breath condensing on cold glass.

'It will all blow over – is what I keep saying to Elizabeth. But there seems no end. Thank goodness we have Rennie. Otherwise, I fear, our sanity would be in tatters.'

Ellen felt a sudden urge to reveal her own news then and searched for the right words, but before they came a door opened and Elizabeth appeared holding a baby. Sidney turned.

'Ahhh, look – Rennie come to say night, night?'

Elizabeth handed the baby to Sidney, and they all cooed at its bewildered face. Then Ellen took a turn and the baby gazed up at her, its little mouth breaking into a gummy smile. They all laughed, and Sidney placed a hand on Ellen's shoulder. 'We know where to come if we need a nanny.'

The baby was handed back and Elizabeth kissed her husband on the cheek and for a while they spoke in German, the baby jigging in her arms. Ellen stroked her stomach and looked around at the large glass cabinets and freestanding vases that graced the perimeter walls. Huge paintings above them of mountains and lakes, solemn and peopleless and washed by golden shafts of light.

'*Auf wiedersehen.*' Elizabeth smiled at Ellen and then left the room.

Sidney and Ellen returned to the table and Collins, the live-in butler, delivered food to the table: haunch of venison, vegetables from the estate, hints of juniper in the gravy. And while eating they spoke of the town and how people were coping.

'Fear of losing loved ones, creates this...' – Sidney searched for words, the loaded fork in his hand held at bay – '...inward-looking stasis. When hanging in such terrible limbo it's natural we find convenient scapegoats -- it will pass in good time, you'll see.'

Main course finished plates were cleared and then Collins returned with cheese, port and brandy.

'I appreciate your visits, although I fear we're putting you in an awkward spot. You must stop coming if it makes life difficult. Thank you, Collins.'

'May I?' Ellen said, reaching for a grape.

'Of course.'

'I can look after myself so please don't worry on my behalf.'

A warm smiled broadened his face. 'Never doubted it, my dear.'

He poured brandy from the decanter. 'Doctor Roberts told me about Muriel. Breaks my heart that working at the mill made her poorly.'

'We're all very sad about it.' Lowering her head she talked to the table. 'Although the situation has improved for the rest of us since losing her.'

'How so?'

She took a small sip of port and swallowed its thick sweetness.

'The colonel had banned us from wearing trousers, but a man from the ministry came and recommended that wearing them with puttees would offer better protection than skirts. So, now we wear trousers.'

'Why on earth did he ban them?'

'Thought them unladylike.'

Sidney laughed mockingly. 'I'm sure the ladies aren't bothered if it stops them from getting sick.'

'Indeed.'

He stood and moved to his spot by the window and swirled brandy in tight circles. 'But, Ellen – I hear from the doctor that women are still falling sick?'

'Protective gloves have been ordered but as Mr Yates thinks the war will soon be over, he hasn't bothered following it up.'

He downed the drink in one then tabled the glass.

Offering out her yellowed hands he took them in his and turned them over, skin of her palms dry and buttery.

'As you can see, handling the TNT doesn't agree with us. Apparently, we're called Canary Girls.'

'Well, something must be done before we lose another soul.'

He poured more brandy. His face flushed and ruddy.

'Mr Yates won't listen.'

'You must go to the colonel.'

'I would, but the block room door is locked and nobody on the office side answers.'

Returning to the window Sidney scowled at the formal gardens. 'Then you must be more strident. You must strike.'

'Walkouts are illegal because of the war. Cedric said we'd be arrested.'

Sidney chewed a thumbnail then slumped in his chair and waved away his irritations. 'Oh, Cedric's a good egg, but he's never been one for rocking the boat. There must be some way to get your voice heard. Some way to protest.'

Sidney pitched forward, head between hands, elbows on the table. 'Why is the world fixated by such bloody-minded deadlocks?'

'I knock on the door every day, Mr Wallis.'

'Well, keep knocking. Don't give up, you must find a way to get this protection.'

For a while there was silence. Sidney's head still down and clamped between his hands.

Ellen looked about the room before her eyes settled on tall windows and the distant troop of elms that silently waved in the wind. She turned back to Sidney.

'The women get together in the church hall on Sundays to put forward ideas for the magazine. Maybe together we can come up with something.'

Sidney glanced up. 'Power of the collective – very good, Ellen. I wish I could join you.'

His hands fell away, his body now free to sit back. 'Doctor Roberts is giving Rennie a once over tomorrow. I'll ask him to nudge the colonel about those gloves.'

'Thank you, Mr Wallis. Together we'll find a way.'

Another silence took hold and Sidney's eyes wandered the room until resting on the landscape of a German romanticist painting.

Ellen pondered robust forms of protest, thought of the Pankhursts and their militant pursuit of the Suffragette cause; storming of Parliament, Downing Street windows smashed, their mantra, "deeds not words" ringing through her head.

'Well, I must be getting back. Early shift tomorrow.'

'Yes, of course. Would you like Collins to drop you in town?'

'No, I'm fine. It's a decent afternoon. I like walking through the estate, easy to forget there's a war on surrounded by its splendour.'

He smiled. 'Just like your mother.'

They stood and she followed Sidney out of the dining room and down the grand staircase and when she was halfway across the driveway he called after her.

'Hope you receive good news about your father. Our thoughts are with you, my dear.'

She called back. 'Thank you, Mr Wallis.'

Her feet crumpled over the gravel for a while and again, he called out. 'We are always here for you.'

She was much further away then, his voice fainter, his figure dwarfed by the columns of the portico.

She waved again and then turned to the road ahead and faced into a freshening breeze.

DEV

Camouflage

I stood beside the canal gathering my thoughts. Still my favourite spot in town. Although, when there on my own, I stayed well away from the edge. It was early and dawn bled through poplar trees that lined the far bank. Their branches stripped by bad weather, twigs lay scattered around the quay. Covered by a blanket of leaves the canal looked walkable, a trick on the eye that faded as a convoy of ducks stroked towards me.

My new hearing aid enjoying the sound of seagulls blown in by the storm, the earpiece like a hi-fi upgrade that shed fresh light on well-worn tracks of the past. It was from Denmark, had digital circuits. Expensive. The audiologist advised that it was only a stepping-stone to the fully digital devices due in a year or so – *probably worth waiting*, he'd said, then – *you can have it for a trial period.*

I bought it.

Swishing trees, nature noises, the higher frequencies in my own and other people's voices. I got them all back.

Neater than my clunky analogue; technology far better. It suppressed background noise; my existence in busy places raised from bystander to participant. Serving customers in the shop I got to know them, the new device giving me fresh confidence, which was all great but since the kiss I had hardly seen Dani.

She'd been busy; I'd been busy. Of course, my doubts crept in. But thankfully Isla was there to curb my sulking, and she reminded me that Dani and her gran were going through difficult times. No doubt she was right. And in any case, I wasn't ready to throw in the towel.

The last time I saw her was when we met for coffee, after which we walked to the spot on the quay next to where her great-grandmother had been found. Then onwards, single file along the towpath, her words robbed by the wind, I'd said *pardon, sorry, what's that again?* way too many times. And then she just seemed offish, seemed obsessed with every nook and cranny of the canal, regularly stopping to peer into the water, as if searching for something. So, I'd assumed that was that. Although it didn't stop me from giving the dice one last roll. I asked, *can I take you out for the day?*

And to my surprise the answer was yes.

And that day was today.

I didn't tell her where to, said it was a surprise. I'd hatched this plan. Our journey, one that would take us back to more innocent times. A walk in the hills to the north where the views were awesome. It would be an hour's journey by car and I guessed getting away from everything would help. I knew a place to park from where we could strike out onto the fell, then drop into the next valley into the town where we'd both went to boarding school. The place where we'd first met.

I tossed the last of the crusts into the canal, seagulls wheeling above, swooping and squabbling with the other birds. I left them to it and drove to the lodges, the van lurching around the potholed lane. Pulling up beside the hedgerow I sounded the horn. Further along, a big tree had been blown over by the storm, its plate of roots perpendicular to the ground and beyond that a telegraph pole tilted over like a giant's fishing rod, the phone lines down and cast into furrows of the field.

Dani appeared from the lodge, skipping over the mud. Climbing in she leaned over and kissed me, her eyes smiling. She looked tired.

As we weaved along the lanes, the interior of the van became an echo chamber of rattles and bangs. Too much even for the new hearing aid. We glanced at one another, smiled awkwardly – she chewed a thumbnail. The smoother dual carriageway eventually coming to my rescue.

'Where are we going then?'

'It's a surprise – okay if you're back late?'

'Of course. Although not sure I can handle any more surprises.'

'Oh?'

'It's been quite a week. The police found...'

'Your great-gran. I heard.'

She frowned, looked perplexed. I pointed at the side of my head. 'New hearing aid. I overheard customers in the shop talking about it. It must have been a shock for your gran.'

Turning off the A road, we followed lanes which led to the hills beyond the Ribble Valley. She briefly explained what had happened and I heard most of what she said.

*

We left the van beside a shepherd's bothy. Dani posted a coin into the honesty box. Cutting through a farm, we found a footpath then straddled a stile. First, we walked through woodland then at the head of the valley trees thinned away, our chatter fading as we focused on the climb.

Towards the brow of the fell the track began to level, and we continued across a moorland plateau, long views abruptly cut short as cloud drifted in, our world reduced to the finer details of drenched grasses and stone walls. We stopped for a breather, and I put on a floppy hat, a sand-coloured boonie from my army days.

'Going on patrol?'

I explained hearing aids need protection from the rain. 'Hoods are no good because they act like a second ear.'

She looked at me blankly.

'They loop the loudspeaker back to the receiver. The feedback can be ear-splitting.'

'Oh.'

She set off.

I followed – the swish of our waterproofs, otherwise silence. Then I talked about my week in order to break the ice. But she remained aloof, used her beauty like a weapon;

enough to halt an invading army. And she spotted my searching questions a mile off, mowed them down with her smoky eyes and one-word answers.

At the top, the air was much colder; lazy snowflakes dabbing around us, a crust of snow plastering two sides of the trig point. Then we descended, snow turning to sleet, sleet to rain.

Then the far side of the valley appeared: slate roofs of a chapel and houses all soaked by the ragged underbelly of lumbering cloud. And below us Witton Road, a swollen river running beside it, the valley floor opening out into a patchwork of sports fields. Dani smiled at me, her mood lifting as she recognised the collegiate campus of our old school.

'No way. I've not seen it from up here before.'

'It's a walk I used to do with my parents.'

'I love it.'

'Schools have merged apparently – officially co-ed now.'

We shared some water and took in the view.

'That last year wasn't the same without you.'

Her eyes fixed me as she swigged back water, her face blank like a poker player. I'd gone too far; touched a nerve. It was like walking a tightrope over a minefield. An awkward stillness descended; our waterproofs pattered by sleet.

'Problems at home – I had to look after my mum.' Her gaze lost somewhere far beyond her dripping hood. 'Home life was a mess. Tried to fix it but failed. I was doing a lot of that at the time…'

'Sounds tough.'

'It was. I mean, school was a good place for me, you know, lots of friends – actually, I regret leaving.' Her face emptying, she wiped her mouth with the back of a sleeve then passed over the bottle. Then she just walked away, occasionally looking back, to check that we were headed in the right direction, hair escaping her hood and whipping back, the shape of her legs hidden by baggy waterproof pants. Her body language solitary and detached – maybe bringing her here had been a huge mistake.

She waited for me at the next stile. Her head above mine we watched the town disappear behind cloud. Then the weather reached us, the drenching mist closing around me and Dani like a secret room.

'I know about your dad.' The words tumbled from my mouth, like it wasn't me who said them. She stared at me, then let out a big sigh. 'Reckon everyone knows about him.' She paused as if waiting to see how much I knew.

'Isla's family talk about the town all the time, you know, the fact it has history. Look, I know that he's in prison.'

She stared into the murk.

'Dani. I don't care about all that. I liked you at school, before I knew all this about your family, and I still like you now.'

Go further. Tell her how you feel. But I struggled to find the right words, and it really didn't help that she'd decided to rip into a snack bar as I fumbled in and out of another inept sentence. Her face softened to a half smile, then she waved the chewed end of an oat bar inches from my nose.

'You're not very good at expressing how you feel.'

'You shouldn't talk with your mouth full.'

Her eyebrows raised; her long lashes jewelled by rain she looked down at me belligerently, took another bite. 'That so?'

I wanted to rant, knock the food out of her hand, grab her, kiss her. But I froze, became drawn in by an oat flake on her bottom lip, my confidence sinking without trace. I looked away to the playing fields that slowly re-emerged from behind broken cloud. But I could sense her gaze upon me, her face much closer. And then her hand was inside the collar of my waterproof pulling me in, the cold press of her nose on the side of mine. She kissed me fully for a few seconds. A pause. Then she kissed me again, chocolatey, reassuringly firm, like she meant it. Our heads still close, we were quiet for a moment. I began to talk, but she placed a finger on my lips and held it there, then she turned and climbed over the stile, and we walked a mile or so in silence. But the silence was fine because the kiss had translated everything.

We were well below the cloud line, views of low fields and dry stone walls uninterrupted. The rain stopped. The narrow path zigzagging down towards the town. My thigh muscles burned, I was cold and wet; my knees hurt. Dani skipped down the path that widened as it levelled. We walked side by side and reminisced about *South Pacific*, decided that Miss Gimmet had been a legend for dealing with our raging hormones so well.

'I didn't think about its theme until much later, you know, handing down prejudice from one generation to the next.'

'Suppose it struck a chord with me, reminded me of my dad and brother,' she replied.

We passed through a kissing gate and continued along the road towards the pub.

'The one you didn't get on with?'

'He was older, but I didn't look up to him. Always thought he was weak.'

'Still in contact with him?'

'He's dead.'

'Oh – I'm so sorry.'

'Don't be, he was just like my dad – bit of a tosser.'

*

The pub was quiet at first, just us on a bench by a wood-burning stove nursing a couple of beers. Shuffling together we studied a menu, then ordered food.

'I like this hiking thing, never really understood the attraction of it. But now, I do. It's like running but the buzz is slow release.'

'Glad you enjoyed it.'

'It's been a pretty heavy couple of weeks. Feels good to get away.'

'How's your gran?'

'Okay, I think. Not really showed any signs of being upset. No dramatic grieving. Kept a close eye on her, though. In a strange way, it's brought us closer.'

The pub got busier, people coming in and shaking off the weather.

'And what about you?'

'Bit numb – but really, it's not been a big deal for me. I just can't believe how together my gran's been. Keep expecting her to unravel, but she doesn't.'

'Made of strong stuff, that generation.'

We sipped beer.

'I'm just glad to be there for her.'

More people came through the squally door. Her body pressed against mine, nudging into me like a cat wanting attention. Then my arm was around her, our bodies compatible, bones and flesh intermeshing, rain rapping the windows, embers glowing brightly through the sooty glass of the log burner. We both ate hot fish and chips.

Our chat nonstop.

Everything logical.

Complete.

No missing ingredients.

Dessert

I went to the bar to order dessert, and while waiting to be served I looked back and watched Dani. She seemed relaxed; her worries melting away. The Moss Side girl, product of a grim upbringing, father in Strangeways, rest of her family deceased. And yet, there she was, charming the couple who sat at the opposite table, listening to them with that genuine look of intent. Identifying my feelings not one of my strengths, but I knew that it was pride that was now filling my chest. She just had something about her and didn't behave like a victim, which made me want to deal with my own demons. No wonder her exercise classes were growing in popularity. Isla said everyone loved her. And of course, so did her gran.

It was clear that Harriette was Dani's guiding light, the person she looked up to. Which turned my thoughts to my Barbadian grandmother and her advice about intuition, respecting the recipe but also one's instincts – *A splash of water, a dash of flour.*

I read the room: old leather, blackened stone, worn floors, everything impregnated with smoky, boozy smells, bowing beams squeezing out burdens, the pub throbbing with a comfy chatter. The mix of ingredients just right, our day improving all the time.

I ordered dessert and went back to the table.

She smiled at me. 'Hello, you.' It felt like my chest was about to burst – *she's literally stealing my heart.*

'Hope you're behaving yourself.'

Disregarding my comment, she turned away and continued talking to the old couple who were now pulling on coats and scarves.

'Congratulations again and have a lovely day.' Dani's last words as we watched them leave.

'Wedding anniversary. Forty-eight years.'

'Mm – life sentence.'

She ignored the quip; silence fell like a sledgehammer. Fumbling for words I spoke of December. I was away for Christmas, staying with my gran in Barbados; something my family did every few years.

A pudding, two forks and coffees appeared before us.

'I've handed my notice in at the pub.'

'Oh, really?'

She cut into the pudding.

'People keep signing up. So I have a class nearly every evening. Was a bit nervy at first but I'm fine now. Actually, I've discovered that I love bossing a big group of people.' Her mouth was multitasking again, I could see custard – *I wish she wouldn't do that*. I moved my rucksack so the landlord could get by. He stoked the wood burner and flames licked up. When I turned back the pudding had been removed from my fork, Dani's shoulders shrugging out laughter, her eyes beaming at me. 'Are you going to put me in the naughty corner?'

And then there we were, behaving like a seasoned couple, forks squabbling over the last morsel of pudding. We settled down, her arm on my thigh, hand on my knee.

'It's not highly paid but I'm really enjoying it.'

'Well, you seem happy enough.'

'Mm.' She nodded whilst sipping cappuccino. 'Rennie's been lovely – sorted everything with the architect. Probably shouldn't tell you this but he's letting me use the space for nothing.'

'He's a real gent. Everyone seems to think he's a recluse, but I see him in town quite a lot, comes into the shop – likes his fresh croissants.'

'Bit of a tormented soul from what I can gather.'

'Oh?'

'His father did a lot of business in Germany and his mother was German. Made them very unpopular during the war.'

'Wow and that still affects him?'

'The town has moved on, but he hasn't according to my gran.'

We sat back, watched the busy pub.

'Gran said he's turning on the Christmas lights, it being Wallis and Hilton's centenary. He's becoming quite a celeb.'

'He should be at the meeting next week.'

'Meeting?'

'At Karl's offices with the heritage people.'

'Oh, the block room meeting – yes, he's invited me along. Are you going?'

'Better had. Karl reckons these expert types are a tricky bunch. Can make life difficult if they're not holding court. Probably show my face then duck out early.'

*

We left the pub. Skies brighter, mid-afternoon shadows subduing the pretty street. We passed Triver's Bookshop, an Indian restaurant, a cafe we often went to during free periods, then we stopped at the road bridge which marked the end of town. The river below in a hurry, chasing itself down the valley, thick woods raking up one side, flatness of sports fields on the other, roof of the school somewhere beyond. Piercing shrieks came from a distant hockey match.

'It's how I broke my nose.'

'Hockey? I assumed you got it in a fight.'

'No. Andela Novak. Nice girl – but a bit cavalier with the hockey stick.'

'Ouch.'

'Broke in two places. Had black eyes for weeks.'

There was a shrill whistle, then a hanging chorus of happy shrieks like the whole valley celebrated a win. Backtracking through town we crossed a little footbridge then started to climb the zigzag path. We stopped about halfway up, surveyed our progress then carried on.

'I'm not like them.'

'Sorry?'

'My dad, my brother – I'm not like them.'

'What makes you say that?'

'People – they assume things.'

'Do they? Well, I don't.'

We stopped. I looked down at her face; her black irises seemed even bigger, jet-black hair shiny – straight.

'Trust me, I've never thought of you in that way.'

I pulled out the hat, beige camouflage unfurling in my hands. 'Does all that stuff about your dad really bother you?'

'Of course it does. It's family.'

'But – you are your own person, right?'

'Yes, I am, but family sucks you in – which is okay if you have a good one.'

Hat placed on head we carried on climbing. I thought of my parents, the cricket team; families sitting around the boundary, well-mannered applause, homemade strawberry flan at the interval.

'When we were kids my brother nicked stuff from the corner shop, encouraged me to do the same.'

I stopped laughing when I saw her face. Hands on hips and breathing hard I shrugged my shoulders. 'I mean, it's hardly a bank raid.'

She pushed past me and stopped.

'It's a slippery slope.'

She looked flustered, like her next words were being hurriedly weighed. 'There was always pressure, you know, to go the same way. Suppose boarding school saved me – not sure what would have happened if I'd stayed at home.'

My thighs were burning. I felt frustrated. Her past dragging her down, dragging our day down. I fixed her eye. 'Well, I suppose you will never know. And as far as I can gather, you've turned out okay.'

A cutting breeze rushed us. I led the way, my mind spinning with mad thoughts of making a new start together: Thailand, New Zealand, Speightstown – maybe that's what it would take to shake off her childhood memories.

We cleared the highest point on the walk, and I looked north, to the flanks of distant fells, their tops dusted with snow glowing in an alien half-light. It was too cold to stop. The silence eery, like time had frozen and the Earth had given up its quest around the sun. The white van below a tiny dot, like a toy. Darkness closing in as we trudged down into the valley. We said nothing.

It took a while for the windscreen to clear.

'I'm so cold.'

She leaned over and I put my arm around her.

'Sorry – I've just had a lot going on,' she said quietly.

'I'm not judging you – in any way.'

'Yeah. I know. Sorry.'

On the dual carriageway we drove through sleety showers. Her head turned away from me – nothing much to see other than orange streetlights and scrolling crash barriers.

'Funeral must have been hard.'

'Mm, yeah. I had a few drinks with my gran that evening, you know, to take the edge off things. She told me about the war years. She wasn't liked in town back then.'

'But your gran's lovely.'

'The Wallises were hated back then. And they raised my gran. So, she got tarred with the same brush. And they looked after my dad, too, when Gran was touring with the Hallé. So as a boy he got the same treatment. Passive aggressive brush-offs, that kind of thing.'

'A soft target.'

'Yeah, not fair at all. I spent years wondering what went wrong with him and she unpicked the riddle in one boozy evening.'

We'd turned off the main road, the van passing through invisible countryside, my eyes straining to pick out the twists and turns. 'Must have been a very different place back then.'

'Well, she said it all came to a head just after VE day.'

'But the war was all done and dusted.'

'Apparently feelings were still running high – local men were killed right at the end of the war. A mob of boozed-up families gathered in the street. It got ugly – windows smashed. My dad snapped, came out of the house with a kitchen knife and slashed one of them.'

'Sounds like he was just trying to protect himself, to be fair.'

'A man nearly died apparently.'

'What happened?'

'My dad ran away to Manchester, was taken in by a gang. Gran was left well alone after that – everyone afraid he might come back with his knife.'

My brain was spinning as fast as the van wheels. None of this was her fault. I just wanted to see more of her – like at first light, every morning. But the gravity of her stories just made every word, every sentence that came into my head seem saccharine. *I need to be patient – give her space. She needs space.*

'Can I stay at yours tonight?'

'No – what? Yes, I mean yes.' Details of grass in headlights rushed past, vibrations striking up from the uneven road filling the van with violent sounds like an animal had gone berserk in the back. 'I'll take the sofa.'

I could sense her eyes on me, a different tone in her voice, so soft my earpiece barely picked up her words. 'No, I mean sleep with you – in your bed.'

The lane weaving and bucking, I slowed, pulled over and stopped, our faces lit by the dashboard.

'Okay – are you sure?'

She gave me that look of intent; sharp, unwavering, like those dark irises were inside my head scanning my soul, searching for any hint of insincerity – a look you would develop growing up with people you don't trust.

'I want to be close.' She wiped her nose like a street urchin then looked back at me. 'I haven't had much of that.'

We looked ahead at approaching headlights, the van twitching in the passing turbulence, red lights fading in the wing mirrors.

'I want that, too.'

*

I dropped Dani at the lodges, turned the van, then parked up and waited. A few minutes later she came out with an overnight bag then skipped over to the other lodge and disappeared inside. After a few minutes more she was beside me again.

'Everything alright?'

'Yeah. My gran said hello.'

It was late, hardly anyone about as we drove through town. The flat was very cold. I drank a glass of water. We stood in the kitchen with our coats on, bare industrial windows borrowing light from the street. We listened to voices spill from the pub until they faded into town.

'I'll put the heating on. Can I get you anything?'

'I'm fine, thanks.'

We climbed stairs up to the mezzanine, took turns in the bathroom, removed clothes, the air so cold we soon found the bed. Dani's front pressing against my side, her tattooed arms around my body, her mouth kissing my scarred ear – pulses of her breath carrying words it couldn't hear.

Then she was on top.

'Is that alright?'

Her voice barely making it past sounds that were harassing my earpiece: a noisy pillow, her swishing hair, her fingers caressing the side of my head like rumbling thunder inside my ear.

'Are you okay?'

I explained about the noises. She smiled, kissed me on the lips then slowly pulled the pillow from under my head, tucked her hair back into a hairband, interlaced her hands with mine.

And in the newfound quiet there was just her movement and the sensation of her lips gently running over my brow, then the bridge of my nose like they were features on a map that led to my mouth. Her rhythm steadily paced. Neither sprint, nor marathon, then her soft, ragged whisper: *I'm coming* tipping me. Four breathless beats of my heart and then – I was back in the room, between the cotton covers, her head buried under my chin, her breath on my chest. The room still cold, but the bed full of warmth. We talked.

She thanked me for listening to her, thanked me for the day. Her fingers stroking the scars on my broken ear, questions about the army coming out of nowhere. She asked if I'd ever fired a gun. I said, of course I have.

A pause.

'Have you ever shot anyone?'

I turned onto my side.

'Not in cold blood, why?'

She closed her eyes. 'Just wondering.' Her sleepy voice fading away. I watched her drift off, studied her sleeping eyes, kissed the side of her downy face. Then lying back, I watched the red plastic lens on the ceiling which should flash in an emergency – but it wasn't flashing.

Removing the earpiece, I switched it off, remembered Miss Gimmet's words: *No kissing.* But they were fainter, fading like a whisper.

I let them go.

Glass Meeting Room #2

To be honest I could have done without the meeting; there was so much to do before flying off to my grandmother's. I was anxious about leaving the business for two weeks and I didn't have time to sit around talking sealed-up spaces. But there I was, in the glass meeting room with Councillor Mike Webster and one of the Heritage experts called Rosemary. They began to chat; I stared at the meeting agenda. We were waiting for the rest to show. Dani amongst the latecomers.

Checking my watch again a wave of tiredness swept over me. Starved of sleep for days, the effects of exhaustion took hold: spiking tinnitus, loss of perspective, irrational feelings steadily rising. The fear of unexplained delays lurking again, a stubborn remnant of the desert kept alive by the absurdity of being shot up by my own side. It was a theory proffered by my therapist, one that had made little difference to my angst, the situations in which it thrived seeming to grow year on year: train stopped at signal, aeroplane waiting for clearance, motorway standstill.

Waiting in a glass box.

My nerves jangled, a sense that something shit was about to happen coursing through me. It took all my concentration to focus on something real. The glass door; glint of a spotlight prisming through it. But glimmer of glass became shimmer of sun; my tired eyes straining to scan a trillion grains of sand for threat – *why didn't I see it coming?*

Then memories. My body dragged over the sand, ears roaring, my head drowning in the wreckage of it all: smell of burning hair, the taste of ferrous metal, bodies around me like discarded dolls. Andy's body under a respectfully laid jacket, his lifeless leg tattooed with the emblem of Tottenham Hotspur Football Club.

Webster's laughter pulled me back and on opening my eyes I focused beyond the glass wall, to the scene at the far end of the office. People arriving. Dani chatting to Shelly, others performing a polite dance around a coat stand. I didn't recognise her at first. Hair up, black 501s, Dr Marten shoes, a tucked-in pullover as buff as the desert. My mind flitting to a tune from *South Pacific* – "There is Nothing Like a Dame" – ringing in my head as I recalled the sight of her prancing around my bedroom, naked apart from my camouflaged hat. Tightness in my neck began to ease.

Councillor Webster nudged me. 'Thought we'd lost you – I was just saying – these wallpapers – not convinced what the fuss is about.'

Mike was playfully teasing Rosemary but not rising to it she smiled, played along, ran circles around him. I sipped water and read the list of attendees typed at the top of the agenda, Rosemary noted as:

Doctor Rosemary Glendenning – Victoria and Albert Research Department
Advisor to the Royal College of Art.

I imagined her to be stuffy, a bit of a bore. Not so. She dressed like a goth, had a sense of humour, was in her early thirties.

'Bomber Harris,' she declared.

For a moment Mike struggled with the riddle. 'Come on now – you're not telling me the RAF had something to do with all this?'

'I am.'

'Well, we're all ears… ex-forces you know.' Mike's thumb jabbed in my direction, as if recruiting me would help flush Rosemary out.

I smiled, took another sip of water. 'Army – not RAF.' Then I drifted back to the list of people, Dani's name appearing at the bottom under Steven Ruskin, handwritten, her surname spelt "*Haye*", not Hey. An error to be later corrected, in the meantime all could meet her, free of preconceptions. It was Mike's idea and his efforts in persuading her to come had obviously worked.

We'd had words about this the night before. I'd argued, *how could you pretend you're someone else?* Yes, people like to pigeon-hole, but that was just laziness on their part, or maybe it was a fear of the unknown but usually people came round to the real you. Then Dani posed the question, *how comfortable would you be, sitting in a meeting room with the daughter of the man who killed your best friend?*

Granted, she had a point.

As Rosemary and Mike continued their chat, I watched latecomers walk through the office. Karl opened the glass door and greeted them in. Dani settled in a chair at the other end of the room. I was ready with a smile, but she just looked at the table and pulled down her sleeves.

So now there was Craig, the planner, Mike, the councillor, and Rosemary, the expert. Rennie wasn't attending because of illness. Steven Ruskin didn't show – no apologies made.

Karl introduced himself and we all did the same, one by one working around the table. Then lastly, 'Guy Froggat... English Heritage, local advisory service.'

He was the one, he was the friend of the murdered man. Spitting out words with vigour it was like he'd apparated from nowhere. Mid-forties, his suit screaming seventies' throwback. Cumbersome, odd, his gaze magnified through thick lenses, the kid who was bullied at school.

Karl apologised for starting late then Mike piped up.

'Rosemary's been filling us in, reckons it's the RAF's fault there's such interest in these wallpapers. Come on, Rosemary, don't leave us hanging.'

But we all watched Karl as he flicked through the agenda notes, the lull coming to an end as he looked up and smiled.

'Sounds intriguing, Rosemary. Happy for you to finish off before we get started.'

Rosemary straightened. 'Yes, of course. Well, W&H wallpapers were largely exported to Germany. Unfortunately, the walls they covered didn't survive the RAF raids. That's why we're so interested in your building, a preserved find if you like, a bit like the Lost Gardens of Heligan. Have you heard of them?'

Mike sat forward on his chair. 'Oh aye. In Cornwall. Go on.'

'The story of this building is similar, in that the Great War also triggered its demise. Wallis and Hilton became a forgotten offshoot of the Arts and Crafts Movement, but the company was probably as important as the William Morris Company.'

We all sat motionless and listened attentively, but Guy shifted in his seat, flicking through the notes. 'Look, sorry, can we please make a start and stick to the agenda?'

There was an awkward pause until Karl stepped in and steered us through the business of the meeting until we became stuck on item 3.1. Guy burbled on, something about protecting elements of historical importance, then he suggested that the building be temporarily shut down until "heritage assets" had been identified.

Mike sat on the edge of his seat. 'Shut down? Look, is this really necessary? People working here are trying to make a living.'

Karl redirected the question. 'Rosemary?'

'Guy's right, we do need to survey the building. But our initial thoughts? We are thinking that actually it's Miss *Hey's* studio that needs our attention. The back wall in particular.'

Rosemary went on to say that they would be able to work around everyone concerned, liaising as necessary. No need for a shutdown.

Silence. Blank faces.

Karl stepped in. 'It's important to mention that what we're working towards here could be a huge opportunity for the town. Guy and Rosemary have invested so much into their research…'

'To be fair we've just picked up where David left off,' Guy interrupted.

'David?'

'David Harrison, the conservation officer. Way ahead of his time – learnt of the block room over a decade ago – dreamt about turning it into a museum.'

A new and heavy silence descended.

'Goes without saying…' Guy paused for breath, '…what happened to David overshadowed everything.'

I thought of the Grahams' grisly story about the body in the reeds. Dani sat stone still, her eyes fixed on the paperwork in front of her. Reflections of serious faces and folded arms in the glass all around us like a courtroom jury.

Mike shifted in his seat. 'David was a good man. We owe it to him, you know, to press on with this.'

Karl rose from his seat, all eyes following him as he repositioned a large white model of the Wallis mill from the side cabinet to the meeting table. He lifted off the roof. We huddled around it, our eyes charmed by the miniaturised rooms.

'Rosemary, I wonder if you would expand on what you were telling us earlier.'

Her finger hovered over the narrow slot. 'It's this space we're interested in. The block room. Sealed and undisturbed since 1915. The mill was requisitioned early on in the war, but before munitions production began, Sidney Wallis insisted part of the building be mothballed, a safe space to store the tools of his business until the end of the war.'

We all gazed into the model agog.

Mike leaned forward, his eyes scanning up and down the slot. 'Never been opened since, you say?'

'The owner says not. We believe it's full of printing blocks, patterns, tools, rolls of wallpaper, who knows what else? You could say a time capsule, stuffed with treasures of the past.'

Mike was stooping now, leaning his weight on the table, peeking through the front windows of the model. 'Now you're selling it to me.'

'I mentioned Heligan earlier.'

'Go on.'

'It's the same deal. Part of our cultural history lost during the Great War. Workforce went to fight in the trenches – none came back. It's a story played out so many times across Britain. Interestingly, like Heligan, the Wallis mill was never sold or redeveloped and the block room within, is – we believe – one of those rare-preserved gems.'

'Enough artifacts to fill a small museum,' Guy added.

'I hear you, but it's too late to turn this place into a museum. It's a place of work now.'

'The station, Mike...' Craig chipped in, '...we're thinking of using the old station. The building is vacant, needs a bit of TLC, but it's available. Ties in with the history and there are plans to renovate the line.'

'Bloody brilliant. We've got the scenery; walkers love it here. Along with the investment at Dardale Hall this could take us to the next level.'

'Heligan has been an incredible commercial success, thousands of visitors. It's the mystery. People love the romance of it.' Karl cherried the cake.

'Heligan of the North, gotcha. Let's crack on with it.' Mike's knuckles rapped on the table.

There was further discussion, the question of Rennie's consent curbing everyone's excitement; Karl and Mike due to seek his permission but only after he'd recovered from illness.

Shelly wheeled a trolley into the room loaded with cakes, flasks of tea and coffee. We all helped ourselves, stood around the table chatting; there was talk of a walkabout after refreshments. I chatted to Karl about my trip to Barbados, Dani on the far side of the table talking to Rosemary and Guy. Everything relaxed and cordial I made my excuses and gathered my things. Dani came over, kissed me, then rubbed lipstick off my cheek. It took me by surprise. Our relationship was supposed to be under the radar. But that's how it was. We'd agree one thing, then spontaneously without warning she'd do the other. It meant we were a bit up and down, but I just went with it, and this was definitely an up, which is where I'd hoped to be before my travels.

'You okay?' Her fingers interlaced mine.

'Yeah, fine, a bit stressed, still got a lot to get through.'

'We could skip tonight if you like.' Her voice like silk, her lips radiant.

'No, seven o'clock is fine – I have champagne.'

She smiled and gave me another peck, this time not removing her mark, then she turned away and chatted to Mike. Thoughts of the desert evaporating; as usual, phobic fears coming to nothing. And feeling suddenly lighter I realised part of my stress was about us, and whether I was reading Dani correctly. But now everything felt certain. Her kisses so fleeting I doubted that anyone had noticed, yet for me it was like she was nailing her colours to the post.

Spilling out of the meeting room felt like I'd escaped from a magnum of champagne, euphoric, buoyant, floating through the office like bubbles in a flute, rising past computer tappers so focused on screens I moved beyond them unnoticed.

I said goodbye to Shelly with such a jovial voice it made her jump. Then I looked back and saw the group moving around the table, the white model caught in the spotlights like a beacon of hope.

Ghetto Blaster

The intercom sounded; I buzzed her in. Her fast steps filling the stairwell, then Dani was there before me, shoulders pulled back by the straps of a rucksack, her fingers gripping handles of a plastic bag.

'Sorry I'm late.'

No eye contact; her coat remained on. Was she staying? She dissolved into the apartment like an exotic breeze. Her perfume like pots of jasmine, a fragrance she wore when we first kissed, a solid memory that settled me. I watched her in the kitchen area, wriggling out of the rucksack, kicking off shoes and removing her coat. The plastic bag limp on the worktop. She'd offered to make dinner. Upbeat and full of energy; *she can't keep still.* Her movement a haze in the dim kitchen light, the line of her figure a mirage in the stark glow of the open fridge. Then she disappeared again, her form untangling from shadows as she moved towards me.

'Harriette said Happy Christmas and a safe journey. You're quite the blue-eyed boy.' Pushing her freezing hands inside my pullover, she smiled when I flinched. Her kiss spiked with alcohol.

'Sadist.'

'It's in my DNA – So, where's that glass of bubbly?'

Pulling away she held up a transparent container.

'Hungry?'

'Mm – what you got?'

'Homemade ravioli. My gran made it.'

Removing the lid, she revealed a dozen or so works of art: pasta parcels gathered at each end like little Christmas crackers, talent captured in Tupperware.

'How long's she away?'

'Until the twenty-second, staying with friends in West Didsbury.'

A long week of work catching up with me, opening the fridge was like opening a heavy hatch. Items behind the door shifting nervously, white interior walls perspiring, foil-capped champagne bottle on its side like a 30mm armour-piercing round.

'How was the end of the meeting?'

'Walkabout dragged a bit. You did the right thing ducking out when you did.'

Hopping onto the island unit, her voice faded as she pulled a sweater up and over her head. 'Starting their investigation mid-January apparently.'

She hopped off again. It was like being in the room with a hummingbird. Moving to the window she hovered by the Christmas tree, its white strips of foil restless above the antique radiator. She studied the shiny objects that hung from branches.

After opening the bubbly, I searched for glasses. 'What are these experts planning to do then?'

'Take samples then separate any built-up layers in the lab.' She took the glass from my hand.

'Back wall of the print room was used as a showcase apparently, so they reckon there's loads of wallpapers layered one on top of the other. They're hoping to display them in the V&A.'

'Mm, we're going up in the world.'

She stood at the big windows looking up at black sky, the bubbly in her hand twitching as trees came to life, every branch in town picked out by the white glow of string lights. She smiled back at me.

'You've got the best seat in the house. Reminds me of Avenue Montaigne.'

'Oh right, where's that?'

'Paris. Went there once on New Year's Eve with college friends.' Her attention returned to the street.

I placed a pan of water on the hob. 'It was good to see Rennie turn on the lights. Thought you were coming to that.'

'Did a swerve last minute as Harriette wasn't keen. Her and Rennie aren't getting on.'

We sipped bubbles. 'I met up with Isla for a drink afterwards.'

'Oh right. How is she?'

'Pretty good. She reckons your father hasn't got a leg to stand on.'

There was no reply.

'That's what her dad reckons, anyway; he knows his stuff. He's a lawyer.'

'Yeah, she told me that, too. Storm in a teacup she said. Cheers.' She swigged back the bubbly.

'Seriously, he reckons the appeal will get laughed out of court.'

Her eyes levelled with mine; her brow pinched as if in discomfort. 'Can we change the subject?'

'No problem. Just thought...'

'Well, thanks for the thought.'

An awkward silence prevailed as we stared at the street, coldness radiating from the windows, goose bumps roughing up her tattooed forearms. I focused on the reflections of the minimalist kitchen that lay behind us. It looked like a laboratory. Vertical plumes of steam rising from the pot; our featureless silhouettes lifeless like products of a fruitless experiment.

'This is going to my head – Fancy something to eat?'

'I'll make a start; all part of the house-sitting service.' Her voice now dull and flat.

I sat on the bar stool; the atmosphere saturated with frustration. Gently stirring the pot, she seemed so far away. Pasta in the pan like sweets in twisted wrappers they rolled over in the slow boil. I felt like an idiot for mentioning her dad. Squatting out of sight, she opened a cupboard and rummaged through kitchen hardware, her voice rising up from somewhere below the island unit.

'Looking forward to seeing your gran? Marion, isn't it?'

'Yes. Can't wait.'

'It's a lovely name.'

She plated up the pasta then added other ingredients:

grated pecorino, crumbled walnuts, a drizzle of honey. We ate in silence, my mouth unwrapping the edible presents. Ricotta cheese and orange zest playing with other flavours, performing dreamy tunes my tastebuds had never heard of. No sooner had she finished eating, her tattooed arms disappeared into the rucksack. She pulled out a small parcel. I unwrapped the brown paper. A small gold angel appeared. A tree decoration, smooth, minimal, the outline of wings tucked behind its tarnished body.

'Gran reckons washing-up liquid would bring out the shine.'

'Real gold?' It was hollow but heavy.

'Plated with low-carat stuff. My gran gave it to me when I was little.'

'Won't she mind?'

'Her idea; the angel baker should have it.'

Kissing it like a lucky charm I hung it on the tree, then picking up a boxy present from under the branches I passed it to her. She tore at the wrapping; the letters *JVC* peeking out.

'You're kidding me.'

'I knew yours had broken – I can take it back if it's not the right one...'

Slumping on the sofa, she read the blurb on the box. 'Absolutely not – it's perfect.'

'It's a thank you in advance for house-sitting.'

She sat crossed-legged on the sofa, her face serious, like she was building up to something, her eyes searching mine.

'Dev?'

'Mm?'

'You're letting yourself in for a whole lot of trouble, being around me.'

'Because of your dad? I'm not afraid of him.'

I sat on the sofa. Her fingers caressed the side of my face. 'You wouldn't see it coming.'

It was like her mind was already made up, was letting go, letting me down gently.

'If he gets out. It will be different... my life will be different.'

'Isla's dad knows his stuff – your dad's not getting out.'

She walked to the back wall and studied the row of audio cassettes on the shelf, the plastic boxes clacking as her fingers ran over them. It was an inscrutable slot of time. The room suddenly airless; something fizzling out inside me. Everything oddly forsaken, as though we were in a hospice, one that nursed our future, not quite departed but in a palliative state of care. Then she turned back into the room, fresh joy on her face, her mood shifting with effortless ease. 'Oh cool, where did you get this from?', the cassette box in her hand the soundtrack to *South Pacific*.

Her low mood magically wiped away, she'd swung back to the earlier champagne moment, but I just wasn't agile enough to do the same. I felt sick. I felt a failure.

'Second-hand record shop on Fog Lane, couldn't resist buying it.'

'What, Sifters? No way. I used to go there all the time. Can I put it on?' She was so excited.

'Be my guest.'

She removed the ghetto blaster from its packaging, the cassette case squeaking open as she loaded the cassette. Music played and we stretched out on the sofa side by side, her back curved into my front, our bodies intertwined like chambers of a heart beating an irregular rhythm. Wedged between her and back cushions, for a moment everything felt perfectly still. The air I breathed filtering through baby hairs that swirled on her neck, her soft perfume like a drug that bribed my mood. "Cock-eyed Optimist" played. We swapped stories.

I told the one of how I got my nickname, Angel, then went on to describe army friends and the tale of Andy's forty-eight-hour marriage to a prostitute in Dortmund. As the song "Bloody Mary" played, she told me about the crooked oddballs who drank in her parents' pub, the parties at Hulme Crescents and her friend called Fez.

The chorus of "Bali Hai" haunting the room we talked about the kiss scene. I reminded her that Bloody Mary believed Liat's only chance of a better life was to marry Lieutenant Cable. She pointed out that Cable wound up dead. Then we lay in a stalemate silence, snug and warm, her restless body occasionally pushing back like a nestling cat, transferring her scent, as if confirming I was hers. Then out of the blue she claimed that fate had drawn us to the same place. Maybe she wasn't breaking up with me after all. My head so tired it had, for now, given up trying to read the signs. The soundtrack fading, I drifted off then found myself sprawled on a beach, my body shaded by palm trees, debris from the swaying coastline lying all around. Then I woke, and she'd gone, the music a faint memory, the dreamy warmth of paradise replaced by the shaky images of Russian tanks in Chechnya that flickered on my pathetically small television. She came back from the kitchen with hot drinks and reminded me that my suitcase was still empty.

I went upstairs and packed clothes. She sat on the sofa flicking through TV channels. We went to bed, but Dani was so restless that it took a while before sleep came.

*

I woke before the alarm. My hearing aid out, my senses foggy, just the rhythm of Dani's purr through the bed. For a few breaths I watched her sleep. If I were an angel, then she was too, but from a parallel heaven. One that I didn't understand. I rolled onto my back, tinnitus plaguing my ear, short buzzes disconcertingly electronic as though in some far-away control room Miss Gimmet pushed a buzzer labelled, "Warn Him".

Dani groaned as if in the middle of an invisible argument, then she mumbled and turned over. I got dressed, left the flat and walked to the quay, the canal stung by cold air. Brambles on the far bank a confusion of black spaghetti that twinkled with glitter. The line of poplars beyond, pre-dawn giants. Everything clinging to life in the frostbitten sump and yet a Caribbean warmth flickered inside me. The thought of my gran's sunny breakfasts of flying fish and mango salsa, served with a jolly demeanour, soothing my soul.

Then my thoughts switched to Dani in my warm bed, her sleep tormented by demons.

Two angels. I loved them both.

Coldness seeped through my clothes and stroked at my bones, the half-frozen runnel that birds used as a landing strip gradually narrowing. Opening a paper bag, I threw bread crusts across the canal, and as they skidded on the ice "Bali Hai" echoed through my mind, the melody thawing my heart as I walked back. *Just keep going.*

When I returned, I could hear that Dani was up. After showering she came down. I gathered my things and soon after breakfast we set off and weaved through country lanes. Dani took the wheel. I gave directions. The conversation was sparse, just a few exchanges about the night before: the old building had kept her awake; creaks and knocks and scrapes. She claimed that the walls and floors were alive with ghosts.

I didn't have the heart to tell her that I had slept soundly; maybe my deaf ears were oblivious to sounds that disturbed her night.

We sped along several roads. Orange-lit motorway, deserted dual-carriageway, winter twilight creeping into the sky as we passed between the fingers of Manchester's palm. The airport not much further. Before long we stood in a multistorey car park and watched a low sun lurk behind smoky skies. And as the strain of labouring jets roared somewhere beyond the terminal buildings, I couldn't help but feel glum; we'd come so far but clearly there was still something blocking the next stage of our journey.

The airport was dead, only a few passengers at check-in. We walked to an open-sided cafe, bought coffees from a bored barista then sat and stared at worn baubles hanging from a dwarf plastic tree, a single length of gold tinsel sagging from the ceiling, everything fidgeting in the whir of the ventilation system. Christmas like a rumour.

I told her that my flight details were on the kitchen worktop. She looked gloomy.

'You okay?'

'I'm fine.'

She asked about my Heathrow connection and arrival time then said she was dropping in to see her Manchester friend before heading back.

We sat quietly again; the last mouthful of coffee was cold.

'I'd better go through.'

She smiled, nuzzled into me. I kissed the top of her head.

She patted my leg, and we stood.

'Have a good one.'

'Yeah, you too. I'll ring you.' I walked towards security. When I looked back, she'd gone.

DARDALE

1915

VII

Blackberry – *Rubus fruticosus*

Study for Wallis and Hilton Wallpapers. Plate No. 107 – Bramble Tangle [see sketch on next page]

Facts: A blackberry is not a single fruit, but an aggregate of individual berries. Each "bobble" in the blackberry bears one seed and is termed a "drupe".

Quaint belief: It was believed that passing sick people under an archway formed of bramble branches could cure (or prevent) all manner of afflictions and illness.

Spurred on by Sidney's enthusiasms, Ellen tested the appetite for action amongst the workforce. Protest, she said, would be the main topic of discussion at the next church hall meeting. At first the women peered at her with a certain amount of suspicion, but then they all worked very quietly as if a giant penny were slowly dropping down through the workshop rooflight.

The once-monthly meetings were normally tame, attended by the same few, what should or should not make it onto the pages of the magazine politely debated. At the next meeting there was a full turnout.

Doors locked, curtains drawn, everyone crowded into the church hall, the vicar's hands outstreched and patting down the pandemonium.

'One at a time. One at a time.'

Yellow hands reached for the ceiling.

'Ethel.'

'Chain ourselves to mill railings.'

Vicar Hodges shifted awkwardly. 'No, no – too public. The aggravation wouldn't sit comfortably with families grieving war dead.'

'Sit comfortably?' a voice bellowed from the back. 'It's not your arse that's turning yellow.'

Brassy laughter.

'What about Muriel Wilson's family? They're grieving too!' another voice shouted. Then Maude spoke of a munitions worker in Leeds who'd given birth to a yellow baby. Then Ethel pitched in and claimed the authorities were indifferent about the worker who'd died at the Barnbow filling factory. 'A cover-up?'

Gasps.

'Throw bloody stones through colonel's window.'

'Throw Harold's bicycle in canal.'

'Throw Harold in the canal!'

Witchy cackles.

Then a lone voice chanted the suffragette motto, *Deeds Not Words*. And soon all the women were chanting. But Ellen remained silent, her mind overrun with all that had happened: Muriel's obituary censored by the ministry, women banned from the offices, Cedric still in Lancaster, Joe in Leeds, no word from her father, a baby inside her belly. And then through the fog of anger that filled the room she noticed Irene wiping away tears, unlocking the door and leaving the building.

The chanting fizzled. Everyone filed out. In the square the consoling crowd surrounded Irene as she sat on a bench and sobbed, her frail voice explaining that one of her brothers had been killed in the biggest battle of the war so far.

Meeting adjourned the group walked up the lane in respectful silence, rooting through hedgerows picking the last of the blackberries, their wrath cooled by a breeze scented with odours of withering bracken. And as they reached the gates and lodges of the Dardale estate Irene said she was alright and insisted everyone returned to the matter at hand. And their wrath did give way to calmness but as they approached the town's square the group had still not settled on an appropriate way to protest. Their outrage rekindled when realising the church hall doors had been locked.

Not until their fists hammered on the doors did the vicar open up, his face startled by the mob of riled yellowness and clenched hands all stained and smarting from the brambles.

The vicar apologised for the lockout. 'In a figurative sense I knock on heaven's door every day to protest about the suffering of my parishioners.'

And that was that. The idea spawned by a man of the cloth no less.

The women emboldened by the divine endorsement.

Two subsequent meetings. Rehearsals performed, a date for the protest agreed.

And when the day arrived, Ellen hurried past the buildings of Main Street in the dim early light, winter trees mere scribbles between them. The mill ahead holding back dank smells of the canal.

Clutching Sidney's key in her pocket she turned off the street and climbed the station steps, a bleak wind squalling up as she turned onto the bridge link. The delicate structure formed by an array of timber stems and tulip spandrels, panels below the handrails carved as ornately as the printing blocks. But like her body the bridge had been ravaged. The whole structure moaning in the wind like an old ship, light of a new day exposing chemical stains on the deck boards and pallet-wagon scrapes on the side panels, its collapse a year after the war an event Ellen would never know of.

She continued on and entered the workshop, the women inside stationed beside benches. Their overalls ill-fitting as if hard labour had withered their bodies, dust in the air above their heads betrayed by light rendered down by the grime-smeared rooflights. The filthy hell of it all, she thought, enough to make Sidney weep.

She closed the door, clunk of the lock prompting the women to simultaneously look up from their work. Everyone poised. Everyone ready.

Ellen gave the nod. Tools were downed. The women filed into the block room, some turning left, some right, Ellen standing firm at its midpoint. Nervous, exhausted, headache throbbing, her scalp itching as if ants crawled all over it. The line of women, a weary variegation of yellow skin and drill fabric, coughing and sniffing as if the block room had been struck down by a medieval plague.

Ellen called the first woman forward. Alice's long brown hair touched by the yellow. Her eyes bright with fervour her knuckles pounding on the door.

'My name is Alice Post. The work I do poisons me because I have no gloves to protect these hands.' She left the block room and lingered in the workshop, biting a fingernail.

The next woman rapped the door so hard she chipped a notch of skin from her knuckle.

'My name is Lizzie Jones. The work I do poisons me because I have no gloves to protect these hands.'

Harold's voice flared up on the other side. Ranting this and ranting that.

Lizzie smiled. 'Tut, tut, Harold. Not in front of the ladies.' Then she turned, walked away and joined up with Alice and they linked arms.

Ethel Hawkins, Margaret Roscoe, Sarah Ann Butterworth also hammered on the door, and recited the same words. And then one by one more women came forward and took their turn.

A barrage of blows that ignored Harold's pleas.

Ellen continuing to calmly call them forward, her block room army advancing in single file, each repeating the same words, each releasing a barrage of thuds onto the door.

'My name is Emily Mary Judd. The work I do poisons me because I have no gloves to protect these hands.'

Then the colonel's voice came from the other side. 'Stop immediately! Do you hear!'

Maria drew her shoulders back, her voice raised over the pompous squawking.

'My name is Maria Haverty! The work I do poisons me because I have no gloves to protect these hands.'

Ada was second to last, her heavily pregnant magnificence perched on a stool throughout, finally she rose and waddled to the door. Her knock twice as hard, her words double the volume. Then with hand on lower back, she rejoined the group, and they all sat holding hands on the grimy workshop floor, their proud buttercup faces forming a circle, rows of pointed shells behind them like some neatly tended meadow of death.

Ellen then knocked and said the lines one last time, her forehead resting against the door, blood in her temples still thudding. Then heavy knocking came from across the workshop. Doors that had been previously locked thumped and rattled and the doorhandles frantically jerked up and down, as though the factory were besieged by angry ghosts.

Ellen felt dizzy as she lurched out of the block room. She tried to fight it off, but the workshop pitched about, and the circle of women seemed all at sea, a wreath of yellow flowers tossed over the railing of a once magnificent ship.

And then Ellen felt her legs give way and she sensed her body collapsing onto the floor. The blackout that followed, an incomprehensible tranche of time into which the world eventually trickled back in. First the sensation of being carried by many hands. Then above her, a small circle, everything spiralling as if she were rifling out of a cannon, the disc of light growing ever bigger. Then the whirling became a hand that swilled a bottle of smelling salts before her face, and the rim of the cannon became a rim of concerned faces that hovered above her.

And all the time, in her memory, she could hear a voice, Sidney's voice that said: *We are always here for you.*

*

Exhaustion was the doctor's blunt diagnosis of Ellen's condition. She stayed in bed for a week. Her aunty bringing hot food every day and the news that Ada had given birth to a yellow baby boy, "a true bobby-dazzler" if ever she'd seen one.

At the end of the week, an internal investigation was launched at the factory. Harold called in the first suspect. Maria sat opposite the colonel; her blinking eyes set in constant awe by heavy prescription spectacles. She waffled a nervy apology and then without equivocation confessed to being the mastermind. Punishment pending, she stood and left.

Knew it all along. Of course, it was her.

Harold gleefully called in the next. She sat on the chair and without equivocation confessed to being the mastermind.

The afternoon ground along like a bicycle with millstone wheels.

Sixty-two women took the chair. Sixty-two masterminds left the room.

Next day all the women were ordered back to work.

The colonel left town, stayed in Bradford for a week, doing what, nobody knew. But they all hoped he'd gone for the gloves. On his second day back, Ellen was summoned to the mill. And when she entered the office, she found the colonel beside the window, gazing at distant moorland that rose beyond town like the shallow grave of a giant. Then swivelling into the room, he confirmed that the army had no place for dissenting voices.

'It was your vicar friend that dropped you in it. Please exercise leniency when deciding Ellen's fate, he'd blurted when I met him at the church. Dropped you right in it, he did.' Returning to the wintery scene he sucked his empty pipe. 'One could say the game's up, dear.'

She looked around the office. No sign of the gloves, not even a mention of them. The protest all in vain.

The colonel droned on.

But she didn't have time for it, because the man before her was a complete idiot. The building she stood in had once been such an honourable ship, Sidney its noble captain.

But it now seemed so unseaworthy, moored up and rotting beside the dank canal.

Her anger growing, she focused on the colonel's holstered gun, lunging for it and shooting him, a fantasy that grew more appealing with every grinding second.

Her heart raced.

'If not for Vicar Hodges' merciful pleas, I would have taken this further. However, if you admit guilt, I have decided to...'

Holding the back of a chair she steadied herself against waves of nausea.

'...exercise leniency and offer you one last chance. How do you plead?'

Vertigo. Panic rising.

'I will only offer you one more chance, Miss Parry. So, I repeat, how do you plead?'

Contents of her stomach rallying.

'Miss Parry?'

Not for one moment did he see it coming.

She managed to hold off for another few seconds. Everything backing up; her cheeks filling. Half-digested braun, mashed potato, green bits she had no recollection of ever eating, it all came out, emulsified like paint tossed from a tin.

The canvas?

Standard army-issue khaki. Perfectly pressed.

DANI

Rubble

After leaving the airport Dani navigated the van towards the address of her Manchester friend. She found a parking space at the bottom of the street then walked the rest of the way. Heavy scent of burning leaves in the air, tree shadows on the walls of grand three-storey houses, the urban neatness of Withington echoing the clipped formality of Fez's letter. As if written by an upmarket alter ego its tone had no hint of his usual jauntiness. Just his telephone number and the ominous words, *need to see you*. She'd called him to ask why but he'd insisted on a face-to-face.

She levelled with his house. A big Victorian bay window loomed above a neat hedgerow, the blink of tree lights inside slow and deliberate. The woodwork tastefully painted with dim nineteenth-century colours. A potted bay tree by the front step, a stained-glass sidelight, a classy wreath of frosted holly on the front door. Everything so unlike Fez, for a fleeting moment she thought it all a scam.

She rang the bell. Nothing for a while, then muffled bumps and shouts. Light and shadow distorting in the wibbled glass until movements converged into an arm that reached towards her. The door pulled back. Fez appeared; his tired eyes lighting up. 'Dani – how yah doin'?' The shrill of children racing through the hallway drowning his words.

'Hi.' She felt a warm rush at seeing her old friend. And like the first time they'd met she couldn't take her eyes off his head. But the mohican had all grown out – his hair brown and curly and a bit thin on top. The clothes he wore nothing like his old punk outfits: soft joggers, converse trainers; the logo *Abercrombie and Fitch* arced across his chest.

'The new you.' She couldn't help but smile. 'Love the hair.'

'Hated my mop as a kid. But curly perms are all the rage now.' He grinned. 'Come in, come in. Good to see yah.'

Stylish objects adorned the walls of a massive hallway: circular mirror, blue Matisse in a white frame, smaller pictures clustered around it. Everything seeming to float above the child-proofed zone. Tickle-induced squeals came from an upper room.

Fez called up the stairwell, 'We're off then, Julie – Julie?'

An upstairs door opened; bootleg denim and big socks descended part way down, Julie sat on a step, her head barely below the ceiling, a neat bob obscuring half her pretty face.

'This is my friend Dani. You know, from the Cressies.' His last word rueful as if referring to an old habit.

'Nice to meet you.'

Dani looked up and smiled. 'Hi.'

There was a thump from above then very dramatic crying.

'We're heading off now – that okay, love?'

'Yeah, fine,' she said, turning to climb the stairs. 'Put Seb in the kitchen, would you? He's been at the tree again. Have a good catch-up.' Her voice growing fainter as her feet disappeared above the ceiling.

Fez coaxed a dog from the front room, the lurcher curling into a basket as he closed the kitchen door. 'Dog's got a taste for pine needles,' he said with an eye roll.

They left the house and walked onto the street. 'Do you mind if we go out? It'll be difficult talking in the house.'

'No problem.'

'Fancy a stroll up the Cressies – for old times' sake?'

'Love to.'

Fez took a deep breath as if relieved to be outside. 'It's good to see you, mate.'

'You've moved on a bit. House, kids, dog – you seem a bit keen to get away from it all, though.'

He laughed. 'They're not all mine, got the sister-in-law's kids round – it's not usually that mad.'

'Oh, I see.'

'We've got twins; bit of a shock to the system at first but that's it now, we're all done and dusted. Julie's not having any more.'

He aimed a key fob at the street; indicators of a BMW flashed.

Dani nodded at the car. 'Doing alright then.'

'Perks of the treadmill.' He shrugged. 'I'm very well

adjusted now, mate. Vagrant punk to executive surveyor.'
He smiled over the car roof before disappearing below it.

Doors closed with a soft thud; the plush interior
library quiet as Fez wheeled the car onto the main road.

'Julie seems nice.'

'She's sound. From Roundhay in Leeds, you know,
the posh bit. She's a buyer for a clothing chain – flies all
over, Hong Kong, New York – right jet-setter. My wages
are pocket money compared to hers. I clear the childcare
costs – she's the one who pays the mortgage.'

The journey was short, one junction on the dual
carriageway. Parking up on a deserted side road they
walked under the Mancunian Way, then deep into Hulme.

'How's life in the sticks, then?'

'Can't complain… it's good spending time with my gran.'

'Sound.' He pulled a packet of cigarettes from his
pocket. 'Fancy a bifter?'

'No, thanks.'

'Got any love going on in your life then, Dani?' The
cigarette see-sawed in the corner of his mouth.

'I'm kind of seeing someone. Briefly knew him at
school; nothing solid – we've both got a lot going on.
Dropped him at the airport before coming over.'

'Travels with his job, does he?'

'No, no – he's seeing family in Barbados. He's a baker.'

'Sound. Reckon you're a match made in heaven.'

'What do you mean?'

He took a deep drag on the cigarette, plucked it from
his mouth, words coming out with smoke. 'You both
having a lot going on.'

'Hadn't thought of it like that, but yeah, I suppose.'

They walked in silence for a while. Light began to fade. The path familiar, she sensed they were close, expected to see the Crescents' grim magnificence at any moment.

'Dani?'

'Mm?'

'I've heard things about your dad.'

His well-meaning tone irked her. Why was it that everyone thought they understood just because they'd heard things?

'Don't tell me this is why you wrote me a letter – anyone with a television has *heard things...*'

No reply. Fez no longer at her side. She glanced back to see him sat on a bench staring into open wasteland. Backing up, she joined him, a look of shock growing on her face as she took in the tartan of rubble and road that unfolded from where they sat to far-off buildings of the inner-city. For a while they remained motionless, their eyes entranced by traffic that coasted across a distant flyover. The dark spire of Salford Cathedral beyond spiking gloomy skies that hung above the Manchester skyline.

'It's... gone,' said Dani, a tone of disbelief colouring her voice.

'It had a slow death, mate. Folks standing at the fence some days, like crowds at a medieval execution, watching that pathetic wrecking ball chipping away at the place. Honestly, could have done a quicker job swinging me own balls against it.' He dropped the fag end and snuffed it out with a twisting foot.

'You're still full of shit.'

He laughed out smoke. 'Yeah, miss you too – feisty little fuckeh. You not going to deck me, are yah?'

There followed a brief silence as their faces stared blankly at the blitzed scene.

'What's going to happen? They can't just leave it like that.'

'Earmarked for regeneration. Lord knows it needs it. Things have deffo got worse here. Drugs, turf wars, it's not called Gunchester for nothing.'

Silence descended again. A dog roamed across the wasteland, stopping occasionally to sniff or pee on piles of rubble. The rubble that her mother's remains were blended into.

Why didn't I scatter her somewhere untainted, like the sea?

'I realise it can't be your favourite subject but just hear me out about your dad. It's something I've heard first-hand. Just thought you should know, that's all, mate – strictly between you and me.'

Sensing his gaze, she didn't return it and tried not to show any expression on her face.

'The police have ballsed up big time.' His hands nervously played with the fag packet.

'Yeah – obviously. They've been in town for weeks trying to find evidence in connection with that body, you know, the murder.'

He let out a short, mocking chortle. 'Murder?'

'David Harrison – twelve years ago.'

'From what I've heard, mate, that's not why they're sniffing around.'

Her hand gripped the bench, her thoughts on the gun. 'How do you know that?'

'One of my best mates is having a fling with a barrister's clerk. Apparently, she works in the chambers, sees all the case notes, CPS documentation, everything. And she talks about work all the time. Obviously not supposed to, but sometimes it just spills out, like a stress release. Well, after a few bevvies she was on a roll, actually wouldn't shut up about it. Bit embarrassing, actually.'

He picked up a small nugget of concrete and threw it at the nearest pile of rubble.

'For sure the bizzies cocked up twelve years ago with that murder; your dad's legal team have got them on that. So, the law has switched tack.'

'Go on.' Shifting on the bench, her body turned towards him.

'Coppers have been scouring the county. If they find what they're looking for, apparently there's a clear link back to your dad and then they've got him. That Harrison bloke – they think he may have been close to uncovering something soon before he died.'

'What have the coppers been searching for then?'

'You heard of the Brink's-Mat robbery?'

Dani looked blank. 'No.'

'Happened twelve years ago. Robbers were caught… but half the loot was never recovered. A crew in the south pulled it off, but all these gangs are networked. The bizzies reckon they're melting it down, laundering it. There's this myth doing the rounds, most jewellery made since then will have a bit of Brink's-Mat in it. So, if you've bought anything from Ratners lately, well, you're a fuckin' accomplice.'

'Melting it down?'

'It's stolen gold they're looking for, Dani, not murder clues. The old bill was tipped off that some of it filtered up to Lancashire. And guess who came up on their radar?'

The next stone he threw bounced off the top of a rubble heap.

'Bingo...' He picked up another nugget of concrete. 'Yeah – yah dad.'

Then as she focused on the wreckage, his rambling chatter about the criminal underworld faded to a vague murmur. The Crescents had protected her, had taken her in and now it was gone, like an old friend wiped out by some terrible catastrophe. Chatter trickled back in.

'Searching for murder clues was just a cover. I mean, the coppers aren't gonna admit to a treasure hunt; they didn't want every looney with a metal detector sniffing around the place, know what-rah mean?'

Body bent double as if sitting on a doomed aircraft, hands over her head as if trying to block out his words, her eyes scrambled amongst details of the weedy path.

'Just thought you should know, mate. Bit of a race against time for the coppers. But so far, they've found nothing.'

He shifted on the bench, his demeanour full of awkwardness. 'What I'm trying to tell you, Dani, is... well, it looks as though he's going to be released.'

There was a long pause. Fez pulled out another cigarette. She sensed something was wrong. Sensed the strain in his voice, the same tightness in her father's words when he lied to her mother.

'And when does this friend of yours reckon that might happen?'

With a fresh cigarette between his lips, his hands protectively cupped a lit match. His first inhalation ecstatic. The subsequent exhalation one of relief as if he were letting go of something long held. But she knew there was something he was keeping from her. His eyes closed as smoke steadily streamed from tight lips.

'Any day although over Christmas more likely – when the whole country's too busy with incinerating turkeys and family arguments to notice.'

Then it clicked and she sensed his dilemma: to warn a friend risked exposing his own deceit. Coming up too quickly, her head and eyes felt drained of blood, distant buildings lost to the dark. Dots of city light swimming in her vision.

She got up and stood on the far edge of the path, the soles of her feet troubled by lumps of rubble. And she felt it then, felt the common place of it – the human condition. Its flawed tendency to inflict pain on the ones who are closest, it was like an invisible wrecking ball that swung through society. Her father soon to be riding upon it like King Kong, the far-off lights of Manchester trembling as if it could sense what was coming.

She turned back to Fez, armed with a question she knew the answer to. 'So, tell me. Who exactly is this *best mate* who's having a fling?' Anger boiling up inside, she wanted to scream, wanted to drag him across the rubble but couldn't, because she saw herself below him, a more toxic scumbag who had done much worse than cheat on a soulmate.

There was no response, just his hand picking at the rotten bench like a child waiting to be reprimanded. His body slumped, his face sullen, there followed an intense pause, their eyes locked, the airwaves between them so full of mutual understanding it verged on the telepathic.

Then he was up, pacing back and forth. 'It's over now, Dani. Julie and me, were going through a bad patch. I just couldn't be myself around her. It was a mistake, I know. I'm a total knob head. Look…'

'I want to go back.'

'Look, please don't say anything to Ju…'

'I want to go now.' Everything complicated and fucked up. She needed space, wanted to be alone, wanted to sit silently in the van and think everything through.

'Okay, fine.'

The walk and drive were conducted without conversation; her heart pounding so hard with twisted anger she could feel it in her fingertips. The intense silence broke as he steered the car onto his street.

'Do you want something to eat? Julie's making a curry.'

She glared at him then.

'Yeah… thought not, no worries. Look, you're welcome anytime. Come and stay for a while if you like.'

Standing in front of his house, orange lights of the car flashed. He said goodbye. She turned and walked and said nothing back.

Strangeways

The interior of the van came to life when she twisted the ignition key, orange lights on the dashboard glowing like embers in the darkness, ice crystals on the windscreen glistening in the lights of passing cars. For a moment it was just her and the Christmas music that played on the radio. The news of her father's release somewhere beyond the frozen glass, unhinged and distant.

Air blasting the windscreen seemed to have little effect on the frost at first. One Christmas song ended; another followed. The urge to do something terrifying steadily gripping every part of her body as clear patches grew bigger and the outside world came into view.

She swiped at the controls and after the wipers had scratched away the remaining ice, she wrestled the van onto the road. Her journey through back streets infected by yuletide songs on the radio, before long she pulled up at a main road junction. A car flashed her out. Her feet jabbed the pedals. The van jerked through the line of cars.

Then she sped towards the city, the lane clear, the oncoming traffic bumper to bumper as if retreating from a war that nobody wanted to fight. Snatching at the controls she joined a much wider road: multiple lanes, tail lights swimming under blue signs. The van pushed to the limit; her anger driving it on. Passing the spire of Salford Cathedral, she went through Blackfriars then turned off towards Strangeways. She knew the way – she'd visited the prison before with her mum.

*

Parking up she remained in the van and watched the gatehouse turrets. The scene oddly barren as if the prison held a terrible gravity that drained life from the street. And then she was out and standing in the middle of the road. The horizontal lines of brickwork either side of her converging like a sketch, everything two dimensional, like she was trapped within a desolate piece of art.

Continuing across the road she squared up to the prison wall and looked all the way up to where the coping stones bulged out. The moment flat and dull and lacking she bumped up against the brickwork and slid down to the ground, her head clamped between hands. *What am I doing here?*

Coldness encircled her. From the wall; from the ground. From a freezing wind that cut through her thin jacket. Maybe she could come back with the gun, camp out in the back of the van, wait until her father emerged. And like she'd tempted fate a group cheer erupted from somewhere inside the prison, like a send-off.

Springing up she strode down the barren street, the huge wall scrolling past until she drew level with the gatehouse. The doors set between turrets big and chevroned and strong enough to hold back gorillas.

She waited, her hands clenched, her heart thudding mad rhythms through her body.

'Come on, then!'

Silence.

'I said, come ON!… It's me! Damini!'

The wind. The distant hum of city traffic. The small motors of a surveillance camera as it swivelled above her head and tilted down. She looked up, the silence see-sawing between her and the camera. Its body motionless, its eye sizing her up for so long that she began to wonder if it had detected traces of her guilt.

Maybe guards would drag her in. Maybe police cars would hurtle down the street.

She waited. Nothing happened. The camera panned back to its original view of baker's van and windswept street.

She lowered herself and sat on the kerb. 'I've got the gun...' – eyes shut tight – '...it was me,' she whispered.

And then as if her confession had triggered an instantaneous response, she heard blue sirens. Faint, somewhere in the city, at one point becoming so loud that she considered sprinting to the van. But as she sprang to her feet they began to fade. The camera mounted above on the turret wall, still ignoring the obvious, indifferent to her confession, focusing on the street. Brushing off her backside she sloped back to the van.

The ignition key twisted, the engine idled, her hands murdered the steering wheel as the blower cleared the glass, the gatehouse slowly coming into view.

'If you so much as lay your eyes on my gran I will finish you,' she whispered.

The van slowly pulled away from the kerb. Its sides adorned with the wings of an angel, it cleared the end of Southall Street, turned left and then flew north.

*

She opened the door to Dev's apartment; the smell of breakfast still lingering inside. The tree lights still on, each pane of the windows reflecting them as if a pattern of galaxies decorated the sky.

The scene appealing to the child within, she found herself gathering cushions and laying them on the floor at the back of the room. The novelty of sleeping somewhere other than bed, something her younger self had done to ease the stress of difficult times. So, it seemed only natural that her mind turned to thoughts of her father, specifically the occasions when he went "away".

The shortest absence most memorable because, ironically, he was on a "business trip" and not serving time in prison. A rare pride welling up in her childish heart when he came back with a tan and sun-bleached hair. The stories that graced the pub on his return ones she would never forget: he'd bought a stretch of paradise on the coast, sea snakes, rivers heated by volcanos, frogs and butterflies the size of his burly hands. He was going to build a place with a pool and hot tub. That snippet of her childhood so memorable because of the hope and the rare sound of her mother's laughter rising up from the bar that lulled her to sleep.

But when his promises came to nothing, she remembered visiting the library and conducting a search for Costa Rica and finding – to her surprise – that it wasn't a resort on the Spanish Riviera – as she'd assumed – but a tiny country sandwiched between the Pacific and

Caribbean. The town of Samara, where he supposedly owned land, a tiny community on its western flank. At the time it had all seemed improbable, just another one of his bullshit stories. But now she clung to the image of Central America that she'd seen in the atlas. And she hoped that after being released he would go directly there, his existence from then on limited to a strand of earth that connected huge continents, his infection contained by the oceans that lay either side.

She lay back on the cushions, pulled a blanket over her body and looked up with wide eyes.

*

She dropped off just before dawn. Her light sleep broken, three hours later she lay awake again staring up at cobwebs in the roof truss and listening to street noises that seeped through the big windows. All night her eyes had searched the tree lights for a solution, the loophole of Costa Rica finally vanishing in the cold light of day; she knew her father would come, somehow, soon. And there was no getting away from what would happen next: the epic fight between father and daughter, Harriette caught in the middle of it all.

Sitting up with her back to the wall she stared blankly across the room. The tree catching her eye, she imagined her name dangling on a branch of its genealogical equivalent. Her part in the family saga studied by some future relative.

A rogue with a conscience... she could hear them muse... *moving on so her gran could spend her final years in peace.* The newspaper cuttings in their scrapbook reporting Dani's surrender to the police, her subsequent confession…

The gun lurched into her mind, still hidden behind the portrait. Incriminating the lodge. *Incriminating my gran… I must remove it… then get far away from here.*

Dani scrambled to her feet and quickly returned the cushions and blanket to the big corner sofa, pausing at the window to breathe. Her panic physical: a twist in the stomach, a coiled-up restlessness radiating through her body. The notion of leaving town spreading its wings, her mind working over the logistics of a rapid exit: a change of clothes, cash from the bedside table, the gun.

She only needed enough to get to Manchester. One night, or maybe two until she was taken in by the police. Grabbing the empty rucksack, she wriggled into the straps.

A quick glance at the window as she shook out her hair and stuffed it into a beanie hat.

The street busy. *I'll take the back route to the lodges.*

Clear of the entrance doors she veered left away from Main Street.

The slope down to the quay, railway arches, towpath, she was soon through the kissing gate and into the field, her stride adjusting to the challenges of the hedgerow path. So occupied with picking a route across the mud, a sudden noise took her completely by surprise. Rude and raspy. Motorbike? Her feet left driverless as she looked up to see a flash of orange through the hedgerow. Her fleeting lapse of concentration enough for an unguided foot to land on a ridge of frozen earth. The agony from her rolling ankle so intense that she screamed out and collapsed to the ground.

Nursing her foot, she glared back. Gaps in the hedgerow revealing two helmeted workmen, their chainsaws letting rip as the unthinkable crept into her mind. The sickening snap, the wrenching of soft tissue: *I've broken it.*

The first attempt to stand cut short by the pain, she sat back and looked around in sheer panic. The line of trees beside the canal, the woods at the top of the hill, the furrowed field that stretched out to the far hedgerow, the moors rising beyond. Suddenly everything seeming so very far away.

Staggering to her feet she cursed the frozen earth and forced back the pain with big breaths. One leg workshy, the rest of her physique quarrelling over the newly acquired workload. And then she was off. Her mind already at the top of the hill, her hobbling figure doing its best to catch up. One… and then two… and then three… and then four… tyre tracks, fallen leaves, smooth stones, sharp stones, a small lump of concrete, a frozen glove; the field full of details previously unnoticed. The distance between Dani and the lodges slowly shrinking. The track, the farmer's gate, the lane, she entered the lodge and slammed the door. Taking a seat in the workshop she slumped down and hinged her head back, her breathing hard, the screams of sawn timber lessened by the lodge walls.

Leaning forward she gently probed her foot. The swelling pushing up behind the fabric of her trainers. She gingerly rotated her ankle one way and then the other, then hinged it up and down. Everything working, the movement unhindered; *not broken,* she hoped. Shuffling through the workshop she removed the gun from behind the portrait and placed it in the rucksack.

She then sat again, the chainsaws wailing, the question *what now?* dragging its heels through her mind. Think... think... think, and then it came, and she was up again and out of the lodge and locking the door. Her body rolling lopsidedly as she made her way past the gateway and through the garden of the other lodge, the gun patting her back well done with every step she took towards the shed. Harriette's lodge empty and lifeless, the half-drawn blinds of the upstairs windows watching on with disappointment as Dani reversed her gran's bicycle.

For God's sake, I'm not nicking it.

And then she was off, the sound of chainsaws fading behind her, the cold air burning her face. The cut-through beside the church, the square, Main Street. The mill. Downhill all the way. She parked the bicycle in the lobby and hobbled up the steps to Dev's flat.

The door closed; the lock turned.

Idiot, fool, imbecile... what the hell have you done?

She gulped water from the kitchen tap.

I can stay here for a few days until the swelling goes down.

She ate a chunk of bread torn from a loaf.

It's fine. No one knows I'm here.

Then grabbing a bag of frozen peas, she lay back on the sofa and pressed coldness onto her ankle. The building uttering creaks and groans, the fridge/freezer whirring. The afternoon marked by chimes of the church bell, the town's recurring rhythm pulsing through the big windows. School kids lingering in the street before heading home, the swell of traffic at the end of the working day. The high street shops and cafes lighting up as the skies were robbed by December gloom. Darkness fell, temperatures dropping below zero. The festive illuminations that graced the trees on Main Street reached into the apartment.

After eating an early dinner, she iced her foot one more time and then lay back on the big corner sofa, her foot propped on cushions, the evening cut short by epic fatigue; sleep falling upon her seconds after closing her eyes.

Her night fitful: crows in a dream eyeing her slow progress across fields, cold sweats, muffled knocks and scrapes that came from somewhere beyond the back wall at three o'clock in the morning. Sounds that bewitched her until, in a moment of madness, she removed the gun from the rucksack and aimed it at the entrance door. Her paranoia gradually draining away she placed the gun on the table and lay very still on the sofa. The gravity of her situation sinking in. Any reservations about handing herself in now put to bed. A strange relief growing inside her because all the running was over, her fate most definitely sealed.

She closed her eyes and before aiming for sleep she gingerly flexed her ankle.

Two days, maybe three... then I'm gone.

Poinsettias

The following morning, she woke with a small cry, who or where she was not clear to begin with. But as the screech of a refuse truck and shouts of the bin men filtered in from the street it dawned on her that she was lying on a sofa.

Pushing on her trainers, she limped a few laps of the apartment. At the window she watched the street: people outside the post office engaged in conversation, sixth-formers in hats and coats larking around a bench. Bruised clouds rolling in from the north.

The snow came from nowhere. Wheeling out of the sky and barrelling over rooftops. So blurred by the murmurations of white that at times the street untethered from time, and Dani imagined her great-grandmother running from wartime resentments. *Did Ellen run; did she stumble, or did she slip on ice; is that how she ended up in the canal?*

The squall passed; tail-end flurries haunting the street; the ghosts retreating into drenched stone and wet cobbles. She glanced back at the antique gun, its barrel oversailing the tabletop, pointing at the back wall like an accusation.

Maybe the sealed room held clues to Ellen's demise. Maybe I could find a way in. Hobbling to the table she picked up the revolver and read the wording stamped into its rusty body, *Webley – 1916.* Dani looked up, her mind wheeling back to Harriette's mention of parish records: *It's the year Ellen disappeared…*

The intercom buzzed.

The gun dropped to the table.

Dani's journey to the handset slow and full of impatience. 'Who is it?'

Traffic sounds hashed through the speaker, as if the caller had fallen victim to rush-hour commuters.

Dani glanced back at the gun.

'Who is it?'

Silence… heavy breathing…

'Parcel… for… One B… needs signing for.'

She searched for shoes. Couldn't find them. The intercom chirped.

'…hello… One B?'

'Give me a second.'

She threw on a leather jacket, Dev's scent swamping her body, steadying her nerve. After struggling down the stairs, she took a deep breath and then opened the entrance door. Cars swishing puddles, hats and scarves roaming the street, smell of warm bread, dripping trees.

There was a feigned cough, a parcel at the end of the postman's arm.

'Sorry. Miles away.'

'Me too at the end of the week. Retiring Friday, then off to Madeira,' he said glancing at her bruised foot.

She took the parcel. 'Sounds nice.'

'Nature lover's paradise, island of eternal spring, that's what the magazine says anyway. The wife's choice – she loves flowers – mad over poinsettias.'

He held out a sheet of paper; she took the pen and squiggled *DH*.

'Need to get through the week before I can hang up my boots.'

But she wanted to stay on the doorstep and hear more about Madeira and poinsettias. Be a part of the normality that unfolded in the street, newly sublime to her because soon she would have to bow out and give it all up.

'Well, best get on.'

'Yes, of course. Have a lovely holiday.'

'You look after yourself now – Have a good life.'

Wrapping the jacket tighter around her body she watched the postman's feet lumber down the steps, his hi-vis jacket flapping in the cold breeze like yellow wings.

Closing the door as the post van pulled away, she limped upstairs, limped across the landing. In the apartment she placed the package on the television and then for a while limped circuits of the living area. Dirty crockery piled up in the sink, ripped wrapping paper on the floor, her encampment on the sofa like that of a hobo. The untidiness shouting out as she inched around. The stabbing pains in her ankle steadily growing as she tidied and cleaned. Kitchen first, then the living space. The bathroom as far as she got before taking painkillers. The postman's words looping through her head as she stared at herself in the cabinet mirror: *You look after yourself now – Have a good life.*

Raising a glass, she swigged back and swallowed a pill. 'Good luck with that.'

It was mid-afternoon before she retired to a chair. A bag of frozen peas on her foot as she watched sleet turn to rain, the rooftops and chimneys of town distorted by the streaming windows. Her mind purged, calmer, more attuned to thoughts of a practical nature.

It would, she thought, be a good idea to cancel her classes. To not show up would only draw attention. Something she needed to avoid at all costs if she were to stay in town for a few days longer.

She needed to go to the information board in the post office and add a note to her flyer that advertised her class. *Sessions cancelled until further notice*, or something like that. Word would soon get around. But for the rest of the day, she just needed to lay low. Rest. Let things heal.

For a while she lay coiled on the sofa and watched the TV drama *Cracker*. Her eye distracted by the little parcel on top of the television. After one episode she ejected the cassette from the video player.

Silence – a memory – an inkling – then she knew.

Inside the package was a hearing aid, a spare that Dev wanted to take on his travels. Removing the wrapping she opened the box to see a plastic tadpole nestled inside.

It wasn't the first time she had considered speaking to an inanimate object. It was something she did when feeling alone and anxious and in need of conversation. She leant towards the hearing aid.

'You recorded the whole series for me. Thank you. I've watched one episode. It's good. We should watch the rest of it together... although... I'm not exactly sure when that might be.'

Shutting her eyes, she pictured the entrance to Longsight Police Station, imagined walking in, standing at the counter, blurting everything out to the duty officer.

Arrest. Imprisonment. Atonement. Her release at some future point in time.

And then just maybe, she would get a second chance.

Dani Hey had a plan.

She almost smiled.

Kissing the earpiece, she replaced the lid and laid the box on a shelf.

And after watching another episode she climbed up to the mezzanine level, slipped into Dev's bed and fell into a deep, unbroken sleep.

*

Within an hour of waking, she had showered, got dressed and was on her way into town. Her foot still painful, but the swelling had gone down, her limp less pronounced now that she'd wrapped her ankle in a bandage.

In the post office she removed her schedule from the noticeboard, replacing it after writing a note across the menu of dates: *All classes cancelled until New Year, due to unforeseen circumstances.*

She headed back to the mill, her journey in the slow lane coloured by details of the street: leaves in the gutter, moss between old cobbles, the ornate railings, the festive display in the bakery window: cake boxes, panettone, biscotti, a gingerbread terrace of houses on a higher shelf, embellished with snowdrifts of icing. The miniature Santa perched on a chimney, the string of fairy lights that framed it all; the moment of wonderment broken when Dani spotted Isla at the till waving frantically, her hands beckoning Dani into the shop with graceful clarity.

Shit.

The bell jingled as Dani opened the door. The shop busy. Customers queuing for breakfast, most of them workmen of some trade or other.

'Dani,' Isla called out.

'I'll come back later.'

'Wait. I've got something for you.' Isla handed her a paper bag. 'Dev asked me to sort breakfast for you. Just haven't had a chance to pop it round – too busy.'

'Thank you.'

'I was hoping you could help me out, just for an hour or so. Work started on the hall today and as you can see everything's gone a bit mad.'

Dani looked at the long queue.

Isla's hands prayed. 'I'll love you forever.'

'We'll all love you for ever,' a gruff voice came from the back.

Laughter. A pause, the shop hanging. Dani looked at the picture of soldiers on the wall, Dev on the back row, head highest, smile broadest, his wholesome nature radiating out.

'My foot's injured.'

Isla patted the stool by the till. 'Take a load off.'

'Okay. Fine.'

Isla kissed her. A cheer went up. Dani removed her coat and worked the till. A warm buzz filling the shop, the morning falling away, the queue elastic, extending and contracting like a muscle, trade dropping off after the lunchtime rush.

Like they always did on Friday afternoon, the bakers deep-cleaned the kitchen then left for the pub. Isla followed them to the door holding a tray of mince pies.

'Can you hold the fort while I take these down to the brass band?'

'No problem.'

Dani ate a chocolate muffin while flicking through a newspaper. The half-eaten treat pushed to one side when she saw her father's name in print. The mishandling of his case exposed by a damning article; her father's legal team had coated him in Teflon, so it seemed. His release set for after the twenty-eighth the last words she read before her eyes lurched off the page.

I could stay a little longer. Spend Christmas at the lodges. Leave for Manchester when Gran leaves for Venice.

Vaguely aware of a voice she looked up to see the landlord of the Nav at the counter. She slammed the newspaper shut.

Dani glared up. The faint sounds of a brass band drifted down from the square.

'You alright, love?'

'Sorry – away with the fairies.'

Geoff placed a basket on the counter. She forced a smile and tapped prices into the till.

'Didn't realise you worked in here.'

'I don't. I'm helping Isla out for a few hours. She got snowed under.'

'Know the feeling.'

'Pub busy, then?'

'Yep, you could say that. You at the party tonight? Kathy's done a grand job of decorating the upstairs rooms.'

The Lassiter's Christmas party had completely slipped her mind. Everyone who worked in the mill had been invited.

'I can't – something's cropped up.'

She took the cash from his hand and returned some change.

'Shame. It'll be a good one.'

Isla entered the shop, the sounds of "Silent Night" following her in. 'Everything alright?'

'Hope you're coming later,' said Geoff as he approached Isla.

Isla held the door. 'Looking forward to it.'

"Silent Night" made way for "Walking in the Air".

Geoff and Isla chatted in the doorway.

Dani disappeared into the kitchenette and when she returned with cups of tea Geoff had gone and Isla was tidying the shop.

Dani sat on the stool and sipped tea.

'I thought you were going to the party,' said Isla as she wiped down the counter.

'Sorry, had to duck out last minute.'

Isla stopped cleaning and looked up. 'Is it because...' She nodded at the newspaper. Dani recognised the assumption.

'No.' The outrage in her voice frail. 'My ankle hurts and... I've still got loads to do before Christmas.'

'You should have said, you needn't have stayed for so long.'

Isla fixed Dani with a look then moved around the counter, opened her arms and pulled her in for a hug. 'You don't owe this place anything. Everyone hates your dad, not you. It's not your fault whenever this place goes over a bump in the road.'

'I know.'

Isla pulled back. 'You okay?'

'Got a lot on. That's the deal when you work for yourself.'

'Oh God, you sound just like Dev. Bloody party poopers both of you – made for each other.' Isla hugged her again. 'Thanks for today.'

'Happy to help. I really should be getting off though.'

'Have a great Christmas if I don't see you before. And make sure you take it easy.'

Isla disappeared into the kitchen.

Dani pulled on her coat, paused at the door and studied the window display. The gingerbread houses open at the back, stiffened by evenly spaced partitions, the rooms cellular and empty. Not having taken breath for several seconds Dani inhaled deeply and then walked out of the shop.

*

In the mill lobby she worked the combination on the postbox and transferred the logjam of letters and flyers into the pockets of Dev's jacket. Bracing herself she climbed the stairs, her ankle throbbing as she opened the door to the apartment, the gun on the table greeting her in, its judging finger singling her out.

'Damn thing.'

Placing the stack of mail on the island unit she grabbed the bag of peas from the freezer and iced her foot on the sofa, the isolation and loneliness she once felt at the Crescents returning. Nobody to talk to, nobody to share her problems with, her eyes drifting across the room to the video cassette, its labelled edge still poking out from the VHS player. The word *Cracker* written across it. A gritty police drama set in Manchester. The main characters Fitzy and Wise – criminal psychologist and detective – working together to solve crimes. Flawed and imperfect but she would have taken either as a father because they both respected the truth. To share the afternoon with them better than moping around, she thought.

After carrying a pot of tea and a plate of mince pies to the sofa she pushed in the cassette and pressed play. Episodes unfolding one after the other until the tape stopped.

The screen blanked; the tape rewound.

She glanced at the gun. Her pulse thumped; the scenes set in police interview rooms had been the most difficult to watch because they had given her a taste of things to come. The police would have so many questions, would want to know everything and she couldn't afford to falter. And it was clear to her now that to prepare well, she would have to relive that terrible day, revisit the painful detail. Practise her side of the story in order to retell it with conviction. And only after it was fresh in her mind would she be able to deliver the whole story in a version that was nothing but the truth.

Her confession was going to be the most carefully planned moment of her life.

DARDALE

1915

VIII

Brown Hare – *Lepus europaeus*

Study for Wallis and Hilton Wallpapers. Plate No. 108 – Narrow Escape
[see sketch on next page]

Facts: Hares are not colonial and don't burrow. Shy, elusive and very fast,
they can travel at speeds of up to forty miles per hour. They frequently
outwit pursuers, by their ability to turn and corner with unrivalled agility.

Quaint beliefs: If a hare runs through a village a fire will break out in one
of its buildings shortly afterwards. [Expression: "Kiss the Hare's foot" –
Meaning to hesitate, after which the opportunity will have gone and all
that will be left is a footprint.]

Joe would often lie on his back in Dardale meadow until
his mind unravelled, eyes detached from the movement
of clouds, hands combing the grass. But lately the meadow
failed to calm his nerve. Weighing every word, every reaction,
every look, an obsession that had grown out of hand.

Cedric's behaviour odd. Abnormally carefree. Could
people see through his calmness; smell his deceit, read his
thoughts?

He was sick of fear. Sick of pretending; most of all he was sick for Africa. So much so he'd contacted his quartermaster by coded message and requested evacuation to German South-west Africa.

The message back – *Meet to discuss.*

He travelled to Leeds. It was the same old routine. Attend a conference organised by the government press bureau where staff officers reported "preferred narratives" of gallantry. And afterwards a drink with journalist friends to swap stories from the front nobody was allowed to print.

Staggering back to the safe house he waited. His feet off the end of the bed, he fell asleep and dreamt of trekking along the Magaliesberg Rand. A step in the earth's crust as far as the eye could see, the flat veld below curving up as if a giant broom had swept the dust of a thousand years against it.

Waking each morning he watched the terraced street for any sign of his contact.

Three days later Sibler showed up. A reticent man. Stick thin, everything about him indefinite. Never a straight answer or clear decision, Joe reckoned that his trail would be impossible to track across the veld.

When Joe announced his intention to leave for Africa, Sibler smirked then delivered the crushing news: German South-west Africa had fallen – invaded by an army of Boer hensoppers who had sided with the British.

Then Sibler laid a new deal on the table. The motherland would offer him asylum, but they wanted more in return. Sibler pulled a revolver from his case and handed it to Joe.

His mission no longer to tinker with fuses and

encourage workers to rebel. His mission now was to destroy the factory.

He caught the train at Leeds Central, more passengers boarding at Todmorden. Seats occupied by chattering women, Joe stared out of the window, his eyes flitting over green landscapes that relentlessly tore back.

The black roar killing conversation when the train entered Summit Tunnel, the carriage consumed in an odd trance, minds wandering away to faraway places.

Joe glared down the aisle, the space long and narrow like the block room, and he imagined himself inside it stockpiling shells and setting charges. And as the sudden blast of a passing train ripped by, he clamped his eyes shut and saw violent reds and yellows engulfing the women, engulfing Ellen.

Daylight exploded into the carriage; stabbing pains sheared through his chest.

The train whistle screamed. And as the carriage came back to life a woman with a concerned face asked if he was alright. He smiled. 'Yes, fine, thank you. Just tired.'

He pretended to sleep for the rest of the journey, but his awake mind grappled with how best to seal the fate of filling factory twenty-four.

*

The day after returning, Joe was summoned to an urgent meeting in the colonel's office.

Why do women lack order and discipline, top of the agenda.

Joe was issued a writing pad and told to take notes.

The "rebellion" yet to be discussed, Harold wittered on about the women he'd caught smoking behind the factory. He placed the evidence on the table. A packet of Black Cat cigarettes.

'Unladylike.'

'Outrageous.'

As the colonel and Harold talked pipes and tobacco, Joe's eye trekked the room: cobwebs sagging with dust, flies on the windowsill now a dismembered graveyard of bodies and limbs. The colonel's desk obsessively tidy. The office sealed and stuffy during summer now chilled by wide-open windows.

The background chatter straying ever further from the point, Joe fixed Kitchener's eyes, his mind skipping back to the day his commando cut telegraph wires. It was the day that Joe shot a British soldier. He'd watched his face hit the dusty ground, saw the big moustache through the sight of his Mauser. And when the day was done, they retreated to the farmhouse, and he remembered – after claiming he'd slain Kitchener – his mother's stoic face sharing a smile with his father. The following day they left at dawn, a long trek in the saddle to rejoin their commando ahead of them. But he would never forget looking back and seeing that last image of his mother out on the porch, her hand waving them off. Only years later did he learn that she perished in a British concentration camp.

The colonel paced back and forth, Harold's sycophantic voice trotting behind.

Joe scribbled another note:

Ellen Parry to receive official caution.

Then the colonel referred to women as "untrustworthy" and announced that a guard would be posted between the block room doors.

Cold air gripped the room. Joe glanced at the windows: treetops in the street a high gallery for a flock of peering birds, their bodies holding fast as branches swayed below them. He placed the pencil down, pushed the pad away and then explained his idea.

The colonel looked astonished. 'You mean permanently fill in the doorways?'

'Yes, sir. A good tradesman should have them sealed up within a couple of days.'

The room fell silent.

'A buffer zone if you like. Soundproof.'

Smugness broke across the colonel's face. 'Like a no man's… or should I say no woman's land.'

Harold's eyes came alive. 'The witches can knock all they like but we won't hear a bloody thing.'

The colonel reached for his empty pipe. 'Block room by name, block room by nature, wouldn't you say, digger?'

'I would, sir, and you haven't even heard the best of it.' Cupping a hand Joe mimicking the act of smoking a pipe. 'With offices totally separate from workshop, there'd be no reason not to.'

Silence.

Joe felt stirrings – two minds slowly wheeling around, then a hand slapping his back.

'You… clever… little… Aussie… digger,' the colonel placing a loving emphasis on each of his words.

*

Two doors – a mere ten feet of block room in between. Office side sealed first. A straightforward job; the tradesman laying bricks for half a day. Workshop side not so simple; the doorway set into a timber frame wall, the infill job entailed sawing, hammering and lime plastering. Risk of creating a spark too great, shifts were cancelled and a twenty-four-hour shutdown was sanctioned by the colonel.

Quotas already falling short slipped even further.

Joe waited on the platform for the tradesman to return from lunch, the sky burnished yellow by winter sun. The train line sweeping out of Dardale like gold seams set into the landscape. A hare sat upright beside the track, its crooked whiskers caught in the low sun, its eyes fixed upon Joe as if sensing foul play.

A creature he would have shot in Africa, but like the tables had been turned, the hare peeled away and ran beside the rails weaving from side to side towards the moors. And Joe envied its freedom, then fantasised about boarding a train and leaving for home, to the wide expanse of hot African savannah.

Cold striking up from the platform he cupped his hands and blew into them, his eye following the tracks out of town and searching for the hare.

'Thinking of leaving us?'

Joe turned and smiled at Mr Barnes, a retired jack of all trades, the handles of a tool bag gripped by his brawny hands.

'All trains have been cancelled – so not today, cobber.'

They carried materials across the bridge link and through the workshop, and then together set about removing the second door frame. Joe sat on a workbench while Mr Barnes filled the opening with a framework of timber.

'I hear this is to keep the Parry girl at bay.'

'You know her?'

'Knew her mother – she taught my children. Sounds like her Ellen went off rails, mind, got mixed up in all that Suffragette business before the war. No wonder it's all kicked off in here.'

Mr Barnes began to nail thin strips of larch horizontally between the timbers.

'Suspended indefinitely so Harold said. Word going around she's got a bun in the oven.'

'A what in the oven?'

'A baby.'

Unbearable sensations rushed through Joe: guilt, twisted exuberance, relief finally elbowing through because he knew the place for an English mother was strictly at home. He wiped his face with a sleeve.

'Blimey, lad – not yours, is it?'

'Nah, dust in my eye.' Joe forced a laugh. 'Not my type, cobber. Too feisty.'

'Well, there was no messing with Ellen's mother, I can tell you that. Had them children in the palm of her hand. The whole town gutted when she died. It was like we'd all lost a mother. Died giving birth she did. Her Tom never bounced back from it. Who would? Losing the love of your life changes a man.'

Barnes mixed lime plaster in a bucket.

'Not sure there's enough after doing the brickwork this morning. May have to come back to finish off.'

Joe glanced into the bucket; obviously not enough. Further disruption? At least another shutdown. His internalised reaction a casual shrug.

'Colonel won't be happy.'

'I'll do my best with what I've got.'

The tradesman trowelled blobs of plaster onto the lath, working in from the outer edges. Joe looking on as the doorway gradually turned into wall; memory of the block room falling away. His mind busy working over his plans, making adjustments, smoothing out complexities.

But his ideas were still peppered with glaring flaws. He was intending to enter the sealed room by way of the floor hatch. Yet he'd not managed to make a copy of the padlock key. And even though quick-fire shells were small, it would be difficult to smuggle them to a lower floor and lift them back up through the hatch.

Barnes scraped out a last trowel of plaster and then tipped the empty bucket towards Joe.

'I'll have to come back to finish off.'

Rubbing his chin Joe sized up the area of unfinished wall. An oval patch of bare lath a foot-and-a-half wide by three high. Better than the hatch.

'That won't be necessary. I've got something I can hang over it.'

'Oh, aye. Like a painting? I can bang a couple of nails in if it helps.'

'A portrait, actually, and yes, would you?'

'Of course.'

'Thanks, cobber.'

*

Later that day Joe explained the situation to the colonel.

'What do you mean, not finished? He can't do half a job then just sod off – another shutdown is out of the question. We need to hit targets, Stander. This is embarrassing.'

'I have a solution, sir.'

The colonel pulled a pipe from a jacket pocket then glared at Joe. 'Well, come on, man, out with it.'

'Yes, sir. One moment, sir.'

Joe stepped out of the room then struggled back in with the large portrait.

'Since being replaced by Lord Kitchener, Sid's been hanging around our office making the place look untidy, so thought I'd put him to some use.'

Joe manoeuvred the gilt-edged frame so that it faced into the room. The colonel's head cocked to one side, a smirk slowly dawning across his face. 'Well, well, well, Mr Wallis has his uses after all.'

Straightening up, the colonel filled his pipe and then struck a match, the flame dancing in and out of the tobacco as he took a quick succession of puffs. 'But will… it provide… enough cover… Stander?'

Joe glanced down at the anti-saboteur poster he'd pasted over the portrait, a margin of oil paint still visible around its edge. Peripheral traces of Sidney peeking out; top of balding head, shirt cuff to the side, trousered leg below.

'Sir?'

The colonel batted smoke away as if dealing with a persistent bug.

'The lath, Stander. Will it cover the bare lath?'

'Oh yes, sir. With ease, sir.'

Murmurs of gratification came from the colonel as he gazed out of the window. There was a brief pause between puffs as he lovingly tamped tobacco into the bowl of the pipe with a little tool. And then as if suddenly remembering he was not alone the tamping stopped and he glared up at Joe.

'That is all, Stander.'

'Yes, sir, we'll hang it up first thing tomorrow, sir.'

*

The women were leaving for a break as Cedric and Joe carried the gilt frame across the bridge link.

They lifted the portrait onto the wall, the unfinished building work vanishing in an instant. Then they edged back and pondered the poster thoughtfully as if standing in an art gallery. Joe's eyes slowly sliding down the "S" of the word saboteur, he saw himself lift the frame off the wall, his hands pulling away the bare lath, his body disappearing through the hole.

'Look out! – SABOTAGE.'

Joe flinched; Cedric laughed.

'Bloody hell, Ced.'

'Sorry. I was just reading the poster.'

'Shouting, more like.'

Cedric continued reading aloud. 'Scotch this by being always alert – Report suspicious things and persons at once – Issued by London Emergency Committee. Well, there you go.'

'Bit dramatic, don't you think?'

'Careful now. You may get locked up by our emergency committee saying things like that. Don't you have emergency committees back home?'

He did.

Branded a marvel for surviving the desert, he was invited by the administration of German South-west Africa to attend committee meetings and advise them on matters of the land, and how best to live beside the indigenous Herero and Namaqua people. But then the German military stepped in and rounded them up and shipped them to concentration camps on Shark Island. The persecution a re-run of his mother's fate at the hands of the British, he couldn't stay and watch it happen again. So, he caught a train from Windhoek to the port of Swakopmund where he began working as a postal clerk for the Woermann shipping line, for years plying the waves between German colony and Hamburg. A simple job at sea. A place without borders, without ties, without committees.

Joe's attention snapped back when he heard the next shift trickling into the workshop. One singer amongst a chatting group, a cough, a laugh. And when they became surrounded by women Joe couldn't help but think of his mother. His heart beating harder with shame he turned to Cedric.

'Search me, cobber.'

DANI

Cracker

She lay on the sofa, a bag of frozen peas wrapped around her ankle, happy voices drifting up from the street; people arriving for the party she guessed.

Removing the bag, it lay semi-rigid in her hands, reused so many times, the contents had pulped to the contours of her foot. She returned them to the freezer, the act of walking a little less painful, her foot bruised and swollen; still weeks away from running she guessed.

Standing by the Christmas tree she gazed out of the apartment window, obliquely towards the Navigation Inn, disco lights in its first-floor windows pulsing to the faint beat of "Kung Fu Fighting". People dancing stiffly in a whirlwind of glitterball spots, a far cry from the parties of Hulme Crescents. She walked a circuit of the apartment, then opened a bottle of wine and raised a glass to old times. 'To, the kitchen.'

She downed it like a shot then sat on the floor beside the tree. Knees to chin, her body rocking, her mind dreading the next step. 'Time to rehearse.'

She thought of the characters of Fitzy and Wise, ghosts of a crime drama still vivid in her memory. Pretending they were there with her in the room, she set the scene for another episode in which she – Dani Hey – would play the accused. On the table she placed a pencil, paper and ghetto blaster that doubled as the interview recording deck.

Fitzy and Wise looking on as she took a seat, her eyes closing, her mind returning to a dark ginnel. Explosions of colour randomly unloading; all the grim details surging back. Her hand reached for the pencil. Rushing into the first sentence, she crossed it out then rewrote it again, three times. The pencil twitching violently for a long time, she shook the ache from her hand whenever reviewing sentences. She reshuffled words and cut out inaccuracies. A second draft, a third, a fourth. Seeing life drain from her brother's eyes over and again filling the hours until she'd got everything straight.

Pushing back from the table she made strong tea and then stood for a while by the window, her nerves calmed by the sight of people enjoying the party. But then the tea was all gone. Wham's "Last Christmas" drifted across the street, a cloud of dry ice consuming figures on the dancefloor. Fitzy and Wise waited at the table, their expectant faces drawing her back, she imagined Wise uttering his lines with a weary calmness.

'I am informing the suspect, Damini Hey, that the interview has commenced, and the recording has now started.'

Returning to the chair she described the night as being cold and smoggy, described how she'd hidden in a spot where the wall kinked in, the gun behind her back. How her brother turned into the ginnel, how she stepped out and startled him.

'Then we argued. And that's when he accused Mum of being a grass.

There were a lot of fireworks. A lot of explosions… He – my brother – was about ten yards away when I drew the gun. I aimed the barrel at the ground in front of his feet. I thought doing that would scare him… you know, stop him dead.

But he kept coming… so I tracked the ground in front of his feet.

He said something like, "Stealing my toys now, are we? Don't make me laugh, piss pants."

Piss pants… he used to call me piss pants. And I did steal the gun. That was true.

Then there was a powerful boom above us and the ginnel glowed green. He lurched towards me.

I panicked – I, just panicked. I aimed at the ground, but the gun kicked up – like it had a life of its own.

The shot was drowned by the fireworks. Then… he was down… on the ground, leaning against the wall. There were more explosions above. His face turned different colours – his sweater was soaked in blood. It all happened so quickly.

But it was obvious what I had done… I had shot my brother… I had shot him in the chest.'

She gagged. Her hands trembled. Then wiping her face, she imagined hearing the voice of Charlie Wise:

'Interview suspended at 11.30 p.m., Damini Hey is taking a short break. The interview is due to resume in approximately five minutes.'

Her face tilted down and she let out a breathless cry. Distant voices sang along to Captain Sensible's "Happy Talk". Gulping deep breaths, she wiped her streaming eyes and nose, then took in a big steadying breath as she straightened.

'He said, "You shot me, piss pants… you fucking shot me."'

Her head swinging slow and heavy, sobs doing whatever they wanted to do. And then she was up and out of the chair, her back to the window, her sleeves wiping away tears.

'…He… he was in shock… trembling. By that point I'd totally lost it… was crying… apologising. But the fireworks drowned everything. He grabbed my arm and pulled me in – my face close to his. He was struggling to talk, gasping for air – his eyes were going. Then his last words, "You're more like him than I am."

I knew he was dead. Everything fell silent. Then I saw people at the head of the ginnel, so – I turned and ran.'

She knew the question would come; imagined Fitzy leaning forward and asking it.

'*Who was your brother referring to when he said –* You're *more like him than I am?*'

'Our father – He meant our father.'

'*And...*' She imagined Fitzy leaning forward, '*...are you more like him?*'

The pub sang louder. Voices more numerous. Drunk. The ghosts of Fitzy and Wise began to wrap things up.

'*We have reached the end of the interview. Do you wish to say or add anything to what has already been said?*'

The partygoers joyfully shouted out the lyrics of "Fairytale of New York" by the Pogues, the song spilling from the pub like an old drunk staggering into the street.

'*...the interview has now ended... The time is 11.57 p.m....*'

Then the ghost of Fitzy and Wise began to fade from Dani's mind, chased away by the rude lyrics that came from across the road, belted out by the lairy pub choir, their voices rising as the Pogues' song got juicier. Dani stood and slapped the table.

'No, wait... I'm not like him... Come back... I haven't

finished. I was trying to protect my mother. I didn't mean to kill him. It was an accident. That's the truth.'

The Irish ballad died away; cheerless house lights came on and spoiled the disco fun. People emerged from the pub. A taxi arrived. Retching sounds drifted up from the street. Dani dived onto the sofa, the cushions pressed either side of her head blocking everything out.

The town fell quiet.

The church bell rang.

Christmas, she thought. *At least I have one more Christmas.*

*

She woke to noises. A dull thump reverberating through the building from somewhere below. Creaks and clicks of old radiators as the heating kicked in. Cats fighting in the street, otherwise, the town at rest now that Christmas Eve had arrived.

Not due at Harriette's until eleven she rolled over and slumbered; hide the gun and pack a few things into a bag was all she had to do before leaving the apartment.

Half an hour later she was up and testing her foot. Less painful, less swollen. After a few laps of the living area, she sat on the bar stool with a coffee and sized up the pile of Dev's post that she'd placed on the worktop the day before. Christmas cards mainly, three official-looking brown envelopes and several items of junk mail.

The elegant handwriting on the uppermost envelope catching her eye. She raised the mug of coffee, but it paused near her mouth when she saw her name written above the address.

Placing down the mug she reached for the envelope, untucked the flap, and slipped out the card. Yellowed with age, the back of it was marked with a royal crest:

By Royal Warrant To His Majesty the King
Hilton and Wallis
Paper Mills Company
Purveyors of Fine Wallpapers
Dardale
Cover Print – Pattern No. 112 – Winter

The front embossed with a latticework of frosted branches and red berries. Inside a message:

Dear Dani

I hope this card finds you well.

Forgive me for contacting you in this way,

but unfortunately, a dip in health prevents me from venturing out.

So, I would be grateful if you could call by, as I have some important news to convey. The subject is of a delicate nature, so I ask that you tell no one about this and that you visit me only after your grandmother has left for Venice.

I appreciate your discretion in advance.

Season's Greetings and Best Wishes

Rennie Wallis

Closing the card, she stared at the print then placed it back in the envelope.

With only a few days of freedom at her disposal, Rennie's words sparked little intrigue. Time with Harriette the main objective. She unloaded the dishwasher, packed her rucksack, plumped sofa cushions and left the apartment. Her journey to the lodges via the quay. A stop-off where she gathered herself. The frozen canal serene, a hazy light softening winter views, air clean and metallic. And the barge was back, moored beyond the railway arches, listing a little as if devoured by the bankside thicket. Threads of smoke rising from its chimney curling down, recharging a mist that shrouded the meadow beyond. A houseboat? – A loner living off-grid?

Good luck to them.

Climbing steps up to Main Street she predicted the pub gossip as she passed the Navigation Inn. *Did you know the mad bitch shot her brother?* Town square deserted. The statue of Sidney Wallis wearing a traffic cone. Everything petrified with frost on the lane.

She opened the porch and was greeted in by the sounds of cello and piano.

'Helloooo,' she sang out while hanging up her coat.

Through the hallway, she glimpsed Rennie at the piano and then Harriette's face appeared at the music room door. 'Happy Christmas, dear.'

'I shouldn't have interrupted. It's good to hear you play.'

Rennie bowed his head and performed a theatrical hand roll. Harriette placed the cello on a stand and then gave Dani a tight hug.

'Not very Christmassy, I'm afraid, but it's a favourite.'

Rennie stiffly rose from the stool. He looked gaunt, his hair whiter, his beard scruffier, his skin a little tanned.

Harriette turned to him. 'Staying for some lunch?'

'No, no, need to get back...' He walked towards the coat hooks.

'Why don't you stay for a bite to eat?' Harriette said, rolling her eyes at Dani.

'Need to work on my speech. No rest for the wicked.'

He shook Dani's hand. 'Get the Christmas card?'

'Yes, thank you.'

'Good.'

Flipping on a flat cap he winked then smiled.

'An original. Probably worth a lot. Keep it under your hat...' – he winked again – '...or else everyone will want one.'

The musicians embraced and lightly pecked each other's cheeks. 'Have a lovely Christmas and good luck with the speech.'

Rennie set off, via the French doors then the garden path. His head and shoulders briefly floating above a hedge, he waved back before dipping below a brick arch and disappearing through a gateway.

Harriette gathered sheets of music. Dani looked blankly at the garden. 'What did he mean, everyone will want one?'

'Don't think he's sent a card to anyone for years. Even I don't get one.'

'Oh.'

She followed her grandmother into the kitchen. 'You two friends again, then?'

'Christmas ceasefire, think he's getting quite attached to you, though. Hungry? Soup and sausage rolls?'

'Yes, please.'

'Prefers to be on his own this time of year. Lost his dad at Christmas, you see.'

Harriette placed a pinny over her head, wrapped the cord around her waist and vigorously tied a bow. 'I'm worried about him.'

'Oh.'

'We all have our off days, but it's every day with him recently.'

Her raised voice came from the larder. 'He's supposed to be doing this speech on New Year's Eve to mark the mill's centenary. I can tell he's fretting about it. Stressing over things like that can make you ill especially at his age. It's too much for him.'

She reappeared holding a loaf of bread.

'Would you do me a big favour?'

'Mm.'

'Will you keep an eye on him when I go away?'

I'll be in prison.

'If I'm around, Gran, yes, of course.'

After lunch they sat in the living room. Doves all around them, the wallpaper pattern like an aviary. The feathered twosomes more obvious in the wash of the table lamp and glow of the fire, as if perching there for warmth and a view of the Scrabble game set up on the footstool.

Time passed. The fire snapping and fizzing, fibres of wood glowing then falling away until the game was done. Then Harriette prepared supper: fish pie with an

Italian twist. Dani stayed in the living room and finished decorating the tree, then curling up on the armchair she gazed at the branches; baubles reflecting the fire, the tree alive with a hundred little flames.

Like two home birds, there was a call…

'It's ready…'

…and a reply.

'…Coming.'

They ate and talked and drank. And after clearing away Dani read out the clues of a Christmas crossword. 'Ten down. Bringer of good fortune. Two words; eleven letters in all. First letter F, ninth letter T.'

There was no response. Harriette asleep.

'Gran.'

She stirred. 'Sorry, dear – think I'd better turn in.' She filled a glass with water. 'Did we finish?'

'One left.' Dani reread the clue; the answer delivered immediately.

'First-footer.'

'Mm. It does fit.' Dani scribbled letters in boxes. 'Not heard that before.'

'First person you let in, on New Year's Day. For luck, it should be a dark-haired man with high-arched feet who remains silent until placing a lump of coal on the fire…' She laughed. 'Or something like that.'

Standing at the door she smiled at her granddaughter who stared blankly into space as if imagining the complexity of organising such an event.

'It's just folklore, dear.'

'I know, Gran. Goodnight. I love you.'

'Goodnight, Dani. I love you, too.'

Dani poked the fire into life then watched a late film called *She Devil*.

Cell Phone

Dani made it to bed at two in the morning, slept through the night without interruption then woke feeling cold. Most of the bedding on the floor, her body curled around a bundled sheet as though she were protecting a night-time pearl. She went to the window and peered into the blackness; timbers creaking as the wind leant against the roof. The room still cold despite the tinkling pipework, the boiler still busy with heating the spaces below, the little radiator beside her legs always last in line for a share of hot water.

Throwing bedding over herself she fell back into bed, her eyes peeking out of the satin-edged blanket. Everything the same: cushioned window seat, slope of the ceiling, wood-panelled walls, the heady smell of furniture polish. It all whispered sanctuary, safety, stability. The rushing wind and ticking radiator lulled her into light sleep. Anything deeper thwarted by her need to go. She shuffled to the bathroom, sleep suddenly a stranger as the cold toilet seat caused her to wince. Elbows on knees, chin propped on winged hands, she tuned into an argument playing out in the room below. Harriette versus radio; the kitchen joining in. Crockery, cutlery, cupboards and drawers caught in a whirlwind of open and shut. Then just the babbling radio.

'Are you up?' Harriette's voice rose from the hallway.

'Just getting in the shower – down in a minute.'

Bathroom window full of Dani's reflection, she imagined the artist's courtroom sketch that would appear on the news. 'Merry Christmas,' she whispered to herself, then showered quickly and dressed smartly. Descending the stairs she paused in the hallway, willow boughs on the wallpaper, baubles glimmering in living room dimness, glossy instruments in the music room. She could see Harriette in the kitchen, standing beside the worktop, her hands busy with pencil and pad, a calm voice on the radio announcing dramatic weather:

'*...warnings of gales in all areas except Biscay, Trafalgar and FitzRoy... The General Synopsis follows.*'

'Happy Christmas, Gran.'

Harriette appeared from behind a cupboard door, her hair a little unkempt, flour streaked across her nose.

'And to you too, dear.'

'Are you alright? I could hear you shouting.'

Harriette appeared shocked as if falsely accused and then, 'Oh that. I was just sounding off. This cash for questions gets my goat. Not sure why politicians think they can get away with it...' She rubbed her forehead with the back of a hand. 'Major should sack the lot of them.'

The radio trundled on –

'*...Rockall, Malin, Hebrides. South-west gale 7 or 8, veering west, severe gale 9. Rain, then squally showers. Moderate, becoming poor...*'

Dani didn't know anything about "cash for questions" or "politicians getting away with it". She never really paid much attention to the news. Surveying the dirty bowls and pans on the worktop, she found herself wanting an opinion, wanting to be on a level with her gran but didn't know what to say. Mesmerised by blue flames under the coffee pot, she didn't hear the hiss and gurgle that came from its lid.

Harriette appeared from the utility room, sleeves rolled up, mild disbelief on her face.

'Do you mind switching it off?'

'Sorry.' Dani crossed the room.

'You're limping.'

'Injured my foot.' She shut off the gas.

'How?'

'Running across the fields.'

'But what about your classes?'

'They don't start again until schools go back. It'll be fine.'

A clowning trombone and applause came from the radio, then... '*We present a special festive edition of I'm Sorry I Haven't a Clue... the antidote to panel games...*'

'I'm up to my elbows in stuffing – make me a coffee, would you, and help yourself to one, there's milk in my cup. Can you zap it in the microwave?' Harriette turned up the radio before returning to the utility room.

'Yes, sure.' Dani set the timer, then watched gusty weather bother the garden. The microwave pinged. Laughter erupted from the radio audience. She placed Harriette's coffee on the worktop.

'I'm going upstairs to do some wrapping.'

'What about that coffee?'

'It's on the side. Don't come into the bedroom.'

Harriette's voice followed her up the stairs. 'What's that?'

'Don't come up, I'm wrapping presents.'

There was a lone voice on the radio, followed by more laughter.

*

Dani opened the bedroom curtains. Dawn a shade lighter; ragged clouds rushing south. Both hands around the cup of coffee she watched a flock of crows land on the furrowed field. Their feathers ruffled by the wind. Hopping and swaggering as they searched for food. A gang of winged gorillas that seemed to move gradually towards the lodge.

Pulling back from the window she laid out Harriette's presents then sat beside them. A pasta cutter and board for rolling gnocchi from Dev. *The Rough Guide to Venice* from herself. Stocking fillers: Half-moon knife, an Italian wine atlas, a tin of Caffarel chocolates.

Her mind drifting as she wrapped, first into the gutter. Then a prison cell where she lay on a bed. Then she imagined pacing back and forth, then she was on the bed again. The paper trembling in her hand. Squawking crows bringing her to, she finished the folding and taping.

Tomorrow can wait – You're not done yet.

Carrying presents downstairs, she placed them under the tree then made her way to the kitchen. Most of the pots already washed and cleared away. The radio silent. Harriette at the table by the big windows.

'I've got pastries here and there's more coffee on the stove.'

Dani refilled her mug then settled at the table.

Harriette removed a cloth that covered the croissants. 'Forgot to ask, how did you sleep?'

'Fine, thanks.' Dani took one and tore it in half.

'The mattress needs replacing – I think the springs are going.'

'No, really it was fine, I slept well.'

'Wish I could say the same.'

'You didn't have a good night? Thought you sounded a little tired.'

Harriette slashed lines through a list, her bespectacled gaze looking up. 'Oh, head buzzing with this and that.'

Dani asked about the news story and then ate more breakfast. Harriette's explanation of parliamentary corruption cut short by uncharacteristic irritation.

'I'll finish off the washing up. Would you prep some veg?'

'Of course.'

Potatoes scrubbed and parboiled, turkey already in the oven. Sprouts ready for the steamer.

They set the table and chatted and then, 'Do you mind if I read?'

Harriette settled with a novel. Dani flicked through cookbooks.

A timer sounded. In went the potatoes.

Then reading resumed. The aromas of cooking heavy and delicious, the air almost edible. Another alarm. Then flurries of activity brought everything together, stuffing and gravy last to the table. They paused for a moment and lit the candles, flames dancing in the big windows. Views of winter heathland solemn. The North Star already striking through a weakening sky.

Harriette picked at food. Dani refused seconds.

'I had too much fish pie. We should have eaten later,' Harriette said, pushing away her plate.

'I ate too many croissants.'

'I'm not a fan of turkey.'

Relief in their laughter betraying issues far greater than the spoiling of a dinner, they retreated to the living room and Harriette lit the fire. Dani collapsed into an armchair, then noticed the gadget on the sideboard.

'I didn't know you had a mobile phone.'

The only people she knew who did were well off. The Graham family had one each, although Isla claimed she only carried hers in case of an emergency.

'Oh, that. It's for peace of mind. Bought one for Rennie, too. So he can contact me while I'm away. Makes me feel better about leaving him. Although it didn't stop me fretting in the middle of the night.'

'You're always worrying about him.'

'He's not been right – lost a lot of weight.'

'He looked fine yesterday.'

'I'm thinking of putting off the trip.'

Dani sat back, a look of disbelief spreading across her face. 'I thought you wanted to get away.'

Harriette stood and gazed blankly at the Christmas tree.

'It can wait.'

A voice screamed in Dani's head: *You're not getting any younger.*

'Well, sorry, but I don't think it can.'

Harriette glared at Dani, her arms folding; her words clipped. 'Well, I'm afraid it will have to.'

'Do you know what? I don't think this is about Rennie. Actually, I think you're afraid of leaving this place.'

'I am not!'

'And what about these friendships you've rekindled? You're not going to just let them go, are you?'

She – the offender – lecturing her respectable grandmother. *But I won't be here much longer – and she needs this.*

'I don't understand why you're pandering to him like he's a spoilt boy. Not to mention he's been lying to you.'

Harriette unfolded her arms. Then she folded them again. 'He made a mistake. That doesn't make him a bad person.' Then she sat down, head in hands.

'Gran?'

'Okay, okay – You're right.'

'Oh – I am?'

'This isn't *just* about him. But I didn't want to bring it up. I wanted our day to be perfect.'

'I knew something was wrong.'

Harriette exhaled and closed her eyes. 'I've been to see the police.'

'What – when?' Dani felt her throat tightening.

'When I stayed with friends in Manchester. They wanted me to visit the station, so they could sign off the case.'

'I don't understand.'

'They're not going to investigate the death of my mother. It happened so long ago there's little chance of discovering the truth. No evidence, so no inquest. Waste of police resources, they said.'

Dani sat on the arm of the chair.

'Oh Gran. Can I give you a hug?'

'I think that's just what I need. Sorry I've been grumpy.'

'I thought you weren't bothered about having any kind of verdict.'

Their embrace gently rocked back and forth.

'Where they found her – it's been playing on my mind. Suppose deep down I wanted a detective or a judge or someone official to solve the mystery. Bestow some kind of justice.'

Dani remembered blood, her brother's wounded face; her urge to vomit bringing an end to the rocking. Harriette looked up.

'You look pale. Are you alright?'

'I'm fine – I just think you'll regret not going.'

'You're right, you're right.' Harriette blew her nose. 'Thank you for speaking your mind. I can be very weak at times.'

'Everything will be alright, Gran – just go.'

'Rennie has been acting oddly though. It's like – he's got this air of finality about him. Like nothing new is worth starting.'

'Well, as you've said before, he is an attention seeker.'

'Mm.' Harriette slowly dragged a hand across her brow. 'Yesterday for example he got all morbid; told me he'd rejigged his will. Silly old bugger started filling up, which then set me off.'

Dani felt her patience slipping. 'Why don't you just talk to him about it?'

'He just clams up – acts all wounded and sorrowful. Look, if I go away, please check on him?'

Dani shifted on the armrest.

'Yes, fine. I'll drop by.'

'Promise?'

'I promise.'

Harriette sighed. 'Then – I'll go.'

Dani gave her another hug. 'Good.'

'There's something else I need to tell you. I'll be right back… don't look so worried. It's good news.' Harriette left the room then returned with an opened bottle of champagne and two glasses. 'Rennie asked me not to tell you. Not yet, anyway – so you must keep shtum.'

'Gran, I'd rather not…'

'Your name appears in his will. You're going to inherit Hunter's Lodge.'

Dani took hold of a champagne flute.

'But… it's your workshop.'

'Oh, my days of mending broken instruments are over, dear.'

Harriette filled the glasses. 'Cheers, to my future neighbour,' then knocked back the bubbly.

Dani sipped from her glass and listened to Harriette talk excitedly about doing up the lodges, took in all the good news and great ideas like a boxer absorbing punches. A voice in her head whispering: *I shouldn't have come back.*

Tip-off

The next two days good; weather bad. They stayed in. Ate food, watched television but mainly enjoyed each other's company. For breakfast Dani made bubble and squeak with leftovers. For lunch Harriette made gnocchi; the radio always on low volume, like a third person in the room, rambling quietly in the background.

Dani thumbed her grandmother's cookbooks and old photo albums. Harriette read up on Venice. A thousand-piece jigsaw something they tackled together.

On the third day they walked along the estate road.

Half a mile in, Dani stopped.

'How's the foot?' said Harriette.

'Stiff. Do you mind if we turn back?'

'Sure. You should take the car when you visit Rennie.'

Dani glanced away so as not to show her irritation. 'I heard you talking on the phone. Is he alright?'

'Bad cold. Doctor was there yesterday.'

'Ah, okay. It's been a while since I've driven.'

'Oh, the Mini's easy. If I can drive it anyone can. And the road will be all yours. The builders aren't back until the new year.'

They walked back. December already robbing light from the day.

'Early night for you then, Gran. Big day tomorrow.'

'Yes, Mum.'

Taking hold of Dani's hand Harriette squeezed and smiled at the same time. 'Don't worry, I'm not going to do a last-minute swerve.'

Back at the lodge Harriette ironed clothes and bed linen in the kitchen. Dani finished off the jigsaw.

After dinner they retired to the living room and watched television, Harriette heading to bed an hour after the nine o'clock watershed, in line with her granddaughter's demands.

Sloping off to bed after midnight Dani woke early next morning to kitchen sounds: the unloading of the dishwasher, cabinets opening and closing. Pulling on a dressing gown she made her way downstairs.

'I can do that, Gran.'

'Just a quick tidy up. Taxi's not due until two.'

'How's the packing going?'

'Not well, the new bag I bought is too small. Do you mind bringing down my suitcase, from the loft? It's cream with brown latches.'

'Of course. I need to go up anyway, for the decoration boxes.'

Unlatching the loft hatch Dani climbed the extendable ladder and carried boxes down one by one and placed them on the kitchen table.

Harriette looked up from a notepad.

'Taking decorations down so soon?'

'Probably in the new year. I've put the suitcase on your bed. Like another coffee?'

'Would you bring it up to the bedroom and keep me company while I pack?'

Dani made hot drinks, took them upstairs and from the bed she watched her grandmother dither at the wardrobe, her hand flicking hangers across the rail, one way, then the other.

'Must be a while since you travelled abroad.'

Harriette turned and smiled. 'On the deck of a troop ship. Slept under the stars with friends from the Hallé. Flying with a budget airline not quite the same, I guess.'

'You'll be fine, Gran.'

'I'll take you next time.'

Dani felt her grandmother's gaze, the room hanging, the moment unable to move on until she responded in some way, but all she could do was stare into the half-empty suitcase because actually, what could she say: *I'll be in prison? Send me a postcard?*

'Tell me… about Italy.'

'Well, there's a lot to tell.'

'Yes, of course. Sorry, maybe some other time.'

Harriette smiled. 'How about I give you the quick tour, starting from the north? How about that?'

As Harriette continued to pack, she reeled off a list of "must-sees", sometimes backtracking and rearranging the order of them according to her memory of the rail network, which, she admitted, after so many years had become a little rusty.

Milan, Bologna, Florence, Siena, Rome.

The selection of clothing for the suitcase becoming effortless as Harriette's anecdotes relating to food and customs seemed to free her mind of indecision.

'Trains are not so good in the south so best to take a boat from Naples if we decide to visit Sicily.'

Then Harriette paused and stared into the suitcase, one hand cupping her chin. 'Mm… I think that should do it.'

She closed the suitcase and clicked the latches. Dani lugged the case downstairs. And as they ate lunch Harriette ran over everything. Again. Controls for the heating and the Aga, how to cancel the smoke alarm when it goes off.

'It will go off.'

Passport – check. Tickets – check.

A car horn beeped three times. They hugged, said goodbye, Harriette's hands waving through the rear window of the taxi until disappearing beyond a bend in the lane.

After closing the door Dani went back up to the bedroom and flopped on the bed, the lodge suddenly cold and indifferent now that Harriette was no longer there.

Small sounds trickled into the bedroom: winter leaves of the copper beech whispering in the garden, the roof timbers conversing with the wind, the far-off sound of a helicopter fading then growing, each riff of beats more definite until becoming obvious it was heading her way, the lodge and garden holding its breath as the downdraft strafed the air above. And even though Rennie had warned them that the Americans would be "buzzing in and out" to check on the progress of their venture it seemed odd to her that they would visit during the Christmas break.

She went to the window to check the extent of the helicopter's onward journey and sure enough it performed a circle above the estate before disappearing behind treetops. Excitement over, she returned to the bed. Her legs unusually at ease, for a moment she listened to her breaths… one… two… three… Time to move. And yet her body, the body that loved to dance and run and inspire fitness classes felt heavy and lazy.

'You've got to move; it's time to get going.'

Slipping off the bed she limped down to the kitchen and began the job of taking down the decorations. Moving from room to room she packed them all into boxes, Harriette's voice prompting her conscience as she carried them up to the loft: *keep an eye on him… please check on him.*

Fine, she would do it. Visit Rennie. Check he's breathing. Leave. Make no mention of his message in the Christmas card. *Important news… delicate matter…*

The will, she thought, *it must be about the will.*

After packing the rucksack, she booked a taxi. The pick-up time early enough for her to arrive in Manchester before nightfall.

One last duty to perform.

Pulling on her gran's quilted jacket she grabbed the car keys, left the lodge and set off along the single track that shimmied through the estate. The cold air rushing in through an open window softening the old car smells that reminded her of Jensen. Her hands busy on the wheel and gear stick, her eyes taking in the winter scenes whenever the road allowed: oaks in the heathland, drifts of silver birch in the dips, streams and clearings, the fallen elm, Dardale Hall coming into view as the car emerged from a hamlet of rhododendrons.

Road became driveway. Gravel clattered through wheel arches. Grand columns and windows of a bygone era scrolled past, the helicopter at rest on the adjacent lawn, its limp rotor blades like an implausible miracle from the future.

She forged on, the road curving away. The stable block

ahead peeking through a grove of winter trees. As soon as she passed through the archway, she saw Rennie behind the glass doors watching the courtyard as if expecting her arrival and then he was out and waving her towards the parking bay, his hand movements overstated as if he were directing a taxiing aeroplane.

'Daft old bugger.'

Dani engaged the handbrake brutally, then stepped out and made her way through the courtyard garden.

'Come in, come in. Good to see you – Harriette said you might come today.'

She followed him into the living area, the hi-tech door sealing shut behind them. 'Coffee?'

'I'm good, thank you.'

'Do you mind if I…'

'Please, go ahead.'

As Rennie filled the kettle Dani scanned the room. Exposed roof trusses, artwork, the space as it was before apart from a metal frame on wheels, a bag full of clear fluid hanging from it, a drip line coiled below, a piece of apparatus you would normally find in a hospital.

'Can I tempt you with a chocolate…' – the shallow box trembled in his hand – '…Fortnum and Masons?'

She eyed the drip stand. 'Are you not well? I can come back another time.'

'Oh, don't take any notice of that. It's a present from Harley Street – just a precaution,' he said, nonchalantly waving it away, but she sensed a mock facade.

'Sure you won't indulge?' He held out the box a little further.

'I'm fine, thanks – good Christmas?'

He popped a chocolate into his mouth, its hard shell clonking his teeth as he spoke, a new confidence in his tone. 'Not bad – I've finished my speech.'

'Harriette mentioned you were composing…'

'Although, alas, I won't be able to deliver it on New Year's Eve.'

'Ahh, right. Why's that?'

'Poor health. My pancreatitis has flared up again. I've been royally ticked off by the doc for over indulging.'

'You're not the only one.' She sat on the sofa and sank back. 'Are you alright?'

'Gives me the run around from time to time.' Rennie tapped his abdomen. 'The pancreas is buried so deep that most people don't know they have one,' he said, returning to the boiling kettle.

'Does Harriette know about this?'

'No, dear – as I said, all fine.' He raised the kettle. 'Sure you won't?'

'Milk, no sugar. Thanks.'

Rennie added coffee grounds and hot water to the cafetiere and after stirring it with a spoon he looked up. 'You know how she worries about me.'

'That's an understatement.'

Rennie smiled. 'She has one of these too, you know – so she can keep tabs on me,' he said, picking up a mobile phone and waving it at Dani.

'I know, she told me.'

Slipping the phone into a pocket he carried mugs of coffee to the sofa.

'Well, I'm glad you caught me before I left for London.'

'London!'

'Mm, London,' he said while handing one of the mugs to Dani.

'Harriette didn't mention anything about you going to London.'

He winced and shifted as he settled into an armchair.

'That's because I didn't tell her. It's my secret little trip, courtesy of the new owners. Really are a smashing bunch, you know, and of course these Americans love to do a deal.'

He opened a bottle of pills.

She wished he'd get to the point.

'Slow-release painkiller... they really are good.' Popping one into his mouth he washed it down with a slurp of coffee. 'I've given them land to the north of the estate in exchange for private health care. Harley Street no less – thrown in use of the whirly bird to taxi me back and forth. Even got my own room and garden.'

Her mind whirred. *I should call Harriette.*

'They've already drawn up plans for a golf course – don't hang around, these Americans. Look – I know Harriette will have asked you to keep an eye on me but that won't be necessary. I'll be in Marylebone later today. In the best hospital money can buy. Councillor Webster will be delivering the speech on my behalf.'

'Is this what you wanted to talk to me about?'

'Pardon, dear?'

'The Christmas card. You wanted to tell me something,' she said before taking a mouthful of coffee.

'Oh, that.' He sat back and folded his arms. 'That's… about your father.'

She spluttered coffee back into the cup. 'What – about my father?'

'Are you alright?'

'Not really, no,' she said placing the cup down.

'A bit of music perhaps. Always soothing at times like this, don't you find?' He pressed buttons on a remote control. 'You see, like my American friends, your father also liked to do a deal. Let's just say – he and I have had a long-standing one. I've agreed to keep his little secret, and well – he's let me live.'

Expensive hi-fi faithfully replicated sounds of an orchestra. The fidgeting display of a graphic equaliser animated the sounds. The music gentle; a classical lullaby. Low volume.

'You could say a beautifully simple arrangement. Until now, that is.'

Dani shook her head. 'Sorry, I don't…'

'I'm not going to be around for much longer. A deal-breaker, wouldn't you say?'

He's dying? 'I don't understand.'

He let out an exasperated sigh. 'No matter. Let us turn to why you're here.'

'That would be good.'

He folded his arms. 'I wanted to warn you… and also present you with what one could call a golden opportunity.'

'Go on.'

'Your father. He will be at the mill on New Year's Eve. In the block room.'

Dani felt suddenly hollow, cavities in her body steadily flooding with dread, her eye drawn to the digitalised columns on the graphic equaliser that were steadily rising in line with the music.

Rennie pulled the mobile phone from his pocket and offered it out to Dani. Fez's voice chattering in her head as she took it from him: *Robbers were caught... but the loot, well, it's never been recovered.*

'Two numbers in the memory. The first is Harriette's. The second a direct line to DCI Craven of the Manchester Police. You might want to contact him on the thirty-first. May I suggest around eleven-ish? I'm sure he'd appreciate the call. Lovely fellow, you know.'

'How can you be so sure that he'll be th...?'

'He'll be there. And this time, my life won't depend on me turning a blind eye.' He chortled and then winced; his glee cut short by a spasm of pain. 'Whilst everyone welcomes in the new year, he'll be helping himself to his end of the deal – his little secret.' He held the bottle of pills and read the blurb on the label. 'Everyone's going to the rugby club, you know. Fireworks, funfair, free grub and booze. It's a sell-out, you can have my ticket if you want. You could call the police whilst eating your complimentary hot dog.'

'No thanks – I'm not a fan of fireworks. Rennie, there's one thing I don't understand.'

'Try me.'

'Why let people use the mill? Surely he wouldn't want that?'

'His idea. Didn't want to risk a break-in. Actually, he

was worried about you youngsters; derelict buildings get used for raves all the time.'

'Why don't you tell the police now?'

He shrugged. 'Too early, dear. He's got contacts on the inside… wouldn't want to risk a tip-off,' he said, tapping the side of his nose.

He settled back into the armchair, a serene smile breaking across his face, the tapping finger now a baton that pretended to conduct an orchestra. '*Cavalleria Rusticana*. Can't beat a bit of Mascagni.'

'How long until you're better?'

'Oh, it's common for malignancy to go undiscovered until very advanced. It seems my body is sneakier than your father when it comes to keeping secrets. So deeply buried, just like the block room. A neat little consistency to my dilemma. A perfectly sublime pattern of deceit, wouldn't you say?'

Glancing at the phone, she had the urge to call Harriette. But to tell her what? Everything he said seemed cursed with ambiguity. *Stiff upper lip, dear. That's, I'm afraid, what our generation do.*

'So, there you go. Glad I had a chance to tell you before leaving.' Rennie closed his eyes and smiled, his raised hands postponing the conversation. 'This piece has the sweetest ending, don't you think?'

They listened to the music, the final moments played by a small section of the orchestra, climbing in unison, softly up and up until a final long, held chord.

Dani glanced at the clock on the wall.

'Well, I hope you have a safe journey. Is there anything I can do?'

Rennie opened his eyes. 'No, no – A nurse is travelling with me.' He placed the bottle of pills on the coffee table, and then fixed her eye. 'You're not like him.'

'Sorry?'

'You're… like Harriette, your grandmother.'

He turned his face towards the window, his brow furrowing before he turned back and found her eye again. 'You will look after her, won't you?'

Dani nodded. 'She'll be fine.'

They shared a brief smile.

'Help me up, dear.'

He held out an elbow and they both tussled with gravity.

'Actually, there is something you could do.'

'Go ahead.'

'If there are any messages from your grandmother, please reply as if everything is alright.'

Rennie's trembling hand gave her a quick lesson on how to use the phone then she placed it in her pocket. And at the door they exchanged goodbyes, Rennie waving and calling out as she made her way across the courtyard. 'We're counting on you.'

Bundling herself into the car she saw that Rennie was still waving. But she didn't wave back. Because there, behind him, was another person. Seat belt in hand, she leant forward and peered through the windscreen, a few seconds passing before it was clear that the other person was a nurse. Her flicker of panic ebbing away, she buckled herself in. Her urge to wave back fading to nothing as the nurse's caring hands turned Rennie and led him away.

Contorting herself around she checked behind and then began to reverse, her mind trying to work out where the nurse had come from as she straightened up and set off.

Trees, gravel drive, columns, windows, rhododendrons, the road curving as it climbed onto heathland. Everything passing unnoticed by her churning mind: *the nurse, Rennie's illness, the block room, the helicopter, golden opportunities, complimentary hotdogs, DCI Craven, undiscovered malignancies, mobile phones... look after her, won't you... look after her... look after her...*

As the road dipped, she approached an S-bend; the memory of Harriette's warnings of ice coming too late as the car skidded and veered onto the grass, slewing and yawing like a boat as it rumbled over the ruts, her attempts to regain control making no difference whatsoever. *We're counting on you... We're counting on you...*

And just when she thought her journey would end in certain disaster the road reappeared. The brakes and steering behaving sensibly now that the tyres had rediscovered steady ground. She stopped the car, sat back and cut the engine. The countryside silent: deer on the heath, crows on the wing, the herniated trunk of an ancient oak inches away from the offside wing mirror.

Idiot.

She closed her eyes. She breathed; all the complications that seemed to plague her life cleared away by the perilous moment.

Take the taxi... or stay until New Year's Eve. Make up your mind.

Picking the phone from her pocket she went to the address book and found the inspector's details.

I could phone the police now and watch them raid the mill.

'…and let my father off the hook – no way.'

Plunging the phone into her pocket she started the car and continued through the estate. And when back at the lodge, she cancelled the taxi; her mind reformulating plans as she sat at the kitchen table and removed items from the rucksack.

She would have to be there in the block room on New Year's Eve. No mistakes, no bungles; the ensnarement of her father unequivocal.

She turned to the back windows as the faint sounds of the helicopter drifted across the estate, the aircraft out of sight because from where she sat, there was not much sky to be seen. The chopping and thudding growing steadily louder, the flight path so close for a moment the lodge seemed to cower below the thrashing blades. The short-lived commotion ebbed away, an expectant stillness gripping the lodge as silence settled back in.

Dani remained on the chair, feeling an urge to take deeper breaths as if levels of oxygen in the room had dipped below normal, her body and legs very still, her eyes fixed on the items that lay on the table: an antique revolver, a mobile phone and a large brass key that unlocked the back door of the mill.

DARDALE

1915/1916

IX

Common Daisy – *Bellis perenis*

Study for Wallis and Hilton Wallpapers. Plate No. 109 – Daisy Chain [see sketch on next page]

Facts: The flower head is not just one flower but a composite of a number of tiny flowers which make up the yellow middle (disc florets) and the surrounding white petals (ray florets). The name daisy comes from the old English, "Daes eage" meaning day's eye, which highlights the fact that petals close in the evening and open at dawn.

Quaint beliefs: It was believed that wearing a daisy chain would protect children from abduction by fairies. [The petal-plucking game, "He loves me; he loves me not" was thought to help confirm the interest of a possible suitor.]

As she always did on November the fifth, Lily called by Ellen's with a tray of parkin. Ellen welcomed her in, and they talked all the way to the kitchen. Lily cut the cake into a grid of squares, Ellen poured the tea and before long they were settled on the sofa, Ellen listening as best she could to her aunty ramble on about this and that: the teething baby, the price of flour, her mother confused *yet again* because the railway had stopped running excursions.

'I keep telling her war is war and holidays will have to wait. She's losing her senses, I'm sure.'

Without adding a word Ellen got up, shovelled a lump of coal into the range and tweaked the airflow. *Tell her. You must tell her.*

'Someone's on edge,' said Lily, as she helped herself to another square of cake.

'Me? – No, I'm fine. It's just…'

'Mm?'

'I have some news.' Ellen's face flushed bright red. Lily looked up.

'Can't be that bad.'

Ellen's eyes searched the floor; pregnant didn't seem to be a word to be said. Too much, too soon for her church-going aunt to take in.

The impasse broken by knocking that rat-tatted down the hallway. The interruption a mercy that Ellen reacted to without hesitation. And beyond the front door she was presented with a group of wide-eyed raggedy children who had gathered under the porch. The first in line brandishing a smartly dressed effigy of Guy Fawkes.

'Like it, miss?'

'Shirt looks new. Does your dad know?'

'We can't burn it, miss. Bonfires have been outlawed.'

'Well, in that case, you better have a piece of this.' Ellen broke up the parkin on her plate and handed a nugget to each of the children. 'The ginger in it will lie on your tongues like embers.'

Cake savoured; the children retreated; a chorus of

thanks ringing out. Their cheery procession already halfway up the neighbour's path as Ellen closed the door. The smile falling from her face as she remembered what lay ahead. And for a moment she listened to her aunty stoke the fire: coal shovel digging in the bucket, the poker stabbing away, the doorway suddenly alight with a devilish glow. Ellen inched along the corridor but as she levelled with the staircase, her body lurched to the right and her feet hurried up the steps. Her escape from the truth ending on a bed face down, her aunt's voice soon calling up from the hallway. 'I thought tha had something to tell me.'

'I have,' said a muffled voice.

Creaking steps. Then Lily's voice, quiet and behind the bedroom door. 'Flower?'

'I've got a headache.'

Lily walked into the bedroom, her niece horizontal in the darkness, face planted into a pillow.

'Better out than in, petal,' said Lily as she continually ran fingers through Ellen's hair.

'I am in desperate trouble.'

'Desperate, you say?'

'Yes.'

'Oh Ellen, there's no point crying over spilt milk. I'm sure your suspension from the mil...'

'I'm going to be a mother.'

And then Ellen awaited scorn, but none came. And then she sensed Lily's weight on the bed. 'Oh, Mary, mother of Jesus,' she said, before sobbing, 'It's my fault. I've been so absent. Your mother will turn in her grave.'

Lily wiped away tears and blew her nose and gradually her distress turned to curiosity.

Ellen rolled her eyes. 'No, it's not Cedric's.'

'A soldier on leave then?'

Ellen sighed. 'He works at the mill, helps Cedric with the accounts. He's new in town so you wouldn't know him. Whatever we had faded and… he's just vanished.'

'Does he know?'

'I went to his digs, but apparently, he's moved on to a place further along the canal. He didn't leave a forwarding address.'

'But he works at the mill, doesn't he?'

'Come on, Aunty – I've burnt that bridge. In any case, the girls tell me the block room is sealed off and there's no way through to the offices. Apparently, he does the number crunching between shifts. Comes and goes at odd times. Look, I refuse to cry over it. There's a war on. I've got to be strong. If he doesn't love me, I can't change that.'

They went downstairs and stoked the fire. Drinking tea and eating parkin, their ginger hot tongues consigned men to perdition. The frenzy eventually subsiding they both sat back, arms crossed, their gaze distracted by a spell of heavy rain that pestered the yard. Lily's voice became calmer then, her eyes lost somewhere outside amongst brick walls varnished by the weather. 'God formed you in the same mould as your mother and she always was stronger than me. But mark my words, if I get hold of him, I'll be crunching his numbers, straight through me bloody mangle.'

Then Lily turned to Ellen. 'I can register the baby in my name. It will dampen the scandal.'

But Ellen wouldn't hear of it and then it was Lily who rolled her eyes. 'Strong-minded just like your mother. Well, we shall just have to hope that the dark shadow of war eclipses tha dilemma.'

And then nothing was said for a short while and Ellen could almost sense the civil war that had broken out in her aunty. Lily, the Sunday worshipper. God and the judgement of others something to fear. And judgements there would be if her niece's shadowy story were to ever get out.

'I won't tell a soul, Aunty.'

Not entirely true; she was planning to tell the Wallises at some point, in the hope that they would offer her sanctuary.

'For the best, I would say. I can offer what I've got. But that isn't saying much. Three kids and a flaky husband is about as much as I can handle.'

What was best for her baby? The Wallises? Her aunty? In any event, for now she was just relieved that her scandal was no longer a lonely secret, Ellen feeling better after sharing her news. And to begin with she carried on pretending nothing had changed. But then the visits from her aunty became less frequent. How was it that she now lived in the world with no one? November solitary and uneventful. December arriving with a knock at the door.

'Miss Parry. May I come in?'

The butler took a seat in the living room and Ellen made him tea.

'Mr Wallis is so shocked at the news of your suspension.'

'I tried to change things for the better, Collins. I really did.'

'And Mr Wallis is grateful for that. And he hopes that you will resume your visits to the hall.'

'He does?'

'Mr and Mrs Wallis invite you to dinner this coming Friday.'

At the door she waved Collins off and then watched his figure until it disappeared beyond the end of the road. Of course, it meant everything to Ellen that Sidney was there for her. To have the support of such a great man gave her strength and restored her appetite for self-belief. In the morning, after chores, she read novels, then walked beside the canal in the afternoon. And in the evenings, she faithfully recorded everything that had happened in a diary: weak governance of the mill, workers falling ill, Muriel's death, her own suspension. And as she reread the pages her feelings of shame switched to pride. Because the wrongs were so clearly obvious. And the protest seemed so right and courageous. It was all there in black and white. Something her parents would have been proud of, she was sure.

And then it was Friday, and the winter light found her striding through the Dardale estate, Collins opening the great doors of the hall before she had chance to knock. He led her up the grand staircase and into the drawing room, the Wallises welcoming her in.

'The heroine returns,' Sidney beamed as he embraced Ellen. The greeting so warm she found it difficult not to cry. They sat and at first there was nothing but small talk and then the tone of conversation changed, and Sidney's posture became upright like a sitting statue.

'Please, Ellen. You must tell us about the protest.'

'Of course.'

Ellen gathered herself and then recounted all that she could, from the church hall meeting to the day of her suspension. And Sidney listened with absolute stillness as if he had turned into a statue and after she finished, he simply said 'Thank you for what you did,' with complete sincerity. And Ellen was grateful to be acknowledged with such simple grace. Emboldened with pride it seemed only natural that she moved on to her own news and he sat very still also then and stared into the middle distance.

'There's something else I wish to share. A personal matter.'

'News of your father?'

'No, he's still missing. I...'

Sidney stood abruptly and repositioned himself at the fireplace. 'This damn war is like slow torture.'

'This is not about my father.'

'Not about your father?'

'No. It is about me. I... I am with child. And in the interest of truth, I must tell you, my baby has been conceived out of wedlock.'

Her eyes filled and then her gaze fell down to her lap. And then she sensed Elizabeth beside her and then heard Sidney's softly spoken voice.

'Ellen.'

She looked up. 'Yes, Mr Wallis.'

'There is no judgement here. Is that clear?'

'Yes.'

'We shall talk this through over dinner. And rest assured we are here for you.'

They moved through to the dining room. Collins served food. Elizabeth offered motherly advice; Sidney reasserted his offer of sanctuary. The afternoon as happy as any moment Ellen had had since the onset of war. And after saying goodbye and while walking across the driveway Sidney threw his lifeline once again. 'We are always here for you.'

She walked through the estate. The landscape all around her subdued by winter's frozen hand and yet she felt very alive. Her body stirring with new life. Her clothes a little tighter; her progress on the winding road a little slower. Sidney's parting words keeping her worries at bay.

Passing between lodges, she trudged down the lane. The buildings ahead looming in dusky light she braced herself for the looks and cold shoulders. But town failed to recognise her. The winter coat and headscarf offering a disguise that allowed her to pass through unnoticed. The town's identity itself somewhat modified by the arrival of Christmas. A large tree erected in the square. Holly wreaths adorned front doors. The post boy cycling past wearing a Santa hat, his bicycle shimmying through the streets as if a sack of seasonal wishes were lighter than a single War Office telegram.

At the house she opened the front gate, the owl always surprised to see her back.

'Missed me? Anything changed while I was away?' she whispered to the brass knocker as she unlocked the door.

But there were no changes. The reality that welcomed her in was a house so cold it took an entire evening for the range to warm the living room. And even after eating well at Dardale Hall she felt hungry. So, she ate bread and butter and four biscuits and drank a glass of milk and then she curled into a ball on the sofa.

Keeping warm, cooking food and washing clothes occupied the days that followed.

And then on Christmas day Ellen set off to Lily's house and sat at the table with her family. The impressive dinner concocted from meagre ingredients, a candle lit to keep the memory of her father alive, Lily claiming no news was good news as she distributed plates of food. But after dinner Ellen couldn't help but scour the newspaper. The pages full of cartoons of red-breasted robins, snowy trenches and soldiers playing games in no man's land; upbeat conjecture that she didn't believe or care for. And where was Cedric? Had he joined up? He was supposed to be home for Christmas. She unwrapped the present he'd left for her. Two novels. Both spy thrillers. Rolling her eyes, she brushed them aside and then spent the rest of December lost in the romance of *Wuthering Heights*.

The first weeks of January so dark and depressing she took to sitting in the nursery. A room locked since the death of her mother. She had found the key in her father's bureau and opened it up. She liked the nursery. The bright daisy wallpaper preventing her spirits from straying too far. A mug of cocoa in hand and a blanket around her middle she shared the lamplight with characters that lurked between the pages of *The Thirty-Nine Steps* and *The Riddle of the Sands*.

But that afternoon she was restless, her eyes merely scanning the words, grasping the story impossible because she could only think of her father.

Had the torment of losing his wife made the prospect of dying in a war so appealing?

The day before, she had sent him a letter, hoped the news of her pregnancy might give him reason to fight on, hoped his reaction would be elation not shame. Wondering if it would ever reach him, her eyes became lost in the bare washing lines that swung back and forth in the yards below. The rain breaking over the terrace behind like spray from a ship's pitching bow. Snuggling under the blankets she recalled the good times before the war and dreamed herself into the quad at Owen's College where she used to sit on sunny afternoons.

But her nap was interrupted by something so rude it was enough to make her jump. The sound just a shadow by the time she came to. The wind? A loud noise? *Isn't the coal delivered on Tuesdays?* Maybe it was nothing.

Then ominous silence.

Then thumps on the front door like a barrage of cannons.

Thump! Thump! Thump!

'On my way. Wait!'

Unwrapping herself, she lumbered out of the chair, trudged down the staircase and opened the door.

'Cedric!'

He stood hunched away from the rain. 'Are you going to let me in?'

'Sorry. Of course.'

She quickly turned and walked into the house. 'What a surprise.'

'Got back yesterday,' said Cedric while hanging his jacket on a hook.

'Tea?'

'I'd love one. Thank you. Keeping well?'

'Not bad. You?' She disappeared into the kitchen. He lingered in the living room.

'I heard about your suspension. Are you alright?'

No answer.

'Like a hand?'

'I'm fine. Make yourself at home.'

'Place looks tidy.'

She could hear the poker stabbing the fire grate. 'Oh, keeping myself busy.'

Shut away for weeks she'd only had her own internal conflict and spy novels for company.

Isolation and stories of espionage had promoted her insecurity and various disastrous scenarios had flashed through her mind: adoption, surrendering herself to an asylum for fallen women, wading into a pond with pockets full of stones.

She was so big already; too far gone to consider abortion.

Lingering in the kitchen she gently agitated the plump body of the teapot and listened to the sound of a shovel rummaging through the coal bucket. 'Seen much of anyone?'

'Just my aunty.'

She walked into the living room and placed the tea tray on the table.

Having just sat down Cedric stood up again, glanced at her belly then quickly averted his eyes.

'Any letters from your father?'

'Not since the telegram.'

She slumped into an armchair. He hovered over the tray, pondering, as if tea-making were a mystifying puzzle.

'We should clear your name. I could ask my father to talk with the colonel – get the suspension reversed.'

'It's not had time to brew, Cedric.'

He fumbled with the milk jug and rambled on about the factory in Gretna and how he didn't share the chief supervisor's fear of Zeppelin attacks. 'A menace on the east coast maybe, but they're so huge and lumbering…' Cedric turned and stared at her middle, '…the RAF would spot… them… a mile off.'

She shifted her appendage into a more comfortable position.

'Please, Cedric. Would you just sit down?'

But he had frozen to the spot; sounds from the mantel clock filling the room. Its busy mechanism marching over the awkward silence, a soft Westminster chime marking the hour. Ellen breathed in, closed her eyes and imagined shells over battlefields pausing mid-flight, charging soldiers momentarily frozen, wheels of the post boy's bicycle barely rotating. The horror of it all suspended because fleetingly she felt empowered and proud to be a woman and glad to be announcing the arrival of a new life at a time when the warring world seemed so intent on destroying it.

'Yes, Cedric. I'm having a baby.'

Placing the cups down, he hurriedly knelt beside the armchair and held her hand.

'Look. Don't worry. We can help.'

'Honestly, I'm fine.'

'My father has connections with lying-in hospitals.'

'I'm due in a few mon…'

'No problem, they take in unmarried women if it's their first one. Happens all the time across the parish, my father…'

'Cedric, it's alright. I'm not destitute.'

He sat back on his heels. 'Oh – that's good then.'

'The Attwoods have offered to take me in.'

'Live on the estate? That's a one-way ticket, until the war's over at least.'

'I wouldn't be living at the hall. Sidney has arranged for me to stay at the lodges. Everyone seems to give the Attwoods benefit of the doubt as they live on the edge of the estate.'

'And they don't have a problem with it?'

'Ecstatic more like. They've tried for years but can't conceive. And Mrs Attwood has experience of midwifery. She helped the doctor deliver baby Rennie.'

'But what about the house?' He looked about the room.

'Sidney's keeping it for us. In case my father comes back.'

'He'll be back, Ellen. I can drop in and check for post if you like.'

She smiled. 'Read my mind. You're a good friend, Cedric.'

Clambering up, he made some more tea and then talked of his thwarted attempts to get home for Christmas. Turned out he'd been called to another munitions factory in Gretna and then couldn't get back because Cumbria was under snow. Stranded in Penrith, he'd stayed at the George Hotel with a couple of officials from the ministry.

'They told me this in confidence so you mustn't mention it to anyone.'

She gently patted her stomach. 'Like anyone's interested in what I've got to say.'

'Not sure filling factory twenty-four has a future. Ministry is pulling the plug.'

'What – why?'

'We keep falling short and apparently they've got all jittery about the factory being so close to housing especially after what happened at the Lee Works.'

'Why didn't they think of that in the first place?'

'Panicky clamour to overcome the shortage. Being next to the station, we seemed a good candidate at the time.'

He poured more tea.

'Production at Gretna is starting next month. The factory is huge, Ellen, makes our little enterprise look like a garden shed. I'll be working there for the foreseeable future.'

'Oh, I see. At least Sidney will get his mill back at last.'

'Little chance of that, I'm afraid.'

'What on earth do you mean?'

'Couldn't believe it either, so I looked into it.'

'Of course you did.'

'As he's married to a German it seems the Aliens Restrictions Act prevents his business from reopening. For the time being his premises are under control of the state.'

*

Two days later Cedric visited again and then departed for Gretna. Two months later munition trains side-stepped Dardale and filling factory twenty-four fell silent. And a week after that Ellen stood in the bay window of her parents' bedroom, her belongings bundled onto a wooden handcart in the street below, Mr Attwood securing everything down before setting off. She opened the sash.

'Go on ahead, Mr Attwood, I still have a few things to do.'

After watching him leave she then waddled downstairs and sat on the settee. The iron range cold, hands of the mantel clock still, utter silence of the house promising last-minute miracles; any time now her father would open the gate, walk up the path and knock on the door. Ellen sat very still and stared at the clock, a loop of hanging moments came and went and yet the door remained silent, and her father did not come. Then she heard the church bell; soft and steady, like an old friend calling her away.

Clambering to her feet she left the house, the brass knocker flipping as she closed the front door. 'Well, you didn't see this coming, did you?' she whispered to the owl as her hand smoothed her bump.

At the gate she turned back. 'If you see my father, would you tell him where I am?'

She stared at the owl. The owl stared back.

She set off; brass animals mounted on other front doors watching her as she passed them one by one. Fox, badger, bumblebee, hedgehog. Their details progressively blurred by a mist that welled up from the canal. The mist thickening on Main Street closing in about her like a secret room as though nature were shielding her lumbering progress from disapproval. Then thinning again in the square; her arrival betrayed by crows. Windows glaring down, gargoyles mocking her slow progress, the church porch a shocked mouth.

And then a weak sun broke through as the rising lane rescued her from town. At the lodges she caught her breath and glanced back, only a few taller roofs visible, the rest of the town obscured by fog.

The Attwoods welcomed her in.

April was boring.

Last days of the month warmer, sometimes she sat outside and read the *Manchester Guardian* front page to back. And then on the first of May Cedric came home for a short break and they sat in Mrs Attwood's garden and talked about anything but war: the survival of Shackleton's crew, uprisings in Dublin, Mexican revolutions, Charlie Chaplin, Einstein's theories.

And then Cedric returned to Gretna and Ellen's world shrank once more; the days dragging their heels through yet another week. And then her waters broke. Contractions mild at first; a whole day passing without progress; hands of the wall clock like vanes of a storm-hit windmill. Another day, another night, the whirlwind of time gradually darkening. Pain like a creeping barrage, her clenched fists worked the sheets as she gasped and reeled and shuddered. And as the anaesthetics flowed and voices in the room faded, her mind roamed the block room, the shelves inside stretching to infinity. The patterns upon them revealing enigmas of creation; the secrets all hers, for a tantalising second, before twisting and warping and exploding into shards.

Then Mrs Attwood's voice came rushing back in.

'Baby crowning. Just a few more pushes, my love.'

Gripping someone's hand Ellen doubled down. Her mouth babbling nonsense through the ratcheting pain. Then she screamed at the passing of a baby's head and then screamed at the passing of its shoulders. A face, a chest, a belly and two legs. A flurry of activity somewhere in the room. Ellen's breathing heavy, her eyes resting on a brightening window; leaves in the garden touched by a golden dawn.

Then a lull.

Then a shriek.

Then Harriette.

Bloody. Crumpled. And lying in Ellen's arms.

DANI

Rollercoaster

She stayed at Harriette's until New Year's Eve. Lying on the sofa she watched television, one hand mauling the Nokia, the other flicking channels, just adverts watched from start to finish: Old Spice, OXO gravy, Milk Tray. Old favourites served with a twist sparking memories of the last childhood Christmas before everything changed.

Her father back for dinner smelling of booze. Dry turkey repelling the gravy. Her parents' after-dinner arguments so scary she'd lie in her room, head buried in pillows. He'd be gone by mid-afternoon – *somebody needs to pay for this*, his parting words. Then for hours Dani would lie across her mum's lap, Deepika's fingers combing her hair, like she was a cat that gave her comfort. And they watched movies and shared Cadbury's chocolates. *All because the lady loves Milk Tray* her mum would say. And then as the days passed her brother would ask when he'd be back – *before you know it*, her mother would reply, followed by *get your coats on* and a bus ride to the shopping centre. Then after a hot chocolate they drifted through shivering tinsel, her mother pawing markdown, Dani and her brother following like weary strays, curiously eyeing other families.

The year that followed memorable because it felt so different: her brother spending more time with her father, no summer stayover at Harriette's, Dani's first year at boarding school. Bruises appearing on her mother's arms.

Dani relaxed her grip on the Nokia and imagined herself in the block room, a phone message to the inspector pre-typed, her finger poised on the send button, enough to stop her father in his tracks; give her a chance to deliver an ultimatum: Hand yourself in.

The mobile phone felt so smooth in her hand, so neat and so powerful, the gun so old-school now.

She navigated to the address book. Inspector Craven, and then Harriette Hey; Dani's finger brushing the screen as she considered composing an apology to her gran. But the phone felt as cold as the gun then. A soulless tool. The sentiment of words sapped by its little digitised screen. Harriette deserved better than that, she thought.

So, Dani went to the bureau and composed a letter: a simple written apology, an appeal for forgiveness, a farewell – I love you.

Then she toured the rooms one by one tidying as she went, breathing in the comfort that she could hardly bare to give up. But soon darkness filled the big kitchen windows, and the time came for her to leave. Not much left to do she turned the heating to low and then placed her letter in an envelope and left it in plain sight propped against a vase. Then she stood in the hallway allowing herself a moment to study the willow bows. Her last few breaths taken with closed eyes, the patterns still fresh and lining her mind like wallpaper. Then after a deep sigh she shouldered the rucksack, locked up the lodge and trudged down the lane. The sounds of New Year's Eve drifting across from the rugby club: the high-pitched shriek of children, the drone of diesel generators; sounds so crazily mixed up by the wind and the trees, she imagined the fun had gone terribly wrong.

Town square asleep. Main Street dead. Rennie's prophecy seeming more and more unlikely. Was the story of her father's return yet another one of his whoppers? Was his illness a lie? Or just another ploy to keep Harriette from leaving town. It had nearly worked, she thought.

The shops of Main Street asleep she crossed the road and gazed into the gloomy electrical shop. The screens that had repeated her father's face like a sick piece of art now silenced. The image that replaced them her own reflection in a window divided by vertical security bars.

She moved on, the mill soon coming into view, a church bell chiming the half hour. Ten-thirty. She stopped and looked around. No sign of thugs loading bars of gold into the back of a truck. And from across the road, she read the flyers pasted on pub windows that advertised the celebrations.

Please join us on New's Years Eve
Pub temporarily relocated to a pop-up bar at rugby club
Complimentary food and drink
All welcome

It seemed as though the offer had drawn everyone away. But her father was nowhere to be seen. Not a whiff. Thousands of miles away on the Costa Rican coastline living the dream, she thought.

'Back to Plan A. Manchester tomorrow then – off you pop, tosser.'

At the entrance to the mill, she pushed keypad buttons, and the entrance door buzzed open. Globe lights hanging in the lobby flickering on; walls pure white like the architect's model.

And after climbing the staircase, she placed an ear against the back wall of the landing, the odd featureless slot in the model coming to mind. Was there really a hidden room on the other side of the wall? *I doubt it.* The silence so reassuring she listened to her own heartbeat for a long time. And then pulling herself away, she continued along the landing and entered Dev's apartment. Then leaning back against the closed door she peered into darkness, her eyes slowly adjusting, furniture in the room like lurking shadows. And through the industrial windows distant coloured lights of a fairground twinkled festively through the night-time trees of Dardale Woods. More forms emerging through the branches as her eyes adjusted further: baby rollercoaster, modest Ferris wheel, the roof of a marquee. Rennie's prophecy ticking inside her head: *Whilst everyone welcomes in the new year, he'll be helping himself to his end of the deal.*

She pressed the mobile phone hard against her forehead. 'Is he telling the truth?'

Then her fingers found DCI Craven in the address

book and began drafting a message, but the little keypad frustrated her efforts, pressing numbers to get letters so hit and miss. Pushing the phone away across the table, she left the message half finished.

Walking circuits of the room not enough to calm her restless self, she stopped at the shelving and flicked through the pages of Dev's scrapbook in search of a recipe.

She'd made soda bread before, with Dev. *Making the dough by hand as good as a run*, she thought. And in any case, she liked its dense texture, a workout for the jaw. Lying heavy in the stomach, it was the kind of food that steadied souls.

She mixed the ingredients together. Heel of her palms kneading rhythmically, her sanity purring, worries falling away: *my father's not here, he's definitely not here.*

Slashing the top of the doughy ball with a knife she placed it in the oven, sat on the floor and through the cooker door watched it brown. And when the timer beeped, she removed it from the oven and cut a thick slice, her mouth working it over as she walked to the back wall and placed an ear upon the brickwork.

Nothing.

She glanced at the clock.

23:35

Then she made black coffee and sat on the bar stool, her ears straining the airwaves for the sound of anything suspicious. Wind stroked the windows, the fridge-freezer hummed; she watched the red digital numbers of the oven clock inch towards midnight; her world steadying with every passing minute.

23:50

Rennie, an attention seeker, a pill-popping hypochondriac.

23:51

Fez's story an iffy second-hand tale, the kind of bullshit mythology born from stories of fool's gold.

23:53

Then she lunged for the phone when its lights flickered on, a tiny envelope appearing in the corner of the screen, a message from Harriette in the inbox:

Good luck with speech.
It's 1995 here!
(Venice one hour ahead)
Hope all ok. Happy NY in advance.
H X

23:55 – Dani drafted a reply:

All good.
Happy NY.
Regards
Rennie

Moving to the window she watched a fox padding along the empty street. The mill silent; its anniversary uneventful. Her father not coming. It was obvious now that Rennie was up to his old tricks.

00:00

She looked at the screen, rechecked her reply to

Harriette then her finger pressed the send button. And as distant fireworks coloured skies over Dardale Woods, thoughts of her father fell away, her mind turning to the next day, her journey to Manchester, her confession. She checked the phone, scrolled back to Harriette's message, reread it, her finger gently sweeping over the letters.

'Happy New Year, Gran,' she said in a tiny whisper.

The mezzanine beckoned. A good night's sleep ahead of her, she made for the staircase, her ankle feeling better, confidence returning to her stride but as her foot met the bottom step a heavy thud came from the back wall.

00:01

McGinty's Cut

There was new stillness, like a shockwave had stunned everything. Her foot welded to the bottom step, she glanced back at the windows; skies over the funfair now a sorcerer's night garden. Glittering stems reaching up; colourful blooms unfurling and popping.

Damn fireworks.

She searched the floor but saw no fallen objects. Books, picture frames, the chess pieces in rank and file, everything in its place on the shelving units. Lurching across the apartment she pressed an ear against the back wall.

I imagined it.

Then another sickening thud. Solid, definite; pulsing through the bones of the building, and into her ear like a smack to the side of her head. She jerked away. Another thud, like a beast awakening. A gorilla. A gorilla in the block room. It's happening.

Rennie wasn't lying.

She glared at the brickwork, her heart galloping, her breathing laboured. And as she hurried to the hallway there was another thud, then dragging scrapes.

Plan B, she thought. *Plan B, Plan B, Plan B…*

She pulled the gun from the rucksack and pushed it down the back of her jeans. And with key and phone rammed into front pockets, she careered down the lobby stairs and plunged into the night.

Hugging the walls of the mill she cut down the side road. The old station high on the right, gable of the mill on the left. And after rounding another two corners she came to the canal, steps to the back entrance coming into view. Feeling her way through darkness she climbed. And on the landing, she searched the far bank, canal and bridge. Still no sign of trouble. Just a moped on the quay below, its poor condition betrayed by the bridge lights: wheel fenders dented, fairings scraped, a rip on the pillion saddle repaired with gaffer tape.

Turning the key, she eased the door open; wisps of dust seeping out like escaping ghosts. The airborne dust clinging to her as she climbed the internal staircase, her body brushing the wall, her feet avoiding the creaks, fine grit underfoot becoming coarser with every step.

Then voices but no people. The light ahead in the print room odd and low. Moving across the top lobby she sneaked through the door then hid behind it and peered into the space. The strange glow – she could see now – was coming from holes that had been smashed through the back wall. Eleven in all, rough-edged, regularly spaced, low down but tall enough to crouch through, the light beaming out onto a moraine of rubble: hunks of plaster, ladders of lath, a torn jigsaw of wallpaper. Trails of dust from each hole like the Amazon delta, all converging into a river of boot prints that flowed towards her and out through the doorway.

And what was that ripe smell? *A box of egg sandwiches?*… and the other wreak… *Petrol?*

Then she saw movement: two people in the block room, at opposite ends of the space, only legs visible behind the holes.

Her father's voice confusing her ears. His rough tone smoothed, his words resigned and full of tiredness. King Kong tamed? The other voice much younger, one she instantly recognised – Steven Ruskin.

She came out from behind the door, and edged into the print room, her hand gripping the mobile phone. Her baby steps freezing when the door at the bottom of the stairwell slammed shut.

'I thought you locked it,' a voice boomed. Holes in the wall becoming a foul-mouthed choir; a pair of legs intermittently visible as they ran behind them. Dani edged back behind the door.

'I did,' grunted her father's voice.

Lunging out of a hole Steven swaggered across the room and passed so close Dani could smell the booze on his breath when he spat on the floor. 'Fucking dust,' he muttered.

Boots clattered down the stairs. A door slammed shut. A key turned the lock. And then up Steven bounded shouting at the holes as he crossed the print room.

'Wide open, Frank.'

'I'm telling you – I fucking locked it.'

Steven crouched and then disappeared into the block room. Both pairs of legs once again busy behind the holes. Steven at one end; her father at the other.

'You're losing it – old man.'

Frank coughed. 'Dust is killing me – and less of the old.' Her father's voice less muscular than she remembered.

'Water bottle's behind you.'

'I'm not blind,' snapped Frank.

'Charming.'

Again, Dani edged out, this time all the way to the middle of the print room, debris piled up in front of her, the glowing space behind holes like a grotto carved by insects. Gun in one hand, phone in the other, her heart galloped.

The holes bickered.

'Can you remember where you put the fucking boat?' said Steven.

'Very funny. Like it could be parked anywhere. And it's a barge, not a fucking boat.'

'Keep your knickers on, Grandad. Ditched the moped?'

'I told you – I'm not walking, you jumped up little cunt. If you don't want a croggy then walk. I'll ditch it when I get to the barge.'

Her father's voice rumbled on, his flow broken by coughing and spluttering. Then Dani heard the words

'McGinty's cut'. And while her father glugged water from the bottle she glanced behind over her shoulder. *There was another? Taking a cut? A getaway driver?* But the doorway was empty; no sign of McGinty.

Steven's cackle snapped her gaze back. And then, through the holes, she saw the big bullets, lying on lower shelves. Bullets you would need both hands to lift. *Cannon shells?*

'Moored,' said Steven.

'What?'

'Boats get moored, not parked.'

'I wish you'd park it. Focus on the job, for fuck's sake.'

Dani glanced at the phone and then held it out as if it were a gun.

'Got the flare?' Frank mumbled half-heartedly.

'How does it work again?'

'Bring it here, fuckwit.'

Steven set off. 'Legs fallen off, have they?'

Dani took a deep breath. 'STOP!'

Steven froze. Wind scuttled across the rooflights.

'Dani?' muttered Frank.

Was that concern in his voice? 'Dad?' she said. 'Is that you?'

'Fuck's sake. Why's she here?'

'Thought you said she was at the lodges,' her father snapped.

Faces appeared in the holes. Dani spat at the floor.

'Nice,' said Steven.

'You shouldn't have come here.'

'Yeah – now we're going to have to kill you.'

'Shut the fuck up, Steven.'

It was like a weird family squabble.

'I know what you've come here for, Dad.'

'Too late. We took it Christmas day... while you were at G-r-a-n-n-y-s,' said Steven, a playground venom poisoning his voice.

'Shut it, for fuck's sake,' barked her father.

She pointed the phone at the artillery shells. 'Why the bombs?'

Frank turned to his daughter. 'We've got what we came for – all that belonged to your great-grandfather.'

'Gran told me about him.'

'Did she really? Then you probably know that he failed to set this lot off. That he ran away to Ireland. That the authorities lost him somewhere in the Western Sahara.'

'No, she didn't tell me that.'

'Oh – so Gran doesn't know everything, then,' said her father, his hands fumbling around the rough edges of a hole as he clambered out.

'I killed our Matt. Did you know that?'

Frank straightened and brushed himself off. 'Actually, I did. But it's fine, we kept it in the family.'

Steven squatted down in one of the holes. 'We found Matt alive. He said it was you.'

'It's not fine, Dad, and we weren't really a family – were we?'

'Ouch,' said Steven.

Frank stared down at the rubble.

'Dad, I've stopped running from what I did. I'm handing myself in.'

'Do me a fucking favour,' said Steven, playfulness missing from his voice.

Frank gave Dani a look; she knew that look. Nothing good ever happened after that look.

'I'm offering you a chance to do the same,' said Dani.

Steven laughed stupidly. Frank took a step closer to his daughter.

'Dani, I can't. Too old for that now.'

She held out the phone with a straightened arm. And as if it emitted some powerful force, her father straightened and winced.

'If I press this button, a message goes to the police. It's over, Dad.'

And then the holes were suddenly alive with Steven's legs, the gap closing between them all. 'Shoot her, for fuck's sake, shoot her.'

Frank produced a gun from nowhere. Dani hit the send button, but the screen failed to light up. The phone dead; battery flat; her finger frantically pumping buttons as if doing so would re-energise the gadget.

Ear-splitting shots. One. Two.

She shrieked, clenched her eyes, dropped the phone. 'It's gone, it's gone! The message has gone – it's over.'

Steven was down, gripping his leg. 'You fucking shot me.'

Frank nonchalantly tossed away the gun and it skittered across the rubble. Holes in the wall now pleading and whimpering, Steven inside the block room but out of sight. 'Frank – you fucking shot me.' His voice scared and tiny.

Her body shaking, she pulled the gun from her jeans and aimed it at her father. But he continued forward until they were only a few feet apart. His manner blasé as if his daughter were pointing a water pistol in his face.

'Careful now – we don't want another accident.'

'Is that how you treat all your friends?'

He looked back at the gun; a wisp of smoke rising from the barrel, then looked back at his daughter.

'We've had a falling out, that's all,' he said with a shrug.

'I meant him, not the gun.'

They both glanced at the holes. Steven beyond them exploring his wounds, a strange whine infecting his voice. Frank turned back and sniffed nonchalantly. And for a second, they both focused on the gun that wavered in her shaky hand.

'It doesn't suit you.'

'What?'

'The gun.'

She held it with both hands then, her aim steadier, 'Fuck you.'

He smiled. 'It belongs to my world.'

His face coated in dust, crows' feet fanning out from the corners of his eyes, the warm smile a stranger to his face. For a moment she thought she saw pride, thought she could trust him. He held out his hand and opened a grimy palm.

'Dani?' He said it softly, his mouth cherishing her name, like she was new into his life, and he valued her more than anything.

Against all instincts, her thumb pushed the release

lever, and the gun hinged open and the bullets spilled into her hand. Then she held it out and his hand wrapped around the barrel. But her grip lingered, and father and daughter remained connected. And for a moment she pretended the gun was a normal everyday thing like a car key, a book or a mug of tea. And then it was just a gun again and she let go. Snapping it shut he swung it behind his middle, conjuring it away like an amateur magician, his empty hands returning to his side. Then one of his hands reached out, his open palm like a plate, his thick fingers asking for the bullets.

'Can I have them?'

'Why?'

'They're no good to you, Dani, that's why. You can trust me.'

'I don't.'

He sighed. 'They're mine. I think you should give them back.'

One of his hands gently closed around her wrist, fingers of the other softly raking bullets off her palm. Then he placed a key in her hand and closed her fingers around it.

'Thank you. Now I think you should go.'

Wind bothered the rooflights and the dusty air swirled as if a ghost danced around them.

'And you?'

He smiled, turned and walked back to the perforated wall. 'Turn myself in.'

'And McGinty, what about him?'

The tone of Frank's laughter was gentle, forgiving not

mocking. He crouched down and re-entered the block room, relief replacing the weariness in his voice, like he was chatting with an old friend. 'God, I hate New Year's Eve, don't you? Always a bloody anticlimax, don't you think?'

Steven yelped, his cries growing more desperate as he dragged himself to the midpoint of the block room. His eyes fixed on the gun Frank had tossed into the rubble.

'Where's McGinty, Dad? You said I could trust you.'

'The McGintys are long gone; they built and worked the canal. The cut is a place named after them.'

'What?'

'A place – McGinty's Cut is a place. You'll find a barge there. I don't need it any more. The key in your hand will start the engine. Check the ballast before setting sail if I were you. Now leave before I change my mind and shoot you.'

She edged back towards the stairs watching her father reload the bullets one by one. Then he picked up a yellow tube, and pulled a chord, the flare fizzing intensely, orange sparks gushing from one end like a Roman Candle.

'What the fuck – Frank!' Steven screamed.

Dani watched her father toss the flare, the arc of its flight lost inside the block room, holes glowing orange one by one as it passed above them. The floor turning to flames as the flare came down and slid through puddles of petrol.

And then a single gunshot.

She flinched.

Steven's wailing abruptly cut short; the hungry flames soon tended to his fallen body.

Another shot. And through a hole she saw her father, waist down, sat on a wooden chest. Legs splayed, arms dangling either side of his slumped middle, gun on the floor.

Then the flames took him, too. Everything in the block room on fire; orange tongues licking through the holes in search of new fuel.

'Dad!'

She wanted to drag him out, but black smoke came tumbling down over the holes like a final curtain.

And it became diabolically obvious then that she'd lingered too long; the oxygen being ripped from her lungs as she fell to the floor with a chest full of gasps. Her escape route earmarked by the river of boot prints. She began to crawl, but with only a few feet to the door hell descended. The first explosion skewing away from her; the second blast ripping through the space like a swiping fist. Her body a feather in the shockwave, thrown forward onto the landing.

The best she could do was to drag herself over the top step and let her body slink down the stairs. Smoke already gathering in the bottom lobby, her fingers blindly scrambled through the murk. *The exit – find the exit.*

Reaching up she turned a key and pushed and then she lay totally grounded, her body all wrong, her legs still inside the building. Canal mist soothing her face as she listened to the mill fight losing battles: groaning timbers, the shattering of glass. Something metallic screeching, it was like a big ship going down.

A minute? An hour? She couldn't tell how much time

had lapsed before smoke that traipsed into the sky became tinged with blue lights.

Then, like a miracle, she felt someone's hand, and it gently squeezed hers.

And for a moment she thought it was an angel.

DARDALE

1916

X

Homing Pigeon – *Columba livia domestica*

Study for Wallis and Hilton Wallpapers. Plate No. 110 – Homing Pigeons – [see sketch on next page]

Facts: They have been known to find their way back to the nest from up to 1300 miles away. The results of the ancient Olympics were carried by trained messenger pigeons. [Charles Darwin owned a diverse flock and was a member of London pigeon clubs. His passion for the birds influenced his 1868 book "The Variation of Animals and Plants Under Domestication", which has two chapters about pigeons.]

Symbology: Pigeons and doves represent peace, purity, faith and fidelity in numerous cultures around the world.

edric closed Ellen's front door then drifted towards town. The end of her street as far as he got before studying the envelopes in his hand. On one of them just Ellen's name, handwritten. A card congratulating mother and baby perhaps?

The other looked official: The King's head. *On his Majesty's Service.* A War Office telegram.

Thoughts churned.

For days he'd heard nothing but bad news: Battle of the Somme a blood bath. Twenty thousand killed on the first day; men who worked in the mill killed the week before. It was obvious to Cedric what lay in his hands, and he wanted to protect Ellen from it. Rip up the envelope. Throw it in the canal. Make it all go away.

And then a ticking sound, and a little voice. And when Cedric glanced up, he saw Harold pushing a bicycle towards him.

'Pint and shilling mix?'

Without answering, Cedric looked back at the envelopes, fragments of Harold's chatter filtering through.

'...town no longer in scheduled area... Nav open at lunch again, but only for an hour mind... landlord still couldn't serve rounds... Lloyd George... Welsh wizard, my arse.'

He slapped the saddle.

Cedric jumped. 'Sorry, who?'

'Lloyd George – bloody teetotal.'

Cedric's face blanked. To which Harold rolled his eyes and swung the bicycle around with impatient verve. 'Oh – forget it. I'll be in Nav if tha changes mind.'

Cedric watched him ride away below the trees of Main Street, their tops flickering in a whispering breeze as if the town held its breath and braced for more bad news. And beyond Harold's freewheeling figure lay the mill. Locked up. Empty. Birds' mess streaked across windows like white tears. Buddleia sprouting from walls. Ducks settling in a sunny spot by the front door. Gaps in paving invaded by meadow flowers, thickest on the steps as if blurring the link between street and entrance. And for a moment it seemed to Cedric that the natural world Sidney depicted on wallpapers was guarding the mill from further misuse.

A squirrel scampered up a gnarly trunk as Harold leant his bicycle against the pub, the branch above him frantically fidgeting as if the tree shook a fist. And as Harold disappeared into the Nav there came a stronger breeze, and the avenue of trees lifted in unison like an inhalation.

Cedric looked down at the envelope once again and thought of Tom, felt the ghost of him about town, could hear his staunch voice say that it was time, time to let his daughter know. Taking deep breaths, he briefly looked up to the flat blue heavens, then crossed the square and turned into the lane that led up to the lodges.

*

Mrs Attwood led Cedric through to the garden where Ellen had fallen asleep in a deckchair, a book splayed across her middle. Mrs Attwood checked a pram that was parked in the shade of a tree. 'Not for long, Mr Hodges,' she said turning back to the lodge.

'Thank you, Mrs Attwood.'

Ellen stirred. 'Oh hello, how long have you been here?'

She yawned then performed a little shiver. A woodpigeon's lecture sleepily looped from somewhere beyond the garden.

Cedric straightened and peered into the pram. 'How's Harriette?' he whispered.

'Doing better than me, so Mrs Attwood keeps telling me.'

Pushing herself up she closed the book. Cedric glanced at the cover.

'*Sons and Lovers*. Very racy.'

A faint smile broke across her face. 'Not for a harlot like me.'

He smiled. 'And how is Mum?'

'Mum.' She laughed then winced. 'That's something I can't get used to.'

'Dare say it takes time.'

'To be honest, not sure I'm cut out for this motherhood lark.'

'Oh, Mrs Attwood will cut you some slack. You should come down to the cottage. I've got some new books.'

She smiled. 'I'd like that. Actually, Mrs Attwood has been amazing… like a mother.'

Ellen held the book above her head like a preacher. 'Have to say, though, I'm not finding comfort in having a child like Mrs Morel did.'

'Mm – well, the book is written by a man, and what do we know?' He placed a hand on his chest, could feel the telegram inside his jacket.

Ellen stood, then looked unsteady. Cedric quickly presented a crooked arm and she held on, and for a moment her gaze fumbled through the flower beds.

'Sorry – got up too quick.'

'It's a beauty,' said Cedric nodding at the glossy blue coachwork of the pram.

'Present from Sidney. Have you heard what's happened to him?' She moved towards the bench. 'Shall we sit in the shade?'

Cedric followed. 'No, everything alright?'

'Hardly. There's no longer a soldier guarding the hall, but the police have put the Wallises under house arrest.'

'Well, I knew that.'

'There's more.'

'Oh?'

'Some windows at the hall were smashed – bricks apparently.'

'What?' Cedric stopped walking.

Ellen turned. 'There's talk of Frau Wallis being deported or interned into a camp or something.'

'Sidney must be going spare.'

'Police claim it's for her safety. Germans in Salford were interned for the same reason.'

'But what about Sidney and Rennie.'

'Don't know whether they're staying or leaving.'

His head pulsed in the midday sun, his mind threatening to boil over. A bead of sweat trickled down his back as he removed his jacket. The envelopes fell from a pocket. He squatted down and gathered them off the grass.

'What's that?'

'Letters.'

'For me?'

'Shall we sit?' He gestured a hand towards the bench.

*

The landlord held a beer glass to the light, his eye magnified as he peered through it. 'You heard about Accrington lads – whole cricket team wiped out at Somme.'

'Aye. Poor bastards copped it first day.' Harold took a sip of beer then licked foam from his lip. 'I hear the Parry girl's dropped.'

The landlord vigorously polished glass. 'God help her when Tom gets back.'

'Father is the Aussie lad, so they reckon.'

'He'll be making honest woman of her no doubt.'

Harold swilled the beer in his glass. 'Will he heck – reckoned he was going back home last time we spoke. Won't see him for dust.'

Stuck for something to say they both looked towards the window, the trees outside sharp green in the sunshine.

'Cedric's back again. Lad's not happy stuck in Morecombe. You know how he loves this place.'

'He should stay home then.'

'He can't. It's Morecombe or join up, so he reckons.'

'Well, he's no fighter, that's for sure.'

Sunshine dimmed; details of the street momentarily flattened before brightening again.

'Ellen's up at the lodges, you know. Jim Attwood was in here yesterday.'

'How's he keeping?'

'Holding up – Had trouble with poachers again. Not that Sid's bothered about all that; he's had some kind of a breakdown apparently.'

'Not surprised the man's lost his grip.'

After drinking the last inch of beer, Harold landed the glass, thin circles of foam slouching down the sides. 'Jim thinks he's gone lunatic. Long hair and beard, drunk his cellar dry he reckons.'

'Sad state of affairs.'

'Tragic. Really tragic.' The landlord placed both palms on the bar. 'Fancy another?'

'Go on then.'

Glass under the faucet, beer frothed out as the landlord pumped the handle.

'Tom will have kittens when he finds out what his lass has been up to.'

'Aye, suppose he will. Well, there's one thing we've learnt from all this.'

'Oh aye, what's that then?'

'Never trust an Aussie.'

*

'They're for me, I saw the address.'

Ellen teased the envelopes from Cedric's hand. Placing one on the bench she held the other in both hands.

'Telegram boy delivered it whilst I was at your house.'

'Why didn't you tell me?'

She opened it, pulled out a slip of paper, blood draining from her face as her gaze flitted back and forth.

Then her eyes stopped and filled, and fast trickles flashed down her tired cheeks. Dropping the telegram, she hurried away towards the far end of the garden.

Cedric picked up the paper and read quickly. Mrs Attwood strode down the garden. 'What's going on?' she said, taking the telegram from his hands, the enormity of the news widening her eyes. Then a latch rattled, and they both looked up to see Ellen disappear through the gate in the wall.

'Poor lamb. We should go after her.'

'Leave her be, Mrs Attwood. Reckon she needs time by herself.'

Ellen hurried through the estate. Heath. Woodland. Soon she came across the pond and collapsed on the grassy shoreline and took in deep breaths of the cooling air. It was a place she had always favoured whenever arguments with her father had pushed her away from home. The romance she'd had there like a daughter's rebellion.

But now those old resentments seemed pathetic and childish.

The landscape she'd previously ignored in favour of a self-centred sulk now looked so beautiful and peaceful, the sanctuary of the glade easing away her shock with every breath.

For a long time now, she had prepared herself for the worst. The odds so stacked against her father, she had rejected any sentiments of hope. But now the news had finally broken she felt incredibly numb and sad and lost. Her eyes stunned by the reflections of trees and sky that seemed so untenably perfect, as if time had stood still. The effect made honest by a surfacing fish; blues and acid greens melding in the ripples. A bee buzzed close by.

Ellen sat very still, her eyes adjusting to the vagaries of nature: swifts skimming water, insects clambering on blades of grass, cygnets bustling behind a pair of cruising swans. And as the glade resonated with life, her own offspring came to mind, and she got to her feet and began to walk. The obligation of motherhood calling her back;

her baby, Harriette, waiting in the garden; her tiny hands and button nose, the smell of bedding on her warm skin. And nothing else dared to occupy Ellen's mind until birds exploded out of trees, the commotion enough to spin her around; wings that swept over the water soon resettling in trees that lined the opposite bank.

Silence.

'Joe?'

The sound of twigs snapping underfoot flashed across the water. Her eyes scoured the shoreline.

'Joe – is that you?'

*

'You'll have to sup it up, nearly closing time.'

'Keep tha hair on.' Harold swigged back then placed the empty glass on the bar. 'See tha tomorrow night then. Seth playing piano, is he?'

'Reckons he is,' said the landlord as he wielded a mop behind the bar.

'Should be a busy one. Well, I'll be off then. Tek care.'

Harold squinted as he emerged from the pub, the warm afternoon made simple by the beer. His world a perfect one until skewered by odd goings-on. The wreak of manure, restless cooing, wings clattering. Then a voice Harold knew but could not place, partly because the voice pleaded with somebody called Fifi, and there was no Fifi in Dardale. *Maybe I'm hearing things.* Maybe the beer was playing tricks on his ears. And then…

'Fifi… now come on then, Fifi.'

Harold turned the corner and saw a horse bridled to a dray. Wicker baskets stacked upfront, beer kegs at the back. Then Harold saw the drayman, could sense irritation building in his voice. A trapped pigeon flapping frantically as the man's hand fumbled inside one of the baskets.

'Come on now, be a good birdie.'

'That you, George?'

The man turned. 'Bit busy at present, Harold,' he said jerking his hand out of the basket. 'She's bloody bit me.'

'Having lady problems?'

'There's always one bugger who won't come out – me quickest bird an' all.'

'Not very far back to the coop from here,' said Harold mockingly.

George abandoned the basket. The pigeon cooed.

'Trying to keep 'em in shape; wings get sluggish without races.'

Harold held the bridal of the horse. 'Army not requisitioned old Titan then?'

'Too old, like us; they want riding horses, anyway. As for me pigeons, have to license them now, otherwise police accuse tha of spying.'

'Give over, what a load of twod.'

'I'm telling tha. They inspect coop, make you release a bird and if it flies towards south coast, you get accused of sending messages to the enemy.'

*

Stepping over black roots and ducking branches Ellen

followed the shoreline of the pond. Woodland on the far side so thick and lush, for a moment she stopped to survey its depths. The scene so quiet she could almost sense the insects at work on the branches and under the leaves.

Then movement; distant, fleeting and at the margins of her vision. The figure of a man running deep in the woods betrayed by daggers of sunlight and the static trunks of oak and beech.

'Joe?' Her voice level and hopeful.

She set off through the wood, soon picking up the trail that led to a gap in the estate wall. A trail she and Joe had followed many times before. And at the spot where the dry stone wall was breached, she clambered over the rockfall and saw a distant figure hurrying across the fields and down towards the canal.

Her shoes slipped and trudged over ploughed furrows as she resumed the chase. The landscape hindering progress until her feet found the towpath; her faster movement soon finding the railway bridge. The shade of its arches providing concealment as she lingered and watched the man as he climbed the steps that led up to the back door of the mill; her heart sinking when she realised the man was not Joe.

Sidney?

Reaching the mill, she climbed the steps all the way up to the workshop. And while catching her breath in the doorway, she studied the room: all the benches and wagons gone, the stink of munitions oozing up from the floorboards like a sick reminder.

Something missing. The omission escaping her

attention at first, but then she spotted the rough-edged hole where a doorway once existed. The oil painting of Sidney that normally hung in the boardroom propped against the wall beside it. The portrait tampered with. A strip of paper with a torn edge stuck across the bottom; words printed across it incriminating the man on the canvas above them.

Look out... Sabotage... Scotch this by being always alert... Report suspicious things and persons at once.

She could almost sense her father in the print room then, his ghost reminding her of the words he once uttered to Lily: *When at war tha has to decide who tha can trust with fresh pair of eyes.*

Her mind wheeled about the room. Why had Sidney escaped house arrest? And why return to a building he shouldn't be in?

'Mr Wallis?' She called out but there was no reply.

The stench of chemicals growing stronger as she drew closer, as if the hole were a mouth that exhaled bad breath, climbing in like entering the throat of a foul monster. She grappled in the dark and as her eyes adjusted, she saw a man standing a few feet away, his hair long and limp, a look of terror on his unshaven face. A timorous beast caught in its lair. A deranged creature she hardly recognised. But there on the shelves either side of him were objects she did recognise. Artillery shells. Neatly stacked. Thirty, maybe forty. Their coned tips pointing inwards, all trained on Sidney like accusing fingers.

'It's not what you think,' he said, taking a step towards her.

'Do the authorities know… about these?' she said, taking a step back.

'I had nothing to do with it. You must believe me.'

Dust spiralled between them like a ghost… *decide who tha can trust with fresh pair of eyes.*

But her eyes were tired, and her legs felt suddenly weak. The chase across the moor catching up with a body wrecked by childbirth.

A silent deadlock ensued until her gaze became distracted by another object. A gun. On the shelf below the shells. Hip height. Her eyes snapped back. But her glance had lingered too long, and Sidney had already traced her line of sight to the same end.

'I've lost so much already, but this, this will ruin me.'

Sidney. Ellen. Revolver. The triangle slowly shrank.

She lunged forward; her hand there first, it gripped the barrel. He grabbed the handle, his finger white on the trigger.

They scuffled like children fighting over a toy.

'Don't… be… a bloody… fool, woman.'

*

The horse bucked; its bridal jangled. Fifi exploded out of the basket.

'What the blazes were that?'

'Sounded like gunshot to me.'

Harold and George walked onto the bridge and watched Fifi fly south, one of her feathers drifting down from the sky, cradling back and forth until making the lightest of landings onto the canal. The quill's graceful ballet across the water gripping their attention. So much so neither of them noticed that the back door of the mill lay open.

'Probably Jim shooting at poachers.'

'Or Sidney taking pot shots at tha birds.'

George smiled at that. 'Wouldn't put it past him.'

They strolled off the bridge and returned to the dray. Harold wheeled his bicycle onto the road and mounted the saddle.

'You here tomorrow night? Seth's on piano.'

'Am I heck. Fixing fence and coop needs a clean.'

'Cleaning coop, tha say,' said Harold rolling his eyes as he tucked trousers into socks.

'Aye. Buggers always spoilin' tha nest.'

'Messy affair, George, messy affair. Well, pass on my love to Fifi, won't tha?'

'I'll pass it on. Tek care.'

And at that Harold pushed off the kerb and the bicycle wobbled a little and he let out a groan as his feet pressed hard on the pedals.

*

After an hour Cedric left the garden and searched the areas immediately around the lodges while Mrs Attwood looked after the baby. Returning empty-handed he and Mr Attwood searched the estate until nightfall but there was no sign of her.

They raised the alarm next morning.

Police notified. Ellen declared missing. A search party formed.

The meadow, the woods, the rolling moor all searched. On the fourth day volunteers dragged the canal with grappling hooks. On the fifth the search was called off.

Ellen, it seemed, had dissolved into thin air.

Enquiries were made around town, but nobody had any knowledge of her whereabouts. The police searched the house on Albion Street but found nothing that helped with the investigation.

And then out of the blue Cedric remembered the other envelope, the one with Ellen's name handwritten on the front. With all the commotion and a baby to look after, Mrs Attwood had totally forgotten that she had placed it in the drawer of her kitchen dresser.

The police opened it and inside they found a card. A Wallis and Hilton pattern on the front. Two pigeons perched on a bough. Inside a written apology, an admission of guilt, and an offer to make things good. All signed off with Joe's declaration of love for Ellen.

I'm leaving... come with me... meet at the canal bridge.

The date and time roughly coinciding with Ellen's disappearance, the theory she had run away with an Australian the best the authorities could do. Police procedure dutifully followed, the search widened, but a merry chase to find two lovers in the end proved too much for a war-trodden country to sustain. And so, the mystery of their disappearance remained unsolved.

But not for Sidney.

*

It came as no surprise to anyone that the police eliminated Mr Wallis from their enquiries; house arrest an alibi nobody ever questioned.

But then nobody knew of the short passage that ran underground between the cellar and the maze at Dardale Hall. A secret folly that had – before the war – left Sidney's German guests astonished; vanishing from the maze only to reappear on the front steps of the hall his favourite party piece.

He'd used it often during his incarceration. To roam the estate and be amongst nature just enough to restore his sanity.

And after the searches for Ellen were called off, he made use of the tunnel again so that his visits to the mill would go undetected. Her body still there, lying in the block room, he wrapped her in oil cloth, tying it fast with bands of rope before lowering her down through the hatch. Her final resting place at the bottom of the canal weighed down by heavy objects discarded by the ministry: a vice, a lump hammer and six empty artillery shells that he filled with gravel. Dirt shovelled into the still waters above the embalmed body until her watery grave disappeared.

The next task – repair the hole in the block room wall.

For another week Sidney shuttled back and forth through the tunnel, popping up in the maze like a mole. The same well-trodden route repeated as he continued overland: heath, wood, over the breached wall, moor, field, towpath. No one noticing him carrying materials and tools to the mill because the canal had been disused and ignored for over a hundred years.

He nailed lath over the opening. Then on went the lime plaster, trowelled smooth. And when dry, he returned with wallpaper. The ragged outline of the plaster repair disappearing below a printed pattern of bumblebees.

War ended.

Elizabeth returned home. A year later she died from Spanish flu.

Sidney mothballed the company. The burden of reparations had killed off the German demand for luxury goods, so he claimed. But truth be told he couldn't carry on. Not after the death of his wife. Not after what he'd done.

His grief so immense he only visited the mill once a year for ten years. A ritual carried out on the anniversary of Ellen's death. Each time adding a new layer of wallpaper over the block room wall. The ten designs chronicling the events that led to her death. Events he'd seen with his own eyes during his secret wartime forays across the estate: Ellen and Joe in the meadow and by the pond, the rest he'd pieced together from talking to townsfolk during the post-war years: doctor, vicar, Cedric, tobacconist, Mr Attwood, Mrs Attwood and Lily.

The process of getting everything down on paper cathartic; journaling the sorry tale into the graphic designs his way of disclosing the unspeakable truth. The first year's bumblebee design overlaid by the second year's design and so on. His guilt laminated between the layers because there was nowhere else for it to go; the gallows waiting for him if he openly confessed to shooting Ellen.

But her death had been an accident – the gun going off as the result of a two-way tussle. There had been no premeditation whatsoever. Both of them had just been in the wrong place at the wrong time.

But who would believe that, and who would believe he was the fall guy for a spy who'd got away scot-free? Friends? He'd been left with very few because of the war.

Ich blieb schtum – Ich hatte keine wahl.

The years marched on. He never told a soul. But he hoped that one day somebody might peel back the layers of wallpaper and read them like chapters in a book; put two and two together and see the story for what it really was.

RENNIE

Pre-flight Epilogue

The nurse and Rennie remained in the doorway as the Mini disappeared beyond the stable archway. Then Rennie sat in the armchair and the nurse covered his lap with a tartan blanket.

'Your car will be here soon. I'll just pack those last items.'

'Thank you.'

The nurse climbed the stairs.

Rennie gazed at the wood burner, the unzipping of bags and clink of toiletries drifting down from the room above.

The stove's iron body still radiating heat from the waning fire, he wondered if the last embers were the remains of his father's journal that had contained such huge secrets. Surely it would burn for longer than wood.

It was a relief that he'd finally disposed of the journal. On several occasions, he'd only just managed to hide it away before Harriette had caught him rifling through the pages. Rennie had found it while clearing his father's study, hidden behind a row of others that were neatly arranged in date order on shelves. Each journal in the library the birthplace of a design. Sketches, notes, stories of folklore. And of course, always a reference to *Gestalt*. A theory his father had brought back from Berlin before the war – *The whole is greater than the sum of the parts* – something that Rennie had heard his father utter many a time.

And of course, he knew of the wallpapers that the secret journal described. Ten post-war designs. One every year. As a thirteen-year-old boy he'd even helped his father apply the last layer to the back wall of the print room.

The Wallis and Hilton company undergoing a brief revival. Limited runs of those final prints sold to an interiors boutique in London. The designs destined for the walls in the well-to-do parlours of Kensington and Mayfair.

But it was the missing journal that told the story. Full of scribbled statements from various characters who had lived in town at the time. Harold, Cedric, the gamekeeper's wife, the gamekeeper, Phillis, the lady who ran the tea shop, a lady called Lily and many others.

The notes describing how everything had gone so wrong back then. The sheer accidental nature of Ellen's death clearly described within. Absorbing the truth almost too much for Rennie's frailty.

His father had killed Harriette's mother. But there was something else. Something just as upsetting.

Because it was clear to Rennie now that the company's post-war recovery was thwarted not by the lack of his ability to take over the reins – as everyone had assumed – but because his father's atrocious secret had prevented the company from moving on.

Back then Rennie had felt as if his father had lost faith in him. The feeling of failure a common thread during his adolescent years, to shrink away and seek comfort within the confines of the estate becoming his fallback. But now he felt a terrible regret and bitterness that he had become a casualty of his father's dishonesty. If only he'd been wise enough to garner the truth from those final designs.

So enchanted by the individual carvings he'd not see the bigger picture when the whole set of blocks worked their superimposed magic. The finished article suggesting more than the sum of its parts escaping him, that theory of *Gestalt* too advanced for his young mind.

He listened to the nurse's footfall across the ceiling and watched her stump back down the stairs carrying a suitcase. She placed it down by the front door and then switched her attention to a small soft-sided bag that she'd left open on the coffee table. Dipping in she pulled out a measuring device. Rennie rolled up a sleeve and the nurse wrapped a cuff around his upper arm.

'Everything alright, Mr Wallis?' she said, activating the machine.

'Oh, just reflecting on the past.'

'You lived in this place for long?'

'Yes, I've been here all my life.'

As the cuff inflated and squeezed his arm Rennie recalled how his father had rapidly deteriorated during his last years; kept himself to himself a lot of the time towards the end. Those last dreadful designs had lacked the playful joy of pre-war offerings. The prints didn't sell. It was the beginning of the end. *I should have seen the writing on the wall. I should have trusted myself; took my chances. I was good enough.*

'Done,' the nurse said as she glanced at a digital readout, the sound of Velcro tearing the air as the collar came off. She made further checks: body temperature, heart rate, level of alertness.

'How am I doing?'

'You're all good to fly, Mr Wallis.'

'The helicopter awaits?'

'We'll get underway real soon. Would you like some tea?'

'Good idea. One for the road. Two sugars for me.'

'Getting into bad habits, are we, Mr Wallis?' said the nurse as she made the tea.

Rennie reached out and took the mug from her hand. She popped two pills from a blister pack, and he swallowed them one by one with sips of tea. Then he pointed at the row of three printing blocks mounted on the wall.

'Tell me, what comes to mind when you look at those?'

The nurse glanced up. 'They're beautiful. They remind me of old tapestries. Do they tell a story?'

In later life Rennie had looked up the word *Gestalt*. But there was no exact translation. It meant something like whole, complete or pattern.

'Probably, but I'm not sure.'

Rennie explained that the set of printing blocks were very old, and some were missing and wallpapers made using them were no doubt lost to decades of redecoration. 'So, if they did, I'm afraid the story may be lost for ever.'

The nurse squared up to the wall and with her head tilted to one side she tried to read the patterns. But the busy carvings were too incomplete for her eye to solve the riddle.

Rennie smiled.

'So, tell me, what lies in the eye of the beholder?'

She sighed. 'Just beautiful patterns, I guess. Maybe the missing blocks might turn up one day.'

'Lost forever, I'm afraid,' said Rennie lifting a leg onto the pouf so his foot could warm by the fire.

'Shame,' she said between sips of tea. 'If only walls could talk, Mr Wallis. If only walls could talk.'

DEV

Ashes

The sky started to spit but the umbrella remained unopened by my side. My dad gave it to me before I left Didsbury. He'd offered to drive, but I'd turned him down, said I needed time alone to clear my head.

But during the journey my mind had run amok, beating myself up for this and that. And now standing on the road bridge I surveyed the mill's charred remains, the counselling I'd received after leaving the army whirling around in my head.

You had no control over events. Feeling guilt was normal but at the end of the day none of it was your fault.

Which was all fine, but I couldn't help feeling bad for asking Dani to look after the flat. It was my attempt to keep her close while I was away, a request driven by my own pathetic insecurities. If only I'd been stronger. If only I hadn't panicked.

A rash of ripples raced up the canal. Rain thickened. Coming to my senses, I opened the brolly. Sky drummed above me; the canal shivered below. And for a while I counted my blessings as the weather swept in. I was due a generous pay-out from the insurance (Rennie had taken out the best cover money could buy). I helped my staff get temporary jobs in a supermarket, Isla was teaching sign language in Manchester and Karl had set up a temporary office in Bolton.

Steven was still missing.

It was noted in the investigators' report that the building had burned with unusual energy. So, most had assumed Steven had died in the fire. Although I hasten to add that no human remains were recovered from the scene. And bizarrely, nobody had any record of what lay inside the sealed room; maybe it had harboured secrets of an incendiary nature. Who knew?

Of course, the bakery going up like that was a disaster. A massive shock. But I was lucky to have friends and family that rallied around me. Needless to say, it was Dani and her recovery that I focused on. And the reason I was here, at the mill, was because she'd asked me to collect a tin of ashes. Odd, I know, but I wasn't about to refuse her anything. Her misfortune down to me at the end of the day.

I stayed on the bridge for a while, Dad's brolly sheltering me from the rain. The mill below an absolute write-off. Floors and roof gone, heaps of rubble on the quay. Anything still standing deemed structurally unsound and cordoned off. Probably foolhardy to go down there but lightning never strikes twice and all that.

So, I walked off the bridge, crouched under the cordon

tape and clambered over blackened rubble. The air so acrid I covered my face with a hanky as I dragged a coffee tin through the sodden ash.

I carried on through the wreckage and stepped onto the quay. Main Street visible from here now that the mill ceased to exist. It was a good view. The town picturesque and certain to survive without its bakery. Tempting to think I'd be back someday, but to be honest I was too numb to consider the future, and, in any case, there were so many questions that remained unanswered.

Why had Dani been on the back steps? What had started the fire? Investigations had, so far, drawn a blank and Dani was not well enough to undergo formal questioning.

January was so dark; it rained nearly every day.

*

I seemed to be at the hospital more than my parents' house. Sometimes Dad dropped me in Manchester, but today I'd caught the bus, sat on the top deck and watched the city go by.

Dani was lucky to be alive. The first crew on the scene had carried her away before they lost control of the blaze. Actually, it was the smoke that nearly killed her and after a month of intensive care she was off the ventilator. Although, for several days she'd barely woken, and I sat next to the bed listening to her rattling chest and sleepy ramblings.

Then as April arrived, she came off the strong drugs

and all week she'd been lucid. Her speech hoarse, but I sensed her old self filtering back in. A spirit, a character that I deeply loved; thank God she'd survived.

I hopped off the bus and walked into the hospital, the route so familiar I navigated the corridors without looking at the signs.

A nurse waved me over as I entered the ward and warned me that Dani was tired. 'She's had a rough night.'

I'd missed the doctor's round, although the nurse flicked through the notes: lung function good, pain relief reduced, no change with the corticosteroids…

While listening to the nurse I watched Dani.

She was on her own, the other beds empty. One of her arms plastered up to her neck and set horizontally, her free hand carefully rearranging plates and cups on the twitchy bedtable. The look of concentration on her face one you would expect to see while playing a game of Jenga.

'…and last but not least she's off the oxygen, so no more nose tube.'

'Progress.'

'All good.'

I thanked the nurse and made my way to Dani's bedside. 'How are you doing today?' I kissed her forehead. Her hair had been tied back and there were crumbs of cake on the blanket; she looked tired.

'Nurses get excited when you visit. You know… look at you in that way.'

'Did you know they're plastering your other shoulder?'

Shuffling up the bed she winced then smiled. 'I can't imagine why.'

'So you can't hug me.'

Her laughter soon fell away. It was clear something was wrong. We chatted, but her voice soon petered out. She sipped water. I carried on.

'Lost my parents' dog in Fog Lane Park. Found Barlow playing in the middle of a football match. I mean he's quick but lacks the ball skills.'

She stared at the window disinterestedly.

'I've brought the ashes; shall I leave them with you?'

'Could you be quiet?' She shifted and winced again.

'Do you need a nurse?'

'No, I don't need a nurse – can you close the door?'

So, I did and then she told me about Rennie's tip-off and the subsequent chain of events that led to the fire. I asked questions to which she muttered yes or no in hoarse tones.

'Have you told the police?'

She didn't answer for a while.

'Yes. But I only told them so much.'

The room felt suddenly hot. Dani broke into a coughing fit.

'I'll get some water.' But her words beat me to the door.

'No, don't.'

Tears came then. Her crying breathless, I gently hugged her wheezing body.

She took a few deep breaths and fought back the tears.

'When I'm better, are they taking me away?'

Pulling back the table, I sat on the bed.

'Dani… why would anyone take you away?'

'Because I told them about my brother.'

'Your brother? What about your brother?'

Her eyes searched the bed sheets and then screwed shut. The hospital bustling beyond the room: the warble of a telephone, sirens striking up somewhere outside.

'I killed him.'

I couldn't breathe, the air bone dry. Her words like a bombshell. The way she was – the ups and downs – it was all clicking into place. 'You…'

'I shot him.' She wiped a forearm across her streaming face then left it there as if to cover her shame.

My mind fumbled around. 'When did…'

'Four and a half years ago.'

She then blurted it all out: the ginnel, the old gun, her plan to hand herself in on New Year's Day, which, of course, she'd not been able to do. I went to speak but she cut me off.

'I've never told anyone.'

'Not even Harriette?'

'Especially not Harriette. Look, I'm going to do the right thing and hand myself in as soon as I can leave here.'

We sat in silence, a terrible chasm somehow growing between us. Tears spilled down her face when she closed her eyes. 'I wouldn't blame you if you wanted to leave.'

I moved onto the bed and held her tight. She buried her head into my neck, and we stayed like that until she fell asleep, her body limp and soft in my arms, her soul at rest now that she'd let go of her long-held secret.

I felt hot and sick, her shock revelation lying indigestible in my head, a future without her unthinkable.

Slipping out of the room I left the ward and disappeared

into the hospital. Drifting without aim it wasn't long before the corridors didn't make sense. Art on the wall, windows onto a lightwell, a bank of chairs fixed to the floor, all landmarks that I'd never seen before.

I should have gone right. Turning back, I took a left. Turning again I paused for breath. Signs were everywhere. Shouting out. Hanging from the ceiling, indexing down the wall, my eyes ignoring everything apart from the word *Emergency*.

'Are you alright?' asked a nurse.

'I'm… lost.'

'The lift?'

'Yes, please.'

I followed her to the lift. She even pressed the call button for me.

'Thank you.'

'Pastoral care is on level one if you need some support.'

'I'm fine.'

She smiled sympathetically and then walked away.

I waited.

One lift out of order, the other stuck at basement level.

Exhaustion took hold: tinnitus, loss of perspective, irrational feelings on the march. I pressed the call button again. The delay unnerving. I thought I'd shaken that kind of fear, but evidently it was still there, deep inside, kept alive by being shot up by my own side and the beige walls of hospital corridors and lift lobbies.

Doors opened. I tilted forward. Doors closed, my stomach confirming the downward journey. Second, first, ground and then I was in the big corridor, two-way traffic blurring past: visitors, medical staff, an electric buggy ahead of me the size of a small car persevering through it all. My panic easing by the time I'd reached the exit. So much so that instead of leaving I turned left and veered into a cafe. Queuing in a line I covertly glanced at people sat at tables: strained conversations, exhausted faces, a weary man gazing at nothing, his fingers playing senseless riffs on the side of a mug. You could almost sense the hard realities trudging through the space. Hospital a place where perspective trumps the frivolous hang-ups of everyday life.

Finding a place to sit I sipped my sugary tea and went over Dani's story about the gun. How she thought it was antique and wouldn't go off. I believed her. Accidents happen in wars. I was living proof of that. And for sure she'd been in her own war. Families turning on themselves the worst form of friendly fire.

I walked back to the elevator. First floor, second floor, doors open. I set off, this time making all the right turns. The ward unusually quiet as I made my way past the other rooms and then I saw two men in suits speaking to the nurse at the desk. The police?

Shit!

They all disappeared into Dani's room.

Mind racing, I paced up and down, a plan of what to say coming to me with every step. But as I set off to defend her name, they reappeared at the door smiling and shaking their heads, the nurse pointing in my direction. They walked over.

'Devon Enoch?'

'Yes, that's right.'

'Inspector Craven, Greater Manchester Police.'

The other suit said nothing.

'If your lass remembers any more about New Year's Eve ask her to give us a call, would you?'

He handed me a card and they both went on their way.

I asked the nurse what had happened.

'She got very upset when they woke her, poor lamb. So, I asked them to leave. She's a bit feverish, you know how her level dips in the afternoon.'

'What did she say?'

'Oh – reminded them about her brother.'

'Reminded them?' I couldn't help snapping out the words.

'I know.' She rolled her eyes. 'Repeats that wacky story every time they come. They've checked it out, of course, but apparently, she hasn't got a brother, right?'

'No, no...' Looking down I shook my head.

The nurse laughed a little, said I had a feisty one on my hands. 'She got a bit annoyed and called them funny names.'

'Names?'

'Called one of them DCI Wise and the other Fitzy. Got cross then, told Fitzy to clean up his act, stop gambling, give up the booze and be nice to his wife. It's okay, I've given her a sedative. She's sleeping again, bless her.'

The nurse put her hand on my shoulder and leaned in. 'I got rid of the old bill. Don't you worry, we'll look after her. Your girl has been through enough already.'

*

Every day I arrived at the hospital half expecting the bed to be empty. And then two weeks later the bed was empty, and I thought the worst as I approached the desk.

'She's showered herself today,' the nurse proudly announced. 'You'll find her in the chair behind the curtain.'

I knocked and entered.

Dani looked up from a book and beamed at me.

'You're looking so well.'

'No pain and my chest is clear and, well, the police telephoned this morning.'

I sat on the bed. 'And what did *they* want?'

'To let me know the only Matthew Hey they know is fifty-seven, lives in Cirencester and has an outstanding parking ticket. Then they asked about my head injuries and wished me well.'

'Weird.'

'Annoying more like. I don't have any head injuries,' she said, shifting from side to side like a bear rubbing its back.

'Wish I could get this off.' She tilted forward. 'Would you?'

I scratched under her plaster cast.

'What are you going to do?'

'The police won't take me seriously. So, what else can I do?'

'I don't know.'

And that's when she told me about McGinty's Cut and her theory of what she thought was loaded on the barge.

525

'The barge.' I'd forgotten about the barge.

'Yes.'

'And the police don't know about it?'

'No, I didn't tell them – I don't trust them.'

I sat on the bed and fixed her eye. She looked glum. 'I'm not telling them, Dev.'

'Why on earth not?'

'It's my chance – my chance to put things right. Just hear me out.'

She explained her idea. It was mad. But I got the logic. And of course, I wanted to support her, so I proposed navigating the barge back to Manchester.

'Is that even possible?'

'Probably.'

Together we hatched a rough plan then I left and went to a bookshop on Shudehill where I found an old copy of *The Boater's Handbook*.

Back at my parents' I grabbed my dad's 1 to 25 000 OS map of the area. But there was no reference to a McGinty's Cut. I called Dani's bedside telephone and told her that I was going back to the canal and if I found the barge, I would bring it to her.

*

The following day I drove north for an hour and parked beside the dilapidated mill. I set off full of hope but no matter how far I walked along the towpath there was no sign of the barge. So, I walked back and drove to the lodges. It was late by then and Harriette insisted I stayed the night. We had lasagne with a glass of wine and talked about Rennie. She said nobody apart from the doctor and solicitor had known of his terminal illness. She seemed pretty together about everything though.

And then for a second time she mentioned Rennie's will. 'Did you know Dani has inherited Hunter's Lodge?' She really wanted me to know about that.

I gulped wine, then bit the bullet and blurted out Dani's story.

Harriette welled up and showed me Dani's goodbye note. I read it. 'Do you think she's going to be alright?' she said.

'I'll help as best I can. If she wants help, that is.'

'Oh, she needs some. Men have not been her best bet in life. She can act a bit cold towards them I've noticed. What I'm trying to say is…'

'Harriette.'

'Mm?'

'I'll look after her.'

Harriette sighed deeply and placed her hand on mine. 'Thank you.'

'Look, I was hoping you could shed light on something.'

'Well, yes, of course. Try me,' she said sitting back.

'Dani confessed to the police, but they insisted her brother didn't exist.'

She glared at the table. 'Good.' Then lighting a match, she held it to the corner of the note and when the flames licked up, she dropped the fireball into a clay bowl, and we watched in silence as Dani's confession turned to ash.

'Well, in a way they're right.'

She poured us both another glass of wine.

'I don't follow.'

'Parents didn't register his birth. No real surprise at the dereliction of duty towards the poor boy, we are talking the criminal classes of Moss Side here, so…'

Walking over to the sink she placed a cloth under the tap. 'Deepika came to see me after becoming pregnant with Matt. She was afraid her family would turn their back on her if they found she'd conceived a child out of marriage, not that that mattered to me of course. And, well, he never went to school. Educated by his father, the Moss Side way.'

She placed the damp cloth over the smoking embers.

'Of course, Dani was the stronger minded of the two, had the sense to break free. She is one of the good guys. You know that, don't you?'

'Yes, I know that. I just hope the police don't change their view.' We both drank more wine, my eyes resting on the wooden blocks mounted on the wall. Impossibly intricate, almost hypnotic. 'I just can't believe they didn't question her more rigorously.'

'Probably just glad to be rid of her father and Steven. Had a string of previous convictions between them – she was a bloody hero for confronting them like that.'

She poured another. I couldn't keep up.

'Not sure she sees it that way. You know – can't shake off what she did to her brother.'

'Well, she bloody well needs to.'

We knocked back the wine. She relaxed into the chair. 'Her brother and father hit Deepika. I mean really roughed her up...' She glugged half a glass then roughly wiped her mouth. '...and the police did nothing. Justification enough, don't you think? At least she tried to stop it. She's a good kid – needs help in seeing that.'

Harriette was right, but how? I didn't say anything, just felt sickened that her mother had suffered. There was an awkward silence.

'You get on well.'

'Sorry?'

'You and Dani.'

'Yes. We get on well.'

I told Harriette about the school production, about the thwarted kiss. She loved that. She knew of the musical and we chatted about the story. She was classy but never stuffy. I really liked her. We were forming a friendship.

'I get the feeling – you've become very close.'

'Yes, that's true – but her past, it's holding us back.'

'I was afraid of that.'

'Well, don't be.'

Placing the OS map on the table I explained about the barge and what Dani wanted to do with its cargo. And for a moment there was complete silence. We didn't have to say a thing; it was obvious the best way to help her break free was to facilitate her intentions.

I unfolded the map, and our hands ironed the creases. Then I asked Harriette about McGinty's Cut. Her eyes searched my face and then switched to the map, her finger soon finding the canal where it cut into the landscape before entering a tunnel, the words *Rushey Mead Hollow* printed on the paper next to her fingertip.

Then she explained that McGinty's Cut was a name long lost.

'The McGintys were navvies who built the canal. Their descendants lived here for years but they either passed away or moved on. Only the older folk in town would remember them now.'

Harriette described how the towpath stopped at the mouth of the tunnel. 'Horses couldn't pull the barges through. One of their descendants nicknamed Legger McGinty would lie on the roof of the freight barges and move them through by pushing the soles of his boots against the ceiling of the tunnel.'

She opened another bottle of wine. 'You'll need a boat if you want to go through.'

*

In Didsbury I strapped a friend's canoe to the roof of Harriette's car, then drove back to the mill. Harriette met me by the quay with some neatly wrapped lunch and a flask of coffee. Shouldering a rucksack, I lowered the canoe into the water and worked my legs into its fibreglass hull. She wished me luck and I paddled away under the railway bridge and out of town. I looked back before rounding the bend to see Harriette still waving. I waved back then carried on through flat meadow and under the broken footbridge.

For a long time, I paddled; rain drizzling down; wet views sliding by. Another slow bend, another long straight and then I was in new territory well beyond the point I'd reached by foot.

It was just me, the canoe and the canal; the paddles near silent as they knifed in and out, the landscape much bleaker as the thin slip of water rounded the shoulders of land like a contour line. Water roughed up. I paddled for thirty minutes. My strokes working hard against the wind. Hips, shoulders, neck. Everything ached; it was like paddling through treacle.

Stopping for a breather, I leant back on the rucksack and took in the view: countryside divided by hedgerows, distant cars silently cutting through it; fast, effortless and light years ahead of my world of hard yards. Outmoded and forgotten, the canal a brilliant way to shift a heavy load from A to B without being noticed. Her old man was smart; you had to give him that.

Pushing myself away from the bank I carried on; the weather hampering progress for at least another hour. Blisters forming on my hands, paddling onwards felt like some medieval penance. Doubts invaded my mind; suspicions that this was a wild goose chase draining my will. Head down I kept going. So busy griping about my aches and pains that subtle changes in the terrain escaped my attention. Not until the wind dropped, did I glance up to see levels on both sides rising up like sheltering arms; undergrowth thickening, trees and bushes crowding the waterside as if the engineered slopes were not to be trusted. Reeds encroaching further in, I paddled along a clear channel no wider than the hull of a narrowboat until a wall of brush completely blocked the way. Faint lines of the tunnel's entrance hidden somewhere behind the tangled mass. It was obvious the barricade was man-made.

The paddle doubling as a machete I inched forward, the canoe almost capsizing as I yanked branches aside, breaking through like I'd been delivered into some dank underworld, silent apart from my lungs gulping in the cool, dark metallic air. Strapping on a head torch I paddled further and further into the gloomy tunnel. The curving walls around me brick then blasted rock then brick again. Trying not to think of the hill above my head I ploughed on, but there seemed no end, a damp breeze whispering in my face like breath from the lungs of a watery demon.

No feeling in my legs, my hands numb, my upper body soaked by water that dripped off the bricks, my teeth chattered as I counted strokes of the paddle. Ninety-seven the last number to pass my lips as a dot of white appeared in the darkness ahead. My arms wheeled and pulled, the dot steadily growing into a disk of light, the pureness of its geometry impaired on one side. The offending silhouette sharpening into the outline of a boat as I drew closer, lurking in the half-gloom, still a good a way off, on the left, somewhere between me and the shimmering corona of bricks that framed the outside world.

It was grey. It had no name. I'd found it.

Pulling alongside I tethered the canoe to a fender and then clambered out onto the barge's back deck and unshouldered the rucksack. Down in the galley there was a coffee pot, a few tins of food and the smell of dampness. The cabin seemed comfortable enough. Cushions and blankets on the bench seat, two bags of coal beside a little stove. Numb with cold my fingers could hardly feel the firelighters and kindling as I made a fire. Flames soon took hold; I added lumps of coal. The sooty stove door alive with orange as I stripped off and changed into dry clothes.

Blanket around my shoulders I explored the barge. Not much to see. A simple bedroom, wash area, a decent amount of kitchenware in the galley cupboards, rings of the hob hissing gas when I turned them on.

The living space well-worn, maintained on the cheap but well looked after. Cabinets and worktops patched up with scraps of wood; the repairs neat and well finished. The creaky floorboards in the aisle mostly covered by a Persian runner. I padded along its length back to the stove, which was now clicking with the heat, the sooty window aglow with orange coals. I added some more.

The boat was no more than a restoration project done on the cheap. There was nothing of value here and my heart sank as I realised that Dani's father had led us on a merry chase.

Warmth from the stove really kicking in now I sat on the bench and ate the sandwiches Harriette had given me. Then putting my feet up, I sipped coffee and surveyed the long, narrow space. Would Dani want to keep the barge? It was just a shabby corridor that floated on water so maybe not. My eye rested on the Persian rug. Perhaps the only item worth salvaging in my opinion. Although even that was worn and frayed. The pile ridged and creased along its length, as if a shoal of snakes had been swept beneath it. Within seconds I'd rolled it up like a big turf.

The floorboards underneath loosely laid, cupped and warped by the damp air. I went for the one that crowned the most, my fingers levering it up. The second board came up easily.

Standing too quickly I stumbled back to the bench. All the time my eyes fixed on what lay between the joists. One or two concrete blocks but it was plain to see that most of the ballast had been replaced with bars of gold bullion. Tightly packed, side by side. Highly polished and irresistible to the eye; a fortune that was already playing havoc with my morals; not until you see such a hoard, do you understand its power.

I replaced the boards, then lifted others. Bedroom, living area, under the kitchen base units; my god, it was everywhere.

The boards went down, the rug reinstated. The raft of gold hidden beneath my feet.

Time to get underway.

Standing at the tiller I slotted the key into the control panel and twisted the ignition. The boat shuddered into life and the engine throbbed through the back deck. A small hole in the hull rhythmically gobbed water over the canoe's pointy end. I pulled up anchors fore and aft and pushed off with my foot.

Opening the throttle, I steered the barge out of the tunnel and into the bright sheeting rain.

*

It took two days to reach the Leeds-Liverpool Canal, guidelines from *The Boater's Handbook* repeating in my head along the way.

Stay on the right.

Don't cut corners.

It's simpler than driving a car.

So, would that be a car with arse-about steering and no fucking brakes?!

I grounded twice, crashed into a lock door and fell off into freezing water when pushing the boat off a grassy bank in high winds.

It was safe to say that me and the barge weren't getting along, and it took days before our disagreements died down. My skills evolving after realising that driving this thing was not possible without first erasing all notions of how long it should take to get from A to B. Nothing happened quickly on a canal; I was gradually adjusting to that. Covering distances just took a very long time. The engine chugged on, and I began to think it was the only noise I knew. Tugga… tugga… tugga… tugga.

I went with the flow. I passed through towns.

Chorley and Adlington already behind me; I chugged through them unnoticed. Next, Wigan. The canal there made famous by a series of twenty-three locks that took six hours to clear.

That night I turned in early, a sense of dread following me to bed. I'd read about accidents in locks. Not surprising that things can go wrong with all that water rushing in and out. My mind buzzed. I didn't sleep well.

I set off early and to my relief a volunteer keeper was at the top lock to help me through. We did the first eight together then he backtracked to help others at the top.

After negotiating the middle section alone, I moored

at lock seventy-nine for a rest and lay on the grass. But no sooner had I closed my eyes a voice came down from above.

'Sleeping on the job, are we?'

I looked up to see the keeper stood on the up-and-over bridge smoking a cigarette.

'Waiting for you to catch up. Can you help me until the Leigh branch?'

He operated the sluices. I adjusted the ropes. And as we descended, the keeper asked searching questions about the "grey lady" to which I could only offer lame answers.

'She looks low in the water,' he said as we passed through the last lock.

'I'm taking it to a yard for repairs. For a friend. Thank you for your help.'

'No problem.'

I opened the throttle and didn't look back and after a few hundred yards I branched off into a canal that led to Manchester. It was plain sailing from there. More locks but nothing strenuous.

The engine chugged on; countryside gradually giving way to bland industrial buildings. Home fans reminding me it was Saturday as I passed behind the Old Trafford stadium.

Then I was in the thick of it.

Traffic streamed across flyovers; trains whistled along elevated tracks. Below it all I trundled between graffitied walls and bridge-supporting buttresses. And just when I thought the city would never end Castlefield Basin came into sight. Once the beating heart of Manchester, now the city's back door; Victorian warehouses gathered around the waterway like merchants harking back to old times. The canal widened, narrowboats at rest along its sides. Finding a gap, I manoeuvred in, secured my lines and then sat on the roof. Momentum of the journey leaving my body, for a while my ears were completely lost without the ever-beating percussion of the engine.

I closed my eyes. Sounds trickled in.

Joggers' feet, bicycle tyres, the shriek of a siren rising above the city's distant hum.

The Wash

My heart sank when I got to the ward. A nurse waved me over and explained that Dani had been discharged then gave me a handwritten message: *Have not been able to contact you, so returned home.*

I phoned the lodges. Harriette picked up.

'How is she?'

'She's just popped out. Where are you?'

'Back in Manchester.'

'You did it then.'

'Yes.'

The line went silent and for frightful moment I imagined her on the floor.

'Harriette?'

'She can't wait to see you. I'll bring her.'

She offered to drop Dani at Deansgate Station the following day and suggested we met under the railway bridge at eleven.

'Safe journey.'

'You too and good luck.'

Back at the barge, I grabbed some cash and went in search of something to eat. The area new to me, I strayed some way before finding a cafe. I was back in the city, and I didn't like it. Its bustle like a slap in the face compared to the peaceful canals. The barge slow and basic but I'd fallen for her old-world charm.

After bacon rolls and coffee, I meandered between the old warehouses and followed the wharf until the barge came into view. Feeling too tired to clear up I sat back on the bench with a novel. A short story, but I was a slow reader and when turning the last page, I realised the portholes had gone dark. So, I turned in for the night and slept deeply, woke early and before setting off I tidied the barge. Everything back in its place, mugs washed up, galley wiped down.

It took ten minutes to find the meeting place. I waited for a while, not sure that I'd got the right bridge and then I saw her in the distance walking up Castle Street. The cast removed from her neck and shoulder but not her plastered forearm which lay in a sling.

'Hello.'

'Hello, you.'

We both winced as a slow passing train screeched on the rails above. I studied her wonderful face; she wore a little make-up, her long hair loosely tied back. A second train lumbered overhead; our kisses oblivious to the screeching.

'Shall we go?' I laughed out.

'Yes!' She laughed back. My heart softening as her slow

thumb wiped lipstick from my mouth. I picked up her bag and we walked to the boat.

'I've never seen you in a dress.'

She angled out her sling. 'Removing trousers in a hurry is problematic.'

We clattered and kissed our way through the barge and clumsily undressed each other in the galley. Our bodies coming together on the small bed. Parts of her still tender, we moved in line with her softly spoken requests, tangling, gently until content. And then, with her head resting on my chest, it wasn't long before we were asleep.

An hour later I slipped out of bed. Dani's sleepy voice following me through the barge calling my name.

'Back in a sec,' I called from the galley, but by the time I'd returned with mugs of tea she was up.

'Where is it?' she said, pulling on her dress.

'There's a bag of cash in the cupboard above the sink, the rest is under the floor.'

She looked around her feet. 'Which bit?'

'Check this out.'

I lifted a board with glee. She took one look then averted her eyes.

'The whole floor. It's everywhere.' My words coloured with foolish joy; I just couldn't help it.

Squatting beside me her eyes fixed on mine. 'I've seen enough, haven't you?' The gold had no such effect on her. 'He put my family through hell because of it.'

I quickly lowered the board and apologised.

'Shall we not lift it again?' she said, pulling on her shoes.

'Let's not lift it again.'

'I'm hungry. Shall we buy some food?'

'Yes, we need food.'

We walked into the city and soon we were pushing a trolley around a supermarket talking excitedly about the journey we were about to undertake. There was no deadline; we were keepers of our own time. Our freedom exquisite. The walk back, a question-and-answer session about boats. On our return I explained how to empty the toilet, how to fill the water-holding tank and how to free the propellor from weed by way of a little hatch.

Over dinner we studied maps and planned the route.

The following day we cast off and left the city. Heading south we continued for days, navigating through the network of canals to Stoke and then, near Lichfield, we turned east.

The pace steady, we trundled on. Dawn until dusk. Canal-side pubs our favourite overnight spot. It wasn't long before we were in the middle of a conversation with others. It was like we wanted to confirm our closeness to the world. And we got attached to the boat even though it wasn't ours. The three of us a four-mile-an-hour tour de force. Casting off, passing through locks, mooring up; after three weeks we were doing it well.

But then the weather broke, and the next morning was full of rain, so we took our time casting off and after a few hours of getting drenched we called it a day and moored up just outside the next town. Dani stayed on the boat and napped. I walked to the shops in search of batteries for my hearing aid and something for supper. When I returned, she was quiet and on edge although she wouldn't tell me what was wrong.

In the evening, we went to a pub and got drunk. Then out of the blue she blurted to people at the bar that we were honeymooners. And as we left, I gave her a look. She pulled a funny face and shrugged her shoulders.

'What?'

I couldn't work out if it was me, her or the canal that was swaying. 'Were you trying to get free drinks – or something?'

I laughed at her bemusement then puked in the canal.

The following day we both woke with hangovers. The weather still poor, we stayed put and fired up the stove. Rain drumming the roof as we made comfort food and played travel Scrabble. It would have been a day of cosy bliss, but I couldn't stop thinking of what she said at the bar. I should have let it go, but during the game it refused to go away. I so wanted to throw down the word HONEYMOON but the best I could do was WED.

After dinner it just came out. 'Are we getting married or something?'

She looked embarrassed and apologised, then said she felt closer to me than anyone else in her whole life, even Harriette. And that at times it was too much, and it made her feel panicky.

'I just keep thinking this is our honeymoon period and we're not going to last.'

I got up from the table and sat on the bench. 'Come here.'

She followed me over and sat beside me. I held her

close, and we stayed like that, holding each other, both of us nestled by that tight narrow space.

'I feel like we're in a bubble,' she said, her flustered face glancing up at me.

'Me too.'

'What happens when it pops?'

'We find a new one.'

She looked down, her head heavy on my chest.

'Like hermit crabs,' she whispered.

'Yes, like hermit crabs.'

Light faded in the portholes. We went to bed, the usual routine kicking in the following day; we carried on in our little bubble. Ironic that her father's boat offered that kind of security. Our life onboard monastic. We shared various battered kitchen items, a dented coffee pot and the inconvenience of a cramped interior. All the time our happy feet only inches above a ballast worth millions. Of course, we made no mention of the cargo and not for one minute did it infect our trip. And yet we couldn't avoid being mindful of how calamitous the end of our journey would be, and the closer we got, the heavier the prospect of its grim conclusion weighed upon us.

Gentle banter and our daily rhythm softening the dread; Dani ditched her sling and most mornings we jogged on the towpath before casting off, those words playing in my head as the days unfolded: *we're not going to last.* Sometimes good things don't. And of course I mourned the bakery almost every day; change is an inevitable part of life. But to be honest, I wanted this journey to last forever.

The following day the land flattened, skies grew big, and the weather turned hot.

With no locks to break the journey, we took turns at the helm; the River Witham Canal guiding us through remote fens.

Leaning over the bow I watched ridges of windy water butt against the hull.

When I steered, Dani sunbathed restlessly. On her front, on her back, up on her feet whenever we passed a building or water tower to check her phone. But out here there was no signal and not being able to contact Harriette made her irritable. We were both tired; it was the furthest we'd travelled in one day.

I searched for a gap in the reeds and manoeuvred the barge alongside the bank and cut the engine. Dani drove mooring pins into the ground, and we lay in silence on the grass, looking up at the sky until sensations of movement faded from our bodies. Finding her hand, I squeezed it and said everything was going to be alright. She thanked me for stopping, and gently stroked the back of mine. We ate dinner sitting on the roof, utterly alone, breezes ruffling along the canal as if it carried on like a watery conveyor belt.

At seven feet above the water, we towered above the surroundings: the canal slicing through the low-lying fields from us to the broad horizon, a distant line of trees and a barn, the earth's meagre offering to coppery blues of a gigantic sky.

'Makes you feel tiny, doesn't it?' I turned to see Dani in tears.

'You okay?'

'Sorry, I'm fine,' she sobbed, then wiped her face on a shirt of mine that was laid out on the roof to dry.

'Do you not like the salad?'

She was laughing and sobbing then.

'Sorry about the tee shirt.'

She brushed a mozzie off my back with a gentle stroke.

'I just, feel a bit overwhelmed by everything. Just feel so together… feel very free.' Her body pressed into mine and the top of her head nestled under my chin. 'It's all just… very perfect,' she whispered.

'Yeah, it's pretty bloody perfect.'

And then for a while just silence; rays of the sun broke below a scant ledge of cloud, insects danced above the barmy fields.

'I've been living two lives for a long time… it's a relief that one of them is over.'

'Must be good to get some closure.'

She thought for a moment. 'Yes, but I'm feeling a little hollow inside, I suppose.'

'More salad, perhaps?'

She laughed. 'I'm fine, thanks.'

'Finer than you know.'

She nestled back in. 'Not sure where I'd be without you and Harriette. She's always encouraging me to be myself. Easier said than done, I find.'

'Saying "I'm good enough" from time to time helps. *My* gran taught me that.'

'You do that?'

'Whenever I'm feeling weak. Filling your emptiness

with a dose of self-belief is no bad thing.'

Her body easing into mine she regarded her toes as they repeatedly curled and relaxed.

'Grans are good, aren't they?' she sighed.

'The best.'

My mind swung between both grandmothers: my gran reminding me to use intuition, Harriette's hands smoothing the map: *She's a good kid – needs help in seeing that.*

I kissed Dani's glowing forehead, nose then lips; sun tangent with the earth we watched low wisps of cloud smoulder on the horizon.

'Standing up to your dad like that is the bravest thing I've ever known.'

She looked at me blankly. 'Sounds like a soldiery thing to say. I don't think sticking a medal on it changes much.'

She said it had all been very scary – but she wasn't sorry that he was dead.

'I don't feel guilty that he is.'

'Well, that's understandable.'

'Not really. I felt like throwing a party.'

I laughed. She gave me a look. I straightened my face. 'Yes – that's a bit excessive.'

The sky singed orange around a semicircle sun.

She wanted to know more about my background. So, I told her stories of my childhood. Cubs, cathedral choir boy, cadets, piano lessons, cricket trials for Lancashire, Caribbean summers spent with my grandmother. Fascinated by all the details her conversation style shifted into the realms of friendly interrogation. I just ran with it, and she listened to my answers so intensely it was like she inhabited my past, sharing the normality I'd been lucky to have. Her face glowed in the evening light.

'Being an orphan isn't so bad. I mean, I spent most of the time running away from my family, anyway.'

'Oh, there's a few of my family I'd like to run away from.'

'But you probably don't feel like wiping them out.'

'Well… yes, that's true. Actually, I'm thinking of getting life insurance before we become any further involved.'

She laughed at that. 'You can't insure against my *pre-existing* conditions.'

The sun made a final bow, clouds blushing within a cobalt abyss.

She whispered a thank you, for not running from her bedside when she'd told me about her brother. 'I don't deserve you.'

'Totally agree, but I think you've earnt yourself a second chance.'

Laughter soon fell from her face and then came that edgy look that was so loaded with intent. Her wild beauty as desolate as the land and sky, for a moment I imagined her aiming a raised gun at my heart, her finger white on the trigger. The thought fading when her hand found my chest and gently pushed me down.

'I don't think you'll regret my second chance.'

We undressed, our clothes sliding off the roof and into the water. Soft warm breezes stroking over us, the silky twilight sky our only blanket. Our warm embrace long, tender and easy-going. And then we lay silently gazing up, our glowing spirits exposed to the stars, gliding satellites catching our eye. The sides of our heads pressed together we picked them out, pointed up at them and for a while nothing else seemed to matter.

*

Up before sunrise, we drank coffee and watched the horizon blush. The river ahead reflecting the new day as if beckoning us on. We ate breakfast on the hop and journeyed without pause. At first it was just me, Dani and a radio that played old hits on a loop.

Both staying on deck, we chatted, fussed each other, waved at cyclists and other boats. Our mood sobering as the breeze carried hints of sea air; the tower of St Botolph's – known as "the Stump" – appearing in the distance, rising from the fen like a broken post. We moored upriver from the tidal lock, the town of Boston a short walk away.

Buying food from a mini supermarket we asked the checkout lady if she knew of anyone in town with knowledge of The Wash. She suggested a pub called The Carps and gave us directions. So, we drank there every night, and I studied the admiralty chart which hung on the wall in the bar. It was the landlord who introduced us to Bernie, a fisherman who'd harvested mussels in the bay most of his life.

When we asked him about taking a narrowboat across The Wash he sat back and gave us a look. 'Not more of yah.'

Over a beer he explained a few friends had taken a small flotilla of narrowboats across in eighty-nine. He'd given them advice and they'd managed to do it. 'They set course for the Nene then upriver to Wisbech.' He swallowed a sip of beer. 'Bit touch and go, mind. Game under in a shallow-drafted boat if the sea gets lumpy. Stick to the canals, that's what I say.'

His mates joined us. We bought a round of drinks; their salty yarns coming at us from all directions as if we were at sea around that beer-marinated table. Then Bernie mentioned our plan and the group discussed the crossing of eighty-nine: three boats, experienced crews, dead flat sea.

One of the drinkers asked if we were sure about crossing the bay by ourselves.

'Yes, we're sure.'

Their offers of an escort ebbing away as we politely declined, everyone agreeing the best conditions for a crossing were forecast for the end of the week. We would have to leave the Haven on a receding tide so the flow behind would take us on our way. The group advised us to stay inshore, and that's when Bernie told us about the Lynn Deeps and The Well. At thirty fathoms the deepest parts of the bay.

We glanced at each other across the table.

*

The galley sang its morning tune: crockery in the washing-up bowl, clap of cupboard doors, coffee pot hissing. And then Dani appeared on the back steps, her hair tied up, eyes puffy with sleep, two mugs in her hand. She joined me on the roof. Our feet dangling off the side as we ate Danish pastries, drank coffee and took in views of a town that was blurred by coastal mist. The air sweet and cool but it was possible to tell the day was going to be hot.

The shipping forecast babbled from the radio; the general synopsis confirming the hot weather; the heatwave set to last for a few more days. The broadcast ran through the coastal areas. Then came ours. *Humber and Dogger: Sea state smooth – wind direction becoming cyclonic later in the day.*

I started the engine, and we cast off. Bernie meeting us at the tidal lock, reminding us again to '…be across before the easterlies'. He and the keeper helping us through and wishing us luck, their figures disappearing as the mist closed in behind us.

Dew settled on our clothes, the laden air shifting aside as the boat pushed us through. We carried on pretending the morning was like any other. Our manner bolder than usual, as if uncertainties beyond the murk were being kept at bay by the power of bright conversation.

But as the visibility improved our chatter thinned to nothing because we realised that the canal was morphing into something bigger, its banks now levees, fenland either side so impossibly low, it was as if we glided over the earth. The route engineered for ships, it felt ridiculous us being there: the barge pretending to be something it was not, taken by a swirling tide that outpaced our lack of speed. Our charade deepening further as the levees pulled back and we headed into open sea. My hand tight on the tiller, Bernie's voice fresh in my mind: *game under in a shallow-drafted boat if the sea gets lumpy.*

But his words seemed overdramatic as we passed unhindered over the dormant sea, water like glass, the grey rubber tubing of the dinghy trailing behind us, skimming effortlessly over it.

Dani climbed up and sat cross-legged in front of me. Her shadow on the roof sharpening as the sun broke through the mist. She scanned the haze with binoculars. I held our course south-east until she spotted the landmarks at Gedney. And then, despite all warnings not to, we steered away from the land, the incessant *tugga tugga* of the engine pushing our comfort zone further and further over watery unknowns.

It seemed to take forever for the fuel to run out, but eventually the engine fell quiet, and the boat glided silently for a short while longer. Mirrored surfaces flexed. The sun burnt the haze; long stretches of water peeking through as if the sea eyed its newfound prey; its lazy tongue licking the hull as we gently see-sawed above the Lynn Deeps.

Dani climbed off the roof and pulled the dinghy in; I fetched a bag of clothes from below. We stood on the back deck looking west. The coastline thin and faint, obscured here and there by mist that clung to Earth's irregularities.

'It looks so far away,' she said.

'It does.'

'Thought I'd be petrified, but it's so peaceful out here.'

'Maybe we should get a boat.'

Her hand ran tenderly through my hair and before she stepped off, we kissed. 'Maybe a sailing boat,' her final words before climbing into the dinghy. I passed over the bag and using the oars she pushed away and skulled close by.

I went below, walked through the barge and stood by the boards we'd lifted the night before. Dani wanted to see the stash for herself. The weight, the eyewatering value of it. Three tonnes, we guessed. Dirty money at the end of the day. Liberating Dani from her past the perfect way to spend it.

Squatting down I angled the drill perpendicular to the hull, leant in and squeezed the trigger; motor brushes flickering behind the gills of its plastic body. Metallic fumes and oily smoke wafting up as the bit screamed into metal plate.

After a few minutes of pressure, the shaft plunged through, jets of seawater spiralling out behind the spinning chuck. I went again. A second. A third hole. One more for good measure; the gold shimmering in the currents, playing with my stupid side. Regard for my own safety waning as my fingers traced over the bars. The spell broken by the sound of Dani's voice.

She called my name again, her intonation full of concern, full of care, the precious metal at my feet suddenly cold and worthless.

Lobbing the drill onto the bench I turned aft and waded past the bench cushions, the stove and the tin of her father's ashes that had sat on the shelf above the sink since Manchester. Zipping up the bag of cash I wedged it tight inside a cupboard then skipped up onto the back deck and took a deep breath of sea air. Doors fastened and locked, I stepped into the *Zodiac* and Dani paddled us clear.

The barge rose and fell, and we too rocked on the gentle swell.

At first nothing happened, but then gradually the stern tipped and the propellor broke above the waterline. The boat continuing to slowly tilt until reaching such an angle that its rate of immersion quickened. Dragged down by its crooked cargo, its length gracefully slid down into the sea, air hissing out as the last few feet of hull slipped under.

The barge had gone; we watched bubbles well up. Sitting on the side of the *Zodiac*, Dani's tattooed arm propped her body as she leant out and gazed into the water.

I said nothing; it was the kind of respectful silence observed at a funeral. Her attention so focused on searching the depths, for a moment I felt invisible. Our existence thinned to such a degree our spirits outshone mere flesh and blood; our souls suspended above a powerful barren place. I fleetingly glimpsed hers; an occurrence that would have been lost to the hum of any hospital; I sensed it healing.

Looking up into the pure blue haze she closed her eyes and took big slow breaths. Then joining me on the plank I felt her body press against mine and she lay the side of her head on my shoulder. Placing my arm around her we sat drifting as one. The mist completely burnt away, the sun's reflection stretching and contracting on the sea's flexing surface.

Lifting her head, she looked at me square on then kissed me. We stowed the oars. She tipped the outboard into the water and pulled the starter cord. Opening the throttle, we wheeled around, our wake briefly cutting a halo before she steered westward. We could see land. Our backs bathed in offshore sun. I turned and looked at her, but she just peered ahead into buffeting spray.

'Are you alright?'

She looked at me, then smiled and shouted back.

'Yeah – I feel good.'

ABOUT THE AUTHOR

After a decade as an architect, Lloyd Harvey became a stay-at-home dad, supporting his wife and two sons. During this time, he worked part-time and pursued hobbies like baking for the Women's Institute and building theatre sets. Lloyd rediscovered his love for writing, resulting in his debut novel, The Block Room.

To learn more about Lloyd Harvey's work, visit his website: www.lloydharvey.com.

ACKNOWLEDGEMENTS

Thank you to both Ann and Tamsin for their feedback and proofreading of the early chapters; to Rosie and Carolina at the Book Guild for patiently guiding me through the publishing journey; and to my wife Ruth for her wise editorial comments and enduring support.